Tail of the Scorpion is many notches above the ¡ ˙igent eye-opening thriller. This is pure geniu¬ cinating, pulse-quickening mystery fi¹¹ 'ntrigue that feels perilously r es you questioning our secui ? You won't put it down...

Renee Richards
Manager of Executive Service's

The author keeps you interested in this real attention getter. You never know what is coming next. You'll be on the edge of your seat waiting to see where these characters lead you. If you like *The Forever Man* you'll love *Tail of the Scorpion*.

Dee Graham
Restaurant Owner

The *Tail of the Scorpion* is a worthy follow-up to *The Forever Man*. C. William Davis weaves a compelling story, which makes you want to read as fast as you can turn the pages, just to find out what will happen next. This book will keep you riveted throughout, and leave you wanting more.

Daniel Bradley
Real Estate Appraiser and Educator

#2

5-31-15

TAIL OF THE SCORPION

From the Author of *The Forever Man*

C. WILLIAM DAVIS III

Word Association Publishers
www.wordassociation.com

ISBN: 978-1-59571-266-0
Library of Congress Control Number: 2008925791

Word Association Publishers
205 Fifth Avenue
Tarentum, Pennsylvania 15084
www.wordassociation.com
1-800-827-7903
Fax: 724-226-3974

For my wife, Linda.

You have spun the fabric of my dreams,
Colored the pages of my books,
And made them real.

I love you.

FOR THE "DREAM TEAM"

Tom & Francine Costello
Jim Baird
Nicole Raymond
Theresa Doerfler
and the staff at Word Association Publishers

for their help in the publication of this book.

The following novel is based on a story originally written by the author during the summer of 1963, between his senior year of high school and college.

Often when the heart is torn with sorrow, spiritually we wander like a traveler lost in a deep wood. We grow frightened, lose all sense of direction, batter ourselves against trees and rocks in our attempt to find a path. All the while there is a path, the path of faith that leads straight out of the dense tangle of our difficulties into the open road we are seeking.

—Helen Keller

One ought never to turn one's back on a threatened danger and try to run away from it. If you do that, you will double the danger. But if you meet it promptly and without flinching, you will reduce the danger by half. Never run away from anything. Never!

—Winston Churchill

They can conquer who believe they can. He has not learned the first lesson of life who does not every day surmount a fear.

—Ralph Waldo Emerson

from *Dale Carnegie's Scrapbook:
A Treasury of the Wisdom of the Ages*

PREFACE

The summer of the murders committed by the media-named "Forever Man" had come to a close. Fall, winter and spring had followed in their usual progression of seasonal change. For the citizens of Smith Falls and the surrounding area, life had returned to its normal pace. There was no longer any mention of the past summer's horror on the daily news. The events of that summer would always lie just beneath the surface of the residents' day-to-day routines, but for the most part, people here—like elsewhere–found a way to push it to the back of their memory.

To the surprise of all, the murderer had turned out to be a long-time resident dedicated to fulfilling a perceived mission of eradicating evil and saving souls. His had been a bloody trail created by a tormented mind. Many lives had been lost over a period of weeks that summer, lost to a killer whose belief was that their tickets must be redeemed.

It was now mid-summer of the following year, but for Sheriff Clive Aliston nothing had ended. He had lost friends to that wave of terror. The loss that affected him most was the disappearance of his second-in-command, his friend and lieutenant Brian Lasiter. Brian had somehow become involved in it all, and even was accused of the attempted murder of an F.B.I. agent. Brian had been wounded in a final gun fight, and then had escaped from the hospital with

someone's help—but whose?

Weeks after the disappearance, Clive had received a note that read: "Their tickets must be redeemed" and a gold necklace with a one-word pendant, reading "Forever." Then nothing for almost a year. For Clive, there was no closure. The thoughts and dreams still plagued him in the night in those quiet times when the routines of life could not mask the void. He was a man haunted by faces in an endless mist.

The horror of the past summer and the unanswered questions would soon be supplanted by a kind of storm unlike any Clive had faced before. It would test Clive Aliston and the people of Smith Falls, even the nation itself. What was coming was a runaway train headed right at them, an event that would bring the nation to its knees. Out there, among those ever-darkening clouds, there could be a connection to the past, to the murders of that bloody summer. The clues, the pieces of that mind-bending puzzle, would remain just out of reach, just out of mind. What was racing headlong at Clive would take all he had to give, but the shadows of the Forever Man would remain ever close…

CHAPTER 1

September

Drifting sand, dunes on the horizon, hot dry breezes that burn flesh like hot polished steel. Blowing tan gritty death as thick as fog. The high-pitched crack of a rifle shot. Matt, lying on his back, rose instantly from the bed into a sitting position. Sweat poured from his forehead and neck, followed by a bone-deep chill that raised gooseflesh over his body. He grasped his throat and sweat-soaked t-shirt, gasping for air, and quickly fell back into his pillow. His eyes focused on the rough plastered ceiling above his bed. The drifting sand, the dunes. All a dream. The creation of his mind in the last foggy haze before he awakened.

His quick waking motion had aroused his wife, Janis. Lying on her side, she rolled onto her back and reached to touch Matt's chest, "Are you alright, dear?" she asked.

"Yes," he answered after a few moments. "Go back to sleep. It's still early." Matt remained flat on his back for a minute or two, then sat up and placed his feet on the floor. With that motion, Beau, their tan-gray tabby cat, leaped from Matt's chest of drawers, scattering aftershave bottles in every direction.

Matt moved his right foot slightly and felt something smooth and cold on the floor. He leaned over; there beside the bed was his golf trophy from five years earlier. The rifle

shot. Beau was the most inquisitive animal Matt had ever owned. He had apparently knocked the trophy to the floor in what was probably his hundredth personal investigation of the dresser.

Matt sat on the edge of the bed for a few more minutes, trying to clear his mind. He finally got up and removed his jeans from the back of the overstuffed chair in the corner of the bedroom. As he pulled on his pants, he turned and looked at his wife Janis. A half smile crossed his face, as if to say how glad he was that she was there with him. He slipped into his favorite shoes, a worn pair of moccasins, and left the bedroom, half closing the door behind him.

As he slowly walked down the short hallway on the way to the bathroom, Matt checked each room. First, Mary and Lisa's room, then Robert's, then Andrew's—though he knew it would be empty.

Matt crossed the dimly-lit living room and stopped at the fireplace. Kneeling, he put his hands down near the grate, where a few embers still glowed orange from the fire the previous evening. The remaining heat felt good on his cold fingertips. He reached for the poker at the side of the fireplace and placed several small logs on the front of the grate. As he pulled a few hot coals over and around the logs, he got his first scent of the coffee brewing in the kitchen. He turned and glanced at the clock on the living room wall: 6:30 a.m. The coffee started by the timer on the pot had been brewing since 6:15. He placed the poker back in its hanger and headed for the kitchen. The aroma of the coffee in the kitchen reminded him of the freshly-ground coffee beans at the corner grocery, on one of the many shopping trips with his mother as a child. He filled his favorite cup then slipped on his denim jacket that had been hanging next to the back door.

Moving the cup to his left hand, he retrieved a double-barrel Remington 12-gauge from the corner by the door. He

carefully slid the large bolt on the door to the left, opened the door quietly and stepped out onto the back porch. Placing the coffee on the picnic table at one end of the porch, he reached into his jacket pocket, retrieving two 3" magnum buckshot shells, placed there the day before. Sliding the release lever on the double-barrel and opening the gun, he then sighted through the barrels for any obstructions. He placed the two shells in the chamber and closed the gun with a quick snap of his right arm. Resting the shotgun in the crook of his right elbow, he picked up the coffee and savored the first warm sip. He stepped through the door of the screened-in porch and from the top step, scanned the brushy hillside behind the house.

After a few seconds, he moved down to the next step and began to sit down. His smooth-soled moccasins slipped slightly on the morning dew covering the stairs. He came down on the top step a little harder than he had planned, spilling some of the hot coffee on his legs. He cursed quietly to himself and brushed the remaining coffee from his jeans. After a few more sips from the cup, he scanned the hillside once again. A movement to his left caught his attention. He shifted the shotgun quickly to his lap and snapped off the thumb safety.

There, standing in the middle of the dirt road that ran beside the house was a fair-sized buck, possibly a six-point, just out of range for him to be sure of the number of tines. His attention was on the deer for a few seconds when he heard a whimpering sound to his right. He turned and there, standing with her front paws on the fence of the pen near the doghouse, was Ginger, their six-month-old golden retriever. For a moment his thoughts shifted to Maggy, the pup's mother. What a hunting dog and companion she had been, and how he missed her. He turned his attention again to the road but the buck was gone. Another sip of coffee and he

snapped the safety of the shotgun back to the "on" position.

His attention again focused on the hillside as he rubbed the L-shaped scar just under his right eye, a lasting memento of his tour of duty as a Navy pilot in the first Gulf War. At just short of six feet tall and about a hundred and eighty-five pounds, Matt was a fairly good-looking middle-aged man. Blue eyes, a mustache and short salt and pepper hair, graying at the temples. He was born Matthew R. Fallon on November 5, 1964, to Joseph & Mary Fallon in Albany, New York. The family had moved to the hills of southwestern Pennsylvania, near Pittsburgh, in 1968. Matt had attended a local high school and moved on to Carnegie Mellon University, School of Engineering, graduating in the upper half of his class. A member of the R.O.T.C. unit in college, he had joined the Navy upon graduation and was recommended for flight school in Pensacola, Florida. He had intended to make the Navy his career, but the air war in Iraq had changed his mind.

In the two short years of the tour Matt had become one of the service's finest F-14 fighter pilots. Everything changed, however, one hot July afternoon in the skies over the border between Iraq and Saudi Arabia. His F-14 took a direct hit from a surface-to-air missile and began to disintegrate. The explosion had caused three wounds: the cut under his right eye from flying canopy glass; a small metal fragment to his left knee; and the most serious, a wound near his right shoulder blade that punctured his lung. The latter had nearly proved fatal. It wasn't the wound or the downing of his plane that made him decide to retire, however. After ejecting from the plane and parachuting safely, he was spotted by Republican Guard forces and pursued through the sandy desert for two hours. He was finally rescued by a platoon of Marines—but not before he was forced to shoot two Republican Guards at point-blank range with his

sidearm. As a pilot, the killing and dying had never been on an up front face-to-face basis as it had been that afternoon in the desert. Because of his wounds, Matt received the Purple Heart and was discharged from the service upon request. After the ordeal, Matt vowed never to kill again. He finally did return to hunting, but the thrill of the sport had somehow changed. Until the events of the previous two months, Matt had hunted more with a camera than a gun.

Matt's father had died in 1994, leaving the business solely to him. His mother passed away the following year. Managed by Matt and Janis, the business had done so well over the past few years that they were able to have management personnel run the plant nearly without them. Having the added free time, he and his family spent many weekends and short vacations at this home in the country. The only member of the family who lived in the city for any length of time during the year was his oldest daughter Lisa, who was attending a private school.

Matt finished the last of his coffee and placed the cup on the side of the top step. With the shotgun in his right hand he moved down the two remaining steps to the ground. Once again he scanned the hillside and the road to the left, carefully searching for movement of any kind. He turned toward the road then walked down the small sidewalk along the house. The walk ended at a limestone driveway at the front of the house. There he stopped, his eyes once again searching the yard, the pines, and the pond in front of him. After a moment he turned to the right and walked to where the driveway met the dirt road. To his right and left was a row of large pines trailing off for forty yards in each direction. The trees almost concealed the house from any point on the road. He paused for a moment, then placed the shotgun in his left hand and slowly stepped out onto the road. Leaving the protective cover of the pines made him a

little uneasy. His eyes searched the road, first to the left, then to the right. To his left was a long, gradually descending hill about two hundred yards long, that bottomed out at the driveway. To his right, the opposite hill was steep; from where he stood, just seventy-five yards of the road was visible. No vehicles, no movement. At a width of about fifteen feet, this country lane was well cared-for and graded well for drainage. The maintenance was supposed to be provided by the county, but Matt had played a large part in its present condition. Both sides of the road were lined by thick forests of oak, maple, dogwood and hickory. The only cleared land was his: the house, outbuildings, and surrounding area.

Satisfied that the road was clear, Matt quickly turned, walked back up the driveway and stopped in front of the house. He looked up to his left, searching the windows of the bedroom where he thought Janis was still asleep. The home was a clean white stucco with red trim. It had originally been a three-bedroom residence, but the sun-porch in front had been remodeled into a fourth bedroom: Matt and Janis's room. It was lined with windows and had a view of a yard and pond that were beautifully landscaped and well-tended.

Matt walked the driveway to the other side of the house, stopped, and once again scanned the area of the pond for anything unusual. He proceeded to the three-car garage that faced the side of the house and paused again. He glanced to his left at the dog pen at the end of the garage. Lying in the doorway of the doghouse was Ginger, her head resting on her front paws. She looked at Matt with sad eyes as if to say, "It's time for breakfast now." Matt smiled, then circled the garage on the pond side and stopped in front of what was left of the storage shed.

All that remained of the once-neat shed was a low brick

foundation, part of the roof, and the charred remains of one wall. To the side of the shed were two burned-out pines and burned grass fifteen feet in every direction. The back of the garage was only eight feet from where the shed had been. Its white aluminum siding was scorched brown and bubbled from the intense heat of the fire. What had been salvaged was in three piles near the foundation.

Matt shook his head again in disbelief and turned to the woods below the buildings at the end of the cleared property. Here, the trees were much thicker and the green canopy of leaves cut the light almost in half. Once again, he searched the tree line, straining his eyes in the dim shadows. Matt walked a few feet, stopped, and sat down on the edge of a large stump that was used for splitting wood for the winter. His thoughts wandered back, back to the many small game hunts he had shared with Andy and some of his friends. He inhaled a deep breath of the cool moist morning air from the wooded valley below him. It was mid-September and although the trees had not yet started to change color, the scent of autumn was mildly present. Another deep breath and he began to daydream.

Back at the house, Janis was in the kitchen setting the table for breakfast. She had been out of bed since Matt had left the kitchen half an hour earlier. As she dressed, she had watched him walk slowly behind the garage on his morning rounds. With the table set, she opened the refrigerator and retrieved a dozen eggs and a pound of bacon from the meat bin. Eggs and bacon, how good they would soon smell and taste. Over the past weeks such normal breakfast fare had been unobtainable. She and Matt had made a trip the day before to the newly-opened Crossroads Store. Many of the shelves were bare, as prepared food was still in short supply, but their menu was much better than it had been in the past weeks. For much of the that time breakfast, lunch and

supper were made up mostly of wild game, fish, and vegetables from their small garden.

Janis placed the bacon in an old cast iron skillet and turned on the front burner of the propane stove. She opened the doors under the sink and reached for an apron and a small walnut box with a brass padlock on the front. After putting on the apron, she removed a jar from the top of the refrigerator. From the jar she removed a set of keys. Placing the box on the sink board she unlocked the padlock and opened the box. From inside the foam rubber-lined box, she produced a small .25-caliber automatic pistol and clip. She checked the pistol chamber for cartridges, snapped the clip into the handle and pulled the slide back in a quick, confident motion, checked the safety and placed the gun in her apron pocket. After re-latching the box, she placed it on a shelf under the sink. She then cracked nine eggs, placing them into a large bowl with a little milk, and proceeded to scramble them.

Janis was a woman of exquisite natural beauty. Blonde hair that fell in ringlets to her shoulders. Eyes the color of crystal blue topaz and a complexion that needed no corrections or additions. With her small frame and pretty figure, she was a storybook princess. To quote Matt, "His dream girl, a goddess of the forest."

Janice A. Boroughs was born in Boston in 1966, and had lived there most of her childhood years. After graduating from high school in a Boston suburb, she had gone to the University of Maryland. Matt was visiting a friend near Washington, D.C., when he met Janice at a party off-campus, just weeks before he left for duty. They were a match from the very start, compatible in every way. When Matt left for duty in the Middle East in 1989, he left her a military forwarding address. Four weeks into his first tour she began

to write letters. On his first leave, she met him in D.C. for ten days and they decided to marry.

Matt was to Janis what all women look for in a man; the chemistry could not have been more right. She tried not to think much about what he was doing and where he was in those months at sea and in the Middle East, but when notification of his plane being downed came to her, she quietly crumbled inside. She had always been a strong, self-disciplined person, but this news was devastating. By the time he was plucked from the desert, taken to a base hospital and identified, five days had passed. To quote Janis: "Five of the longest twenty-four hour days on the planet." She was there upon his arrival in Washington, D.C. and remained with him through those early days of recovery at Walter Reed Medical Center. Once Matt had regained his strength he was flown home to a veteran's hospital, and once released from the hospital and the military they spent a ten-day honeymoon in the Poconos. They returned to Pittsburgh and to the home Janis had started, with hopes of a new life and a family.

After months of what seemed like an endless battery of tests, they were told that Janis might not be able to bear children. Deeply in love and desiring a family, they turned to adoption. The following months were a drawn-out, endless session of meetings and interviews, but in the end they were awarded the custody of a one-year-old baby boy, Andrew. The baby was special from the very beginning, quiet and well-behaved, in control almost from the start. He was a perfect baby boy, a mother's and father's dream. Some months later it was discovered that Janis had a chemical imbalance that had prevented any pregnancy. Once corrected, Matt and Janis were ecstatic and started on the family they had wanted from the start.

In the next few years the family was increased by the

births of Lisa, born in 1992, followed by Robert in 1999, and finally Mary in 2001. As the family grew, Andrew was the focal point of the children's interest and their leader in almost everything. He seemed to grasp almost any situation, any moment, for what it was. It was like he could feel life in advance of itself. It was Andrew who renewed Matt's interest in hunting and fishing and in the sheer beauty of nature itself. Matt began to realize that Andrew had a special gift of communing with nature. He was a hunter's hunter and could catch fish like a pro. Andrew could blend into the forest like the wind through the trees. He had a sixth sense when in the forest that had to be seen to be believed. He was much older than his years, already a strong man; Matt knew he could rely on him for almost anything.

As the children grew, so did the family ties that would prove so vital in the years to come. Andrew grew into a young man, tall and slim, with light brown hair and brown eyes. The focus of every girl in school, a class athlete. He was never in trouble, loved his family, and, like Matt, placed his family and friends above all else. More than anyone, Matt could see the man who was emerging from this child. Although Andrew was not his biological son, Matt felt part of him, a feeling that grew as Andrew grew.

Janis also could see that her special little boy was becoming a man. She had watched him in the yard of camp from the quiet of her bedroom window. He would be feeding a squirrel, or just standing motionless in the evening haze staring at the golden sunset over Scorpion's Tail. Andrew was a part of it all. He could see and feel what no other person could. To Matt and Janis and his sisters and brother, he was a bridge to a world that few had ever seen or lived in. He was in touch with life and all its wonders; he was Andrew Fallon, and they loved him.

Matt's daydream was quickly ended by the sound of a vehicle coming down the dirt road. Janis also heard the sound and retrieved the pistol from her apron pocket. Matt jumped up from the stump he was sitting on and raced back to the side of the garage. He slipped the safety of the shotgun to the off position and waited for a sign of the car. Ginger was barking and racing around the fence of the pen. Matt tried to calm her with a few soft words but to no avail. Janis turned the flame off under the almost-completed breakfast, opened the back door and slipped out onto the back porch, pistol in hand.

Lisa, Robert and Mary raced into the kitchen and Mary began to scream wildly. Janis pushed the kitchen door open, placed her index finger in front of her mouth and announced, "Shhhh." She followed that brisk command with, "Get into the living room and don't talk or move until you're told." Once again, she closed the kitchen door, slipped the safety off on the .25-caliber and peered out over the railing of the screened-in porch in search of the approaching car.

Matt moved from the garage to the side of the house in six or seven quick steps. He peered around the corner of the house, scanning the road. The car was still not in sight, but the sound was getting louder and he could see dust among the trees at the top of the hill.

Janis turned her back to the porch rail, closed her eyes tightly and whispered, "Please God, No!!" She opened her eyes, recomposed herself and turned once again to the road. She could see the dust trail moving down the hill toward camp. She clenched her teeth and wrapped her index finger around the pistol trigger.

Matt raced from the house to the row of pines at the side of the road, stopped on his knees, shotgun in hand, and waited for the car to reach the driveway. Janis slid the screen

on the side of the porch open and braced the pistol on the porch railing. The car was only fifty feet away and slowing quickly as if prepared to make a turn. Matt leaned forward and placed both elbows on a chest-high cut-off stump beside the pines. He raised the shotgun, leveled the barrels at about window high on an automobile and stared down the ramp to the front bead. A second later, the front end of the car rounded the trees. It stopped just inside the driveway, directly in front of Matt, who never moved from his position.

There was a moment of silence and Matt squeezed the trigger more firmly. The latch of the driver's door clicked and began to open slowly. The curved glass and the reflection on the side windows prevented either Matt or Janis from identifying the driver. The car was an unmarked late-model white Ford with black-wall tires and little in the way of trim. The door swung fully open and the driver began to step out.

From the distance of the porch, Janis was unable to identify the man at first and again closed one eye and sighted down the short barrel of the pistol. The man stood fully erect, with his back to Matt, and stared at the porch. Matt raised the barrels of the gun above the roof of the car and directly at the man's back. Janis slowly began to lower her pistol as a half smile began to develop across her face. The man turned slowly toward Matt. He was wearing mirrored sunglasses which he slowly removed; he placed both hands and the glasses on the car roof. Matt also lowered his gun slowly as the man spoke, "You always greet old friends this way, or is this just a bad morning?"

Matt did not immediately respond but stood up slowly as he continued to lower his gun. He broke into a full smile and in a totally astonished voice said, "Clive Aliston, where the hell did you come from?"

CHAPTER 2

July 30, 2:30 a.m. Pacific Time – the Arizona/Mexico border

A jeep came up over a rise along the fence line on the American side of the Mexico border. It moved slowly, headlights on, raising a small dust cloud behind it in the light of the moon. It traveled the line for about a quarter of a mile, then slowly came to a stop on a high flat area next to the fence overlooking a small ravine that led down to the river. At the wheel was Ross Gibb of the U.S. Border Patrol, and his partner Jim Bellows. As they came to a stop, Jim had his night vision binoculars trained on an area just to the bottom left of the ravine. "What the hell do you think you saw now?" Ross said as he clasped his hands and placed them on the top of the steering wheel.

"I'm not sure," Jim said, as he climbed out of the jeep and walked to the fence. He turned, looked at Ross and said, "You know not everything that moves out there is a coyote."

Ross just laughed and said, "Yeah, and you know as well as I do that we never see anyone trying to get across in this section. It's so damn remote, not even the illegals will walk all the way out here to try and get across. I can't remember the last time we even saw anyone else out here."

Jim just shrugged his shoulders, turned back to the ravine and placed the binoculars back to his eyes. "Well, I know I saw something out there—and remember, I wasn't the one who was out all night partying before coming to work."

25

"Hey man, it was a family party and I only had three beers. Not exactly putting on a drunk, you know," Ross said as he turned in the seat toward Jim.

"Just kidding," Jim said as he lowered the binoculars, turned to Ross and laughed. "I just think that between the two of us, I would be the most reliable right now at what we see."

"Yeah, yeah, right," Ross said as he slid up the back of the bucket seat and sat on the top, his feet on the bottom of the bucket. "Reliable, your ass," Ross laughed. "I've got two years on you running this damn fence. Just who is the pro here, you pompous ass?"

Jim, laughing too, turned once again to Ross and said, "This pompous ass old timer!" Jim was about to turn back to the fence when in the light of the moon and the dash lights he heard a thud and saw Ross jerk backward. He watched as Ross, his eyes wide open, slowly looked down at his chest. He saw Ross place his hand on his chest then put it out in front of him. It was covered in a dark, almost red smear. Ross slowly turned his head toward Jim, his eyes and mouth wide open, but no sound came from him. Suddenly, a red dot appeared on Ross's forehead and there was another thud, as Ross flipped off the seat backwards. Jim moved quickly to the jeep and yelled, "Ross. Ross!!" He reached for the flashlight on his belt, snapped the switch on and pointed it at Ross, now lying face up in the back of the jeep. What Jim saw sent a wave of fear down his spine. Ross lay on his back, his uniform shirt soaked in blood and a small but deep hole in the center of his forehead. Jim reached for his service revolver, quickly turned back toward the fence, then dropped to one knee beside the back wheel of the jeep. He scanned the area in front of him, trying to make out any movement; he saw none. He was about to raise the night vision binoculars to his face when he saw three red dots on his chest. As he slowly looked up there were three distinct

thuds and Jim fell back against the tire of the jeep. He struggled for one more breath, then slid over to his side and to the ground. Minutes later there was a snapping sound as a man using a wire cutter clipped the links of the fence. A gaping hole opened in the fence and men began to pass through, one at a time in the beams of the jeep's headlights. One of the men stopped and pointed a handgun with a silencer attached at the jeep. There were two distinct thuds and the headlights went out.

July 30, 3:35 a.m. Eastern Time—Michigan

Betty and Frank Lehane had been awakened by the thunder and rain from a mid-summer storm. It was 3:35 a.m., hours before their normal wake-up time but they had both lain awake for nearly half an hour before finally deciding to get out of bed. Betty had made coffee and was trying to get the weather report but the signal for their TV dish was still not coming through due to the high storm clouds. Frank put on his raincoat and, coffee in hand, prepared to go out to the pump station at the end of the low dam that held back the reservoir for the city water system. Frank had been the engineer in charge of the reservoir and pump station for the last ten years. He and Betty had lived in the old two-story farmhouse for that same period of time. Frank walked over to Betty and kissed her on top of the head as she sat in the recliner playing with the TV remote. "You know that you're wasting your time, dear. Ain't gonna be no signal till the storm passes."

"Yeah, but it ain't even raining now. Damn dish," Betty said as she looked up at him with a smile. "I think the old antenna rotor was better than this."

"Yeah, right," Frank said with a chuckle. "And when the weather is good and you get those stupid soap operas you couldn't get with the antenna rotor, you don't seem to be too

upset with the dish then."

Betty looked up from the chair with a sort of smirk on her face and said, "Frank go out and check your damn pumps and gauges. You've been away from them much too long. I'll start breakfast and give you the weather report, if I ever get it."

Frank smiled and sarcastically said, "Yes, dear." He turned and walked to the front door then stopped and took a recording instrument in a leather case from a hook by the door. As he opened the door, he turned back to Betty with a smile and said, "I'll be back in half an hour, dear. Try waking up again—only this time on the right side of the bed."

"Oh, just go, you big pain-in-the-butt, and be careful near the water. It's dark, slippery and wet out there."

"Yes, dear," Frank said as he blew her a kiss and then turned and walked out the door, closing it gently behind him. Betty played with the TV remote for several minutes then gave up, went to the kitchen and started to prepare breakfast.

Frank walked down the long path that ended at a pair of steps just below the pump station at the top of the dam. When he reached the steps he looked up the two flights to the top. He was about to start up the steps when, in the glow from a light at the top, he saw the dark silhouette of a man step into view. He stopped momentarily and spoke, "Hey, who are you and what are you doing here? This area is off-limits except to authorized personnel." He was about to continue up the steps when he heard a noise behind him. He turned and saw another man just inches away and was about to repeat his question when the man made a quick move and Frank felt a sharp pain in his abdomen just under his rib cage. He tried to speak again but the man moved again with two more quick thrusts and Frank felt two more searing pains.

Betty had just put bacon in a skillet and was about to cut two English muffins when she heard a sound at the front door. She turned and just looked at the door for a moment then went back to what she had been doing. There it was again, the sound, almost like a thud. She stopped again and then started toward the door. Halfway there she heard two more thuds as if someone was pounding on the door. "Hold on Frank, hold on. I'm coming. You forgot your keys again didn't you?" she said as she reached for the doorknob. She unlocked the door and slowly opened it, saying, "When will you ever remember those keys?"

What she saw took her breath like a thief. Standing in the doorway was Frank, his eyes and mouth wide open as if frozen by fear. Blood covered his chest and ran from both corners of his mouth. He moaned and fell against her, knocking them both to the floor. She screamed and rolled over and up onto her knees. She rolled Frank over onto his back, screaming, "Frank, Frank!" She placed her hand on his chest then raised it in front of her face. It was covered in thick red blood. She was about to scream again when she realized someone else was standing in the doorway beside her. She turned in that direction and looked up to see the business end of a handgun, only inches away. The last thing Betty saw was the muzzle flash.

Five minutes later, two men crossed the walkway at the top of the dam to about its center. One took a pack from his back and handed it to the other man. He opened the pack, retrieved a small keypad and punched in a set of code numbers. He placed the keypad back into the case and passed it back to the other man. That man took a plastic garbage bag from his pocket and placed the pack into it. He gathered the bag together at the top, placed it at his mouth, and started to blow into it like a balloon. When the bag was half inflated he wrapped a wire tie around the top of the bag

and with the help of the other man cinched it tight. He retrieved another bag from his pocket, placed the first bag inside and once again sealed it with a wire tie. The two men walked a metal walkway to a pump about one hundred yards into the reservoir. When they reached the end of the walk one of the men took the double bag and threw it out into the dark water with all his strength.

Ten minutes later, the two men, driving a car along a dirt road near the reservoir, pulled over to the side of the road. The man in the passenger seat pulled a remote control from his pocket and the two men looked back toward the reservoir they had just left. The man behind the wheel spoke softly in a foreign language the word, "Now." The other man pushed a lighted red button on the remote and at that instant, in the direction of the reservoir, was a flash of light and a muffled bang. The car returned to the road and sped away from the area. Back at the reservoir, near the pump where the bag had been placed, a large orange stain spread slowly over the surface of the water.

CHAPTER 3
September

Clive turned away from Matt, and looked up at Janis on the front porch and with a wide smile said, "You're not gonna hurt me with that little pop gun are you?"

Janis slid the safety of her pistol on, jumped up and bolted through the porch door and in two leaps traversed the stairs to the sidewalk. She ran across the yard and leaped into Clive's arms. With her arms around Clive's neck she kissed his cheek. "It's so good to see you. We've missed you so very much." Matt held the shotgun in his left hand and rounded the car with a smile as big as Janis's.

Clive lifted Janis off her feet and kissed her cheek. "It's only been three weeks, babe, but had I known what I've missed, I'd have been here sooner." Setting Janis down, he stretched out his right hand to meet Matt's and shook it wildly. He put his left arm around Matt's shoulders and hugged him. "How have you been, buddy?" he asked.

"We've been fine." Matt answered. "But we've missed you. How the hell have you been feelin', Clive?"

With that same big smile he answered, "Much better. Takes more than a bullet and a crack on the head to stop this old sheriff." With Janis on one side and Matt on the other, her arm around Clive's waist, they slowly walked across the yard to the back steps. They stopped at the bottom of the

steps and Clive brushed his hand through the front of Janis's hair, "You're just as beautiful as the first time I saw you." He turned to Matt and slapped him on the shoulder, "And you're as ugly as ever." He smiled and they all broke into laughter. Clive turned his back to the stairs and sat down on the second step. "The place looks good. It feels good just being here." His eyes scanned the back of the property. "I guess we never did get the chance to catch any of those large bass in the pond. They still there?" he asked.

Matt smiled, "Yeah, they're still there. When you feel up to it, we'll drink a few beers and wet a couple of lines."

Janis expression changed and with a surprised look toward the kitchen, she exclaimed, "The kids."

"What about the kids?" Matt asked.

"I told them to get into the living room and not to come out until they were told." Janis yelled up toward the kitchen door, "Lisa, Mary, Robert, it's okay. Come on out."

After a moment the kitchen door began to open slowly as three heads appeared around its edge. When the kids saw Clive they trampled over each other trying to get to him first. Seeing the oncoming stampede, Clive got to his feet as fast as he could and in less than a second was smothered with hugs and kisses from Mary and Robert. Lisa stopped about halfway down the steps and just stood there with tears running down her cheeks. "Uncle Clive," was all she could say.

Clive stared at her with admiring eyes. "Hi honey, how have you been?" She stepped slowly down the next two steps and put her arms around Clive's neck as his big arms lifted her from the stairs and turned her toward Matt and Janis. After what seemed like minutes, he let go of her and lowered her to the ground. "Sure is good to see you, honey. God, you're as beautiful as your mom."

Lisa was beautiful and looked as much like Janis as any daughter could. Blond hair, blue eyes, and about the same

height and build. As Matt had always jokingly said, the only thing she ever got from him was her stubborn streak. Janis took Clive's hand in hers and winked, "Your timing is still right-on."

"Timing, for what?" Clive asked.

"For breakfast, of course."

He smiled again and said, "I thought something smelled good." They all turned and with kids hanging all over Clive, moved up the stairs and into the kitchen. Matt placed the shotgun in the corner after carefully unloading it and then took Clive's service revolver and holster and hung them on a hook in the corner. Janis returned the pistol to its box, relit the burners under the food, and started with Lisa's and Mary's help to set the table.

Clive walked into the living room and stood at the side of the leather lounge chair that sat in front of the fireplace. He turned to Matt, who had just entered the room, and said "I spent a lot of time in this chair." Matt smiled as Clive looked around the room. "It feels good here," he said as he slowly moved his hand over the soft leather of the chair. "It feels like home."

Matt placed his hand on Clive's shoulder as he passed. "That's the way we want you to feel." Clive sat in the big chair and Matt moved to the couch. Beside the chair was a family picture that Clive picked up and stared at. Matt, Janis, Mary, Lisa, Robert and Andrew all looked back at him, smiling from the picture. Clive felt tears coming to his eyes and returned the picture to its resting place before his emotions had a chance to show. Matt looked at Clive as if he knew how he was feeling.

"How have things been here?" Clive asked.

Before Matt could answer, Robert walked into the room and up to Clive. "You feelin' okay now, Uncle Clive?"

"Yes, Uncle Clive is fine…My but you have grown over

the past few weeks."

Robert put his arms around Clive again and hugged him. Robert was eight years old, and like most boys his age, never seemed to stop moving unless he was asleep. "Glad you came to visit," Robert said, looking into Clive's eyes. "Can you stay? Huh? Please, huh? Come on, Uncle Clive, please?"

Matt smiled at Clive and responded first, "You can stay can't you?"

"Well," Clive said with a pause. Janis, who heard the question from the kitchen, glanced around the doorway and stared at Clive, who stared right back. "Depends on how good the cook is."

"Yeah, right," answered Janis and returned to her work.

Robert turned to Matt and asked, "Can I go outside till we eat, Dad?"

Janis in the kitchen responded, "On the porch only."

"Aw, Mom," Robert said with a frown.

"You heard Mom," intervened Matt. With that, Robert touched Clive on the shoulder and left the room for the back porch.

Clive turned to Matt with a more serious look on his face, "How is everybody taking all this?"

"Well, better than I figured," Matt answered. "Janis doesn't cry at night anymore, but I know it's always on her mind. Mary still has nightmares now and then, but not like before."

"And Lisa?" Clive asked.

"Well, she has wanted to go up to the ridge but I don't think it's a good idea just yet. Not safe, you know?"

Clive shook his head in agreement. "It's better out there now, but it's not back to normal yet…"

"I am worried about Robert," Matt added. "He keeps it inside and there are times in the evening I've seen him just stand out there on the big stump and stare at the sunset over

the big oak on the ridge. I guess it's just too much for him to grasp. I don't think it has all settled in yet. I know in my heart that we will resolve this about Andy. I'll never stop looking, but I worry about what it has done to my children."

Clive stared right into Matt's eyes, "And you, what about you?"

Matt cast his glance to the floor, took a deep breath and once again looked at Clive. "I'm managing," he said with a slight smile.

Janis looked around the door and yelled, "Food's on the table and no one eats with dirt on their hands. Let's wash them good."

"I guess she means us," Matt said, and with that Matt and Clive got up and headed to the bathroom. Janis opened the back door and called Robert inside. Lisa pulled some chairs from along the wall and moved them to the table. Clive and Matt returned from the bathroom and were greeted by Robert and Mary arguing over who would sit by Uncle Clive.

"Uncle Clive sits at the head of the table and you can sit on either side," Matt replied quickly to end the argument.

Mary pulled the chair out from the end of the table. "Sit, Uncle Clive," she said, looking up at him smiling. Mary was also a beautiful child, six years old and trying her best to be ladylike. She was also blue-eyed, but had more of a strawberry color to her hair than either Janis or Lisa. She had straighter hair than either her mother or sister and was an equal combination of both her parents. She was very lovable and emotional and had a fondness for reading.

Clive sat down and kissed her. "Thanks, honey."

Lisa placed a heaping, full plate of home fries, bacon and eggs in front of Clive and leaned over and kissed him on top of the head. "Now finish all of it or you do dishes."

"Okay, Mom," Clive answered as he reached for the toast.

Once seated and eating, Matt asked, "You are staying aren't you?"

"Well," Clive said once again, "I have to deliver some papers to the county station up the road, but I could swing by here on my way back. Only take a couple of hours and it's still early yet."

"You're on," replied Matt. "Could possibly even find a bed if you had some time to stay the night. It is Sunday tomorrow, you know?" With a little more badgering from every member of the family, Clive finally agreed to stay. But only if he could reach his office from his police cruiser. Telephone service was still at a minimum, and he had to report in to his office before he could make a commitment. The breakfast was a spur-of-the-moment reunion that could not have been planned any better. There was laughter, joking and a sense of love between family and friend that had little resemblance to the fear and disaster of the previous six weeks. There was little mention of the hardship and sacrifice that had affected all of their lives. There was a strong bond between them, a feeling that could not be put into words.

Clive was not truly related to Matt and his family but could not have been more involved in their lives. He had met the Fallon family in typical police fashion. Janis had run a stop sign on a nearby crossroads shortly after they had began to use the newly-constructed camp, several years earlier. After writing a warning ticket, Clive discovered his police cruiser would not start. Embarrassed, he returned to Janis's car to ask if she could help. She had no jumper cables and asked if he would return to camp with her to seek her husband's help. Matt willingly assisted him and somehow the ticket seemed to vanish into thin air, a phenomenon that Matt needled Clive about from that day on. Clive seemed to be around from that time on. It was as if the friendship was needed by all. There were picnics, parties and hunting trips,

campouts and sometimes just a talk around the fireplace on a winter evening. They had become friends, family people who needed each other.

Clive rose from the table, "Well, as much as I don't want to leave, I do have to deliver those papers. This has been one of the best mornings I've had in a long time. Janis, the food was great, as usual."

Janis walked up to Clive and hugged him. "You come right back here Clive Aliston. No excuses."

Matt got up from the table and retrieved Clive's gun from the hook behind the door. "You need some company to the station?"

"No, you better stay here where you're needed. I'll be fine." Clive took his gun and after what seemed like an eternity of kisses and hugs, walked out of the kitchen and onto the back porch with Matt and Janis.

Janis once again gave him a kiss. "You know I don't like goodbyes. See you in a couple of hours." She turned quickly and entered the kitchen.

Matt and Clive stared at each other for a moment then slowly shook hands and briefly hugged each other. "Right back now, remember," Matt said. They walked out to Clive's police cruiser and once again shook hands. "Be right back, friend?" Matt said. They smiled at each other and Clive got in his car and started the engine. Matt followed in front of the car as Clive backed out onto the road. Clive paused briefly, waved at Matt through the window and then slowly drove up the steep hill away from camp.

Matt stood in the middle of the road in dust the car had left and watched him disappear over the hill, "Carefully, my friend. Carefully," Matt whispered. He slowly turned back down the driveway to his house and paused a few feet from the sidewalk. He turned to his right and slowly looked up toward the big oak on the ridge at Scorpion's Tail. Tears

began to fill his eyes but he managed a smile. With a low whisper he said out loud, "Good morning. It is a beautiful morning, but I miss you…"

CHAPTER 4

July 30, 3:40 a.m. Eastern Time—near Buffalo

On a ridge in a wooded area just off Highway 90, fifteen miles south of Niagara Falls, four men unpacked equipment from the back of a truck. The lights they used had red filters on the lenses so they could not be seen from a great distance. They unloaded the boxes from the truck and walked to an open area in the brush overlooking a deep valley. It was too dark to see all of the valley floor but they knew what was at its bottom. Numerous sets of power lines snaked along the valley floor to a large distribution complex just below them. They could see the lights from the buildings and the iron work from a large complex of substation-type structures that spread out in all directions from the center building complex. One of the men watched the movement of a few workers below with night vision binoculars. As the other men began to open the boxes, the man with the binoculars walked to the other side of the ridge and scanned the valley on the other side. He was there for several minutes when he noticed several small flickering lights midway up that side of the hill and a little to his left. He watched them for several minutes, then in a foreign language called to one of the other men with him to come and take a look. The two men passed the binoculars back and forth several times then the first man, the one who seemed to be in charge, said one word:

"Campfire." They looked at each other; the second man reached behind his back to his belt, pulled out a handgun and then took a silencer from his coat pocket and threaded it onto the gun. He looked again at the other man then took one of the red-lens covered flashlights, nodded to the man in charge and walked away down the hill into the darkness.

Along the side of the same ridge, about midway between top and bottom was a large flat area almost like a shelf on the side of the slope. Several small fires flickered in the darkness at various spots, and eight or ten small tents sat in a row on one side of this flat field. At the opposite side of the clearing was one larger tent with two flags standing in holders at its front entrance.

One of the front flaps of the larger tent flipped open and a man in tan shorts, knee socks with moccasins, and an undershirt stepped out. He closed the flap and with a shirt in one hand stretched his arms above his head and yawned. He shivered all over, put the shirt on, then shivered again. As he started to walk slowly away from the tent, he tripped on something in the dark, bent over, quickly put his hand over his mouth, and mumbled something about the pain in his toes. He stood up straight again, retrieved a flashlight from his back pocket, snapped it on and pointed it at the ground. He bent over again, picked up a metal backpack frame, held it out in front of his face and looked at the tag on its side. He got a disgusted look on his face then whispered, "Walker. I should have known." He took the pack frame, walked to one of the small tents on the other side of the clearing, placed it on the ground beside the tent, then yawned and stretched again.

He slowly turned and started again in the same direction he had been walking in when he came upon the pack rack, then again shivered all over and mumbled, "Scout camping trips. One of the things I hate about scout camping trips is

having to take a piss in the middle of the night. I gotta get out of that warm sleeping bag early enough as it is. I sure as hell don't need this." He continued to mumble to himself as he walked to the far edge of the clearing to a brush line, then around the brush to a latrine hole that had a roll of toilet paper tied to a post next to it. He unzipped his shorts and started to urinate as another shiver ran through him.

A few seconds later he looked up at the night sky and an "ahhhhh" of returning comfort came from deep inside his chest. After a couple of minutes he rezipped his shorts and turned back in the direction of the campsite. He had only gone a few steps, looking at the ground in the light from his flashlight, when suddenly two feet appeared in front of him. He slowly raised the flashlight up the legs and body of the person standing in front of him. When he reached the man's face, the man stared back at him. With a questioning look on his face he said, "Who…" and was abruptly stopped in mid-question by two flashes of light and two thuds. He dropped to the ground where he stood. Minutes later, small flashes of light followed by more thuds came from the campsite. On the ridge above, in the light from the red flashlights, the other men continued to assemble military-style weapons on three tripods.

July 30, 3:40 a.m. Eastern Time—the Louisiana coast

Under a bridge that spanned a section of swampy river delta, near the Louisiana coast, two men in camo clothes, their faces covered in camo paint, worked steadily. One of the men was packing small bars of what looked like a gray or tan putty around the supports of the center span of the bridge. The other man stood at the center of a catwalk under the bridge, holding an AK-47 and keeping watch on both ends of the bridge. The man placing the bars took a small electronic instrument out of his pocket and pushed a button

that lit a set of digital numbers on a display on the face of the instrument. He punched in several number sequences, then taped the instrument to the pack of bars now taped to the bridge pier. When he had finished, he pushed a button on the instrument and digital numbers began to count down. He climbed to the catwalk and met the man with the AK-47. They conversed for several seconds in whispers, then the man with the gun took a cell phone out of his pocket and dialed a number. When the party at the other end answered he said, "It is finished," and hung up. He and the other man then slowly walked the catwalk to the other end.

Two miles away, at a long straight dirt road in the middle of a swampy forested area, a small plane sat on the dirt as three men attached brackets to the wings. Once the brackets were attached, the men opened a long wooden box that sat in a box truck next to the plane. The side of the truck had lettering that read, "Bio-hazard Medical Waste." From the boxes, the men lifted rockets one at a time, two men on each of the heavy rockets, and latched them under the wings of the plane. In the cockpit, the pilot sat watching the men as they loaded the rocket brackets. His cell phone rang, and when he answered it he heard the words: "It is finished." He hung up, opened the door of the plane, and in a hushed foreign voice told the men, "They are finished at the bridge." The men continued to load the rockets and the pilot went through a check-list on his lap.

The man who had been driving the truck walked to the plane, opened the door and spoke to the pilot. After several minutes, he walked away from the plane and down the road about a hundred yards. He stopped at an open area at the edge of the swamp. He placed a pair of night vision binoculars to his eyes and looked out toward the bridge where the other men had been working earlier. At one end of the bridge near the end of the catwalk he saw three flashes

of light followed by a pause then three more. He lowered the binoculars and smiled, then turned to his left and looked out over the vast flat swampy area in front of him to a glow of lights just at the edge of the horizon. In the distance, some four miles away, stood one of the largest oil refineries on the Gulf Coast.

CHAPTER 5
September

Matt wandered around the driveway for a few moments, holding back his tears as his memories flashed back chaotically. He had been thankful to be able to spend a wonderful morning with his good friend, but the time with Clive had brought back the events he had tried to keep inside for the last few weeks.

He walked up to one of the shag bark hickory trees beside the house, placed both hands palm down on the tree at about eye level, leaned forward and placed his forehead on the back of his hands. He pushed hard against the tree as if trying to uproot it, his face never leaving the back of his hands. Suddenly the tears came in a rush he could not hold back. He made no sound but slowly turned, placing his hands over his face and his back against the tree and sliding to the ground. He remained there for a moment or two before he could finally regain his composure. He wiped the tears from his eyes but remained seated, and just stared at the surface of the pond in front of him.

Janis had been working in the kitchen. As she leaned over to wash the table she glanced out the side window at about the same moment Matt reached the tree. She stopped, motionless, and with tears welling up in her own eyes, watched as her husband finally broke under the pressure of

the memories she knew must finally resurface. She stopped what she was doing, and with both hands flat on the table, she bent over slightly and turned her head toward the back wall. She began to cry softly. Lisa, Robert and Mary started to enter the kitchen when Lisa realized that Janis was crying. She quickly turned to stop her siblings, then turned in front of them and whispered, "You two go clean your rooms. We need to help Mom. I'll be there in a moment to help you."

Mary, realizing that something was wrong, looked over Lisa's head toward her mother then quickly looked back at Lisa. "Come on, Robert. Bet I can be done before you."

Lisa touched her cheek and smiled, "Go on now." The two children turned and left for their bedrooms. Lisa slowly turned and walked to her mother. "What's wrong, Mom?" she asked as she leaned over and slowly ran her fingers through her mother's hair.

Janis was sobbing quietly as she turned and looked at Lisa. "Nothing. Everything's fine," she said as she wiped her tears, and turned her back to the window and hugged Lisa. Lisa returned her mother's hug and as they stood there holding each other, she glanced out the side window just in time to see Matt slowly get up from the ground and wipe away the last of his tears. She just held her mother for a moment as she watched her father through the window. Janis finally looked at her face-to-face and whispered, "Thanks, honey. I'm fine, really."

Lisa smiled and wiped the last tear from her mother's face. "Well, I guess I made a promise. I better keep it." She smiled and turned and left for the kids' bedrooms.

Janis once again turned to the window but Matt was not in sight. She took in a long deep breath and returned to her work. Matt was a strong man both physically and emotionally, and she knew that when he finally needed her he would come to her on his own, in his own time.

Matt had walked to the dog pen and was petting Ginger through the holes in the fence when he finally returned to reality. He looked down at his empty hands and then around in every direction. He realized he had left the shotgun in the house when Clive left. He shook his head and looked straight up at the sky, "You ass. No gun..." He looked down at Ginger, "Well the least you could have done was remind me," he said as he smiled. Ginger just sat and looked up at him with her eyes wide open and her head tilted to one side as if she knew exactly what he was saying. Matt turned and started to walk away toward the house when Ginger let out a bark. Matt stopped and turned back and smiled at her, "Yeah, I know. Forgot your food too. Good thing my head's attached." He turned once again and walked back toward the porch.

Matt entered the kitchen then walked through the living room to his and Janis's room. From the top drawer of his dresser he removed a 9 mm semi-automatic pistol and belt holster, slipped it through the belt on his jeans then pulled his denim jacket down over it. He then removed the loaded clip for the pistol from another drawer, placed it in his pocket and left the room. As he passed Lisa's room, he looked in on the kids cleaning the room as fast as they could. "Hi, Dad," they all said in unison.

He smiled and asked, "Where's Mom?"

"She's in the bathroom, I think," replied Lisa.

Matt smiled again and turned to the bathroom door. He knocked gently on the door and entered. Janis was in front of the mirror, combing her hair. "Hi, honey," he said, as he put his arms around her from behind and kissed her on the back of the neck. "I'm going to feed Ginger and then cut some more wood for the fireplace. I'll be out behind the garage if you need me." He walked back out of the bathroom, then stopped and put his head back around the

corner. "Everything okay?" he asked.

Janis smiled in the mirror and replied, "Okay." They stared at each other in the mirror's reflection for a moment, then Janis added, "I'm going to clean up around here a bit, then I'll be out. I want to do a little more on my painting." Janis was an amateur artist and enjoyed the quiet and relaxation of painting landscapes and nature scenes.

"Do you want me to get your easel and supplies from the garage?" Matt asked. She nodded in agreement and he smiled and left the house, first retrieving his shotgun and a dish of dog food and table scraps from the kitchen. He crossed the back yard to the pen, unlocked the gate and placed the bowl of food on the ground in front of the doghouse. Ginger jumped and pawed at his pant leg while her tail wagged wildly. He patted her on the head and left the pen, locking the gate behind him. He entered the garage, picked up all of Janis's art supplies and a folding chair, and after setting his shotgun in the corner, carried all of her equipment to a shaded grassy spot near the pond. He returned to the garage, took an ax and a logger's maul from a hook on the wall, picked up his shotgun and walked out behind the garage.

When he reached the wood-cutting area he braced the shotgun in the Y of a nearby tree and removed the 9mm from the holster on his belt. He took the clip from his pocket and slipped it into the pistol handle, then pulled back the slide bolt to chamber a shell. He placed the gun on top of a small stump next to the wood-cutting area. He picked up eight or ten pieces of hickory from the nearby wood pile, carried them to the splitting stump and dropped them to the ground. As he picked up the ax, his eyes scanned the property around him. He looked at his watch: 10:30. "Clive, you should be back here by noon," he whispered as he set the first piece of wood on the cutting stump. He took in a

deep breath and began splitting wood. As he worked splitting and stacking his mind began to drift back to that day when the nightmare began. It was the first time he was able to really face the memories he had so successfully learned to block out. His friend's visit had given him something he knew he needed: the courage to relive it, if only in his thoughts. He drifted back to that mid-July Sunday.

CHAPTER 6
September

Clive was on the road to the sheriff's station to deliver the paperwork he had with him. He was feeling a lot more comfortable after the great breakfast he had had at the Fallon camp. It had been so good to see them all again. What a great morning it had been. In his heart he loved them all as if they had always been family. Thoughts of what they had been through over the past weeks came back to him. They were a tough family both physically and emotionally, yet it had been tough on all of them, including him. Who would ever have believed that this all could have happened? He even thought back to 9/11, what had transpired from that time seemed more like a mystery or action novel than true life. His thoughts went back to a little more than a year before, back to Smith Falls and the murders that had taken place. Thoughts of the faces of the victims crossed his mind. What an unbelievable thing to happen in a small, out-of-the-way place like Smith Falls. He knew that those events had changed his life forever.

The tragedy of 9/11 was national, the events of Smith Falls were very personal and the events of the last two months had hit home both ways. My God, how things had changed. He had lost so many close friends both to the disaster and to the murders. He had always thought of

himself as a tough cop—on top of it all, where he needed to be—but he had learned that like the country itself, he had not been truly prepared. He knew in his heart that he was changing, yet he knew he could not let what had happened push his feelings away. He knew that he had become tougher than he ever thought he could be; he had become more hard-line and intense in his police work. He would never be caught off guard again. The Clive Aliston of the past was no more. He had become what he needed to be and if death came to him because of it, then so be it.

As he drove on, Clive began to think back about the previous two months, back to that fateful day in mid-July. His mind moved through time from 9/11 to the murders in Smith Falls and to those recent days of chaos and terror. As his thoughts moved back and forth in time, there was a feeling that tugged at his insides. The past weeks had been, to say the least, horrific in themselves, but there was something else that lay heavy on his mind. Something about parts of it seemed to say, I'm there right in front of you, like a bright red thread through the center of a black swatch of cloth. It was as if the murders from the year earlier still haunted him and kept pushing clues at him from out there somewhere. Through all this there was something, but what? What did "Forever" mean now and "Their tickets must be redeemed," and most of all, where were Brian and Max?

CHAPTER 7

July 30, 5:00 a.m. Eastern Time—central Pennsylvania

Two guards walked out of one of the guard towers at the entrance to one of the largest correctional institutions in Pennsylvania. Bob Delano and Jim Smith were on an early-morning break. They both needed to get some fresh air and they wanted to continue with their heated discussion about the upcoming football pre-season in August. "I don't care if they did lose some prime players," Bob said. "They'll still make a damn good run at another title."

"Bullshit," Jim said. "You can't lose people at those key positions and expect to repeat as Super Bowl champions. It's just wishful thinking on your part."

"Why am I even discussing this with you?" Bob said. "You didn't pick them to win last year. Shows how much…" His statement trailed off as he looked over Jim's shoulder to a woods line three hundred yards from the front gate of the prison. He just stood and stared in that direction with a questioning look on his face.

Jim, seeing Bob's face, just said, "What?" and turned to look out in the same direction. Bob was still quiet but walked the couple of feet to the wall and leaned out, straining his eyes at the tree line. "What?" Jim repeated as he joined him at the wall and looked out at the dark tree line then back at Bob. "What the hell do you see?"

"I don't know," Bob said as he turned back to Jim. "I thought for a moment that I saw lights in the trees."

Jim looked out again in the direction of the trees, straining his eyes. After a few moments he looked at Bob and said, "I don't see anything out there. You're nuts. The edge of that tree line is one hundred yards inside the first fence. Who the hell could get in there without being caught? Jack Kimble and five other guys are out there. They just ain't gonna let someone stroll in here on their own."

Bob finally stopped staring at the dark tree line and turned to Jim, "Yeah, I guess you're right."

"Yeah, I'm right. Just like I'm right about the loss of those key players. I tell ya it ain't gonna be the same season this year."

"Yeah, yeah right," Bob said. "You're always right. Come on Mr. Know-it-all, we gotta get back inside. I've had enough fresh air and your style of football, you big stupid."

"Yeah, big stupid, your ass," Jim said as they opened the door and started back inside.

Bob stopped just inside the door and once again looked back to the tree line with the same questioning look on his face. A moment later he just clenched his teeth in a half smile, shook his head and continued on inside.

Fifteen minutes later, Bob was back at the desk at the end of one of the prison rows. He had just filled in some reports and leaned back in his chair, rubbing the back of his neck. He started to think again about the light he thought he had seen. He picked up the phone and called to the outer perimeter fence to where he knew Jack Kimble would be. The phone rang about ten times with no answer. Bob placed the phone back down and sat back in his chair. After several seconds he said, "Must be at the bathroom." He picked up the phone again; it rang ten more times and he hung up. He sat motionless for several more minutes then called Jim on

the walkie-talkie and asked him to come to the desk.

When Jim arrived, Bob asked him to stay at the desk for a few minutes. Jim just looked at him with a curious look on his face and said, "Why? What's up?"

Bob said, "Jim, just stay here. I gotta check something out. Be right back." With that he got up and left before Jim could speak again.

Jim sat in Bob's chair and mumbled to himself, "What the hell is he up to now?"

At six a.m. Eastern Time, cell phones began to ring in various places across the United States. Each person who got one of these calls from a group leader heard four short phrases: "It is finished. Their time in hell has come. Soon we will all be joined in heaven. May our cause be blessed."

Bob Delano walked out of the guard tower again and to the rail at the top of the wall. He placed a pair of binoculars to his face and scanned the guard building at the first security fence. He could see the lighted office window and the desk inside but there was no one there and no movement. He watched for several minutes then lowered the glasses and whispered, "Okay guys, where are you?" He put the glasses back to his face and scanned the tree line. There was nothing in sight, no movement and no lights. He lowered the binoculars again and just stood staring out into the slowly lightening sky. He was kind of admiring the orange glow on the horizon when he raised his arm and pressed the light on his wrist watch. It was 6:01 a.m.

Bob looked back at the road that led to the front gate and saw headlights from a large vehicle coming down the road at high speed. "What the hell are they doing?" he whispered to himself. "You can't drive that fast or that close to the prison gate. They'll never get stopped." Just at that moment three bright flashes lit up the tree line and three white lighted streaks shot toward the prison gate. Bob watched as they

disappeared below the wall. He stepped forward to look over the edge of the wall when three loud explosions shook him off his feet. He rolled over and got to his knees as debris landed all around him. He jumped to his feet, reached inside the guard tower and pulled the alarm lever. As the alarm sounded, three more lighted streaks passed over the wall and into the buildings behind him. The buildings erupted in three explosions. Bob was thrown against the wall. As he got up again he turned toward the road just as the truck disappeared from sight below the wall. He leaned out over the wall just as the truck hit the main gate. Bob's mouth dropped open and his eyes opened wide as a brilliant flash enveloped the entire wall. The last thing Bob heard was the thunderous explosion as the entire wall he was standing on collapsed.

CHAPTER 8
September

Clive and Matthew were now a distance apart: Matt at camp cutting wood and Clive on the road to the police station. Their minds however were joined, back at that day when it had all begun weeks earlier. For Matt, there were memories of a beautiful July day, the morning cloaked in a crisp sparkling mist that danced and dazzled the eye like diamonds shimmering on the leaves and branches of every tree. The Fallon family had planned a picnic at their favorite place on the ridge at the big oak on Scorpion's Tail. They had left the house about 8:00 a.m., just as the patches of sky began to peek through the mist and the rays of the sun pierced arrows of light through the canopy of green leaves above. A cool gentle breeze made ripples on the pond as they started up the path through the lush green forest of the valley. Robert and Mary raced up the path ahead of the rest in a foot race, to see who could get to the picnic grove first.

Janis and Matt slowly walked hand-in-hand behind, watching the children far up ahead. Andrew was lagging behind as usual, watching for any sign of wildlife and scanning the woods for another of the secrets he was so fond of learning. Matt and Janis talked about almost anything that came to mind. They wished Lisa could be with them. She was in summer session in a private school in the city and

was not able to come home to the camp on weekends. Matt and Janis carried the picnic basket and cold drinks. Andrew had a bag of games, yard darts and his compound bow and a quiver of arrows.

Janis and Matt reached the picnic table under the big tree long after Robert and Mary did. The children were sprawled out on top of the table, trying to catch their breath and arguing over who had gotten there first. Janis chased them off the table, spread out the tablecloth and set the basket and drinks on top.

Robert ran to the swing that hung on one of the large branches of the tree and sat down as Mary began pushing him. "Higher, higher," he yelled.

Matt looked at Mary, "Not too high, you hear?"

Andrew was still not at the top of the path so Matt walked over to see if he was coming. He was nowhere in sight. When he returned to the table, there sat Andrew with a wide smile. "I fooled you again, Dad."

Matt looked at him shaking his head. "I swear you could sneak up on an Indian and give him a heart attack." Andy laughed, then walked over to the far side of the open field to a stack of straw bales and started to put up an archery target. Matt noticed Janis standing alone on the edge of the steep ridge near a big rock overlooking the valley. He walked over to her and put his arms around her waist. "Beautiful, just beautiful."

"Our valley is beautiful, isn't it?" she said.

"Not the valley," he answered with a smile. "You. I mean you." He pulled her closer to him, kissed her lips, and whispered, "I love you."

She closed her eyes and ran her fingers through the back of his hair, "I love you so very much, too..."

The valley in front of them was beautiful. A steep hill descended in front of them into a lush green valley below. In

the distance, you could see the house and the outbuildings of camp, the pond and the creek behind that meandered through the valley and off into the distance. There were no other buildings in sight, which made their camp appear like small sparkling pieces of opal, cast on a thick forest green carpet that stretched for miles in every direction. Scorpion's Tail was not only a favorite picnic ground for the Fallon family but was the agreed-upon place to meet in the event any misfortune or emergency should befall them—a place of safety that few people outside the area knew existed. The area around the massive oak had a mystical feel about it that went hand-in-hand with stories told by the locals Indian tribes who had lived in the area eons ago. To those Indians, Scorpion's Tail was a magical place of spirits that guided the forces of nature to protect the tribe from evil. The Eastern tribes of long ago had named this place Scorpion's Tail, and the origin of the name was a mystery still unsolved to that day. The ridge was the highest ground for miles around, and from a topographical map you could plainly see it was indeed in the shape of a coiled tail of the scorpion. How did the early natives know? It was a place of unanswered questions and exquisite beauty, with a feeling of safety and peace about it.

The remaining part of the morning was a devoted to family fun and games. They all ate lunch together, then Matt and Janis stretched out on a blanket and watched Andy showing Mary and Robert his expertise with his bow. He was an accomplished archer, and at times his ability with the bow even astonished Matt, who was himself a good shot. Andrew stood fifty paces from the target and grouped arrows in the center bull with deadly precision. Andy was making an attempt to show Robert how to draw back the bow when he stopped and turned his attention to the northern sky. Matt noticed the rolling thunder approaching

from the same direction. He got up from the blanket and stepped out from under the tree. With his hand over his eyes to block out the sun, he stared at the sky to the north. The thunder grew louder and Janis got up and walked to his side, "What is it?" she said.

Matt was about to speak when Andy yelled, "Look, just above the horizon." Matt and Janis strained their eyes to make out what he saw. Matt noticed six small black dots that were quickly growing larger. In a matter of seconds the rumble was directly overhead as six F-18 Hornet fighters raced through the sky just above the trees. The sound was deafening and the ground shook beneath their feet. The children raced back to Matt and Janis and held onto them in a sort of panic. Andy just stood there and watched them disappear over the trees. In less than a minute, a second flight roared overhead and into the distance. Matt stood there with a puzzled look on his face.

"What is it?" Janis asked again.

"I don't know, but I swear they were armed to the teeth."

"Why?" Janis asked with a surprised look on her face.

"I don't know," he replied. They calmed the children and sent them back to Andy, who was standing there bow, in hand, looking strangely at Matt.

Janis returned to the blanket, followed by Matt, who still looked puzzled. "Never seen them before?" Janis questioned with an uneasy look on her face.

"I have," Matt said. "They are stationed at a base in New York, just east of Lake Erie. They usually don't fly this far south." He laid back down, folded his hands behind his head and stared at the huge oak branches above him.

Janis, lying beside him, kissed his cheek. "Guess they're just on maneuvers, huh?"

"Yeah," Matt answered, but inside he wondered. Quiet returned for about half an hour, while Matt and Janis napped

on the blanket under the tree.

Matt suddenly opened his eyes as Andy gently shook his arm. "Dad, I think you better come see this."

Matt quietly stood up and walked to the table where Robert and Mary were coloring in some books. He smiled at them and said, "Keep quiet. Let Mom sleep a little longer. I'll be right back." He and Andy walked to the very end of the ridge to a cliff overlooking the valley to the south. "What is it?" Matt asked.

Andy pointed toward the small village of Dawn, about five miles away. Thick clouds of black smoke rose in the afternoon sky from six or seven different places. "I've seen more jets to the east and maybe half a dozen helicopters—all military. There, there's one now."

Matt stood and just stared. "If only I'd brought my binoculars," he said. A moment later he heard the sound of helicopters coming from the west. He and Andy turned and saw three armed gun-ships not half a mile away in formation, headed south in the same general direction as the jets. "Andy, something is wrong," he said with a worried look on his face. "I'll wake Mom. You get the kids' games and things together."

Matt and Andy ran back to the picnic area to find Janis standing in the middle of the open field waiting for them. When she saw them at a full run she knew something was wrong. "What? What? What is it?" she yelled as they approached.

Matt stopped in front of her, placed his hands on her shoulders and tried to catch his breath. "It looks like the town of Dawn is on fire and there are military aircraft everywhere. I just don't know. Something just isn't right." Janis started to say something but Matt interrupted her. "I'm going to run back to camp to get the jeep. You and Andy and the kids stay here. You will be safe up here. I want the jeep

to get back home quicker. I don't want to get caught in the open on foot with the children. I'll come back up to the ridge on the back dirt road."

"But Matt."

"No, please listen to me," he said, interrupting her. "It may be nothing, but I'm not taking any chances." They quickly walked back to the table. "Andy, you stay here with Mom and the kids. I'll be back in half an hour."

"You want the bow?" Andy asked.

"No. You keep it here with you." He whispered in Janis's ear, "Keep the kids calm and quiet. I love you." Before she could respond he turned and ran to the top of the path, down the hill and into the wooded valley below. The farther he ran the faster he moved, aided by the downhill slope. He dodged branches and over and around logs as he cut corners off the winding path. He was about three quarters of the way down the hill and had cut off the path once more to save time, when his foot caught on a rock under the leaves that sent him tumbling headlong into a small stream at the bottom of the path. He landed face down in the water and onto a large rock that knocked the wind out of him. He pulled his knees to his stomach and gasped for air, his face and hair still partially in the water. He straightened out, dragged himself to the side, grabbed a root at the top of the two-foot high bank, and peered over the edge. His eyes were still filled with muddy water but he could see hazy green foliage around him. Suddenly, a lone figure appeared through the dense underbrush and walked slowly toward him, followed by another. A wave of dizziness passed over him and he lowered his head. When he raised it again the green was gone and he saw the sand dunes of a desert. He rubbed his eyes to clear away the mud and dirt and looked again. Standing not ten feet from him was an Arab man in light, loose-fitting camo clothes, holding something in his

hands. He rubbed his eyes again and focused on the second man, dressed the same. In his mind, he heard the unmistakable click of a gun bolt. He glanced again at the first man, who was slowly turning a clip-fed, automatic weapon toward him, an AK-47. Republican Guard, his mind flashed. He rolled off the bank into the water, and grabbed for his side to retrieve his service weapon. Nothing there but wet denim jeans.

He leaned back on his elbows, closed his eyes and waited. Nothing happened. After a second or two he slowly opened his eyes and crawled back up over the bank. He wiped his face and once again stared at the spot where he had seen the men. No one there. Only the trees, a few birds chirping and the gentle rustling of the wind in the leaves. He put his forehead down in the mud on the bank for a second and breathed a sigh of relief. A flashback from his past. A phantom out of the dark recesses of his mind. A memory he thought was long forgotten.

Suddenly, he remembered his family and dragged himself painfully to his feet and started to walk toward the path. After a few feet he began to run again and soon was moving as quickly as before. He rounded the next bend and there before him was camp. His feet pushed harder as he passed the pond and ran up through the yard to the garage. He reached the jeep in the garage and then remembered the trouble he'd had starting it the day before. He tried once, twice and a third time. "Not now, you piece of junk," he yelled. He tried again and the motor turned over. He quickly backed out of the garage, turned around and sped down the driveway to the road. He stopped for a brief second to check the road in both directions, then accelerated out of the driveway. About a hundred yards up the road he turned into a field on the left that led to an old logging road that curved up the hill toward the ridge.

The jeep stalled out just after his turn. He was about to curse the machine again when he thought he heard something in the distance. He paused and turned his head in the direction of the sound. Nothing but silence. He reached for the key again, then stopped. There was that sound again: Tat-tat-tat-tat, a pause, then the same. It was the unmistakable sound of gunfire. He reached for the key and again restarted the jeep, slapped it into gear and floored the gas pedal. The vehicle jumped forward as the rear tires dug into the soft topsoil of the field. The jeep fishtailed back and forth, throwing mud and weeds high into the air. He straightened it out and turned onto the road, up the hill and into the forest. The road was narrow and winding, with just enough room for one vehicle. The limbs hung low over the middle and weeds grew high in the center. Branches slapped against the windshield, across his shoulders, face and arms. Though each branch stung his flesh and partially blocked his vision, he continued on at a fast pace.

Suddenly, the foliage opened and there before him was the small stream he had fallen into minutes before. He jammed the brake pedal to the floor and the jeep skidded to a sideways stop just short of the creek bank. He stood up in the front seat and looked over the windshield. No way to cross; the bank was too high on his side. He sat back down with a puzzled look on his face, then put the jeep in reverse and backed up to the edge of the trees. He clenched his teeth and mumbled to himself, "If you can't drive, fly." He pushed hard on the gas pedal and the wheels spun and then dug in.

"Speed, come on speed," he yelled. The vehicle covered about fifty feet and out over the creek bed. The opposite bank was much lower but was covered with large rocks. The rear wheels left the bank and the engine screamed as the traction of the ground disappeared. He cleared the creek but the jeep nosed into the other side with a loud, bone-crushing

thud. Matt was lifted from his seat and almost out over the windshield. He came back down so hard into the seat he thought he landed on the floor boards. The jeep tried to stall again, but he depressed the gas pedal quickly and bounced over the large stones on the opposite bank onto the forest floor and up the road once again. The road on this side of the creek wasn't much better, but he continued his fast pace. He was about three quarters of the way up the hill when suddenly the trees opened up once again, just in time for him to see that the right side of the road had been washed out. It was too late to stop and the wheels of the right side were already in mid-air. The jeep, now two feet off the ground, began to roll to the side and turn over when the wheels hit the earth again. The impact ripped the steering wheel out of Matt's hands and tossed the jeep sharply to the left into a large mud-filled puddle. It ground to a stop and sank in. The impact yanked Matt out of his seat and half into the mud and water of the large pool. He wiped the mud from his face and crawled out into the ankle-deep black ooze. The jeep was still running but the mud and water were near the axles of the front and rear of the vehicle. "Shit," he yelled as he rubbed his sore ribs.

Matt looked his situation over for a second, then slapped the jeep on the hood, "Now, let's just see how good you are." He jumped back into the jeep on the passenger side and moved over the shift and into the driver's seat. He wrapped his fingers tightly around the steering wheel and looked at himself in the rearview mirror. He shifted into gear and whispered, "Let's do it…" He eased the pedal to the floor and the wheels began to turn slowly in the mud. The jeep started forward and then slid back. He took his foot off the gas and once again said, "Do it." He shifted into reverse, started to back up and then quickly returned the shift to first gear and the jeep began to roll forward. Mud and water flew

onto leaves, trees and the forest floor in all directions. Slowly, he moved forward out of the grasp of the black, sucking ooze and onto the solid ground of the road. Once out of the mud, he stopped and put his arms on the top of the steering wheel and placed his head on his arms. He paused for a moment, then raised his head and brushed his hand across the front of the dashboard, "Good job." Once again he pushed the gas pedal to the floor and continued up the hill toward the top of the ridge.

A few moments later Matt reached the field at the top. As he drove to the picnic area around the tree, he realized that his family was nowhere in sight. Where had they gone? What could have happened to make them leave the safety of this area? He stopped the jeep near the base of the tree, then climbed out and stood there and searched the landscape around him.

He thought he heard a sound from above, like a squirrel chattering. He looked up into the thick green of the oak and there, standing on one of the large limbs, was Andy, bow in had. He had an arrow in the ready position. He smiled and then quickly moved down and out of the tree with the agility of an animal. He swung down from a lower limb and landed on the ground beside Matt. "Where's Mom and the kids?" Matt asked.

"There is a safe place just over the edge of the ridge in a cave."

"What cave?" Matt asked, looking puzzled.

"It's there. Believe me," Andy replied. "Dad, what happened to you?" Andy said as he looked up and down Matt's body. That's when Matt realized how dirty, scratched and welted he was. "The road is bad, real bad. Can't go back that way."

"But what happened to you?" Andy asked again.

Matt just smiled. "Small accident. I'll explain later. Let's

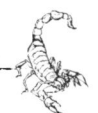

get Mom and the kids home. Have you seen or heard anything else?" Matt asked, as he looked to the south toward Dawn.

"Haven't seen anyone or any other aircraft since you left, but I did hear gunfire."

"Yeah. Me too," Matt replied. Matt started to walk toward the edge of the ridge and motioned for Andy to follow. "Let's go, Son. Show me this cave."

CHAPTER 9
September

Matt had finished his second glass of iced tea out on the porch and was brought back to reality by the children. They had tired of the puzzle-building and wanted to go outside. Robert and Mary asked if they could play in the yard.

"Can we play outside now?" asked Robert.

"Yeah, Dad," Mary chimed in. Matt looked up at them both and nodded an okay. The children ran out through the doorway, slamming the screen door, down the stairs and into the yard.

"Stay in the yard and in sight," Matt added quickly.

The kitchen door opened again; Lisa walked out onto the porch and stood behind Matt. "Where's Mom?" she asked as she placed both hands on his shoulders.

He leaned his head back, looked up into her eyes and smiled. "She's down at the pond, painting, honey."

"Guess I'll go down and keep her company," she said as she kissed him on the forehead. She walked around his chair and stopped. "Do you want something else to drink?"

"No. I've had enough, thanks." They smiled at each other and Lisa left the porch and walked to the pond. Matt inhaled deeply, wiped his face with his hand and rubbed his eyes. "Well, Beau, guess I better get back at it. That wood won't split itself." He placed the glass on the table, picked

Beau up from his lap and put him on the table. He stood up, stretched his arms up over his head and yawned. "Boy, I better get going before I fall asleep," he said, as if Beau understood. He picked up the shotgun and yawned again, then rolled his shoulders to loosen them up, opened the screen door and left the porch.

Matt walked around the house on the road side, stopped at the driveway for a moment, then walked to the road. He looked up and down the road in both directions, then looked at his watch. It was 11:45 a.m. "He should be here soon," he said in a whisper, referring to Clive. He raised the shotgun about waist high with his right hand and wiped some dust from around the front bead. He raised the gun again, rested it upside down on top of his right shoulder and walked back the driveway toward the garage. He stopped at the dog pen, opened the gate and grabbed a dog leash from high on the pen fence. He clipped the leash to Ginger's collar and led her outside as she jumped and barked in excitement. She tugged at the leash, pulling him down past the garage in the direction of the wood-cutting area. He stopped momentarily at the side of the garage and held Ginger back with a steady pressure on the leash.

He looked toward the pond at Janis and Lisa sitting near the water, talking as Janis painted. "Do you two need anything?" he asked.

"No, Dad," Lisa answered and they continued their talk. Matt walked Ginger to a tree near where he was working and tied her up, then set the shotgun down again and placed his pistol on the same stump. He picked up all of the already-split pieces of firewood and placed them on the pile he was building. He gathered six or eight rough pieces and set them near the stump. He picked up the ax and examined the edge, then placed the head of the ax on the ground leaving the handle against his legs. He spit into his hands

and rubbed them together, picked up the ax and began to work again. As he worked, memories of the picnic returned and he remembered the cave Andy had shown him.

July

They walked to the edge of the ridge and Matt stopped and scanned the thick brush in front of him. "Where is this cave?" he asked Andy, who was standing behind him.

"Over here, Dad," Andy replied as he walked a few feet to the right. Matt followed him and when he stopped, Andy raised the branch of a small tree on the edge of the ridge. There before them, under the thick foliage, was a narrow path. It curved down and around the side of the hill and out of sight. Andy looked at Matt, "Go ahead, Dad." Matt bent low and started down the path. As he moved down and along the side of the ridge, he realized the path was completely hidden from sight in all directions. Moving forward, he noticed many deer tracks in the soft earth at his feet. He continued on across the side of the ridge for about fifty feet, bending low under the thick branches. He stopped suddenly as several deer jumped up ahead and bounded into the valley below. "Hey, Dad. Back here," Andy whispered low. Matt turned and looked back at Andy, who was standing about twenty feet behind him. Andy motioned with his arm to come back to him.

Matt complied, and stopped in front of Andy, "Well, where are they?"

Andy smiled and then with both hands pulled back some branches to his right. There before Matt was the opening of a cave. It was concealed so well he had walked right past it. The entrance was about ten feet wide but totally covered by the thick green leaves. The entrance curved downward for about ten feet then leveled out.

"Let's go," said Andy as he held the branches back for

his father. Matt descended into the cave, followed by Andy. When he reached the bottom he could smell something burning and see light just ahead and around the bend. They walked about twenty feet toward the light and turned the corner. There, in a large room, were Janis, Robert and Mary, sitting at a homemade log table and bench with a torch burning in a holder on the cave wall.

Janis jumped up and ran to Matt, followed by the children. She threw her arms around Matt's neck and hugged him. The children hung onto him, one on each leg. "I'm so relieved you're here and alright," she said as she squeezed him even harder. She let go of the hold she had on him, put her arms on the sides of his shoulders and looked into his eyes with a worried look on her face.

"We heard gunfire just after you left, so Andy brought us down here for safety. He went back outside even though I told him I'd go," as she gave Andy a scolding look. "What is going on out there?" she said as she glanced back at Matt.

"I still don't know, but I want to get us all back to camp. Come on. Son, let's get going," he said to Andy as he slapped him on the shoulder. Andy walked over to the table, retrieved the torch from its resting place on the wall and led them out of the cave.

He stopped for a moment, put out the torch and placed it in another holder at the entrance. They walked the path to the top of the ridge with Andy in the lead. At the end of the path, Andy stopped and put an arrow in a ready position in his bow. He slowly crawled out of the brush and into the field. He remained on his stomach as his eyes scanned the field and the forest in all directions.

All clear. He stood up and pulled back the tree limbs and motioned them forward, then they crawled out of the brush and trees one at a time, with Matt bringing up the rear.

Janis turned to Matt as he stepped out into the field. Her

eyes grew large and surprised when she saw the condition of his clothes and face in the bright, afternoon sun. "Honey, what happened to you?" she asked as she touched his face.

Andy looked at Matt and they smiled at each other. "Small accident," he said to Janis. "I'll explain later. Let's go." With that, they all ran to the jeep and climbed in. Andy sat beside Matt in front and Janis and the children sat in the back. Matt turned to the children. They both stared at him with a terrified look on their faces. He realized they had not spoken a word since he got back. "Are you scared?" he asked. Neither replied, but they both nodded their heads in confirmation. He smiled reassuringly at them. "We're going home now. Everything will be fine." He looked at Janis, who did not smile, but just stared back at him. Matt turned to Andy, who was once again putting an arrow into his bow. "When did you find that cave?"

Andy looked at him and shrugged his shoulders. "Oh, about two years ago. One day when I was tracking some deer."

"Did you furnish it also?" Matt asked.

"Yeah, it's kind of my private place."

Matt smiled at him again and slapped him on the leg. "Good job, Son. You kept them safe." He reached for the key and started the engine.

Janis tapped Matt on the shoulder. "Are we going home on the logging road?"

"No," he said as he turned his head back toward her. "The road is almost impassable."

"That small accident?" she replied.

"Yeah," he said with a sort of laugh. "We'll drive through the woods and down to Hadley Road then to the highway and straight home. It's the shortest way I can think of." He put the jeep in first gear and headed out across the field to the tree line on the south rim of the ridge.

"If you keep to the left you can get over the edge much easier," Andy said. "The trees down there are further apart and the brush is not too thick."

"Okay, Son, you lead," Matt replied. They left the field a few moments later and started through the forest and down a gradually descending hill. Matt drove back and forth between trees and around large rocks in a snake like fashion down the hill and into the valley below.

"Stop! Dad," Andy said suddenly. "The road is just beyond that big rock. Let me take a look."

"No," Matt replied. "You stay here. I'll look." He stopped the jeep and stepped out, then walked to the huge rock formation in front of him. He crawled up the back side of the massive boulder and slid on his stomach to the top to look over the edge into the valley in front of him. A single-lane, dirt road came from his left, passed in front and below him and then turned left and straight away from him into the trees. It was Hadley Road. The road was at the bottom of the valley and ran from the town of Dawn to the crossroads known as Hadley crossing about two miles ahead. He lay there searching the road and the forest for a few minutes. Nothing was moving. Satisfied that the road and valley were safe he slid down the rock and returned to the jeep. "Looks okay," he said to Andy. He put the jeep in gear and drove out and around the rock and down the hill to the road.

Once on the road surface, he turned toward Hadley crossroads and picked up speed. He drove the road at only a moderate pace to allow Andy to watch the forest on both sides. They were nearly to the end of the forest and very close to the crossroads when Andy noticed a car up ahead and off to the right side of the road in a ditch.

Matt stopped the jeep about fifty yards away and he and Andy stepped out. "Stay here," he said to Janis. "Come on, Andy. Let's take a look." They walked slowly to the car, a

late-model Chevy. As they got closer, they noticed steam coming from under the hood and both doors were open. Andy raised his bow halfway up his chest in a ready position and stopped about five feet from the car on the road side. Matt moved around the car and into the ditch and looked inside. No one there. He rubbed his hand on the side of the car, "Andy, come look at this." Andy walked around to where his father was standing; they both looked in amazement at the half-dozen holes in the car body and door.

"Bullet holes I think," Matt said.

Andy moved to the front of the car and looked at the grill. "Same here, Dad," he said as he stared at Matt.

Matt reached inside and touched the leather of the seat. He moved his hand near his face and rubbed his index finger and thumb together in front of his eyes. A thick red fluid ran down the front of his thumb. He looked up at Andy in complete amazement. "It's blood." They both turned, their eyes scanning the forest and road in all directions.

Matt wiped his fingers on his pants and again looked at Andy. "Do you recognize the car?" he asked.

"No," Andy replied.

Matt looked inside again and pulled the front seat forward. On the floor in the back he saw something shining. He reached down and picked it up and held it up to the light. It was a brass shell casing. He looked at Andy, "7.62," he said, "AK-47 brass, automatic weapons." He looked again into the back. "The seat and floor are covered with them," he said. He paused for a second, then said quickly, "Let's get out of here." They started back to the jeep. "Don't say anything to Mom. I'll explain."

"Okay, Dad," Andy replied.

"Did you see the license plate?" Matt asked.

"Yeah, Pennsylvania, and the dealership tag is from Pittsburgh." About halfway back to the jeep, Andy stopped.

"Wait a minute Dad," and he ran back to the car. He bent down in the middle of the road just a few feet from the vehicle, and studied the road surface.

Matt also returned, "What is it?" Matt asked.

"Shoe prints going up the road toward the crossroads," Andy said as he followed them a few feet further. He bent down once again. "More blood," he said as he touched the road surface then turned his finger toward Matt. His index finger was red with thick, muddy blood.

"Someone is hit bad," Matt added.

"I count three people," Andy said. "And another thing, they are all wearing the same type of shoe."

"Come on," Matt said, and they returned to the jeep.

"Is anyone hurt?" Janis asked as they climbed back into the vehicle.

"No," Matt answered.

"What were you looking at in the car and on the road?" she added.

"Just looking around," Matt said as he looked at Andy. Janis didn't ask any more questions, but Matt knew inside that she had not fully accepted his answer. He drove the jeep past the car and on up the road. As they passed the car, Matt was happy the bullet holes could not be seen from the roadside. Janis stared at the car as they passed. A chill came over her and she shuddered and then turned her eyes back to the road ahead. Matt looked at her in the rearview mirror, just as Janis noticed his eyes looking back at her in the reflection. Neither of them said a word; they just drove on.

CHAPTER 10
July

The one-lane road ended at a two-lane blacktop road about half a mile from the crossroads. Matt paused for a moment and checked the road in both directions, then turned right and continued on at a faster pace. They came up over a small hill and the crossroads lay just ahead. Matt stopped on the shoulder of the road, about a hundred yards from the intersection. "We'll wait here for a few seconds and watch the road." He stood up in front and leaned on the top of the windshield. "Andy, you watch the rear."

"What are we waiting for?" Janis asked.

"I want to see if there is any traffic on the highway," he replied. After about five minutes, he sat down. "Let's take a look." Not a single vehicle had passed in front or behind, which had Matt wondering even more than before. As he drove slowly to the intersection, he looked at his watch. It was 2:30 p.m. In his mind, he questioned why the roads were deserted at that time on a Sunday afternoon. They stopped at the main highway and he checked once again in both directions. Still no cars or any signs of movement in any direction.

He looked across the intersection at the crossroads store on the opposite corner. It seemed to be deserted. "Andy, we're going to stop at the store to see if the Johnsons know what is going on."

Matt drove quickly across the highway and stopped at the gas pumps in front of the store. He noticed the hoses of two of the pumps were lying on the ground instead of in their holders. He got out of the jeep and picked one up and placed it back into its holder on the pump. "Andy, let's check the store. Janis, stay here with the children. We'll be right back."

Andy climbed out with bow in hand and followed Matt. They walked to the steps of the small porch in front of the store and looked around. Matt walked up to the door and tried to open it, but it was locked. "They should be open at this hour," he said as he turned to Andy. "I need you to go see if the back door is open. I need Mom to stay with the kids. Be careful. Anything wrong and you get back here," he added as Andy turned and walked around the side of the store.

Matt stepped off the porch and walked over to one of the large windows in the front. He placed his hands on the glass to block out the reflection and looked inside. The store was empty and dark but he noticed cans and boxes lying all over the floor and shelves turned over in the middle of the aisle. He caught movement in an aisle near the back of the store. He strained his eyes to see and then realized it was Andy.

He knocked on the glass and motioned to Andy to come to the window. Andy moved slowly toward him, stepping over and around the debris in the aisle. When he reached the window Matt tapped on the glass again. "Open the front door," he said. Andy moved to the door and Matt stepped up onto the porch again and waited in front of the door. The latch clicked, the door opened, and Matt stepped inside. "How did you get in?" he asked.

"The back door is about ripped off the hinges," he said. "Doesn't seem to be anyone around, but it looks like a war went on in here."

Matt walked over to the check-out counter. The cash register was sitting open and empty. "Get Mom and the kids

in here," he said to Andy. "I'll look around a little more."

Andy went out to the porch and motioned for Janis to come in. She and the children got out of the jeep and ran across the lot and into the store. Her eyes were wide with surprise when she saw the mess inside. "Andy what's going on here?"

"I don't know, Mom. Something weird."

Matt returned from a room in the back and walked over to Janis. "There is no one here. I don't know," he said shaking his head. "Andy, did you check the garage out back?"

"No. Not yet," he replied.

"Go have a look, and please be careful."

Janis looked at him. "Andy, you heard your dad. Please be careful." She turned to Matt, "Where are the Johnsons?" she asked.

"I don't know," Matt replied. "There just doesn't seem to be anyone here. Even the cash register is open and empty. There is still plenty of food left around here. You and the kids get some boxes. Take whatever you think we might need."

"But Matt, we can't just take it," she said.

"Please, Janis, just fill some boxes. I don't know what the hell is going on around here but we might just need all we can get. I'll pay the Johnsons later."

"But Matt," she said.

"Please, Janis. Please," he said firmly. "I'm going to look in the basement. Get what you can and we'll get out of here." Janis got two or three boxes from behind the counter and she and the children began filling them. Matt walked to the back of the store and opened the cellar door. He reached for the light switch at the top of the stairs and switched it on. No light. "Power's off," he whispered to himself. He walked back into one of the aisles and got a flashlight and some batteries from a shelf. He ripped the packages open and put

the batteries into the flashlight. He tried the light then returned to the cellar stairs and proceeded down into the cellar. Once in the cellar, he found the fuse panel and checked it. There was nothing wrong. The power had to be off. He searched the entire cellar and found nothing.

Matt returned upstairs, just as Janis and the kids returned from the jeep to get another box. "Janis, get some of those cans of Coleman fuel off the shelf behind the counter and I'll get some lanterns. The power is off here so it's probably off at home too. He got three new lanterns from a shelf and put them into another box, then walked behind the checkout and grabbed a half dozen boxes of twelve-gauge and 9 mm shells and placed them into the same box. He turned behind him to the rack where Mr. Johnson had his guns for sale. It was empty, and the chain that locked them in was broken on the floor. He turned again to the shelf under the counter and picked up six boxes of .30-30 ammo and put them into the box with the other supplies. He picked up the box and headed for the front door. He just stepped out onto the front porch and was about to say something to Janis, who was placing the last box into the jeep, when he heard something down the road. There it was again: Tat-tat-tat-tat, gunfire and the sound of a police siren.

Matt set the box down on the porch, put his hand above his eyes, and stared down the road. Janis, standing beside the jeep, did the same. Suddenly, a truck came into sight, followed by a police car with lights flashing. Janis yelled, "Mary, Robert, into the store." The children got out of the jeep and ran to Matt, screaming wildly. Matt opened the front door and pushed them inside.

In a few seconds the truck was at the crossroads. There were three men in front and at least three or four in the truck bed behind. Janis stood frozen in place beside the jeep. The men in the back of the truck were firing automatic weapons

at the police car behind them. Matt could see the bullets hitting the car's hood and windshield. The officer behind the wheel and the man beside him were returning the fire with hand guns. Two or three shots fired by the police broke the back window of the truck and it skidded to a stop in the middle of the intersection. The police car headed straight at them. One man in the back of the truck stood up and fired a long burst at the oncoming cruiser. The hood of the car popped up and both front tires blew out. Janis suddenly heard Matt screaming, "Get in here, Janis. Get in here!" She turned and started to run to the store just as the police car swerved into the dirt hillside across the road, up the bank and flipped over onto its roof. She turned back to the road as she ran and tripped on something and fell to the ground between the gas pumps and the store. The man in the truck reloaded his gun and once again emptied it into the police car. Glass, dirt and pieces of car flew in all directions. Matt jumped off the porch and raced to Janis. Just as he reached her the man in the truck saw them and turned his weapon toward them.

Matt grabbed Janis by the back of her shirt and picked her up. As he did, he looked straight at the truck, the man squeezed the trigger and bullets hit the ground in front of them kicking dirt up in little puffs in a line headed straight at them. Suddenly, a man beside him screamed and grabbed his shoulder. As Matt and Janis turned to run, Matt saw the man fall back into the other men with the feathers from an arrow protruding from his shoulder. When he fell, he knocked the weapon from the other man's hand and onto the road. As Matt and Janis reached the front door of the store, Matt saw Andy step out from behind the side of the store with the bow at full draw. The bow string sang as another arrow flew toward the truck. The second arrow hit high on the back of the truck cab and bounced off. One of

the men in the back yelled, "The cop's done. Let's get the hell out of here." The truck backed up quickly then raced forward and down the road, just as Matt and Janis dove through the door and onto the floor of the store.

Andy suddenly burst through the back door and yelled, "Are you alright?" He ran over the boxes and cans on the floor to Matt, who was on his knees holding Janis.

Janis was crying and screaming, "What's going on?" The sobbing children ran out from behind the counter and over to Andy, who knelt down and took them both into his arms. Matt and Andy calmed everyone down. Matt stood up, still holding Janis. He looked at Andy and breathed a long sigh of relief. Andy walked the children over to Matt and Janis. They continued to comfort each other as Andy walked to the front door. He stepped out onto the porch and checked the road in both directions. It was all quiet again.

Matt suddenly remembered the police cruiser. "Andy, the police car. Is anyone moving?"

Andy placed his hand on his forehead, shading his eyes, and looked toward the police car. He noticed a hand and arm moving outside the broken windshield.

"Yes," Andy screamed back toward the store. "Someone is trying to get out." He jumped off the porch and ran toward the gas pumps, then stopped and yelled back to Matt, "Hurry, Dad. It's Uncle Clive."

Matt looked into Janis's eyes. "Clive. Oh, Matt, hurry," Janis said as she ran to the door with him.

Matt stopped her at the porch. "Stay here with the kids. I'll help."

Andy had already reached the car and was shouting into the broken windshield. "Uncle Clive, hold on. We'll get you out." He turned back to his father, who was just crossing the road. "Come on, Dad. They're hurt." He got down on his stomach, put his bow on the ground and started to crawl

into the window.

Matt reached the car and got down on his knees and looked inside. Andy was between Clive and his partner, trying to get a seatbelt unbuckled.

"Matt pull me out of here," Clive yelled as he stretched his arms out of the car. "We gotta get Parker out of here. He's hit bad."

"Are you hurt?" Matt asked as he pulled on both of Clive's arms.

"No, just my ego," he said as he rolled over on his stomach and slid out onto the dirt shoulder of the road. Once outside, Clive sat back and leaned against the fender of the car. He was bleeding from the left side of his forehead and his left arm.

"You hurt bad?" Matt asked again.

"No. Just hit my head when we rolled over," he said as he wiped the blood from his face.

"What about your arm?" Matt asked.

Clive raised his left arm as he winced with pain. Just caught a piece of me. I'm okay. Get Jerry out."

Matt returned to the window just as Andy cut the seatbelt with his knife. He braced Jerry Parker's body against his own to prevent him from falling to the roof. "Dad, he's hit in both legs pretty bad and he's unconscious."

"Can you slide him over to me?" Matt asked.

"Yeah, but you'll have to pull him from there. The bank is too close on this side to get out." Clive rolled back over to Matt in an effort to help.

"No," Matt said as he pushed him back. "I can get him."

Clive sat back against the car and wiped his face again. Matt crawled half into the car and put his arms under Jerry Parker's and around his chest and began to pull as Andy carefully straightened out his legs. Jerry suddenly awoke and screamed in pain then passed out again. Andy stopped

quickly and looked at Matt. "Go on, Andy. We can't help but hurt him. We've got to get him out now." They worked a few more minutes and finally got Jerry out on the ground.

Andy crawled out next and rolled over onto his back to catch his breath. "Dad, I smell gasoline. We gotta move."

Matt stood up and helped Clive to his feet. "Get over to the store. Janis is there. We'll get Parker."

"Get my gun. It's in there somewhere," Clive said as he stumbled across the road. Andy looked inside, in front. No gun. He looked through the back windows and saw the gun outside the car in the dirt of the embankment. He got up and ran around the back of the car, picked it up and stuffed it into his pants. He searched for Parker's weapon for a moment but could not locate it. He glanced up and down the highway then moved around the car returning to Matt.

"Help me get him onto my shoulders," Matt said as he turned Parker toward himself and raised him part-way up. Andy grabbed him from behind and pushed him up and onto Matt, who bent over with the weight of his body. "Got your bow?" Matt said as he turned and started across the highway. Andy readjusted the gun in his belt then picked up his bow and followed Matt.

Clive staggered to the gas pumps and then to the jeep. He stood there for a moment then looked toward the store, just as Janis stepped off the porch and started across the lot toward him. He wiped the blood from his eyes, then began to stagger back and forth and slid down the side of the jeep to the ground. Janis reached him just in time to stop his fall. "Clive," she said as she placed his head on her shoulder and eased him to the ground. She pulled back his hair, exposing a two-inch long gash just above the hairline.

Clive opened his eyes again as she wiped his face with her handkerchief. "Hi Darling. Nice Sunday, huh?"

"Not quite," she said. "You sit still. I'm going to get

something from the store." As she stood up, Andy and Matt reached her and she helped them lower Parker to the ground beside Clive.

Clive leaned over and patted the unconscious Parker on the head, then looked up at Matt. "He's a good kid. Never been in a firefight before, but he kept at those bastards even after he was hit twice. He's got guts. Good kid," he said again as he sat back against the jeep and held his arm and closed his eyes.

Janis turned and ran back to the store. "I'll get some first aid supplies." She jumped up onto the store porch and through the doorway, slamming the screen door behind her.

"Give me your knife, Son," Matt said as he lifted one of Parker's eyelids to check his pupils. "Eyes not responding to light the right way. He must have a bad concussion." Andy gave Matt his knife and Matt proceeded to split one of Parker's pant legs to check the wound. "Man, this leg is broken up badly. We gotta stop this blood." He quickly split the other pant leg and checked that leg. "This one's not as bad. Just a flesh wound." He then moved over to Clive and split his upper shirt sleeve.

Clive opened his eyes again. "I'm okay. Just take care of the kid."

"I want to see this a minute, Clive. Just hold on," Matt said as he checked his arm. "Looks like a clean entrance and exit, not too bad, just got the side of your arm." He then reached and held Clive's face into the sun and checked his eyes. "You're okay, I think. Doesn't look like a concussion."

"I'm just a little dazed and out of it. I'm okay," Clive said again.

"Andy, put some pressure on Parker's leg just above the wound. I'll run in and give Mom a hand." Matt stood up then ran to the door just as Janis was about to come out with an armload of bandages and medicine. "Janis, where are the kids?"

"They are over there behind the counter" she said as she stood looking at him. "Matt," she whispered.

"Yeah, I know," he answered as he touched her face. "Go on and help Andy. I'll be right there." Janis left the store and Matt walked over to the checkout counter and looked behind it. There, sitting on a box holding each other's hands, were Robert and Mary. They just sat and looked up at Matt. He walked behind the counter and bent down on one knee. "You two okay?" he asked. They didn't say a word but just looked at him and shook their heads. "We seem to be having a little problem here. Don't know what yet, but I know you two will be grown up and help, won't you?"

"Yeah, Dad," they both said in quiet uncertain voices.

He brushed his hand through their hair and smiled. "Uncle Clive is outside, but he and his friend are hurt a little and we are taking care of them. We'll be going home as soon as we make them feel a little better, okay?" They both nodded again and they all smiled at each other. "I'm going back out to help. You two can come out from behind here and wait by the door, okay?" They all got up and he walked them to the door and stepped outside. As he stepped off the porch, he looked back at the two children standing with their hands pressed on the inside of the screen. He winked at them and smiled and they half smiled in return.

Matt turned back to the jeep but was met by Janis halfway. Her hands and clothes were marked with blood as she wiped sweat from her forehead with the back of her hand. "Matt, Jerry is in bad shape. He's still unconscious, but I think I got the bleeding stopped. I think the leg is broken, I can see bone, and there may be an artery nicked. The other leg is not too bad."

Matt looked past her at Clive. Andy was putting a bandage on his arm. "How's Clive?" he asked as he stepped toward Andy.

"He seems to be okay, but we've got to get them both to a doctor."

Matt knelt down in front of Clive. "Hey buddy, we gotta get you both to a doctor as soon as possible."

"No," Clive said as he looked up at Matt. "You won't find a doctor open for miles around here. They either went home or to the city where they are needed."

"Clive, what's going on?" Matt said. "We have been on a picnic at the ridge. We know now that something is going on, but what? We haven't had TV or radio on since yesterday afternoon."

"Well, you won't get radio, TV or much cell phone service for who knows how long now. It's all down—along with the power in most places," Clive said, holding his head. "I wondered why you were out here on the highway with all this going on."

"What's going on?" Matt asked again.

"It's a long story," Clive said as he leaned back against the jeep. He closed his eyes and shook his head back and forth. "You ain't gonna believe this one."

"Believe what?" Janis asked.

Clive opened his eyes again and looked at Matt. "No time to tell you the whole story now. We gotta get off this open road. It's too dangerous."

Matt stood up and turned to Janis. "Get the kids and we are out of here." Janis ran to the store and got Mary and Robert and came back to the jeep. Matt retrieved the box he had placed on the porch earlier and returned to the jeep. He and Andy helped Clive into the front seat, and then with Janis help picked up Jerry and put him in the back. Janis crawled in and put Jerry's head in her lap and told the kids to get on the floor in the back.

Andy crawled up onto the back of the jeep and sat beside the spare tire. He put the bow over his shoulder and pulled

Clive's pistol from his pants and checked the cylinder. The shells were all used. "Uncle Clive, you have any more cartridges for your gun?" he asked as he pushed the empties out of the cylinder and onto the ground.

"Yeah, here," Clive said as he looked over his shoulder at Janis and gave her a quick loader of six more .357 cartridges. She took the loader and handed it to Andy. "Can you use that thing?" Clive asked as he slid down into the seat.

"Yeah," Andy answered as he placed the cartridges into the cylinder, spun it and snapped it closed. Janis just looked at Andy as he put the gun back into his belt. He looked back at Janis, then toward Matt. "Come on, Dad. Let's go home."

Clive looked over at Matt. "The kid's right. It's the only safe place and we've got to get Jerry to where we can help him." Matt looked back at Clive, then started the jeep and pulled away from the store and down the road toward camp. Neither of them said a word; they just drove on.

CHAPTER 11
September

The ax slammed down through a piece of firewood one last time and the two split halves dropped to the ground on either side of the cutting stump. Matt stuck the ax into the top of the stump, then arched his back to stretch out the muscles. He wiped the sweat from his face with his shirttail and then checked his watch. It was 12:45. He picked up the last of the split pieces of wood and placed them on the pile near the stump. The sun shone brightly overhead and a gentle breeze moved through the leaves of the forest around him. Ginger was lying where he had tied her, head on her paws, half asleep. He looked toward the pond where Janis and Lisa were still talking and painting. He walked to Ginger and sat down on the ground beside her. She placed her head in his lap as he began petting her. The afternoon was warm and quiet as he watched the forest below him. He checked his watch again then thought to himself that Clive should be back by now.

Clive was returning from delivering the papers at one of the other county stations and had made several stops on his way back. During the ride, he had hashed over his thoughts about 9/11 and of the murders of a year ago that the press had dubbed the "Forever Man Murders." He had also spent a lot of time thinking about the unbelievable events of the

last months. At times he tried to stop thinking about all of it, but just as he would think of something else it would all come flooding back into his mind. He was driving down two-lane blacktop Boyers Road, when up ahead he saw the entrance to a small dirt road that he recognized. He began to slow, then made the turn to the right and up a steep incline, raising tan-colored dust behind him. He drove for about a quarter of a mile, then pulled off to the left in a small parking area.

It was called the overlook. Clive knew exactly where he was. He parked the car and then waited for the dust cloud to pass. He lowered the two front windows and unfastened his seatbelt. He slid down in the seat and then picked up what was left of the coffee he had bought and took a sip as he looked around at the forest on either side. He remained in that position for a few minutes, finished the coffee, turned off the ignition and sat up in the seat and looked out the windshield at the view in front of him. Extending for several miles in all directions was what appeared like a lush green carpet with tinges of yellow and orange scattered about. He looked into the deep valley to his left and thought about the Fallons' camp that lay just ahead near the valley bottom. He raised his eyes to just above the valley and stared at the ridge far out in the distance. The ridge was somewhat higher than his position and even at this distance he could see a huge tree near its edge, a spot he knew well. My God, what had happened here in this beautiful place seemed unreal. It played out in his mind at incredible speeds and then stopped abruptly in his mind at that ridge in the distance.

Clive took a deep breath then folded his arms across the top of the steering wheel, lowered his head to his arms and slowly let the air out. His thoughts focused on what had happened in the last weeks. He thought about the Fallons and their nightmare and about the journey that some of

them made to save one of their own. He thought about how it had all played out: the events, the places and the people who became a part of it all. He thought about Madison Lynn and the unbelievable way they had met. What an unusual person she was and what she had seemed to know about him. He thought about the church and the priest, and what he had told him about the things that had happened there. He remembered that valley, that horrible place that he hoped he would never see again.

Clive squeezed his eyelids tight as he remembered the ridge and the big tree at Scorpion's Tail. How could it all have been real? Yet he knew it was. All of it was real. They had all lived it. It would forever be etched in his memory, all of their memories. He raised his head slowly, and as he did he remembered the last thing that Madison Lynn had told him. What did it mean and how did she seem to know what she knew? It was something, but what? He knew even she was not sure. In his mind there was a mass of loose strings, strings that needed to be tied up, but how? Somewhere in all those thoughts, in all those memories, that bloody thread wove its way through his mind. At one end was the beginning of it all and at the other end was that phantom pulling it along in the place of shadows, where the answers lay. Inside him burned a fire that tormented his mind. What had taken place in the last weeks had been like throwing gasoline on that fire. He raised his hand and squeezed his temples, closed his eyes and just sat motionless for a few minutes. He looked at his watch and then snapped his seatbelt, started the car, rolled the windows up, and turned on the air. He took one last look out toward the ridge and the massive oak at its edge, shook his head, then put the car in reverse and backed up. He drove back down the dirt road to the blacktop and headed in the direction of camp.

The grey squirrel appeared again on a limb of one of the hickory trees near Matt's position, then ran down the trunk and onto the ground. He sat quietly and watched it searching for nuts on the ground. Suddenly, Ginger began a low growl. At first he thought she was growling at the squirrel, when suddenly she jumped up and began barking in the direction of the road. The squirrel raced up the tree and disappeared in the thick branches above. Matt jumped to his feet and retrieved the 9 mm from the top of the stump beside him and slipped it into the holster. He quickly walked to the tree where the shotgun was leaning and picked it up. He couldn't hear anything, but Ginger was still barking and growling with her eyes and ears fixed in the direction of the road. Janis and Lisa had heard the dog and were standing up looking toward Matt. He made a quick motion with his arm in the direction of the garage. They both looked at him puzzled and just stood there. He motioned again and mouthed the words, "Get inside."

Janis whispered to Lisa, "He wants us in the garage. Let's go." With that they moved quickly away from the pond, up through the yard and into the garage. Matt left Ginger tied up and walked past the garage and down the driveway toward the road. He crossed the driveway over to the row of pines just above the pond, concealed himself between two of the trees, and waited. He looked back at the garage at Janis and Lisa, who were standing behind one of the doors, looking out of the windows. He motioned for them to get down when he suddenly remembered the children.

Matt left his position and ran to the back of the house. Robert and Mary were in the sandbox in the back yard, looking at the road. They also had heard the car approaching. Matt whistled at them and they both turned. He waved them toward his position and they dropped their toys and began to run in his direction. When they reached

him he whispered, "Into the garage with Mom." They ran to the garage door and were met by Janis. She moved them both inside and out of sight. Matt ran back to his position between the pines and waited. The car moved down the hill and turned the bend into the driveway. It was Clive.

Matt breathed a sigh of relief then yelled in the direction of the garage, "It's okay. Clive is back." Matt stepped out from behind the trees, placed the shotgun on his shoulder and walked to the driveway as the car came to a stop. The children ran past Matt and toward the car. The car door opened and Clive swung his legs out, just as Robert and Mary got to him. Matt waited for Janis to walk to him, then they both headed toward the car. Clive picked up two small bags from the front seat and a couple of magazines. "You're late," Matt said as he and Janis reached the car.

"Easy, boy. Settle down. I had a special stop to make on the way back." He looked at Robert and Mary and handed them the bags. "Got something for you two."

"Candy," they both said as they looked into the bags.

"I figured they hadn't had any for a while, so I picked up a little. It's okay, isn't it?" Matt smiled and nodded his approval. "And I picked these up for you, dear," as he handed Lisa the magazines. "They're a little old. About a month but it was all they had. Hope you like *People*. Didn't have much of a choice."

"They're fine," Lisa said as she kissed him. He turned and retrieved a large, white package from the floor in the back of the car and handed it to Janis. "This is for all of us."

"A roast!" Janis said in surprise.

"You think you might be able to do something with that for supper tomorrow?"

"You bet I can. Where did you get this?" she said as she felt the weight of the large roast.

"Oh, just a farmer I know on the road back here."

She smiled at him, "You're something."

Clive walked around the back of the car and opened the trunk. "And this is for you and me, buddy," as he pointed into the trunk. Matt walked up to the back of the car, reached into the trunk with one hand and brought out a case of beer. "Now you think you might be able to find those fishing poles? Those bass ain't gonna wait forever you know." Clive reached into the trunk and removed one more item, a brown paper bag, and handed it to Janis. "If I remember, this is your favorite."

Janis opened the bag and pulled out a box of chocolate-covered cherries. "Clive Aliston where did you get these?"

He winked at her and smiled. "That's a secret."

She put her arms around him and kissed his cheek. "You sure know how to spoil the Fallons, don't you?"

"No, it's just that I'm a great guy, that's all." They all laughed and started toward the house.

"I take it from all these gifts that you're staying?"

"You bet. I got a call through to the office just after I left. They said they will handle things till Monday. Besides, I'm still on light duty."

"Great," Matt said as he slapped Clive on the back. "Let's see if we can find those fishing poles." Matt and Clive started slowly up the sidewalk beside the house. Clive took Matt's shotgun and Matt hoisted the case of beer onto his shoulder. They talked and laughed as they moved to the back porch. Janis and Lisa followed behind, still looking at their gifts and whispering, with smiles from ear to ear. Robert and Mary raced past all of them and across the back yard to the swing set beside the sandbox. They frantically opened the bags of candy and began picking out favorite pieces, stuffing several into their mouths and trying to talk at the same time. Matt and Clive stopped at the back stairs and Matt placed the case of beer at his feet. He raised his

hand to cover his eyes, blocking the sun as he looked toward the swing set. "Robert and Mary, you two share the candy evenly. I want no fighting."

They both looked up momentarily and yelled, "Okay," then returned their total attention to the bag.

Janis and Lisa stopped beside Matt and Clive. Janis added, "Lunch is very soon, so not too much candy now. I want you to eat."

Uncle Clive chimed in, "You heard your mom, guys."

Robert and Mary stopped again, somewhat disappointed, and said in unison, "Okay, Mom."

Matt turned again to Clive, "Have a seat here on the step for a minute. I'll get the poles and a couple of lawn chairs from the garage. Be right back."

Janis picked up the case of beer after handing her candy and the roast to Lisa. "I'll put this away."

"Not too far away," Clive added, as he sat down on the steps.

She laughed and said, "Yeah, I know, but it's not cold yet."

Clive looked up at her and said, "Who needs cold? We're gonna be fishin'. Can't do that without a beer."

Janis smiled again, "Oh, I'll get a six pack out of the case and bring it down to you two overly-thirsty guys." She and Lisa went up the steps, across the porch, and into the kitchen. Lisa placed the candy and the roast on the table and Janis began to open the case of beer, retrieving six cans. "Lisa, get some ice from the refrigerator and put it in a plastic bag with two glasses. Put them in a paper bag with these beers and take them to your uncle before he dies of thirst." She smiled at her and said, "Tell him he'll just have to drink them on ice until the beer is cold."

Lisa complied and as she started out the door with the bag, turned and asked, "Do you want to start lunch now?"

"No," replied Janis. "When you're done, go ahead and

enjoy your magazines. I'll start lunch in a little while."

Lisa turned and took the bag out to Clive, who was still sitting on the steps. She handed him the bag, placed her hand on his shoulder, smiled and said, "Thanks again, Uncle Clive."

He looked up at her, returned the smile, and patted her hand. "You're welcome, baby."

Lisa returned to the kitchen, where Janis was putting the roast and the remaining beer into the refrigerator. "Mom, I think I'll go to my room and read a little, okay?"

"Sure, honey. I'll call if I need you."

Matt had returned from the garage with the two poles, chairs and a box of lures. "Well, are you ready?" he asked Clive, who was getting up with the bag and the shotgun.

"I am now. I got the refreshments." They both laughed, then started down the sidewalk toward the pond.

As they passed the kitchen window, Janis opened it. "Remember, lunch is in a short while, you guys."

They both stopped and looked at her in the window. "Yes, dear," they both said, then laughed and continued toward the pond. She closed the window, then turned to the back door to see the children. They were still sitting on the swings, bags in hand, talking. As she turned back to the kitchen she heard Lisa's bedroom door close. She stopped at the table and picked up a chocolate-covered cherry from the box, then crossed the living room, entered the bedroom and looked toward the pond as she took a bite of the candy. She almost dropped the candy as the cherry syrup ran down her chin. She wiped the syrup from her chin with her thumb, then placed the rest of the candy in her mouth and licked her thumb as she savored the taste she had not had in what seemed like years. She watched as Clive and Matt placed their chairs on the grass near the pond, opened their beers and began rigging their fishing equipment. Clive sat in one

of the chairs and Matt stood beside him preparing his pole. She saw them talking and laughing, something she had not seen Matt do for a long time. It made her feel almost relaxed. She stood for a moment in the warm rays of the sun that penetrated the window and smiled. Her comfortable feeling slowly disappeared, however as she saw Matt pick up the shotgun and lay it against the lure box on the ground before sitting down. Clive also removed his service revolver from its holster, checked it and placed it on the ground beside him. She saw Matt turn in his chair and look up and down the road in both directions before returning his attention to the fishing and conversation.

Even on such a beautiful, sunlit day, with friends close at hand, the past seemed somehow to creep into their lives—a past she knew had somehow changed them forever. She turned and re-entered the living room, walked to the bookshelf on the wall adjacent to the fireplace and fingered through the CDs. She turned to the component stereo between the bookcases, knelt down and opened the glass door, and placed a CD in the player. She turned on the power and pushed "play." She stood up, walked to the kitchen and pulled two large cans of soup from the cupboard above the sink but did not open them. Instead, she placed them on the table, pulled out one of the chairs and sat down. She pushed the curtain at the window aside, giving herself a view of the yard, the road and the forest behind. Reaching again for a piece of candy, she began to daydream as she stared out the window. The view in front of her began to fade as her memories returned. Like Matt, she had found a way to push them from her thoughts. They had been filed away in a dark place in the back of her mind, but now it was time to relive them, time to remember. As she stared into the past, strains of the old Skyliner's recording, "Since I Don't Have You," filled the quiet afternoon air. As the present faded and the

past emerged, she remembered that day when they returned to camp in the jeep with the seriously wounded Jerry Parker in her arms. That day when all their lives changed forever…

CHAPTER 12
July

The jeep rounded the curve at the top of the hill overlooking the valley and the camp road. Matt slowed, then came to a complete stop at the crest. The dust trail that followed them up the road enveloped the jeep momentarily. As the cloud passed them, Matt stood up in the front and checked the descending hill in front of him. Andy jumped off the back of the jeep and walked around to his father. Janis asked in a low voice, "What is it?"

Before Matt could answer, Clive did. "The road is narrow here and darkened by the forest cover. We gotta take this slow. See anything?" he asked as he looked up at Matt, still scanning the hill road in front of him.

"No. All seems to be quiet. Andy, you take the wheel and give me Clive's gun." Matt climbed out of the jeep and Andy got in, then handed the revolver to his father. "I'll walk the road in front of you several yards out. If we run into any trouble, you hit reverse and back up over the crest of the hill. Don't wait for me."

"But Matt," Janis said frantically.

Matt didn't respond but just raised his hand and waved her off, stopping her in mid-sentence. "Andy, if anything, just move, you hear?"

Andy looked at Matt and nodded. Matt reached out and

placed his hand on Janis's arm. "I'll be careful." She did not respond, but just returned his stare. Matt once again looked at Andy, then at Clive. "Ready?" he said as he moved out in front of the jeep and down the center of the road into the valley. At a distance of about thirty yards, he raised his hand above his head and, without looking back, motioned to them to follow. Andy put the jeep in first and began to slowly move down the hill behind Matt. They continued down the hill, moving and stopping, moving and stopping, as Matt scanned the woods on either side, searching for anything unusual.

Janis kept her eyes fixed through the windshield at Matt, even as Jerry Parker began to moan. She just patted his forehead, ran her fingers through his hair and whispered "Shhhhhh…" never lowering her line of sight. The ride down the three hundred or so yards of hill seemed to take forever, but soon the lower end of the pond was in sight just around the trees.

Matt stopped and stood motionless in the center of the road. Andy also stopped. After a few moments, Matt bent down on one knee and looked under the tree branches at the edge of the pond, giving him a view of the house. He remained there for several moments, then stood up and turned to the jeep and motioned for Andy to move toward him. Andy moved the jeep down the road until he reached Matt. As the jeep came to a stop near Matt, he stepped to Clive's side. "Well, what about it?" Clive asked.

Matt said, "It looks quiet but you guys stay here. I'll check it out."

As Matt turned, Clive asked, "You want me to come with you?"

"No," Matt replied. "Stay here. I'll be just a minute." He moved down the road alongside the pines to the driveway, then stopped and looked around the last tree toward the

house. He turned again and disappeared up the driveway.

Moments after Matt disappeared, the dogs began to bark with excitement. They sat in the jeep for several minutes, minutes that seemed like an eternity. Parker moaned again and Clive turned to Janis. "How's he doing?"

"He's bleeding through the bandages again and he's still unconscious. We gotta get him to the house."

Clive looked at Andy. "Five minutes. No longer, and we move."

Andy continued to stare in the direction he had last seen his father, and answered, "Okay." Several moments passed, then from behind the row of pines Matt stepped out onto the road, raised his hand and motioned them toward him.

"Thank God," Janis said with a sigh of relief. Andy started down the hill to Matt, then turned into the driveway. He stopped in front of the house and switched off the ignition.

Matt circled the back of the jeep over to Clive. "Come on buddy, let's get you out."

"I'm okay, Matt. Just help Janis with Parker."

Matt paid no attention to Clive's comment and helped him out of the jeep. "Andy, help Uncle Clive to the house. I'll help Mom with Jerry." He tapped both children on the top of their heads. "You two kids get out and follow Andy and Uncle Clive." Robert and Mary got out from behind the seats and ran to Clive, each taking one of his hands as he slowly walked up the sidewalk, followed by Andy.

Matt then climbed partway into the back seat and began helping Janis move Parker. As they removed him from the back and placed one of his arms around each of their necks, he began to awaken. They each took one of his legs into their hands and picked him up in a two-man carry. He opened his eyes, rolled his head back, and moaned, "Oh, my God." As they slowly and laboriously walked him up the sidewalk to

the porch, Janis could feel the blood from his leg running between her fingers. Reaching for strength and gasping for breath, they started up the back steps just as Andy reached them to take Janis's place. She passed Jerry's arm and leg to Andy, and he and Matt moved him into the house.

Janis stopped at the top of the steps to catch her breath, then crossed the porch into the kitchen. Once inside, she helped Andy and Matt place Jerry on the kitchen table so they could work on him. Andy returned to Clive, who was on the living room couch with Robert and Mary, on either side. Janis went to the sink and tried to fill a pan with water, then she realized the amount of blood she had on her. It was soaked into her jeans and ran down her hands and arms to her elbows. She turned to Matt, who was placing a rolled-up towel under Parker's head. "Matt," she said as she showed him her hands and arms. "He's bleeding to death. We gotta work fast."

"Andy," Matt yelled. "Get in here, quick." Andy came running into the kitchen and Matt handed him another towel. "Put as much pressure on his leg as you can while I get something for a tourniquet." He quickly opened the door under the sink, retrieved a short piece of clothesline, and began wrapping it around Jerry's leg above the wound. When finished, Matt tried the water faucet. No water. He said, "The generator," and quickly left the kitchen for the garage. When he returned, he just said, "Okay, water's on."

Janis finished filling the pan of water then ran through the living room to the hall cupboard and got a clean bed sheet. She ran back through the living room, passing Clive, who was trying to get up again. "Sit down," she yelled as she passed. "I've got my hands full now. I don't need another patient. Kids, keep Uncle Clive on the couch." She ran into the kitchen as Matt checked the rope on Jerry's leg. "Andy, relieve the pressure on his leg and let me look," Janis

said as she ripped Jerry's pant leg open further down below the knee. "Okay, the bleeding has slowed up. Andy, rip this up into strips for bandages," she said as she handed him the sheet. "Matt, to the bathroom and get gauze pads, antiseptic and alcohol. Matt and Andy looked at each other momentarily They complied without saying a word. They both knew that Janis was in control now and arguing was pointless. As Andy tore the sheets into pieces and Matt went for the first-aid supplies, Janis opened a drawer at the sink and retrieved a pair of scissors. She began cutting off the remainder of Jerry's pants. As she worked, Andy heard her whisper, "Jerry, don't you give up. Don't you die on me now. Please, God, help me, help me."

Janis and Matt continued to work on Parker for over an hour. They cleaned and bandaged his wounds, then with Andy's help moved him to their bedroom. Through the entire ordeal, Jerry never regained consciousness. As they worked, Clive and the children just sat on the couch in a sort of a daze. Andy had put temporary bandages on Clive's head and arms but now it was Clive's turn to be tended to. As Janis slowly closed the bedroom door, she stopped and looked at Matt, "He's so pale Matt, and his breathing seems to be so shallow. I just don't know."

Matt shook his head in agreement. "I know, but without the assistance of a doctor I don't know what else we can do for him, but pray." He held her in his arms for several minutes, then whispered in her ear, "We gotta clean up Clive and bathe the children and get them settled in for the evening."

She raised her head from his shoulder to look at Clive and the children on the couch. "I'll get the kitchen ready for Clive, could you and Andy take care of the kids?" She kissed him, then turned and entered the kitchen, where Andy was in the process of cleaning up. "Andy, can you give Dad a

hand with Robert and Mary? I'll finish this. Then we have to help Uncle Clive."

"Okay, Mom," he replied as he turned and entered the living room.

She noticed a sort of uneasy sick look on his face as he left. She shuddered and felt a chill run down her spine. What must be going through his mind, she wondered. She turned to the table and continued to clean up. The table top was littered with bloody pieces of sheet and a large pool of blood ran from the middle of the table and down one of the table legs to the floor. The blood on the floor was tracked everywhere from Matt's and Janis's shoes, and lines of blood streamed down the front of the sink. She took a washcloth from under the sink and began to wipe the table and the front of the sink.

In the living room, Clive suddenly seemed to come out of his half trance, as Andy and Matt took the children to the bathroom. He stood up and steadied himself on the arm of the couch, then proceeded to the kitchen. In the bathroom, Matt had begun to run some water in the tub. He turned to Andy, who was helping Robert undress. "Can you take care of this son? The water pump must need adjusted. The pressure is dropping. I'll go check it then I want to help Mom."

"Yeah, Dad, go ahead. I'll handle this," Andy said, as he looked up at his father.

Matt told Mary to go to her room and prepare for a bath also. As Matt was leaving the bathroom he turned and spoke again to Andy, "Son, are you okay?"

"Yeah, Dad. I'm alright, but what is going on? How could anything like this happen?"

Matt shook his head, "I don't know, Son, but we'll talk to Uncle Clive in a bit and find out. Sure you're okay?"

Andy kind of smiled. "Yeah… okay…" As Matt turned to leave again, Andy stopped him outside the bathroom

door. "Dad, what about Lisa?"

Matt stared at him then lowered his head and sort of spoke to the floor. "I don't know. She's been on my mind since the crossroads. Go ahead with the kids for now. We'll figure out something." He turned and headed out to the garage and Andy re-entered the bathroom.

On his way to the kitchen, Matt once again stopped at their bedroom and looked in on Jerry. He was still pale and unconscious. Matt checked him for fever, lifted one of his eyelids to check his pupils, and listened for his breathing. As he left the bedroom he whispered, "Hold on, kid. I know you can make it." He crossed the living room toward the kitchen but was met at the doorway by Janis.

She looked around at Clive, who was wiping his face with a cloth. She looked at Matt, tears beginning to fill her eyes. "Matt, we have to get Lisa. What about Lisa?" she whispered.

Matt stared over her head at Clive wiping his face. He then moved his eyes back and met her stare, "I know, honey. It's been on my mind for hours. We have to talk to Clive now. We gotta get the whole story, then make some kind of decision—and the sooner the better. Just remember, the one thing we cannot do is panic. We're a family and we will get through this as a family." He placed his hand on her shoulder then walked out to the garage to check the well pump. Janis stood there for a second, her back to the door, wiping her tears, then turned and entered the room just as Clive seated himself at the table.

Matt returned from the garage and as he entered the kitchen he said, "Well, buddy, I guess it's your turn." He then helped Clive remove his shirt. Janis was finishing the cleaning of the sink. When she reached up and turned on the light switch, nothing happened. She turned to Matt and was about to speak as Matt spoke first, "Yeah, I know. I should

have finished those emergency lines from the generator to the house. I put on the generator for the pump and the refrigerator in the garage. After we finish with Clive, I'll go to the shed and see if I can find those old oil lamps. I just hope I have the fuel for them. If not, I guess it's candlelight dinner tonight," he said as he smiled at Clive. "Speaking of food, we gotta keep this refrigerator closed as much as possible till I can move the food. The cold will last much longer that way."

"I hope it's not off for that long," Janis added.

Clive looked up at Matt as he un-bandaged his arm. "It could be a lot longer than you think with all that has happened."

Janis turned away from the sink to the table with clean bandages and alcohol. She set the articles on the table, then placed her hands palm down on the table top and looked at Clive. "What has happened? Please. I have to know." Matt also looked intently at Clive, then at Janis.

"What I am about to tell you sounds like something out of a fiction novel. It's still hard for me to believe."

Janis's nerves had about reached their limit. She spoke again before Clive could continue. "I want to know and right now. I have a daughter who may be involved in this mess and I must know." She just stared at him with an almost terrified look on her face.

Matt spoke first as he placed his hand on her back. "Janis, it's not Clive's fault."

Clive put his hand on the back of hers and looked up at Matt, as Janis turned her head toward the table and began to cry quietly. "It's okay. Matt, I know what she's feeling. I've had Lisa on my mind too, since I realized she's not here with you. She's still in the city, isn't she?"

"Yes," Matt answered. "She took those special summer classes that were offered on campus for exceptional students.

She is in a dorm on the college campus in Oakland. She isn't due to come home until two weeks from now. Can we go get her?" Matt asked Clive anxiously.

"Yes, but not tonight. It's too dangerous. First thing in the morning."

"Why can't we get her now?" Janis asked, as she continued to stare at the table top and cry.

Clive stretched out his hand, placed his fingers under her chin and raised her face toward his. "I want her home too, but believe me, we can't go at night. We'll get her home and safe as fast as we can."

Janis wiped her tears again with the back of her hand, then looked into Clive's eyes. "I'm sorry, but it's just that I am so worried. I want my baby home. Please tell us what happened."

Matt turned to the doorway of the kitchen and there stood Andy. "Yeah, Uncle Clive, tell us what's going on," he said as he entered the kitchen and pulled out a chair at the table and sat down. "Please, tell us," he said again.

"How are the kids?" Matt asked.

"Robert is finished and Mary is almost done. I told them to play in their rooms until we eat, if that's okay?"

He turned once again to Clive as Janis spoke, "Please, Clive, please."

As Janis and Matt cleaned and dressed his wounds, Clive began his story of the day's events. "I can understand why you don't know what has happened, if you have been here at camp for a few days. It all began in the early hours of this morning, maybe around 6 a.m., our time. Well," Clive said as he took a deep breath when Janis poured alcohol over his arm. "Easy girl," he said as he pulled his arm back away from her.

"Sorry, Clive."

He placed his arm back on the table and continued. "We

have been hit by another terrorist attack."

"Again?" Matt said, with an astonished look on his face.

"Yes, again," Clive said as he sat shaking his head. "And as bad as 9/11 was, this attack makes that look like a small brushfire. They caught everyone off guard. This had to be in the works for years, maybe even before 9/11. 9/11 may have been just a test to see what kind of havoc it would play with our infrastructure. I think they wanted to find out back then what would happen to the stock market, the economics and the panic. I guess they must have thought the test worked well enough to continue on with the master plan."

Janis looked again at Clive. "What's all the problems we have here to do with this situation?"

"Yeah, Uncle Clive, what about Johnson's store?" Andy asked.

"And the power outage?" added Matt.

"What I've told you isn't the whole story," Clive said as he got up and walked to the sink for a glass of water. After he filled the glass, he turned to the three of them at the table. "There's one more little twist to this whole nightmare, the one I've been involved with." Andy, Matt and Janis didn't speak, they just sat and awaited Clive's next comment. Clive finished his water then returned to the table. As he sat down he took in a deep breath. "It's the part I haven't wanted to tell you since I realized Lisa wasn't here."

Janis suddenly stood up and quickly turned to the sink and placed her face in her hands. Matt got up and went to her side, putting his arm around her shoulder. He turned to Clive. "Tell us Clive, now."

Clive began again. Janis turned away from the sink. There were no tears on her face, only a look that spoke for itself. Clive looked up at the stare of those ice blue eyes and he knew she would not rest until she had the answers she needed. Matt looked at Janis, then back at Clive. "Finish it

Clive, please."

Clive turned again to Matt then continued. "They must have infiltrated from everywhere, Canada, Mexico, and maybe even Cuba. They probably held jobs here and were students and maybe even teachers. No one knows for sure how many or how long."

Andy spoke again, "Why do they think they can win, especially here?"

"They don't, Andy. They just want to pay us back, to hit us and hurt us wherever they can, and that's just what they did. They hate us and what we stand for. Turning the U.S. into a third world country would be a win for them. They hit power stations, airports, train stations, bus depots, ship yards, phone lines, key cell towers and oil refinery reserves. They even made attempts at several nuclear reactors."

"Did they succeed?" Matt asked.

"No," Clive answered. "From what I've heard on the police emergency radios that are operating, at least not the reactors. Except one in California. I don't know much about that. As for the rest, they just raised holy hell."

"Didn't the C.I.A. and the F.B.I. or someone know about this?" Janis snapped.

"Apparently, not enough," Clive answered. "They must have used decoy groups and diversions to keep our guys busy over the past year or so. The one place they hit that we didn't expect was something I would never have thought of."

"What?" asked Andy. Clive looked at Andy, then Janis and Matt. "The prisons."

"What!" exclaimed Matt.

"Yeah, you heard. The prisons. One third of the prisons on the east coast are empty, and who knows out west. We got all types of degenerates on the loose out there. That's what my men and I have been doing non-stop for hours now. It's what I didn't want to tell you. Most of the terrorists'

hits were far enough away not to affect this area that much, but this part is right here at home. They hit a prison just north of here and several near Pittsburgh and in West Virginia."

"What could they possibly gain by that?" Matt asked.

"Well, we have the largest prison population in the civilized world. A lot of those behind bars could care less about this country. What better way to create chaos and maybe even get some recruits."

Janis sat down but continued to stare at Clive. "What else?" she said softly.

Clive sat back in the chair, then started again. "As for us here locally, they hit the Keystone Power Station."

Janis looked over at Matt as another chill raced through her.

"And?" Matt added.

"Well, you know now why the power is off. Don't know when it will be back on. Cell phone use is spotty at best. I don't know when that will be up and running entirely."

"And the city?" Janis asked.

"Janis, Matt," Clive said with a pause. "It's bad. Real bad. When I left Smith Falls, I heard on some police emergency radios about fires burning in Pittsburgh, and we got all manner of nut cases out there."

"What about what we saw near the town of Dawn from the ridge?" Andy asked.

"Andy, after they hit the power station and the prison, I guess, they regrouped and headed north. Dawn is where the state police, the National Guard and the Air Force caught up with a group of them. After the fight was over, there wasn't much left of the town. As for any more terrorist activities around here, I doubt it. But we still have the prison problem. That and any other would-be criminal who wasn't behind bars. Anything from looters to bike gangs." Janis got up from the table, walked to the back door and opened it. She just

stared out at the back yard as the last rays of the afternoon sun shone through the leaves.

Matt looked at Janis, then back at Clive. "Is that it?" he asked.

"Yeah," Clive responded. "That's about it."

Andy got up and walked to his mother, who was still just standing silently staring out the door. He then turned to Matt and Clive. "What do we do?" he asked.

Matt looked at Andy then back at Clive. "We can't use our cell phones here. We never had coverage in this area, even when things were good. I picked up the land line phone. It's dead. It's the reason we always use CB radio here at camp. So what do we do next?"

"We get ready tonight," Clive said.

"Yeah," Matt said as he stared back at Clive. "In the morning we move."

Janis did not turn around, but they all heard her whisper, "Lisa." The room fell silent.

CHAPTER 13
September

Janis was preparing lunch; Clive and Matt were still sitting by the pond, fishing. They had caught a few fish but it was now mid-afternoon and the fish had slowed somewhat. They sat and drank their beers and discussed almost anything. Then there was a pause and Clive asked Matt, "How are all of you really doing? I mean, really."

Matt looked up at the sky for a moment then lowered his head and stared out at the surface of the pond. "I guess we are still living but I can't say much more than that. It's hard, so very hard. The not knowing, I mean. There is no closure and that leaves such a gaping hole in our lives. Janis doesn't talk about it much but it has to be on her mind every minute of every day. Mary and Robert, they play, they try to have fun but I know a huge hole has been torn in their lives too. Just hope it doesn't leave scars that will follow them the rest of their lives."

"And Lisa?" Clive asked.

Matt turned to Clive and shook his head. "I think she blames herself. I've tried to talk to her about it but she feels it was all her fault. She says if she hadn't taken those summer classes, we would have all been home together and it may have turned out differently."

"And you?" Clive asked. "What about you?"

Matt kind of pressed his lips together, as if holding back his emotions and once again turned toward the pond. "I don't know how to put how I feel into words. I feel this could have all been different too. But how and what else could we have done? I ask myself, did we think this out right? Did we do all we could have done? I think of it one way, then another. I try to explain it to myself, but in the end I just can't put it into words, not even for me. The one thing that burns in my mind is, did we make the right choices? Did we do all we could?" Clive took in a deep breath then he also turned and looked out over the surface of the pond. "I think about that too and I also question myself. We, I think, did all we could at the time. Not many people have had to face what we had to face just five or six weeks ago. Our choices were made fast and under pressure. We have never had to deal with this before, and when you choose you can change things forever for good or bad. I once read something that I think puts it best. Every time you make a choice you are turning the central part of you, the part of you that chooses into something a little different from what it was before."

Matt turned to Clive and with a somewhat surprised look on his face said, "C.S. Lewis."

"Yes." Clive said, "C.S. Lewis."

Matt turned a little in his chair and smiled. "You read C.S. Lewis?"

Clive continued to stare at the pond. "You would be surprised at what I read when I get the chance." He slowly turned to Matt, who had a smile on his face. "Even law enforcement people like to read. It calms my soul. It is a place that I can go to get away from it all, and believe me there are times when I desperately need that." Clive's expression then changed to a more serious look. "Matt, I have never faced what you are facing now, not to the degree

that you are. I try to feel what you must be feeling but I can only guess. I have had losses in my life and I know in a smaller way what it means to have no closure. The murders of a year ago still haunt me. I lost friends, some close friends, to that horrible time and there is no closure to me. One of my friends is gone and we have never been able to find a trace of where he may be. Even if I did find him, I would have to put him in prison. There would be closure to some extent but what kind of an end would that be? I guess part of me is glad that he is missing. I would not want to be the one to put him away—or worse, to end his life."

Matt turned his face to the pond again and said, "I know how close you and Brian were. I didn't know him as well as you, but he was your friend. I guess we both have huge holes in our hearts, ones that may never be filled. I think you feel and understand my hurt as much as I feel yours. I can only stop this hurting when I know what happened to Andy. And you, my friend, if it is to be prison or death you must know what happened to Brian. Both of us chose and we are changed for it. It is out of our hands and only God knows the outcome." Matt slid down in his chair and they both sat silently and watched the wind blow ripples across the surface of the pond. They both remained silent for about ten minutes, then they heard Janis call them for lunch. They picked up their weapons, reeled in their lines, turned and walked toward the house, leaving their chairs and fishing equipment at the pond.

Lunch was a time of laughter and talk about anything but the past. As Clive ate and talked and laughed, he would think of what they had talked about at the pond. The Fallons were all hurting deeply and yet he knew they still had room in their lives for him and he for them. He knew Matt was right. They all needed closure, but how could they find it? When lunch was over, Clive and Matt sat on the back steps

and talked to Robert and Mary for a time. When the kids returned to their play, Matt told Janis they were going back to the pond. He got six more beers out of the refrigerator. They walked back to the pond, once again put their weapons on the ground beside their chairs and continued fishing. They talked for a time, then they both just sat and fished. Clive was about to say something else to Matt but when he turned to speak he realized that Matt had fallen asleep. He smiled and said, "You rest, my friend. You need it." He reeled in his line, checked his bait and cast out again. He sat quietly and began to think back to that day when they had left camp for the city.

July

Clive was awake first and he checked his watch. It was 5 a.m. He had not slept well and he knew Matt had not either. He had lain awake for some time in the middle of the night and had heard and seen Matt get up and go to check on Parker. The house was quiet now and he got up from the couch and walked to the kitchen and splashed water on his face. He found a tube of toothpaste in the cupboard above the sink and used his finger to brush his teeth. He wiped his face and then went back to the living room, put on his shirt and buckled on his gun. He went to the refrigerator and poured a glass of orange juice. He quietly opened the door and stepped out onto the screened porch. He was about to sit down when he thought he saw a light out near the garage. He walked to the side of the porch and watched for a few minutes. All seemed dark and he could hear the sound of the generator running. He was about to turn away when he saw it again: a light from what seemed to be a flashlight coming around the side of the garage. He placed his orange juice on the picnic table, unsnapped his holster and checked his revolver. He moved quickly but quietly to the screen

door and down the steps. He watched from the corner of the house as a dark figure moved around the front of the garage and then entered through the man door at the front of the garage to the left of the two large garage doors.

Clive remembered the dogs in the pen and wondered why they were not barking. He could see the light flashing around inside the garage as if the person was hunting for someone or something. He moved quickly to the garage. As he passed the dog pen he looked at the two dogs as if to say, bark, do your job. They just looked back at him and sat there. He slowly opened the door that was already ajar. He could see the person near the back of the garage looking at the gas cans near the back wall. The person picked up one of the cans and shook it, as if checking for gas. He slowly and quietly moved closer to the person, his gun raised and pointed at the person's back. When he was about ten feet away, his foot hit something and made a noise. The figure in front of him froze in place, then slowly lowered the can to the floor and swung a long gun off his shoulder and stopped. Clive cocked his .357, which made a click, and then sternly said, "Freeze." The figure stopped and did not move.

Clive said, "Lower the weapon to the floor."

The figure did not move but instead replied, "No."

Clive repeated himself. "Drop the weapon."

Once again he got, "No."

Clive then said, only this time with a shout, "I said drop the weapon now."

The response this time was "Okay, Okay." The figure slowly lowered the gun to the floor and then stood up. Clive said, "Now don't move." He backed up about ten feet and then flipped on the light switch. To his surprise, the light came on. It must have been on the same circuit as the refrigerator. Once the light was on, he moved again to the man in front of him. He stopped about five or six feet behind

him then said, "Put your hands on the back of your head and slowly turn around." He watched the man slowly turn and as he did, he moved his gun up to the level of the man's face. When the man was facing him he realized that it was an elderly man with gray hair and a mustache, somewhat on the heavier side. He was wearing a plaid ball cap, old carpenter jeans, and a well-worn Carhartt coat.

As he turned to face Clive he sarcastically said, "Look Sonny, you really don't want to piss me off."

Clive said, "Just shut up. Now tell me who you are and what you're doing here." The old man started to lower his arms, but Clive shouted, "Keep the hands where they were and tell me who you are and what you want."

The old man tilted his head and kind of squinted with one eye and said, "The name's Coop and what I'm doing ain't none of your business, Sonny."

Clive said, "Back up from the gun to the wall." The old man shook his head in disgust but complied. Clive bent over while still watching the old man and picked up the gun. It was a 10-gauge pump shotgun with a shoulder strap. Clive slipped the gun over his shoulder and then asked again, "I said name and what do you want?"

The old man was about to answer when a voice came from behind Clive. "His name is Marion L. Cooper and he's a friend, Clive." It was Matt.

Before Clive got to say anything, the old man lowered his arms to his side and snapped, "I told you the name is Coop and you use that first name he just gave you and I'll blow a hole in your middle just about where your buckle is."

Clive just looked surprised and said, "Hey, old man, who's gonna blow holes in who here?" Cooper was about to speak again when Matt walked to Clive's side and reached out to push Clive's arm and gun slowly down toward the ground. He turned and smiled at Clive then took the

shotgun off Clive's shoulder, walked to the old man and handed it to him. He shook the old man's hand and then turned to Clive and said, "Let me introduce, Dr. Marion L. Cooper, as you now know as Coop. And, by the way, he means what he said about the first name."

Clive lowered the hammer on his .357 and holstered it, then took the couple of steps toward Coop and stuck out his hand. Clive said, "Now I know why the dogs didn't bark." The old man just looked up and down and hesitated to shake his hand but finally and reluctantly did. "Sorry about that," Clive said with a smile.

Coop dropped his hand quickly then stepped away. Looking back at Matt, he said, "Where did you get this cowboy?"

Clive turned to Matt and Coop and said, "Hey. I said I was sorry."

Coop then stared at Clive and asked, "And just what might your name be, Sonny?"

Clive looked somewhat disgusted and said. "It isn't Sonny. It's Sheriff Clive Aliston. Glad to meet you, I think."

Matt, now smiling somewhat, said, "Okay, guys. We're all on the same side here. Let's put the hair back down and remain civilized."

Clive smiled at Coop and said, "Truce?"

Coop forced a return smile and said, "Yeah, right."

Clive then said, "You said Dr. Cooper?"

"Yeah," Matt said. "He is a doctor and maybe we should have him look at Jerry?"

"Good idea," Clive said and they all left the garage with Matt in the lead.

As they walked to the house, Coop asked, "Who's Jerry?"

Clive responded, "He's my partner and he has been shot up badly. You think you could look at him?"

Coop said, "Yes. Where is he?"

A voice from the porch said, "He's up here in our bedroom. Come on up, Coop." It was Janis. Coop picked up his pace and got out ahead of Clive and Matt.

As Clive passed the dog pen he whispered, "Good watch dogs." Clive walked with Matt then said, "Boy, I guess it's lucky for Jerry that a doctor is your friend?"

"Friend and neighbor," Matt said adding, "Well, he isn't exactly your normal doctor."

"Not normal?" Clive asked.

Matt turned to Clive and walking backwards with his hands up, palms out toward Clive, said, "He's a vet."

"A what?" Clive said in surprise.

"I said a vet, as in veterinarian."

Clive looked at Matt and said, "You're going to have a vet look at Jerry?"

"Hold on a minute," Matt said as he turned and started up the back steps. "Coop's a good doctor and he's probably treated every animal and person in this area for years. I mean minor things you know."

"I know it's not legal," Clive said. "And I think Jerry's condition isn't exactly minor."

Matt stopped Clive at the back door and placed his hands on Clive's shoulders, "Clive, he's a great guy if you get to know him, and right now he's all Jerry has."

Clive looked at the floor and shook his head, "I guess you're right."

Matt smiled and said, "Let Coop do what he has to. Let's eat, get some food and water and whatever else we need to go for Lisa. I want to leave as soon as possible."

Coop tended to Jerry with Janis's help. The children were still asleep and they decided to let them go. Matt and Clive got some breakfast and packed some food and water and then went to Matt's gun cabinet, only to find Andy already there. They picked out a 12-gauge pump shotgun and Matt's

9 mm handgun and the .30-30 lever-action Winchester that was Andy's. Clive saw a black 12-gauge shotgun in the corner of the gun case. It was a stockless model and he asked Matt if he could use it. "Have at it." Matt said. "I figured you might prefer that. There's some double ought buckshot shells in our bedroom." Minutes later, Matt was packing the ammo in a small knapsack when Andy slipped two boxes of .30-30 in the sack also.

Matt looked up at Andy and said, "Son, I don't think you need to pack those. Keep them and your .30-30 here near you."

Andy looked at Matt, then Clive and said, "Dad, I'm not staying here. I'm going with you and Uncle Clive."

Matt put his hand on Andy's shoulder and smiled. "Andy, I know you want to go, but I need you here to stay with Mom and the kids. Clive and I will get Lisa."

"But Dad," Andy said as he stood up. "I want to go help get Lisa. She is my sister and I want to go. Besides you may need more than the two of you if it's as bad as Uncle Clive says it is out there."

Matt stood up with the knapsack in hand and said, "Andy, who's going to stay with Mom and the kids? We can't leave them here at home alone."

Just then a voice came from out in the hallway. It was Coop. He was standing there with his shirt sleeves rolled up to the elbows, wiping blood from his hands with a piece of white sheet. "I'll stay. The kid's right. Where you are going, you're gonna need all the help you can get."

Matt looked at Clive with a frustrated look on his face. Clive looked at Matt and said, "Coop's right, but he's your son. It's your choice."

Janis then moved in behind Coop and said, "Matt, you need Andy with you and Clive. Believe me, I don't want him out there anymore than I want Lisa out there but at least we

are at camp here. I can handle a gun and I'm not afraid to stay with Coop. The camp is in a remote place. There's less of a chance of any trouble here. You need more than two of you." Matt looked at Clive again. Clive said nothing. He just shook his head and looked back at Matt.

Andy reached out and put his hand on Matt's shoulder. "Dad, you know I have to go. Mom and the kids will be fine here with Coop."

There was a moment of silence then Coop spoke up. "Matt I'll go back to my place and get food, gas and ammo and be right back." He looked past Andy and Matt to Clive and said, "The gas is what I was looking for this morning. I knew they might need more and I have an underground tank. There's just me back at my place and I can be more help here. You need Andy, both of you."

Matt looked at the floor and shook his head, then said, "Okay, okay. He goes—but I'm not sure how much I like this."

Clive looked at Coop and asked, "Jerry. How's he doing?"

"Not good, but okay for now. I think he will be fine. It's gonna be a long road back but I think he'll make it." They all left the gun room and Janis went back to Jerry's room, followed by Matt and Andy. Coop said to Clive that he was going home for supplies and they both walked to the kitchen.

Clive stopped Coop at the back door and put out his hand and Coop did the same. "I think Matt's right about you Coop. Sorry for the way we met."

"Don't worry about that, Sonny. I think you might be okay too."

"The name's Clive, not Sonny," Clive said with a smile.

"Yeah, Clive, and the name's Coop, not Marion."

They both kind of smiled and Coop went to leave but turned and said, "I'll be back in half an hour. Keep your eyes

open."

"Done," was all Clive said as he walked away. Clive, Matt and Andy packed the jeep and put what gas Matt could spare into the tank. Coop, as he promised, was back in a little more than half an hour in his flatbed truck. He had more ammo and several large gas cans. He gave one can to Matt for the jeep and they pulled the packed jeep out into the driveway. They all checked in on Parker and, to their surprise, he was awake. He seemed to be a little better but he was still weak from blood loss. The kids were now awake and they all gathered in the living room and talked out their plans.

As decided, Janis, the kids, Jerry and Coop would remain at camp. Matt, Clive and Andy would get Lisa. They expected the trip to take one day, two at the most, allowing time for any road problems. When all was finalized, Matt and Janis went to one of the bedrooms and said their goodbyes. Janis cried but she knew Matt had to go. The last thing she said to Matt was, "Come home safe to me, both of you. And bring my girl back here safe." She held him for what seemed like minutes, and whispered, "I love you," several times. He told her the same, then it was time to part. She held Andy and kissed him several times and Matt picked up the children one at a time and held them and told them to help their mom.

Janis hugged and held Clive and kissed him, then looked into his eyes and whispered, "Bring them home to me safe, and I want you home too. You hear me, Clive Aliston?"

He smiled and hugged her and said, "Yes, dear. I hear you." They walked out to the jeep and Matt slipped into the driver's seat with Clive beside him. Andy climbed into the back then remembered something and ran back to the house. He returned a minute later with his bow and arrows in hand.

"Sure you want that?" Clive asked.

"You bet," was all he said as he climbed into the jeep. Janis, Robert, Mary and Coop followed the jeep out to the end of the driveway and said their final goodbyes. Matt put the jeep in gear and headed up the hill away from camp, with the four of them waving goodbye until they disappeared in the dust cloud that the jeep left behind.

CHAPTER 14
July

Matt, Clive and Andy drove out the dirt road to the blacktop Route 8. Matt stopped about a hundred yards from the highway and sat and listened. Andy, sitting in the back, said, "Dad, do you hear that?"

Clive answered before Matt did. "Yeah, we hear it, Son. That's what your dad is waiting for." In the distance they heard a police siren that was coming closer.

Matt picked up the 12-gauge pump and stood up in the jeep. Clive pulled out his shotgun and did the same. Andy remained seated in the back but he checked the .30-30 and sat and waited. In a matter of minutes a dark car flashed past out ahead of them on the highway. Seconds later it was followed by two police cars, lights and sirens on, traveling at high speed. They all stayed in their positions and listened as the sound of the sirens faded into the distance. Clive then slowly sat down in his seat. He looked up at Matt, who was still standing looking out at the highway in front of him. "Matt, it might not be a good idea to use a main highway like Route 8 to head south to the city. When I came this way yesterday, most of the trouble was on roads like 8 and some of the four-lanes. I would think most of the bad guys out there are going to use those to get out of this area as fast as they can. Some of the back roads might trap them and they

know it. I realize it's going to take longer to get to the city but I think it's better if we make it there with less trouble."

Matt looked down at Clive but didn't say anything.

Andy looked up at Matt and said, "You know he's right Dad."

Matt slid down into the seat and for a second he just stared out the windshield at the highway in front of him. He took a deep breath then looked at Clive. "I want to get there a.s.a.p. but you're probably right. Better to get there safely than not at all."

He put the jeep in drive and was about to pull out when he heard a voice on the CB radio under the dash. It was Janis. "Fallon 2, this is Fallon 1, do you hear me?"

Matt looked at the radio then at Clive and picked up the mike. "This is Fallon 2, Janis?"

"Yeah, this is Janis," she answered. "I put the CB on before you left. I wanted to try it but I guess I forgot to tell you."

Matt looked again at Clive, then answered, "Good idea. I guess I didn't even realize it was on till now. I'm not going to leave this on in the jeep. We could get too much background chatter and there will be times that I may not want the noise. You get what I mean?"

There was a pause, then Janis answered, "Yeah, I get you."

He paused, then added, "I'll call you again at 2 p.m. or close to that time and let you know where we are."

Clive tapped Matt on the shoulder. "Tell her we may get out of range or have some other communications problems. If she doesn't hear from us, not to panic. Now set up two more contact times."

Matt nodded and said, "Got ya." He keyed the mike and told Janis what Clive had said. They agreed on every four hours from 2 p.m.. He said a few more things about the CB then added, "Move the food in the kitchen refrigerator to the garage. I forgot to do that before we left. You should have

enough gas to run the generator till I get back."

There was a pause, then Janis answered, "Coop says he's got that end of it covered. Not to worry."

Matt said, "See you soon. I love you." He shut off the CB then looked at Clive. "I know a back way around Butler."

Clive looked at him and said, "Through West Sunbury?"

"Yeah," Matt replied. Clive shook his head in agreement and Matt pulled slowly out to the highway. When he reached the road, he checked in both directions then turned right headed north toward the small town of Harrisville. He traveled two or three miles on Route 8 then turned to the right onto a small two-lane blacktop Boyers Road and headed east toward the small village of Boyers. They drove the six to eight miles of that road without passing a single car. When they reached Boyers they drove slowly through the town. There were no people out anywhere and no cars on the road. As they moved slowly through the town they saw people looking out their windows at them. They could see that some of those people were holding guns.

Clive looked at Matt and said, "If they're smart they'll stay in their homes till it's all clear." Matt just looked at Clive and shook his head in agreement.

At Boyers they picked up Route 308 and headed south toward the town of West Sunbury, some fifteen miles ahead. Route 308 was also deserted until they got near a large body of water to their left, the Butler Glades. As they came up over the hill on the road, they were passed by a county sheriff's car. When Clive saw the car he waved and asked Matt to pull over to the side of the road. Clive stood up, turned, and looked back toward the car that had just passed them. He looked down at Matt and said, "That's one of our cars, and if I'm not mistaken it's Jack Duff, one of my officers." They were only waiting for about a minute when the same car came up over the rise and pulled in behind them.

As Clive had suspected, it was Jack. He got out of his car and walked to the jeep. "Clive, boy am I glad to see you. We have been worried sick about you since we lost contact yesterday. One of the Butler police officers reported finding your car early this morning and that it was shot up bad and blood inside. Are you okay?"

"Yeah," Clive said as he climbed out of the jeep.

"What about Parker?" Jack asked.

Clive shook his head and said, "He's not good. He got shot up badly, but I think there's a good chance he'll make it. He's back at the Fallons' camp and he does have a doctor—well, sort of. Jack, you do know Matt Fallon and his son Andy?"

"Yes," Jack said as he shook Matt's hand.

Clive looked up at the rise in the road not one hundred yards behind them, then looked down the road in the opposite direction. "This is a bad spot to be talking. We can't see beyond that rise. Let's move up to that pull-off a quarter mile up the road. It's a better spot." They all agreed, and moved up the road to continue their conversation. Clive spoke first. "Jack, let everyone know I'm okay but I'm not coming back to the station—not just yet. If you can send help to Matt's camp, at least medical help, it would be great."

"Well," Jack said. "I'll try, but every police officer in the area is out there now and we are spread thin. I mean thin. As far as medical help it's pretty much the same, and ambulances—forget them. It's still bad out there. We never know where we'll be needed next."

"How are our guys doing?" Clive asked.

"Good," Jack responded. "At least so far. I guess none of us would ever have expected anything like this."

"You got that right," Matt said. "How bad is it out there, especially in the city?"

"You mean Butler?" Jack asked.

"No," Matt said. "I mean Pittsburgh."

"Well," Jack said as he pressed his lips together and shook his head. "I don't know any first-hand info but we've heard that it was bad last night. Some fires, looting and the escapees, that's the biggest problem. I guess the Pittsburgh police and the county and sheriff's department have their hands full. Last I heard this morning was things were better, but I don't think normal is going to be where we are for a while yet."

"What about the rest of the country?" Clive asked.

Jack looked at Clive, then Andy. "I guess they laid us out real good as you know Clive, but one thing I think those asshole terrorists didn't count on was the resilience of the American people."

"What do you mean?" Andy asked.

Jack said, "Well Andy, they hit us and hard, but if what we're hearing is correct the good people of this country won't stay down for long. I've heard of some pretty heroic things happening, mostly near here but also rumors that that's the case all over. Everyone is fighting back. I even heard some of the prisoners that could have escaped, stayed and helped in any way they could. I guess for some people being American comes first."

Clive turned and walked a few steps toward the highway and looked in each direction. He paused, then turned around and said, "Well, I guess they found out."

"Found out what, Uncle Clive?" Andy asked.

Clive walked back to the cars and said, "Andy, have you ever seen two brothers fighting and you stepped in to take sides? I hope you didn't, or ever do. When it comes to brothers, they might fight each other, but when someone from outside attacks one of them you'll have both of them on you before you know it. It's just like this country. We can fight among ourselves but when it comes to being attacked

from outside, personal matters are set aside. Apparently, we are all still Americans at heart. You attack some of us, you attack all of us."

"Amen," Matt said as he sort of smiled.

Clive then asked Jack, "Where are you coming from?"

"From Butler," Jack said. "I was there when this all started. You remember you sent me to get that evidence on that robbery? I got stuck there for awhile and helped out as much as I could. I'm on my way back to Smith Falls but I heard about your car being found so I came this way instead of up Route 8. Don't use the main highways, Matt. There seems to be more trouble along them."

"Okay," Matt responded, then Jack looked at Clive.

"Where are you going, Clive?"

"To Pittsburgh," Clive responded. "Well, actually to Oakland. I'm going with Matt and Andy to get his daughter, Lisa. She's in school there. I'm not going to let them go on their own. Tell them back at the station that I'll be back a.s.a.p. and if you can, see if you can get someone to Matt's camp to help Parker. I know I need to get back to the station but I'm not letting them go get Lisa on their own."

Matt then cut in, "Clive, if you need to go, go ahead with Jack. Andy and I will be fine."

"No," Clive said sternly. "I'm staying with you until Lisa's home safe. Now, we've gotta get going Jack. Give them the message at the station and be careful yourself on the way back. I'll see you soon." They all shook hands. Jack headed north, while Matt, Clive and Andy headed south again on Route 308. They traveled the five remaining miles to the town of West Sunbury and were met at the town line by a local police roadblock. Clive conversed with the officers for a few minutes then they headed through town and south in the direction of Butler. They were about five miles down the road just east of Unionville when they passed a

farmhouse on the right.

As they drove by, Clive looked up at the house just in time to see a man hitting and pushing a woman in torn clothes back into the front door. Andy saw it at the same time. "Uncle Clive, did you see that?"

"Yeah," Clive responded. "Matt, I don't want to stop again, but I have to. Something's wrong here. Pull off in those trees up ahead." Matt turned quickly off the road and into the trees. Clive climbed out and took his shotgun and checked his revolver. "You two stay here. I'll check it out as quick as I can."

"No," Matt replied. "You go, we go, and don't argue."

"Okay, okay," Clive said. "Matt, you and Andy stay near that stone wall at the front of the house. Don't let anyone get out that way until I see what's going on. I'll come in from the back." They started toward the house when they all heard a woman scream.

CHAPTER 15
September

Clive's daydreaming and Matt's nap were interrupted when they heard Janis call from the house. She wanted Matt to come up for a minute to help her with something. They both got up but Matt turned to Clive and said, "No, Clive. Stay here and enjoy the afternoon. I'll handle it and be back in a few minutes. Do we need any more beer?"

"Yeah, maybe a couple," Clive said. "Sure you don't need my help?"

"No. I think I know what she wants and she doesn't need both of us. Be right back." Matt turned and left for the house and Clive stood for a few minutes and stretched, then sat back in the chair. He picked up his rod and started to reel in when he realized he had a fish. He reeled it in slowly and then realized it was a small bass. He pulled it from the pond, unhooked it and released it.

He smiled as it swam away. "Go back and grow up. See you in a couple of years." He re-baited his hook and cast out again. He drank the last of the beer in his can, then crushed it in his hands and dropped it beside his chair. He reached into the bag of ice, popped open another can, took a sip, then slid down in the chair. He stared out at the forest behind the pond as his thoughts drifted back to that day on the road.

July

As Clive had asked, Matt and Andy moved through the trees toward the house and then ran one at a time to a stone wall that was about four feet high and at the foot of the front yard. Clive moved up through the trees to the left of the house and then behind a row of pines behind the house. He was about to move across the back yard when he heard a woman scream again. He curled his lips and said, "Ah, shit," and made a dead run at the back porch of the house. He covered the yard and the back steps in what seemed like only five or six steps. He never stopped his forward motion and slammed into the back door. The door flew open and in a split second he was inside the kitchen. He looked down the hallway and saw a man standing, looking back at him from the living room with a large knife in his hand. Clive quickly raised the shotgun at the man and yelled, "Freeze."

The man's face suddenly showed total fear as he stood there looking back at Clive. Clive slowly started down the hallway toward the front room, the shotgun pointed at the man's face. As he moved toward the man he said, "Drop the weapon on the floor and back up." The man did not move except for his eyes. They made a quick move to the left then moved back to Clive. Clive continued to walk slowly toward the man, when in the reflection in a mirror on one of the living room walls he saw a second man holding a half-naked woman with a gun pointed at her head. He saw the first man glance once again in that direction and he stopped. He repeated to the first man, "Drop the weapon and back up." He once again glanced at the mirror and realized that the second man did not realize that he had seen him. He paused for a moment, then told the man holding the knife, "I'll count to three. If you haven't dropped the knife, I'll blow your head off. One, two…"

"Okay, okay," the man said, throwing the knife to the floor.

Clive did not move, but stayed out of the sight of the second man. He repeated to the first man, "Back up," and the man complied as he glanced to his left a third time. Clive said, "Turn around and open the front door." The man just stood there. Clive screamed this time, "Damn it. I said open the front door." The first man turned quickly and opened the front door and then stood there. Clive then said, "Turn to the wall and place your hands behind your head and don't move." The man did as he was told then Clive glanced into the mirror again. He saw the second man pointing his gun in his direction with his hand over the woman's mouth. He was waiting for Clive to clear the corner of the hallway wall. Clive did not move but instead yelled out the front door. "This is Clive. Leave the boy at the wall to cover the front and come on up to the porch. I got him."

He watched the first man but glanced again at the mirror. The second man was getting nervous and kept pointing the gun first in Clive's direction then at the front door. He then realized that the woman who was being held saw him in the mirror also. He could tell by her eyes that she thought he didn't see the second man so he winked at her in the mirror. He was sure that she saw him. He nodded and smiled.

He yelled again at Matt and Matt yelled back. "I'm at the porch. I'm coming in." When the second man heard Matt's footsteps coming up the front porch steps he made a quick move toward the door with his gun. A second later, Clive stepped out from behind the wall and leveled the 12-gauge at the man's head. When the woman saw Clive move she bit down on the man's fingers that covered her face. The man screamed and let go of her and she dropped to the floor. In a split second, the man turned again toward Clive and moved the gun in his direction. Clive did not hesitate. He dropped the barrel of the gun to the man's chest and fired. The blast picked the man up off his feet and threw him into

the wall behind, smashing the plaster, and then onto an end table and finally to the floor. Clive then turned toward the first man, who was just running out the front door. He only made it about two feet out the door when he ran into Matt, who raised his shotgun and slammed the side of the butt into the man's face. He flew against the wall of the porch and slid to the floor unconscious.

Clive turned to the woman on the floor. She was naked except for underpants and she quickly grabbed what was left of her blouse and covered her breasts. She slid away from the man on the floor up against the wall, then put her face in her hands. Matt looked inside, first at Clive, then at the woman on the floor. "Should I call Andy up?"

Clive looked at Matt then back at the woman. "Yeah, but only to the porch." Matt stepped out and called Andy. When he got to the porch he told them to hold the .30-30 on the man unconscious on the floor and not to come inside. Andy looked through the window and saw Clive and the man on the floor and the woman sitting against the wall. Matt repeated, "Stay out here on the porch. If he tries to get away, shoot him in the leg." Andy just nodded and Matt stepped back inside.

Clive walked over to the man on the floor, rolled him onto his back and checked his pulse at the neck. "Is he dead?" Matt asked.

"Yeah," was all Clive said as he got up and shook his head and pressed his lips together as if upset. "I didn't want to have to do that but he gave me no choice."

Matt looked at Clive and said, "There's nothing else you could have done."

Clive took a deep breath then said, "Yeah." He turned to the woman on the floor and knelt down beside her. "Ma'am, are you alright?" He got no answer, so he repeated, "Ma'am, are you alright?"

This time she raised her head and just glared at him. She was a shapely, very pretty woman with long blonde hair and blue eyes. Clive guessed that she was in her early forties. She slowly began to stand up, still holding the remnants of the shirt to her breasts. She was about five foot seven, and looked like she was of Scandinavian descent. Clive began to say again, "Ma'am, are you…"

She stopped him in mid-sentence and sternly replied, "No, I'm not alright and my name isn't ma'am. It's Maddie."

"Maddie?" Clive asked.

"Yes," she replied. "As in Madison Lynn Devereaux, and what the hell took you so long to get here?" Matt and Clive just looked at her with a surprised look on their faces. She repeated. "Well, what the hell took you so long? I know you can talk. Can you hear? I asked you a question."

Clive, still looking surprised, just backed up and said, "Ah, ah…"

She cut in again as she slowly walked toward him, stopping right in front of him. "I've been fighting off these two assholes for nearly half an hour now. What did you two do, stop for brunch?"

Clive put up one hand, palm out toward her and said, "Whoa, lady. Hold on a minute. We just saved your butt and you're mad at us. Besides, how did you know we were coming?"

She turned away and walked to the wall, exposing her bare back, then turned back to Clive and said, "Don't ask me how I knew. I just knew. If you don't mind, would you find me something to wear? Enough men I don't know have seen me naked for one day."

Clive just opened his eyes wide and said, "Okay, lady." He aked Matt, "would you check around and see what you can find? I'll tie up the other guy." Matt headed to the second floor to a bedroom while Clive went out to the porch and,

with Andy's help, tied up the other man. Andy asked if he could come inside and Clive said, "Give us a few minutes, then yes, you can." He left Andy out on the porch and went back inside. Maddie was standing in the corner of the room, holding the shirt and looking at the man on the floor.

Matt returned from upstairs and handed Maddie a pair of faded blue jeans and a light blue short-sleeve man's shirt. "It's all I could find that I thought might fit you."

She looked at the clothes then said, "Well, I guess they'll have to do." She then looked at both of them, as if over a pair of glasses, then said, "Well are you two going to turn around or are you going to watch me dress?"

"Okay, lady," Clive said as they both turned around. Clive then asked while she dressed, "How did you get here?"

As she pulled on the jeans, she said, "Three of them stopped me out on the road and said they needed help and that's when they grabbed me and took my car."

"Your car?" Clive asked. "Where's your car?"

"I don't know," Maddie answered as she pulled on the shirt. "The third guy left in it about an hour ago. That was about half an hour before these two decided they wanted a piece of me. As I said, I've been talking and fighting my way out of it until you got here—late, I might add again."

Clive turned his head toward Maddie just as she was about to pull the shirt over her head, and then quickly turned back and said, "Hey lady."

She cut in again, "Oh, don't 'hey lady' me. I told you my name and you were late."

Clive just took in another deep breath and then continued, "Do you know who lives here?"

"No, and you can turn around now," she said, adding, "I don't know who lived here but I think if you look in the basement you'll find them. I think they are both dead."

Clive and Matt turned around, then Clive asked, "Were you in the basement?"

"No," Maddie said as she stood with her hands on her hips. "I just know they're there."

Clive looked at Matt now, even more puzzled, and said, "Would you go take a look?"

"Sure," Matt said as he went to the kitchen and then opened a door that he figured led to the basement.

Clive stood and stared at Maddie as she walked to the front window and looked out at Andy on the porch. "Is that Matt's son?"

Clive had taken a cover off the couch and was placing it over the man's body. He stood up and turned to Maddie and said, "Yeah, that's Andy, Matt's son. How did you know Matt's name?"

She turned to Clive and crossed her arms and stared at Clive. "Let's just say I guessed."

"Yeah, right," Clive said as Matt walked into the room.

"Clive, she's right. There are two people down there. A man and a woman, maybe in their fifties, both dead. I think shot."

Clive turned again to Maddie and said, "Okay, lady, who are you and how do you know all of this?"

Maddie walked to Clive, her arms still crossed, stopped and looked up at him and said, "I told you the name is Madison Lynn Devereaux."

Matt cut in. "Clive, I hate to break this up but I gotta get Lisa. Can we go?"

Just then, the door opened and Andy stuck his head in. "Can I come in?"

Before Clive or Matt could answer, Maddie did. "Yes, Andy. You can come in." The door opened and Andy stepped in. Maddie unfolded her arms, stepped away from Clive, walked up to Andy and shook his hand. "Hi Andy,

I'm Maddie. Nice to meet you and thanks for coming to my rescue."

Andy gave her a strange look and said, "Uh, yeah, sure."

Matt said, "What about the other guy?"

Clive thought for a minute then said, "They killed those people more than likely. We have to take him till we can drop him off with some of the other police." He then turned to Maddie and said, "You go too until we find someone to take you to a safe place."

Maddie again folded her arms and glared at Clive. "You're right I go with you, but I stay with you."

"Like hell," Clive said. "You get dropped off at the first safe place."

Maddie walked quickly to Clive again and just glared at him. "You are the only safe place—and besides, you're going to need me. Now that's settled and I don't need any more argument from you. I'm headed with you to the city. You can drop me at home later."

Clive stared down into those deep blue eyes and said, "Where do you live?"

She stared back and replied, "Twenty miles north of Smith Falls. The wrong direction for you to take me back. As I said, I'm going with you. You need me. Case closed." She forced a smile then walked out the door to the porch.

Matt looked at Clive. "That woman is just plain weird."

"You think?" Clive said as he headed for the door, shaking his head. They picked up the half-conscious man on the front porch and they all walked to the jeep. Matt and Clive sat in front and Maddie and Andy sat in back, with the man between them being covered by Andy with the .30-30. As they pulled out of the trees, Clive looked back at Maddie, who was staring at him, smiling. He just shook his head and turned back toward the front. Matt pulled out onto Route 308 again, headed toward Butler.

CHAPTER 16
September

Clive's daydreaming was interrupted again when Matt returned from the house. As Matt sat down again in the lawn chair, Clive got up. "Well, buddy, it's my turn. I think I need the little boys' room and, to tell you the truth, a big glass of water before I drink any more of that beer. I caught a small one and put him back. Maybe you'll do better while I'm gone."

Matt put the extra beers on the ice bag and said, "I'll see if I can do better. There are some monsters out there."

Clive stretched, then slowly walked to the house. When he entered the screened porch, Janis was setting the picnic table for supper. "Give up on those fish already?" she asked.

"No," Clive said. "Just needed the little boys' room and actually, I could use a big glass of water. Re-hydrate, you know."

"Be my guest," she said as he entered the house. When he returned, she wasn't on the porch; he saw her at the dog pen, petting Ginger. He walked to her side and she put her arms around him and hugged him for a few moments. She looked up into his eyes and smiled then looked down at the dog. "I miss Maggie. She was a good dog."

"Yeah, I know," Clive said. "Me too." She turned away from Clive for a moment and then wiped a tear from the side

of her face. Clive reached and placed his fingers under her chin, turning her face toward him. "I know it's hard, Janis, especially the not knowing. But you're at least trying to get on with your life. It's what he would have wanted."

Clive and Janis walked around the front of the pen and stopped. Clive looked toward the pond at Matt and made a motion as if he were catching a fish then extended his arms out to his sides as if to ask, "Well?" Matt just shook his head. Clive turned back to Janis. "I can only imagine what you all must be going through. In a small way I do understand, from the no closure point of view—but it can't even compare with your situation. Just remember, I'm here for you, all of you. I won't stop helping to find an answer, not ever."

Janis looked up at him and smiled and said, "Yeah, I know Clive Aliston. I know." Her expression turned a little more serious. "How could they, I mean the government, have let this all happen? I felt safe before all of this, but now I'm scared, Clive, and I mean scared to the bone."

"Yeah, I guess a lot of people didn't expect this. The government should have known and I don't know why they didn't. I guess sometimes a message of warning will not be so easily received by the people who need to be warned. The danger signs were all right there on the horizon, from porous borders to a faulty immigration system, to spreading our resources too thin. I think maybe they said, 'We've had our 9/11, our Pearl Harbor. It can't happen again, not on our watch.' Well, thinking like that will get you bitten on the ass faster than you think. All I can say is thank God for the American citizens. They stood shoulder to shoulder and fought back, no matter what it took. I hate to say what might have happened if total panic would have set in, that and if they had been disarmed like so many wanted. Our forefathers that started this nation would have been proud of them. I know I am. Janis, we'll keep looking to find an

answer, no matter what it is. We've got to hang in there and keep on living. It's what all of our new heroes would have wanted. It's what Andy would have wanted. Well, I guess I'll get back to those fish." Janis hugged him again and he turned and headed to the pond. She watched for a few minutes, then turned and walked to the back steps. She didn't go up to the porch but instead sat on the bottom of the steps and looked up at the blue sky above the field and forest behind the camp. Her thoughts drifted back to that afternoon at camp after Matt, Andy, and Clive had left to get Lisa.

July

It was getting close to 2 p.m., the designated contact time, and Janis left the house and walked to the garage. She went to the work bench and opened a large wooden box. Inside was the CB base station. She turned on the set, waited several minutes, then keyed the mike. "Fallon 2 this is Fallon 1. Do you hear me?" She waited but there was nothing but a hash sound and total silence. She waited a couple of seconds then repeated, "Fallon 2 this is Fallon 1. Do you hear me?" There was a pause then Matt's voice came through. "Fallon 1 this is Fallon 2. Janis this is Matt. Is everything alright there?"

"Yes," Janis replied. "We are all fine. What about you?"

"Fine. All fine," Matt said.

Janis added, "Where are you?"

Matt replied, "We are on Route 308, just north of Butler."

"That's all the further you are?" Janis asked in a kind of panic.

"Yes," Matt replied. "We ran into a little trouble that slowed us down. That and a couple of road blocks."

"Are you sure you're alright?" she asked again.

"Yes. We are fine," Matt said. "We have a prisoner, and I

guess you would call her a victim, with us. We are going to drop them off as soon as possible but we'll get Lisa a.s.a.p. I mean that."

"A prisoner?" Janis asked, sounding even more concerned.

"Yes," Matt said. "But as I told you, we are all fine. We will be fine. Now are you sure all is okay there?"

"Yes, we are fine," Janis said, then added, "The kids are in the house playing and Coop went for one more load of gas. I told him I thought we had enough but you know him. Parker seemed a little better but we need to get him to a hospital or something sometime soon."

"Okay," Matt said, then added, "Hope to be home by dark. I'll talk to you again in four hours, okay?"

"Okay, honey," Janis replied, then added, "Please be safe, all of you. I love you all. Talk to you soon."

Matt said, "I love you too, dear. We'll talk at 6 p.m. Stay alert, Fallon 2. Out."

The set went back to hash and Janis put the mike in the box, shut off the set and closed the box. She stood and leaned on the top of the workbench for a few minutes with her eye closed and whispered, "Please God, keep them all safe. Bring them home to me." She turned and walked to the utility room and opened the door. Inside was the gas generator and when she opened the door the noise of the generator got much louder. She walked to the gas tank and checked it. It was still half full. She closed the door and walked to the refrigerator to check on the food. As she did, she heard the dogs bark. She looked out the door window and listened, then went back to check on the refrigerator. When she was satisfied that all was okay, she closed the refrigerator door, walked back to the work bench and picked up the four tomatoes that were sitting on the bench. As she did, she heard the dogs again—only this time they sounded like they

were more upset than before. She walked back to the door of the garage and looked out.

She saw the dogs racing around the pen and looking toward the road. She thought to herself, if it was Coop the dogs wouldn't even have barked. A chill ran through her and she reached behind her back and pulled out the .25-caliber automatic pistol from a holster on her belt. With the gun in one hand and the tomatoes in the other, she slowly opened the door and stepped outside. She stood at the door and looked in every direction, but saw no one. The dogs were still looking toward the road and racing around the pen, barking. She stepped out away from the garage, then felt a little uneasy being away from the security of the building and stepped back against the garage. She moved down the front of the garage toward the driveway so she could see out toward the road. When she reached the front corner, she leaned out and looked past the front to the entrance of the driveway. No one there. She took in a deep breath then stepped away from the garage headed toward the road.

She had only taken two steps when she was grabbed from behind. An arm went around her neck and another knocked the gun from her hand. She grabbed at the arm around her neck with the now-free gun hand and tried to scream but nothing came out. She couldn't breathe as the person wrestled with her. Suddenly, the person let go and spun her around. She found herself face to face with a crazed-looking man with a bald head, goatee and two gold front teeth, laughing at her. He quickly reached up and grabbed the front of her blouse and pulled her close to his face. So close she could smell his bad breath. "Hi honey," was all he said as he laughed a hideous kind of laugh. Janis, without thinking, reached up with the other hand and smashed a tomato into his face. He didn't move; he just spit

out part of the tomato into her face and laughed even louder. His face then suddenly went stone serious. He screamed, "Bitch," and slapped her with the back of his hand. She fell back to the ground, very close to where the .25 auto lay. She reached quickly for the gun but as soon as it was in her hand a boot smashed her hand to the ground. She looked up just as another backhand hit her again. She went face first into the driveway and started to move again when she was grabbed by the back of her hair and pulled up and pushed toward the garage. The dogs were now in a frenzy as if they would crash through the fence. She managed to turn a little toward the man who had her in his grasp just in time to see him point a handgun at the dog pen and fire. Maggie let out a yelp and fell to the ground. Ginger ran into the doghouse and went silent.

The man yanked hard on the back of her hair and pushed her toward the garage door and then inside. She tried with all her strength to get free but it felt as if all the hair on the top of her head was being pulled out by the roots. Once inside, the man pushed her toward the workbench then let her go. She spun around and faced him. He was about five feet ten, and wearing a prison uniform. He just glared at her, then began that horrible laugh. He abruptly stopped laughing then walked closer to her and said in a voice with a strong southern accent, "Well, darling, how do you do?"

Janis screamed, "Go to hell," and spit in his face. He started to laugh again then stopped and wiped his face with the back of his hand. He sort of growled and leaped at her. He grabbed her blouse and ripped the front of it almost completely off. She pushed him back and started to claw at his face, leaving three blood-red scratches on the left side. He pushed her back against the bench, reached for her shirt a second time in an attempt to pull it off. He then pushed

hard up against her. She could feel his hands against hers and she screamed and pushed as hard as she could. He backed up two or three steps and stopped. He laughed again and started toward her. Janis reached back on the top of the workbench, looking for anything she could find. What she came up with was a rubber mallet used for putting hubcaps on a car. She swung it at him but missed and he grabbed her hand and laughed again.

He was about to push against her again when they both heard a voice coming from the front of the garage. It was a voice with a heavy Scottish accent, "Bobby Ray, let the lady go."

The man confronting her didn't even turn around. He just laughed again and said, "Screw you McRoy. This one's mine."

The man spoke again, only this time with more authority. "Bobby Ray, don't make me ask you twice."

The man in front of Janis just laughed and reached for her again. There was the sound of a gun shot and a bullet hit the wall not three feet from Janis. The man attacking her stopped and turned toward the man in the doorway. "You asshole. I'm tired of taking your shit. You don't run me. Find your own woman."

The man in the doorway walked slowly toward the two of them. He was a man of maybe mid-forties or early fifties, with almost-white hair and a beard. He was also in a prison uniform and he was holding a large-caliber handgun pointed at the man he called Bobby Ray. He walked toward Janis, then said, "Bobby Ray, leave the woman alone and get outside. Don't make me ask you again." The man called Bobby Ray yelled a mass of profane words at the older man, then turned and left the garage, slamming the door behind him. The older man walked to Janis as she made an attempt at covering herself. He stopped a few feet from her and then

lowered his gun to his side and in a much gentler voice asked, "Ma'am, are you alright?"

Janis just looked at him and sneered. "Do I look alright?"

The man said in a soft voice, "Stay away from Bobby Ray. He's just plain loco crazy."

"Who are you?" Janis asked as she continued to cover herself with the remainder of her shirt.

"Just some people who need a place to rest for awhile and maybe some food and water."

Janis just looked at him and snapped, "Looks to me more like prisoners that escaped."

"Yeah, that too," the man replied. "But you won't get hurt if you just do what we ask. Now please go to the house. We have a wounded man that needs help." Janis just stood and glared at him. He once again asked in a soft voice, "Please go to the house."

Janis walked away from the bench and headed for the door. As she stepped outside, followed by the man, she looked at the dog pen. Maggie lay dead in a pool of blood and Ginger was inside the dog house. Janis stopped and looked at the dog for a second. "He didn't have to do that," she said as she turned to face the man.

He just shook his head and said, "I'm really sorry about that. As I said, stay away from him. He's an animal." Janis began to feel tears running down her face but quickly wiped them and turned and walked toward the house, followed by the man with white hair.

Coop was on his way back from his place when he reached the top of the hill above camp. When he saw a strange-looking truck parked in the grass in the backyard, he stopped his truck and watched. He saw Janis followed by a man with a gun walk to the house and up the steps and go inside. Coop put the truck in reverse and backed up slowly over the edge of the hill and into some trees just beyond the

field behind camp. He got out of his truck and put a large caliber handgun in his waistband, picked up his 10-gauge shotgun, and checked it for shells. He quietly closed the truck door and then turned and headed through the low trees toward the house.

CHAPTER 17
July

Janis crossed the porch and entered the kitchen, followed by the man with white hair. When she was inside she saw Bobby Ray looking in the empty refrigerator and another man slumped in a chair at the table with a bloody piece of rag or sheet tied to his shoulder. Bobby Ray slammed the refrigerator door and stepped directly in front of Janis. He smiled again, exposing the two gold teeth and said in a sinister voice, "Where ya put the food, honey?"

The man behind Janis stepped beside Janis and Bobby Ray and said, "Bobby Ray, I told you to leave her alone. If you had any brains in that empty head of yours you would have realized the power is off and the food's probably in the refrigerator in the garage. Didn't you hear the generator running?"

Bobby Ray looked at the man but did not move. "Can't say I did, McRoy. I was occupied, if you know what I mean. I told you, you ain't my boss." He pushed Janis to the side and said, "Get outta my way, bitch. I'm hungry." He stood beside her and directly in front of McRoy and turned to Janis, "When my belly's full then I'll have some of you."

McRoy looked down at Bobby Ray. "I told you, leave her alone. If you're going to the garage, get food for everyone."

"Screw you," Bobby Ray said, as he tried to pass McRoy.

McRoy reached out and grabbed Bobby Ray and slammed him up against the wall. "Bobby Ray, I've had about enough of your mouth. Now I said go get food and for all of us. You don't want what happened back at the cell block to happen again, and my patience is getting real short. Now go before I just put you out of your misery." Bobby Ray didn't say anything else; he just stared back at McRoy. When McRoy let him go, he turned and walked out to the porch, laughing like a crazed fool. McRoy looked at Janis and said, "Remember. Stay away from him."

Janis still holding her shirt, turned and looked up at the man and said, "So your name's McRoy?"

"Yes," he replied. "Sean McRoy," as he stuck out his hand. "It's a pleasure to meet you, even under the circumstances. I've always had respect for a classy woman."

"And then what, will you want something from this classy woman?" Janis asked.

"Never, ma'am," he replied. "If I can't win you, then I guess I can't have you. I am a gentleman, no matter what you think of the crowd I happen to be with."

Janis looked down at his hand, then reluctantly shook it. "Well, I guess I should thank you for what you did back there." She let go of his hand quickly then added, "But that's all." She looked at the man at the table and said, "He looks like he's in bad shape. I think he needs a doctor."

"No, no doctor. You can play doctor for now." Sean said. "I mean, please, could you help? He's just a kid, and a good kid I might add."

Janis looked back at Sean. "A good kid, but in prison. Yeah, I'll bet real good."

Sean didn't respond but just looked down at her shirt. "You better go change before Bobby Ray comes back. We don't need to entice him anymore than he already is."

Janis said, "Where are my children?"

"In the living room," Sean said. "They are fine and they will be fine. All of you will be fine. Just do what we ask, please."

Janis turned and entered the living room. Seated on the couch were Robert and Mary between two men, one white and one black. The children looked pale and scared. Mary got up and ran to her mother and Robert tried to do the same, but the white man held him. He yelled and started to cry. Janis, holding Mary to her leg, turned and glared at Sean. He looked at the white man and said, "Corbin, let him go." The man complied, then sat back and smiled. Robert also ran to her side. She tried to comfort them while still trying to keep herself covered.

The shirt slipped off somewhat and the young black man slid forward on the couch and started to get up. "Oh baby," was all he said.

Sean looked at him and said, "Joey, sit down and be the gentleman that I know you can be."

Joey just continued to stare at Janis as she pulled up the shirt. "Hey Sean, I was just going to help the lady. That's all, that's all. Cool down, man." He smiled, first at Janis then at Sean, and sat back down on the couch.

A second later, another black man, an older man with gray hair and a short cropped gray beard walked into the living room with one of Matt's shotguns in his hand. "Hey Sean, there's a gun case back in that room. Got all kinds of guns but can't find no ammo. Had to bust the glass to get this. He then turned to Janis and to her surprise took off his hat and said, "Howdy, ma'am." He stuck out his hand and said, "Name's Darnell, Darnell Moseman. But you can call me Mose. Near everyone else does. Well, all 'cept Sean here. Seems he likes my first name, Darnell, you know? Ain't that right Sean?"

Sean just looked at Janis and smiled, "Just call him

Mose." He then added, "Where is the ammunition? Remember, I said do what we want and no trouble."

Janis said, "It's in an ammo box and the key's in our room. I'll get it."

She turned to go when Sean said, "Hold on a minute. I'll go with you."

Janis and the kids and Sean started toward the hallway when another man came out of Janis's room on a run yelling, "Sean, Sean, there's a cop in that room in the bed and I think he's been shot." The man stopped in front of Sean and then looked behind him at Janis and the kids. "Ah, and what do we have here, my pretty?"

He tried to step past Sean toward Janis when Sean put out his arm to stop him. "Herman, she isn't your pretty, and what about the cop?" Herman looked up at Sean. He was a short, slightly fat man of maybe late forties. No hair except for a band of brown short hair around his head at the ears. He wore thick glasses like the bottom of a Coke bottle, so his eyes looked twice their size in the magnification. He had a large belly that hung between his shirt and pants and he was sweating profusely. He looked back again at Janis, then Sean asked again, "The cop? What about the cop?"

Herman looked back at Sean. "He's in there and he tried to get up so I hit him. I saw his shirt and badge on the chair."

"Damn it," Janis said as she pushed past Sean and Herman and the old black man, Mose. She hurried with the kids to the door of her room then turned to the kids and said, "Go to one of your rooms and stay there till I come and get you."

Sean said, "Wait a minute," and looked at Mose. "Darnell, go with the kids." He looked at Janis, who was staring at him. "They'll be fine with Darnell, believe me."

Mose pushed past Herman and Sean and stopped in front of Janis. "They'll be fine, ma'am. I'll take care of them.

None of this dirt is going to touch them, not while Mose is watchin'." He smiled and Janis told the kids to go with him. Mose took both kids by the hand and walked them to one of the other bedrooms while asking them their names.

Sean looked into Janis's eyes. "They'll be fine with him. He will protect them."

Janis looked back and said, "I suppose he's one of the good guys too?"

Sean then smiled and reconfirmed, "They'll be fine."

Janis cringed and then turned into the room and moved to the bed where Parker was now unconscious and bleeding somewhat from the corner of his mouth where Herman must have hit him. She lifted one of his eyelids and then bent down to listen to his breathing. She took a Kleenex from a box and wiped his face, then quickly turned toward Sean while still holding the shirt to her chest. "No one touches him again, you hear?"

Sean put up his empty hand and said, "Okay, lady. Okay. I'll tell them."

"No," Janis said, "You're supposed to be in charge. Make sure."

"Okay, lady. Okay," Sean said.

"And the name's Janis, not lady," Janis said as she turned to the chest of drawers and got out a bra and pullover short-sleeved shirt. She then turned to Sean and just stared at him.

"What?" Sean said, looking puzzled.

"You going to stay here while I change?" she asked, holding the clothes up to her chest.

"Janis, I'm not leaving you alone in here."

"What, you don't trust me?" Janis said with a sneer on her face.

"Not just yet," Sean said, crossing his arms while still holding the handgun. "You're a little too feisty for me to trust you just yet."

Janis just looked at him with a cold stare, then said, "Fine." She dropped the bra and shirt to the bed, pulled what was left of her clothes off and proceeded to put on the clean bra and shirt. As she did, Sean's face got a little red and he turned away from her somewhat.

Outside, Coop had moved down to the edge of the field and got a better look at the truck. It had bullet holes all over and the back window was gone. He moved down through the field parallel to the house and then circled behind the garage. Just before he moved behind the garage he saw Bobby Ray come out of the garage with an armload of food and then drop it on the ground. He saw him walk two or three paces to the left and bend down to pick up a small caliber gun and stuff it in his pants. He then got an empty box from the side of the garage and walked to the pile of food and proceeded to throw it in the box, cursing to himself the entire time.

When he went back into the garage, Coop moved around to the side of the garage and waited. He realized that the long barrel 10-gauge was going to keep him from moving quickly, so he leaned it against a bush on the side of the garage and pulled out his handgun and waited by the side of the garage near the man door. Minutes later, Bobby Ray came out the door with more food and walked the two or three paces to the box and started to drop in the food, still cursing to himself. Coop moved from the garage behind Bobby Ray. When he stood up, Coop placed the cold end of the gun barrel just behind Bobby Ray's ear and pulled the hammer back with a click. "You move sonny, and there's only gonna be air where your head was."

CHAPTER 18
September

Clive had returned from speaking to Janis and sat for awhile talking to Matt. After about half an hour he got up and said he was going to walk around to the other side of the pond and try his luck there. Matt told him to try near a large cypress tree at the corner of the pond and Clive slowly walked in that direction. Matt took a long drink from his can of beer, then sat back in the chair and looked up toward the ridge to his right. He sat quietly but questions started to enter his mind. Had they done enough that day to prevent what had happened? Did they look long enough and far enough before they gave up? Did the authorities do all they could have, even with the chaos of those first few days? In the weeks that followed, did they do all they could have, even with all the hardships and the dangers out there? How could he and his family carry on with this terrible weight of not knowing? What would life be like if no closure ever came to them? What should he be doing now? Surely not fishing and living life as if it was normal again. And yet, he knew in his heart that no matter how much pain there was, he had to make life as normal as possible for his family. He and Janis had to hold it together. He also knew that even if it consumed the rest of his life, he would never give up. Yes, this was the hardest thing he had ever done in his life, even

harder than that day in the desert. The search would go on. It had to go on. For the children, his family, and even Clive, life had to go on—even if it was just a shadow of its former self. They had to keep it together but they also all needed this time to think, this time of rest and calm, this time of faith and prayer.

Matt looked back at the pond and at Clive as he cast his line out to the corner near the tree. There was one thing he knew: that Clive Aliston was the best friend he had ever had. He also knew he could count on him any time, especially at a time like this. Clive would not stop until they had an answer. They had a strong bond; Clive was like family and they would never give up. Even with all that had happened, Matt knew that he was a fortunate man; he knew that it was faith that held them all together. As he sat, his mind seemed to settle somewhat and he began to think back about that day and the ride into the city to get Lisa.

July

Matt had driven the jeep farther south on Route 308 toward the city of Butler. Close to the junction of Routes 308 and 422, they came to another police road block. Clive knew some of the officers and explained what had happened at the farmhouse, what they were doing, and where they were headed. He turned the prisoner over to them and they gave him an idea of the route they thought would be the safest. When they were about to resume their trip, he asked one of the police officers if he would take custody of Madison Lynn and see that she got home. Maddie, who was sitting some distance away in the jeep with Andy, suddenly got out and turned to Andy and said, "I told him I was going with him. I guess your uncle doesn't listen too well. I'll be back."

She turned and walked to where Clive and Matt were standing. She looked at the officer they were talking to and

said, "I won't be going with you. I'll be going with them. They need me." She stopped directly in front of Clive, crossed her arms, and just stared up at Clive with those deep blue eyes.

Clive turned and looked at Matt, who just said, "Hey, don't look at me. You're the sheriff," then turned and walked back toward the jeep.

Clive looked back at Maddie and shook his head, then placed both hands on her shoulders and said, "Ms. Devereaux, you can't go with us. We don't know what we will be running into. It's not safe out there."

She looked down at his hands then back into his eyes with an even more determined look on her face. "That's exactly why you need me with you. Now, I'm not going to argue with you or Matt or this officer." Matt had stopped about halfway to the jeep and was looking back at Clive and Maddie. She turned to him and added, "Matt, it's not only about you three. It's about Lisa, and we are wasting time."

Clive removed his hands from her shoulders, placed them on his hips and just stared at her. He started to say, "Maddie," when she turned to the other officer, stuck out her hand to shake his, and said, "Thank you for your help and concern, but I'll be leaving with these gentlemen—even if I do have to go with this one." She then turned to Clive as she started to walk toward the jeep. "Let's go, Aliston. We are wasting valuable time. You can visit with the officers some other time." Clive turned and watched as she walked away toward Matt and the jeep.

The officer he was talking to just smiled and put out his hand to shake Clive's. "Good luck Clive. I think you're gonna need it with that lady on board."

Clive just shook his hand and said, "Yeah, right."

As Maddie passed Matt on her way to the jeep, she said, "We are wasting Lisa's time. Tell our sheriff there it's time to

go." She continued on to the jeep and climbed in beside Andy. She sat down, then turned and looked back at Clive with her arms crossed over her chest.

Clive looked at the ground and shook his head, then said to the officer, "We might be luckier than you. We got her to protect us." He smiled and walked to the jeep, picking up Matt on the way. Matt was about to say something when Clive said, "Please don't say anything. Just drive."

Matt followed Clive to the jeep and they drove east on Route 422. They followed Route 422 for several miles when they turned off to the right on a road that said Herman, Marwood and Cabot. They followed the road through those towns and saw little to no traffic except for police cars. They stopped twice to confer with those police, then moved on.

When they reached the town of Sarver, Clive told Matt to pull over at a building that looked like an old fire hall, near a railroad bed that had been converted into a rails-to-trails path. He looked at a map from the jeep's glove compartment, then told Matt to drive out to Route 356. They turned south on 356 and then right and finally ended up on a small blacktop called Lardintown Road. It was a winding road through the back country, but it cut off several miles and kept them off the main routes. Lardintown ran into a two-lane blacktop, Bull Creek Road, at a "T." Clive turned to Matt and said, "I think this takes us out to the expressway. If it looks okay, we can make up some time and get to Oakland sooner. If not, it's more back roads."

Matt pressed his lips together, then looked at Clive. "Better to get there, as I said, than not at all." He looked at his watch. It was four o'clock. Still two hours until time to contact Janis.

Clive, looking concerned, said, "Yeah, I know. I'm worried about them too."

He looked back at Maddie as if to say, "Well, you seem

to know everything. Is all okay back at camp?"

She just folded her arms across her chest again and said, "I don't know everything."

Andy, sounding a little frustrated, said, "Come on, Dad. Let's go get Lisa so we can get home."

Matt looked in each direction then turned left on Bull Creek Road headed toward the expressway. They had only gone about a mile on Bull Creek Road when Clive turned and looked to the left. In the distance he saw a large, gray building with a small lake in front of it. "I know where we are now," Clive said as he tapped Matt on the shoulder and pointed toward the building. "That's the Outdoor Life Lodge. I was there a couple of summers ago at an F.O.P. picnic. We can't be more than five miles from the Route 28 expressway. If we can use part of the expressway, we'll be there in less than an hour." They came to a large bend in the road and as they passed the Outdoor Life Lodge sign they saw a road block, made up of several trucks, just out ahead of them.

Matt hit the brakes and said, "Wow," as he slowed quickly and came to a stop about fifty yards from the trucks. Matt picked up his shotgun, as did Clive.

Clive stood up and looked out over the windshield at the group of men standing in front of the trucks, holding guns. "Wait here a minute," he said as he placed his hand above his eyes to shade them from the sun. For a moment the men at the block just stood and stared back at them. Then the man in front started to walk toward the jeep, followed by three other men, all armed. Clive lowered his hand from his eyes then placed his shotgun on top of the jeep windshield and watched as the men came closer.

Matt looked up at Clive and said, "What do we do?" Clive didn't look at Matt but just kept staring at the approaching men. He reached into his shirt pocket and took

out a pair of sunglasses, placed them on his face, then raised his shotgun to a ready position. Matt stood up and held his gun across his chest. As the men came closer, he asked again, "What do we do?"

Clive started to lower his gun and his facial expression seemed more calm. He took his left hand and placed it on Matt's gun without taking his eyes off the approaching men. "Wait. Don't do anything." Matt looked back at Andy and Maddie. Andy had the .30-30 across his lap in a ready position.

Maddie looked up at Matt and said, "It will be okay." He didn't answer. He just gave her a questioning look and turned back to the four men who were now just twenty-five yards away.

Clive slowly removed his sunglasses and lowered his gun as the lead man came closer. "Matt, the big guy in the front. I know him." Matt started to lower his gun. When the man reached the jeep, Clive said, "Shane, how the hell are you?"

The man he called Shane motioned to the three men behind him to lower their guns and they slowly walked to Clive's side of the jeep. Shane stuck out his hand. "Clive Aliston, long time no see. How the hell are you?" Clive shook his hand as Shane motioned for the other three men to step up. "This is my brother Eddie, and my buddies Al and Van."

They all shook Clive's hand and Clive pointed to the others in the jeep. "This is my buddy Matt, his son Andy, and Maddie."

Shane and the other three nodded a hello. "I haven't seen you in what, two years?" Shane said. "Good to see you again."

"Yeah, been at least that long," Clive said. "What the hell are you guys doing out here on the road?"

"Keeping the peace," Shane said. "The police here are busy as hell. I'm quite sure you know. We had some trouble

right here in the area. Had to give them a hand."

"Still have trouble?" Clive asked.

"No," Shane replied. "We sort of took care of it. Those who caused it won't be doing so anymore."

Clive looked at Shane with a sort of half smile and said, "I guess I don't ask anymore about that?"

"Yeah, right," Shane said as he smiled back.

Clive then asked, "How many men do you have?"

Shane said, "Well, the four of us and three more at the trucks."

Clive stepped out of the jeep then added, "You took a real chance walking up to us that way. We could have opened, fire you know. I mean if we had been the wrong kind of people."

"Don't think so," Shane said as he pointed to the tree line on the hillside behind the jeep. Clive, Matt, Andy and Maddie turned around to look. In a tree stand about thirty yards up the hill they saw a man in camo clothes wave at them, then raise a semi-automatic weapon above his head. Shane took a walkie-talkie he was holding and spoke into it, "Hey brother, it's Clive Aliston."

The man in the tree stand began to wave again and then put his fingers to his mouth and whistled. "My brother Aaron," Shane said, as Clive and Matt waved back.

"Okay, you got me on that one," Clive said. He smiled and added, "You know on any normal day I'd be telling you to take your guns and go home, but I think not today. We can use any good help we can get."

"When it's over, the job's yours again," Shane said with a smile. "Don't think I want the job on a regular basis." Clive got more serious and explained what they were doing and where they were headed. Shane told him he would run into another road block at the expressway, manned by the local police. He also said that as far as he knew the expressway

was clear only as far as Oakmont.

Clive turned to Matt. "We can cross the Allegheny River there and then hopefully down the other side to Washington Boulevard and into Oakland."

Shane shook his hand again and wished them all luck. They said goodbye and were led around the road block and continued on toward the expressway.

CHAPTER 19
July

Matt drove another two or three miles toward the expressway. As they rounded a bend in the road they passed a sign that said, "You are leaving Fawn Township. Come back and visit us again." Just under that sign was an orange traffic cone with a sign that said, "Slow." Out ahead about a quarter of a mile was another police road block. This was a major block and as they drove in closer Clive could see ten or twelve police cars, some state police and other local police parked above and below the expressway overpass. Clive told Matt to drive slowly up to the road block, then he stood up in the front of the jeep so that the officers up ahead could see him. Two officers were just out ahead of the main block, standing behind a state police car. As the jeep started to get closer, the two officers motioned for them to come to a stop.

Matt stopped the jeep about ten feet from the car. Clive got out of the jeep. One of the officers told him to stop and show some identification. The other officer with him said, "Never mind, Dave. I know this guy." The two officers came around the car and walked up to Clive. They shook hands and talked for a few, brief moments, then one of the officers called to the others at the road block on a walkie-talkie and told Clive to continue onto the block.

Clive got back into the jeep. They proceeded to the road

block, then stopped again. Clive knew several of the officers there from the Tarentum and Brackenridge police departments, and a couple of the state police. The state police officer in charge walked up to Clive and shook his hand. "Name's Ron Evans, and you, I hear, are Clive Aliston."

"Yes, I am," Clive responded.

The state officer continued, "What are you four doing out here at a time like this?"

"Well," Clive said with a pause. "We are on a sort of a rescue mission. We need to get to Oakland to a school dorm to get Matt's daughter." Clive introduced Matt, Andy and Maddie.

Ron looked at Clive a little more seriously, "You sure you know what you're getting into here? I mean, I can understand your concern but things are not good, and the closer you get to the city the worse they get. Fortunately, I haven't heard much about any trouble in the Oakland area. Some looting and a few fires and some trouble with escaped prisoners—but as far as I know nothing concerning the terrorists.

Matt spoke up, "Thank you for your concern, Ron, but I have to get my daughter. I just can't leave her there. I don't think I'd be able to go home to my wife unless I have her with me."

"Understood," Ron said. "I'm just telling you this isn't going to be any picnic you're headed to. If you didn't have Clive here with you, I'd be apt to tell you no. I'm just letting you know, Clive, that you had better have eyes in the back of your head and I mean all the way in there and on the way out."

"We will be careful," Clive said, then stepped out of the jeep. He took the map he had and unfolded it on the hood of the jeep. Matt got out and walked to his side, and they started to study the map.

Ron looked at the map and said, "I think the best and safest way there is down the 28 expressway to Oakmont. The highway is clear till there, as far as I know. Beyond that point, it's still not safe."

"Where from there?" Matt said.

"Cross the Oakmont bridge," Ron said. "Then I would follow the other side of the river down to Washington Boulevard. It's not bad till there. Once you're on Washington Boulevard, be careful. There were a few bad places there. Not sure about now. Once you are in Oakland, you are probably going to run into a larger police presence, so expect to get stopped often. I'll give you a color card to place in your vehicle. It has a number on it that they will check. It's been set up by the local homeland security office. Do not use the card until you are stopped. We don't want them in the wrong hands. You will also be asked two questions that I will give you the answers for, and given a code number. When asked for the information, give it right the first time or you may all be stuck in Oakland or Pittsburgh for longer than you want to be. That's about it. Is there anything else I can help you with?"

"No," Clive said. "You have been a great help. The route you gave us is the way I expected."

"Wish I could send some men with you," Ron said, as he shook Clive's hand first, then Matt's. "I just can't spare anyone right now. This point is the cutoff for the southbound and northbound end of the expressway. We sort of have watch on the middle ground, if you know what I mean. Anyone headed north or south gets stopped here."

"Understood," Clive said. "We will follow your directions. Thanks again for your help. Now, about those answers and the code number." Ron took Clive aside and quietly gave him the information he requested. Matt returned to the jeep, and a few minutes later so did Clive.

Clive put a pale blue card in the glove box and then told Matt to head south on the expressway. They waved goodbye to all the officers, then the road block was opened and they drove up the ramp and headed south.

They drove about seven to ten miles to an exit marked Harmarville, seeing very few cars in either direction. About halfway there, Andy said to Matt and Clive, "Wow, this is really eerie. I don't think I've ever seen a major highway this deserted."

"Amen, son," Matt said.

Clive looked at Matt and said, "They must have this total area in major lockdown." Not one more word was spoken until they got to the exit. As they drove down the exit, they were stopped again at a road block. This one was manned by the Army Reserves. After a few minutes, they continued onto the Oakmont Bridge, which was deserted, and then ran into another block. They were passed through and told to turn right just after the railroad tracks and go through town and down along the river toward Washington Boulevard.

As they passed through Oakmont, the streets were almost deserted except for a police car parked across the road about halfway through town. Two officers were behind the car and a third was just coming out of a storefront, The Mystery Lover's Bookstore, with several coffees in hand. Apparently, the shop had some type of power for its café. They stopped and were once again questioned, then offered coffee and told to continue on. They drove through town and then on a two-lane along the river. No one said anything until they got to Washington Boulevard. When they reached the intersection, they were again stopped and passed through—only this time the blue card was used and placed on the windshield and the questions were asked. As they started up the Boulevard, Maddie slowly lowered her head, placed her hand on her forehead and squeezed, then sort of moaned.

Andy looked over at her and then put his hand on her shoulder and leaned close and asked, "Maddie are you alright?" She did not respond but just moaned again. Andy tapped Clive on the shoulder and Clive turned around. Andy pointed to Maddie and, with a puzzled look, shrugged his shoulders.

Clive reached around, took Maddie's arm in his hand, and said, "Maddie, what's wrong?" She took her hand away from her head, squeezed her eyes tight, opened her mouth, and clenched her teeth as if in pain.

Clive asked again as Matt turned and looked back quickly, then said to Clive, "Should I stop?"

"No," Maddie said as she sat her eyes still tightly closed. "It will pass."

"What will pass?" Clive asked.

Maddie paused then opened her eyes. She looked at Clive and said, "It happens sometimes."

"What happens?" Clive asked, looking concerned.

"The pain in my head," Maddie said, as she sat back in the seat and brushed the long blonde hair out of her eyes. "Sometimes I get the pain. When it happens, it will pass."

"When what happens?" Clive asked, somewhat stressed.

"You wouldn't understand," Maddie said.

"Look, lady," Clive started to say as Maddie interrupted.

"Clive, don't be concerned about me. It's not me you have to be worried about. What you will soon face will take all the emotional strength you have left for today. Don't waste it on me."

"What the hell are you talking about Maddie?" Clive said, even more frustrated.

Maddie put her hands on top of his shoulders, stared into his eyes, and calmly said, "Please, Clive. For your sake, listen to me. I'd tell you but I'm not sure you would understand or, for that matter, accept my explanation. I'll

save that for later."

Matt spoke up, "Is it about Lisa?"

"Yeah," Andy said, "Is it about my sister?"

"No," Maddie said, staring at Matt. "It's not Lisa. As I told you, she is fine. She will be fine." She then looked back at Clive, "Please, Clive. Do not be angry at me. Please just take my word for this and calm down. I'm sorry for the way this happens. I know you don't understand. I will tell you, but not now. You will be needed—and soon. I just can't tell you more than that for now." She looked away from him out the side of the jeep and removed her hand from his shoulder. She whispered, "It is evil you will face and soon they will need you. He will need you." Andy just stared at her, as did Matt in the rearview mirror. Clive was going to say something else then decided against it and turned to face forward in his seat. He looked at Matt, shrugged his shoulders, and shook his head.

They all sat silently as they continued up Washington Boulevard toward Oakland. The streets along the way were mostly deserted except for police and firemen. There were several cars either smashed or full of bullet holes. One car sat near the side of an intersection. It was on fire and a group of firemen was trying to put it out. At every block there were police cars and fire equipment. Police tape was stretched in every direction and they were told more than once to keep the speed low. They were checked at least every two blocks, but the sky-blue pass on the windshield and the answers to the code questions gave them access to the area.

Once they reached Oakland, the police and fire presence was even more noticeable. There were two or three houses that were burned out, as were dozen of cars. Two buildings on one side were still in flames and they were stopped for several minutes for fire equipment to be moved. Clive looked back at Andy and Maddie. Maddie just sat calmly

and said nothing. Andy had a shocked, almost fearful look on his face. Matt leaned forward, placed his arms on top of the steering wheel, and watched the buildings burn. Clive could see the concern in his face. He reached over and touched Matt's arm. "Matt, she will be fine. I just know she will be fine."

Matt turned to Clive and said, "I just want to get there. It can't be more than three or four blocks." Clive could see the frustration on Matt's face. He was about to say something else when Matt put the jeep in neutral, pushed the emergency brake, and jumped out. He walked around the front of the jeep, then turned and said to Clive, "I can't wait anymore. You drive."

Clive stood up and said, "Matt, wait. You can't go out there with no identification, especially carrying that shotgun."

Matt said, "The hell with that, Clive. I'm going to find Lisa." He looked at Andy, who was standing up and starting to get out of the jeep. "No, Son. You stay here with Clive and Maddie. I'll be fine."

"But, Dad," Andy started to say.

Matt then repeated himself more sternly, "Andy, you stay here."

Clive stepped out of the jeep and walked to Matt. "Matt, you can't just walk around here armed and not identified. They will shoot you. They have no idea who you are. Now if you must go, wait one minute." He left Matt standing in front of the jeep, walked to a fireman who seemed to be in charge, and spoke to him for several minutes. When he returned, he handed a fire/police armband and another blue card to Matt and said, "You're in luck. I told him the situation and he took my word for it. Now he is sticking his neck out for me and you. You go no further than the dorm. Makes no difference if Lisa is there or not. To the dorm only

and I will give you the two answers and the code number. You tell no one else, is that clear?" Just then part of the building nearest to them collapsed with a loud roar and a ball of flames that shot high into the air. It surprised all of them and some of the firemen nearest to the building started to run toward them. The fireman in charge who had talked to Clive ran to them and stopped. He removed his hat and wiped the sweat and dirt from his face. Clive reached into the back of the jeep and got a bottle of water.

The fireman turned toward the flaming building and spoke into a walkie-talkie. "Bobby, did all the men get out of the way?"

"Yes," was the reply.

"Thank God," the fireman said. When he turned to Clive, Clive handed him the bottle of water. "You look like you could use this."

The fireman took the bottle and drank half of it, then said, "Thanks man. I needed that." He then turned to Matt, "Your sheriff friend here says you are alright. Please make sure you are, and be careful out there. I've had several of my men shot. It's more under control now than yesterday, but it's still not a hundred percent. You get my meaning?"

"Yeah," Matt said, shaking his hand. "And thanks again."

"Believe me, I understand," the fireman said. "I have a daughter at school too."

"In Pittsburgh?" Matt asked.

"No," the fireman replied. "In New York, and I have no idea where she is or if she's okay. Just go get your daughter and do what you're told if confronted by police. You may need your daughter—but she needs you in one piece."

Just then a voice came over the fireman's walkie-talkie. "Hey, Cap, we need to water down that adjacent building. It's starting to smoke from the heat."

He answered, "Be right there." He shook Clive's hand, then Matt's, and said, "I gotta go. Good luck. I hope your daughter is okay."

Matt said, "Thanks," as the fireman put on his hat and ran back to the fire.

Clive looked at Matt and said, "Now go, but remember what I said. We'll be right there."

Matt looked at Clive, then Andy. "Son, stay here. I'll be fine."

"Okay, Dad," was all Andy said as he sat back down.

Matt turned back to Clive. "It's about four blocks down, right side, red brick, number 312, second floor front."

"I'll find you when we are out of here. Now go," Clive said. Matt nodded and turned, crossed the street and headed down the sidewalk, gun in one hand, putting the blue card in his pocket and the armband on his sleeve.

As he disappeared behind a fire truck, Maddie spoke up. "He will be okay, he and Lisa." Clive and Andy both looked back at her but said nothing.

CHAPTER 20
September

Janis had watched Clive walk back to the pond, where he talked to Matt briefly then walked around the other side of the pond. She walked slowly back to the house and continued to set things up for supper. Lisa came out onto the porch and asked, "Mom, do you want to cook that roast for dinner today or are we having something else?"

Janis thought for a moment then said, "No, I don't think we'll have the roast today. How about just some of those pork chops I got at the farm the other day? We'll have the roast for dinner tomorrow before Uncle Clive leaves. What do you think?"

"Sounds good to me," Lisa said. "I'll take them out of the freezer and put them in cool water to thaw. What else do we want?"

Janis thought for a second then said, "Canned corn and I guess those canned potatoes. I don't like them much but we don't have any others."

Lisa started into the kitchen, then turned back to Janis. "Hey Mom, how about we put those potatoes in a skillet with some onions from the garden and make homefries?"

"Good idea," Janis said. "They would be better that way." Lisa started into the kitchen but Janis called her back. "Lisa, it's still early, too early to cook. Just get things ready

and we will start later. If you don't mind, keep an eye on the kids. I think I'd like to do a little painting."

"Okay, Mom, go ahead. You need a little break. I'll handle it." Lisa entered the kitchen and Janis finished setting the table then took a broom and swept the porch steps and headed for the garage to get her painting supplies.

She got all she needed, then walked to the pond where Matt was fishing. Matt looked up at her from his chair and smiled. "Hi honey, decide to take a break?"

"Yes," she said. "It's early and we don't need to eat just yet. Lisa is watching the kids. We'll start supper in an hour or so. Is pork chops, corn and homefries okay?"

"Saving the roast for tomorrow?" he asked with a smile.

"Yes. I think it would be good to have that before Clive leaves, don't you think?"

"Yeah, good idea," Matt said. "Sure hate to see him go tomorrow."

"Yeah," Janis said. "Me too. It's been great having him here again."

There was a moment of silence then Matt asked, "You okay?"

"Yeah, I'm fine," Janis answered.

"Sure?" Matt added.

"Yes, dear. I'm fine, and you?"

"I'm good. I'm really enjoying this. I think we all needed this. All of us, even Clive."

Janis bent over and kissed Matt on the lips, then ran her hand across the side of his face. "We will end this. We will find him. It will all come to a close and I feel more positive about all of it. I don't know why but somehow I just know. We have to keep faith in that thought and in each other. We will all be together again."

Matt smiled and reached up and touched her face and whispered, "I love you."

She smiled, then pinched his nose between her fingers and said, "Yeah, I know." She walked to the side of the pond in a shaded area and began setting up her painting supplies. She waved at Clive, who had just caught a fish and was holding it up for her and Matt to see. She yelled, "Too small," and laughed.

Clive laughed and said, "You're right," then went back to fishing. She sat down on her stool and started to open her paints. She turned on her CD player and slipped in a CD. She began to think back to what had happened after the convicts had come to camp that day weeks ago. As she painted and her mind drifted back, the sounds of "The Rose" by Bette Midler drifted across the pond and filled the air with music.

July

After Janis had dressed, she and Sean returned to the living room. "What about my kids?" Janis asked as she sat down in one of the chairs.

"They'll be fine with Mose," Sean said, adding, "Where did the cop come from?" Janis did not answer but only stared back at Sean.

"Hey, lady, Sean asked you a question," Corbin said as he stood up.

"Take it easy," Sean said, motioning with his arm to Corbin. "First, her name is Janis, not 'lady,' and let her have time to answer."

Corbin turned to Sean. "Hey McRoy, a cop here in the house. This don't look good, man. What if there's more around?"

"There isn't any more," Janis said, looking at Corbin.

"Hey, Sean, Corbin's right," Joey said as he slid forward in his seat.

"Where there's one cop there's always more. Hey lady,

your old man a cop, or is that your old man?"

"No, that isn't my old man. He's too young to be my old man. And no, my husband isn't a cop. And my name's not 'lady,' it's Janis."

Corbin then started toward her and said, "Yeah, lady, where is your old man?"

"Sit down," Sean said, as he stepped between Corbin and Janis. "Let the lady, or I mean, Janis, answer the questions." He looked at Janis and said, "Well?"

Janis composed herself and said, "My husband and his brother own a business and they are out of town. I don't even know if they are alright."

"Anyone else?" Joey said.

"Yes," Janis said, now looking at Joey. My older son and daughter. No, they are not here. They are away at school. There's just us here, me and the kids."

Herman, who had been walking around the room picking up almost everything and looking at it, turned and said, "Hey Sean, you don't believe the lady, do you? Looks like a lot more people in these pictures than she said, and one's a cop and it ain't the one in that room." He looked at Janis and laughed quietly, exposing some brown decayed teeth.

Sean said, Who's the cop in the picture?"

Janis paused then said, "He's dead. He was killed a year ago in an investigation about a serial killer."

"Good riddance," Herman said as he set the picture down. Herman walked to her side and leaned over next to her ear and said, "Do you miss your friend the cop that died? I hope he burns in hell. Did the killer cut him up? I hope he cut him up real good."

Janis leaned away from Herman and his bad breath and said, "You pig."

Herman laughed then reached for her neck. As he did, Joey jumped and pushed Herman back and yelled, "Get

away from her."

Herman backed up several steps, picked up a poker from the side of the fireplace, and started after Joey.

Sean turned to Herman, pulled the hammer back on the handgun, and yelled, "Drop it." Herman stopped and so did Joey, who had moved toward Herman.

"Go ahead, asshole," Joey said, sneering at Herman. Herman sneered at Joey, then raised the poker again.

Sean moved in right in front of him and put the gun in his face. "I said drop it and I mean now. I knew bringing you and that maniac Bobby Ray was a bad idea. You two cause me any more trouble and we'll bury both of you right here."

"Let me put a cap in him," Corbin said as he stepped up behind Sean.

"No one gets capped unless we have to," Sean said. "And for your sake Herman, don't make it a have to." Herman laughed again, then threw the poker to the side and laughed at Joey, who tried to push past Sean.

Sean stopped him and said, "Okay, let's all just calm down. We got enough to deal with. We don't need any more problems. Corbin, go check on Mose and the children. Joey, see what else we have in the way of weapons, and Herman, just stay out of trouble. I meant what I said."

Herman turned and walked to the kitchen. Janis stood up and started to follow Corbin but Sean put his hand up and said, "You stay here. The kids will be fine. I gave you my word."

"Your word," Janis said. "That makes me feel real good. You're the only one that's holding this zoo together. What if they get you? Where does that leave me and the kids?"

"They won't get me," Sean said. "They need me and they know it."

"Need you?" Janis said. "Need you? What about Bobby Ray and Herman? They would cut your throat in a second if

they got the chance and I'm supposed to take your word that all will be okay. If you were as smart as you claim to be, why would you bring them with you anyway? You are either very stupid or not as in control as you would like to believe."

Sean took in a deep breath and started to say, "Janis, no need for you to get nasty. I…"

Suddenly, there was a thud from the kitchen. Janis and Sean turned in that direction then walked to where they could see. Lying on the floor was the wounded kid who had been sitting at the table. "Jimmy," Sean said as he quickly walked to the kitchen, followed by Janis. Jimmy was lying on the floor moaning and Herman was sitting in a chair laughing. Sean picked up Jimmy with Janis's help and put him back in the chair. He then turned to Herman, who was still laughing. "Shut the hell up, you piece of shit," Sean said. "You could have helped him." Herman stopped his loud laughing. He just sat and chuckled quietly, but did not move.

"Oh, you're in control," Janis said. "Anyone can see that." Sean just looked at her as they held Jimmy in the chair. Janis looked in the kid's eyes and whispered, "Can you hear me?" She got no response. She looked at Sean and said, "He needs a doctor."

"No doctor," Sean said. "You be the doctor for now."

Janis stood up and looked at Sean. "You tell me he's a good kid like you care about him, but apparently you don't care that much or you would turn yourself in and get him help."

Sean just looked at her and said, "Janis, I said see what you can do for him."

She glared at him, then turned and started to remove the bandage from Jimmy's shoulder. As she did, she asked, "How did he get hurt?"

Sean sat down on one of the other chairs and said, "We were being chased by a cop car and ended up in a shootout at some crossroads near a gas station. Some people there at

the station decided to help the cop. Somebody shot Jimmy with an arrow. Imagine that."

Janis did not show any expression and did not turn toward Sean. She just kept removing the bandage, but in her mind she knew it was Andy's arrow from the confrontation at the crossroads store. As she worked on Jimmy, he started to moan as if in pain. Herman got up from his chair and walked to where he could see what Janis was doing, then laughed and said, "Aww, Jimmy, does it hurt? I could make it hurt real bad." He began to laugh even louder.

Sean got up and started to say, "Herman get the hell out of here and…"

Just then, Joey came into the kitchen and said, "Sean, there's a car coming down the hill toward here. What do you want to do?"

Outside, between the house and the garage, Coop had taken the guns away from Bobby Ray and pulled him back to the woods side of the garage, just out of sight of the house.

Bobby Ray had stopped talking for only a few minutes when he started on Coop. "Hey old man, you're gonna wish you didn't do this. You're outnumbered and when we get done we are gonna feed you to the snappers in the pond out there. Why don't you just gimme the guns and forget this, and maybe I can talk my friends into bein' easy on you. We won't hurt you too much."

Coop pushed him face first into the side of the garage and said, "Shut the hell up, you son of a bitch."

Bobby Ray tried to turn toward Coop as he said, "Listen you old fart." Coop pushed him into the garage siding again and cracked him on the top of the head with the side of the handgun.

Bobby Ray bent over and grabbed his head and started to curse again, when Coop put the muzzle of the gun in his ear and said, "One more word and I clean out those ears

with lead side to side." At about that moment Coop also heard a car coming down the road. He grabbed Bobby Ray by the back of the collar and moved around the front of the garage and then quickly through the man door and on inside. He moved to the other side of the garage, to the windows in the roll up door, pushing Bobby Ray in front of him. He held Bobby Ray against the wall and held the gun to the side of Bobby Ray's head. As he looked out the window to the end of the driveway, Bobby Ray started to curse again and Coop pushed the muzzle of the gun hard into the side of Bobby Ray's head and said, "I said shut the hell up." Bobby Ray got quiet except for cursing to himself in a low whisper. Coop watched the end of the driveway as the car got closer. In a matter of seconds the car turned into the driveway. It was a county sheriff's car.

CHAPTER 21
July

Janis stopped her work on Jimmy and started for the living room when Sean stood up and sternly said, "Stay here till I tell you to do otherwise." Janis turned and looked at him. She could tell by his expression that he meant it. She stopped and returned to what she was doing.

Corbin, Mose and the children came down the hall, with Corbin in the lead, holding a single shot shotgun. "Sean, a car just entered the driveway," Corbin said, as he placed a shell in the chamber of the gun and snapped it closed with a quick jerk of his arm. The children ran from Mose and into the kitchen to Janis.

She stopped again and was about to speak when Joey, who had been looking out one of the front windows yelled to Sean, "Sean it's a cop car."

Sean gave Janis a disgusted look and said, "No more cops, Aaa?"

Janis held the children to her and said, "I told you the truth. I have no idea who that would be or why he's here."

Sean just shook his head and then looked at Mose. "Darnell, take the children back to the bedroom and keep them quiet.

Mose said, "Come on children," and proceeded to turn them away from Janis. As he did, they both began to scream and cry.

Herman, who had been standing in the corner of the kitchen, started to panic and yell, "Get them away from me, get them away from me." He put his hands to his face and slid to the floor, curled in a tight ball, his legs and arms drawn into his body as he kept repeating, "Get them away from me, get them away, get them away."

Joey yelled again from the living room, "Sean he's about to get out of the car, man. What the hell are we gonna do?"

Sean walked to the corner where Herman was in a frenzy, kicked him solidly in the side and then bent down to Herman's ear and sort of growled at him. "Shut the hell up you crazy old bastard. Those kids are not going to hurt you. Now shut the hell up, you asshole," as he kicked him again. Herman stopped screaming and turned his covered face to the corner and started to cry like a little child. Sean slapped him across the top of the head and repeated, "Shut the hell up." Herman got quiet and just sat and sobbed. Sean looked at Mose, who was still standing there with the children. "I said, to the bedroom." He walked to the children as he looked at Janis, who was trying to calm them. Sean bent down on one knee and got the children's attention. In a very soft voice he said, "Listen, children. You go with Mose. He is your friend. Your mommy will be okay. She is going to help us with our sick friend, then you can come back to her. It will only be a few minutes. Now, go with Mose. He knows some really good games to play."

They looked up at Janis. She also bent down in front of them and said, "Sean is right. You go with Mose. He is a good man and you'll be okay."

Robert, still crying, said, "But Mommy, I want to stay with you."

Janis hugged him, then said, "It's okay, honey. I'll be okay. I just need to help this sick man then you can come back and stay with me. Now go. It's okay."

Sean nodded to Mose and said, "Go." Mose took the children and left for the bedroom. Janis and Sean both started to stand up as they stared into each other's eyes. Sean said softly, "It will be okay."

Janis said nothing but in her mind was the question, "How could a man be so violent with someone like Herman and so gentle a second later with children?"

Corbin came into the kitchen while Joey watched from the living room. Joey said, "Sean, he's getting out of the car."

Corbin stared at Sean and said, "What do you want to do?"

Sean thought for a second then turned to Janis. "Jimmy okay for now?"

"No," Janis said. "I just started."

"Well, he'll have to wait," Sean said. He took Janis by the arm and pulled her close to his face. "You go out and talk to him. Make sure he knows all is okay—and remember, we have the children."

Janis looked at him with a cold stare and said, "You hurt them and I'll see you dead before this day is over."

Sean squeezed her arm, pulled her closer, and said in a stern whisper, "I said go talk and make it good. I want him gone and he better not come back with help. You got me?"

Janis pulled her arm away from him and said, "I heard you the first time, or maybe you want to put me on the floor and kick in my ribs."

Sean just sneered at her and said, "Go and make it good."

Outside, in the garage, Coop still had Bobby Ray pinned against the garage wall and had watched as the cop got out of the car and looked around the front of the house. He was about to pull Bobby Ray away toward the garage door when he saw Janis step out into the driveway and begin speaking to the cop. Janis had left the house. As she walked down the

sidewalk at the side of the house she said, "Hello, officer." The officer turned and started to walk toward her. When she reached him she stuck out her hand to shake his.

"Are you Janis Fallon?" the officer asked as he reached for her hand.

"Yes, I am," she responded.

"Name's Lenny, ma'am. Glad to meet you," the officer said. When he looked down at her hand, he saw blood on her fingers and then he noticed some blood on her clothes. "Ma'am, is there a problem here?" he asked, looking somewhat concerned.

"Yes," Janis replied, trying to look and act calm. "I have one of your men here and he is badly wounded. Could you call an ambulance? You won't be able to move him in your car."

"Well ma'am, I mean Janis, that's why I'm here. We got a message from Sheriff Aliston that Jerry Parker was here and wounded. I came to see if I could get him back to the hospital. You say we need an ambulance?"

"Yes," Janis said. "He's better now but you can't move him in a car. We need an ambulance."

Lenny looked a little puzzled, then looked down at her hands again at the blood. "You say he's better now?"

"Yes," Janis said as she noticed him looking at her hands. She started to wipe them on her shirt as she nervously said, "Yeah, he is somewhat better."

Lenny looked her straight in the eye and then asked, "Ma'am, that looks like fresh blood. You sure all is okay here?" She started to reply when Lenny looked over her shoulder and saw part of the back end of the truck parked in the back yard. He then noticed the bullet holes in the tailgate. Lenny started to walk around Janis toward the truck and Janis tried to step in his way. "Officer, we are fine here but you need to get an ambulance for Jerry, please."

Lenny looked at her, then side-stepped again and

headed for the truck. When he saw the blown-out back window and more bullet holes, he started to unsnap his holster as he said, "I don't think all is okay here, ma'am. Now you stay here."

Janis started to walk toward Lenny as he drew his gun. "Officer, we are fine here. Please go get an ambulance."

In the house, Joey looked from the living room to the kitchen, where Sean and Corbin were standing. He put out his arms and whispered, "What you gonna do?"

Sean looked at Corbin and said, "Step out onto the porch and watch him, but don't shoot unless you have to." He then turned to Joey and pointed to the front windows, "Keep an eye out there." He looked down at Herman, who was still in the corner with his face covered, and knelt down for a second and said, "And you, shut the hell up unless you want to see the inside of that cell block again." Herman did not answer but just continued to cry. Sean stood up and looked out the kitchen window as Corbin moved out to the porch.

Janis started to follow Lenny as he moved toward the truck. "Officer, don't worry about that. We just need an ambulance."

Lenny looked at the truck, then at Janis and then toward the house. "Looks like you need more than that, ma'am. Now stay there till I check this out." Janis did not stop but slowly followed Lenny. Just as Lenny got to the truck, Corbin stood up on the back porch and pointed the shotgun at Lenny and fired. The pellets hit the truck and Lenny in the right upper leg. Lenny screamed and dropped to his knees while turning toward the porch. He saw Corbin and fired one quick shot in that direction that hit next to Corbin's head on the side of the house wall.

Corbin dropped to the floor of the porch and reloaded the gun. Janis ran to Lenny but as he got up to his feet he looked back at her and yelled. "No, stay there." Just then

Corbin raised up and aimed again. Lenny saw the move, and dragging his wounded leg, ducked behind the corner of the truck just as Corbin fired. The shot sprayed across the back quarter panel of the truck but missed Lenny. Corbin dropped to the floor again just as Lenny fired. The shot tore through the side wall of the porch right beside Corbin's head, spraying wood splinters into the side of his face.

Corbin yelled, "Son of a bitch," and winced in pain, then continued to load his gun.

Lenny got up and, dragging his leg, headed back to the police car. Janis started to get up, but as Lenny ran past her he yelled, "No, stay down." He ran to the far side of the car, opened the door and reached in for the shotgun clamped to the dashboard. He paused for a second as the pain burned his right leg. When he looked up he saw Corbin come around the corner of the house, the gun pointed at him. He ducked down just as a blast from Corbin's gun shattered the side window of the car. He looked up and saw Corbin reloading again; he stood up and pointed his shotgun at Corbin. He was about to fire when one of the front windows of the house broke out and Joey pointed and fired a handgun at Lenny. The shot hit Lenny in the left shoulder, knocking the shotgun from his hand. Lenny fell back, but quickly returned to the side of the car and picked up the gun in his right hand.

Janis was screaming, "Stop, please stop." Corbin fired another shot into the side of the car and Joey shot two more times, hitting the hood just above Lenny's head. To both Joey's and Corbin's surprise, Lenny stood up and fired one shot at Corbin, missing but driving him to the ground then he quickly turned and fired two shots at the window, hitting the shutter on both sides. Those two shots forced Joey to the floor. When Lenny looked at Corbin, he was up and running toward a large tree near the road. He realized that Corbin

was trying to get around the side to get a better shot. He knew he would be out-positioned in seconds, so he fired another shot at the windows, blowing the curtains back, then yelled to Janis to stay put and ran toward the garage as fast as he could move his bad leg.

Coop had watched most of what had transpired from the garage. It had happened so quickly that he had little time to react but now he was on the move. He grabbed Bobby Ray by the back of the shirt and pushed him out the door toward the driveway and the running Officer Lenny. Just as Lenny saw Coop with Bobby Ray, Coop yelled to Lenny, "I'm on your side," and stopped with Bobby Ray in front of him and placed his handgun to Bobby Ray's head. Lenny stumbled as he got close to Coop. Corbin had run to the back of the police car then out into the driveway and was raising the gun toward Lenny when Coop yelled, "Put it down or I shoot your friend here." Lenny got up slowly, blood covering his right leg from thigh to knee and blood over most of the left side of his shirt. He moved toward Coop and Bobby Ray. He looked at Coop, not knowing if he should believe him or not. Coop just pushed Bobby Ray forward, keeping the gun to his head and yelled again at Corbin, "I'll shoot him. I mean what I say."

Suddenly, a voice came from Coop's right side. "Go ahead, you'll be doing us a favor." It was Sean and he had a gun pointed at Coop. Coop looked first at Sean then back to Corbin, who still had the gun raised and pointed at Lenny while moving in closer. Lenny had his handgun pointed at Corbin while trying to maintain his grip on the shotgun with the other hand. He stood bleeding and weaving back and forth in the middle of the driveway.

Seconds later, Sean was joined by Joey, also pointing a gun at Coop. "Put the gun down and let Bobby Ray go," Sean said as he and Joey moved in closer to Coop.

"I'll shoot him," Coop said again as he pulled the hammer back on the gun.

Corbin yelled to Sean, "Who do you want me to shoot first, the old man, the cop, or Bobby Ray?"

"Hold on," Sean said as he looked at Corbin. He then turned to Coop and Lenny and said, "You're outnumbered and out-positioned. Now put the guns down and back away." No one moved. Sean said again, "Put the guns down and move back."

Coop was about to answer when another shot rang out from behind Corbin. Corbin ducked and turned back as the shot whizzed past his head and hit the garage behind Lenny. It was Herman and he had a handgun. As he fired again, he yelled, "I'm comin' Sean. I'll get them for you." The second shot came even closer to Corbin and he dove to the side. The second shot hit at Lenny's feet and he stumbled back and fired back at Herman, missing him.

Sean and Joey turned their attention to Herman and Sean yelled, "Put that gun down, you asshole." Coop wrestled with Bobby Ray, who was trying to get away as he pulled him toward the garage. Joey turned toward Coop and kept his gun on him. Sean yelled again at Herman, just as he fired again. The third shot went through Lenny's pant leg but did not hit him. He began to run toward the back of the garage, firing another shot toward Herman. Herman heard or felt the shot go past his head; he screamed, dropped the gun, ran to the police car, and hid behind it.

Corbin, who had run back toward the house, now came into sight. He had Janis by the arm, the shotgun pointed at her head. He looked at Coop and said, "Drop the gun and let Bobby Ray go, or I do her." Coop just looked at Corbin but did not move. Corbin yelled again, "Okay old man, her blood's on your head."

Sean yelled, "Corbin, no."

Just then, Coop let go of Bobby Ray and turned to Sean and said, "Tell him not to shoot."

Sean looked at Coop and said, "Put the gun down and she's gonna be okay." Coop slowly bent over and placed the gun on the ground then stood up and put up his hands. Bobby Ray turned around and picked up the gun and also took the small .25 auto out of Coop's pocket. As he did, he laughed, then spit in Coop's face.

Coop just closed his eyes, then looked at Bobby Ray and with a cold stare said, "I get the chance and I'm going to kill you, sonny."

Bobby Ray laughed then hit Coop across the side of the head with the gun. Coop went down on one knee and Bobby Ray yelled, "How's that feel, old man?"

Corbin pushed Janis across the driveway and over to Coop. She helped Coop get up then turned to Sean and screamed, "Enough, he's the doctor you need!"

Sean looked at Corbin and Joey and said, "Go, get that cop."

Before they could move, Bobby Ray said, "I'll get the bastard." He ran, gun in hand, to the side of the garage and looked around the corner. When he did, a shot rang out and hit the corner of the garage. Bobby Ray backed up, then turned to Sean and said, "Still some fight in the pig."

Sean looked at Corbin and Joey and told them to go around the other way and get him.

Janis, holding onto Coop's arm, said, "No. There's been enough shooting. Let me talk to him."

Sean said to Corbin and Joey, "Hold up. Let's see what the lady can do."

Janis let go of Coop, then said, "Are you alright?" as she looked at the red welt on the side of his head.

"Yeah, okay," Coop said.

She looked back at Sean then said, "Well?"

"Go Janis," was all Sean said as he followed her to the corner of the garage. She stopped at the corner then yelled out. "Lenny, it's Janis Fallon. I'm coming around. Don't shoot." She hesitated then took in a deep breath and stepped out. She walked down the side of the garage to the back but did not see Lenny until she looked at the shed. She was followed by Sean, Corbin and Bobby Ray. Joey stayed and held a gun on Coop. Janis saw Lenny holding onto the shed, weaving back and forth as if ready to pass out. He was covered in blood. He raised his head and looked at her as the shotgun slipped out of his hand to the ground. She held out her hand and said, "Lenny, give me the gun and come to me slowly." He looked at her and then looked at the ground and started to breathe as if he was struggling to get air. She repeated, "Lenny, come to me and give me the gun." Sean and Corbin moved in behind her, their guns pointed at Lenny.

Sean said, "Lenny put the gun down and do as she asks." Lenny looked up again, held out the gun as if to give it to her, and started to stagger toward her.

Suddenly, Bobby Ray jumped out from behind all of them and yelled, "Pig, bastard," and fired, hitting Lenny in the chest and driving him back through the shed door and onto the floor inside. It took all of them by surprise.

Bobby Ray fired again into the shed and Janis yelled, "No, there's gasoline in there." Bobby Ray fired two more times and one of the cans ignited with a thunderous roar. They all were knocked back and turned to run as the remaining cans exploded. In seconds, the shed and surrounding trees were in flames, as a fireball rose high into the air.

CHAPTER 22
September

The afternoon was warm. Matt stopped his daydreaming, put down his fishing rod, and leaned back in the chair. He raised his arms above his head, stretched and yawned. He picked up his beer and took a long drink, then just sat and watched Janis painting on one side of the pond and Clive fishing on the other. Deep in thought, he had questions still running through his mind. Had they done enough? What should they be doing now? He closed his eyes, raised his hand, and squeezed his temples. What a horrible feeling, this not knowing, and worse yet, not knowing what to do. He calmed himself by taking several deep breaths, then whispered, "I've got to do for the rest of the family. I can't lose control. Yes, we have tried and tried hard for the past six weeks. Clive helped for as long as he could. But I know he had to return to duty. And now we need this break. I'm not shirking my responsibility. I'm taking pause for rest and thought. Now Clive's back for a time. We'll begin again. I will not stop until we have an answer. Matt, calm down. Rest and think. Rest and think." He took another drink of beer, stretched again, took several deep breaths, and whispered again, "Calm." He did not pick up his fishing rod, but instead tilted his head back and looked up at the tree branches above his head and the

cloudless blue sky beyond. He felt the cool breeze as it came across the pond to him. He closed his eyes and his mind wandered back to that day in Oakland. He remembered walking away from the jeep, across the street and down the sidewalk toward the dorm.

July

Matt moved down the street in the direction of the dorm. He saw no one except police and fireman. Several of them looked at him somewhat suspiciously but when they saw the armband they continued on with what they were doing. About half a block from the dorm building, a police officer sitting in a patrol car along the curb saw Matt coming and got out and stepped in his path, his hand on his gun. "Can I see some identification please, and not the armband?" Matt slowly reached into his pocket and retrieved the blue card. He showed it to the officer, answered the questions, and gave the code. The officer asked for his personal identification, then let Matt move on. As the dorm building came into view, Matt started to jog, then broke into a run. When he reached the sidewalk in front of the building, he slowed to a walk again. The building looked deserted but in good shape except for a couple of broken windows.

As he slowly moved up the sidewalk he raised his shotgun across his chest in a ready position. He scanned the building windows but all was dark. He stopped in the middle of the sidewalk and looked up at one of the second floor windows. He whispered, "Lisa, please be here. Please do what I told you." He saw a young man look out of the window. When the man saw him, he waved and turned and yelled something back into the room. Matt heard someone yell, then the sound of a door slam and footsteps as if someone was running down a flight of stairs.

Suddenly, the front door flew open and Lisa came

running out the door and straight at him, yelling, "Daddy, Daddy." Matt lowered his gun and shifted it to his left hand in anticipation. When Lisa was several feet away she leaped out and landed in Matt's arms, her arms around his neck and one leg wrapped around his. She kissed his cheek and whispered, "Daddy, you're here. You're finally here."

Matt held her tightly with one arm for several seconds, then released his hold on her and looked into her tear-dampened eyes. "You knew I'd come for you baby. I told you if anything happened I'd be here as soon as I could get here. You did exactly what I asked. You stayed inside and locked down."

Lisa wiped the tears from her face and said, "We talked about leaving and some of the kids did. I hope they made it home or to safety. I almost left too but then I remembered. Me and half a dozen others are still here. Dad, it was bad last night. I mean really bad. Gunshots and screaming and police cars and fire trucks. Some of the fires were really close."

"Yes, I know, dear. We just drove through some of it, but you're okay and that's what matters, now. We can get you home until all gets back to normal. We have the jeep just up the road."

"We?" Lisa asked, with a questioning look on her face.

"Yes, we," Matt said. "Me, Andy, Uncle Clive and a sort of new friend named Madison."

"Uncle Clive is here with you?" Lisa asked, looking somewhat surprised.

"Yes," Matt said, adding, "It's a long story on how that happened but I'll explain later."

"And Andy's here too?" Lisa said with a smile.

"Yeah, he's here," Matt said as he hugged her again. "He wouldn't have it any other way. He's been worried sick about you. We all have. But now I know you're alright and as soon as we can we'll be telling Mom."

"Telling Mom, but how?" Lisa said as she looked at Matt again.

"The CB in the jeep," Matt said. "That's if we can get a call through."

He looked at his watch. "It's almost time to call. She'll be so happy to hear your voice."

Lisa asked, "Who's home with Mom and Mary and Robert? Dad, you didn't leave her alone?"

"No," Matt replied. "She's at camp and she's with Coop. You know Coop; he'll protect them like they are his own."

Lisa smiled, then turned toward the dorm. "Dad, what can we do for the rest of my friends? We can't just leave them. They don't know if or when anyone is coming and we are getting low on food and water."

Matt put his arm around her shoulder and they started to walk toward the dorm. "Don't worry, honey. We'll talk to them and figure out something." They walked to the front door and were met by several of the other students. Back up the street the jeep was given the all-clear and Clive jumped in and drove around the fire truck and headed toward the dorm.

Several minutes later, Andy spoke up, "Uncle Clive, that's the dorm just ahead on the right. Pull in, pull in." Andy stood up in the back and said, "Where's Dad and Lisa, where's Lisa?"

Maddie pulled on his pant leg and looked up and said, "They are fine, Andy. Just fine." He looked down at her and smiled briefly. As the jeep came to a stop he jumped out. He picked up the .30-30, then changed his mind and handed it to Maddie, who took it with a surprised look on her face. He picked up his bow and slowly started around the jeep toward the sidewalk.

Clive got out and grabbed his shotgun and then said, "Andy, not alone. You go with me. Maddie, will you be okay

here for a few minutes?" Maddie got out and stood beside the jeep holding the .30-30 as if it would come alive and bite her on the hand. Clive looked at her, then the gun and said, "Maddie, put it on the floor in the back. Better yet, give it to me."

She stepped forward and handed him the gun, then smiled and said, "They are okay for now. All is okay."

Clive looked at her and smirked and said, "Yeah, right, okay. You stay here while we go see if all is okay?"

Maddie looked at him sternly and once again folded her arms across her chest, saying, "Aliston, go. I'll be fine. As I said, all is fine for now." Maddie leaned against the jeep, while Clive and Andy slowly walked up the sidewalk to the dorm.

As they got closer to the building, Clive kept scanning the front of the building with a questioning look, then he heard something and said to Andy, "Stop." He was about to add something else when the door opened and Matt stepped out. No sooner was Matt outside, when Lisa came running out from behind him and straight to Andy. Andy ran toward her and they met and hugged and held each other for several seconds. Lisa was crying and Andy tried to wipe tears from his eyes in a way that no one would notice. After a few seconds, she kissed Andy on the cheek then let go of him and turned to Clive, who was walking slowly toward her with a broad smile on his face. She walked slowly to him and then ran the last few steps and into his arms. He tried to hold her but with a gun in each hand he just held his arms out. Matt and Andy stepped up and each took one gun. He then wrapped his big arms around her and lifted her off the ground. He kissed her cheek and whispered, "Thank you, God." She held him for a time and Matt could see the tears welling up in Clive's eyes. Clive finally let go of her, then tried to draw the tears back without touching his face but then, realizing he couldn't, he used his shirt sleeve to quickly

wipe them as if they didn't really happen. He placed his hands on her shoulders and looked into her eyes. "I knew you would be okay. I just knew."

A voice came from behind Clive. "No, Aliston. I knew. I knew and I told you." Maddie stepped out from behind Clive and put out her hand toward Lisa. "Hi Lisa, I'm Maddie."

Lisa slowly put out her hand and shook Maddie's, then to her surprise Maddie pulled her close and hugged her and held her for a few seconds. Lisa looked over Maddie's shoulder at Clive and sort of asked a question with her eyes like, "Who is this?" Clive just shrugged his shoulders and shook his head and smiled.

When Maddie let go of Lisa, she just stared at her with her hands on Lisa's shoulders and said, "I'll explain all of this on the way back to camp. I want to make sure you get the right story, not someone else's version." She turned and looked back at Clive and raised one corner of her mouth in an exaggerated smirk.

Lisa just smiled and said, "Glad to meet you, too."

Matt spoke up. "Clive, we have six other students here and one counselor, and we have no way of knowing if or when their parents or someone is coming for them, or how long the counselor needs to stay. He wants to get home, too. We need to talk to someone. They are low on food and water."

Clive took both guns back from Andy and Matt, and said, "Why don't we go inside? It's much better than out here." They all turned and walked back to the dorm.

After about fifteen minutes of discussion with the other students, Clive decided to go find help while Matt watched from the open second floor window. Clive left the building and walked out to the jeep. He was about to start it when a fire truck pulled up beside him. Seated in the passenger seat

was the fire captain they had spoken to earlier. Matt watched from the second floor window as Clive conversed with the fireman. Clive looked up at the captain, smiled and said, "Hey, thanks for all your help."

"No problem," the captain replied. "And is she okay?"

"Yes, she is," Clive responded with a smile. "She and six of her friends and a counselor, all okay. But we need some information on where we can take them. They have no idea if anyone is coming for them and food and water is getting to be an issue."

"Well," the captain said as he removed his hat and scratched his head. He thought for a few seconds and said, "Yeah, I think I know exactly where we can take them. I took a couple of my injured men to a Catholic church just around the block from here. The priest is a good guy and they do have food and water. He's taking good care of my men and I don't think he'll mind taking in a few more."

"Thanks so much," Clive said. "The only thing is if someone does show up for them how will they know where to find them?"

"Well," the captain said as he replaced his helmet. "I think we can cover that too. It's getting late and we are going to place police and firemen all along this route for the night. We will be setting up generators and mobile lights. We're not going to have a repeat of last night. The escapees and looters have had their fun. I'll station one of my men here. In case someone shows, I'll have him send them to the church. Will that work?"

"Amen," Clive said as he shook his hand again. "I'm sorry, Captain, I didn't get your name before. I'm Clive Aliston. Sheriff Clive Aliston."

The captain broke into a smile and said, "I'm Jonas. Jonas Walker. I thought you looked familiar. Are you the Aliston from, what were they called, The Forever Man murders?

Yeah, that's it. So you're him?"

"Yeah, I guess that would be me," Clive said with a sort of half smile. "Something I would like to put in the past, if you know what I mean?"

"Yeah, I got ya," Jonas said, then added, "Come on. Let's see if we can get these kids a place to stay."

He and Clive walked back to the dorm and Clive asked, "You hear anything about your daughter?"

Jonas looked down at the sidewalk, pressed his lips together and shook his head. "No, not a word and I'm really starting to get worried."

"I can imagine," Clive said as they reached the dorm door. They paused for a second and Clive said, "I'll pray for you and her. We all will."

"Thanks, Clive," was all Jonas said as they entered the building. After several minutes of discussion and explanation to the students, they all left the building, the students taking what they could with them. They all climbed into the fire truck except for Clive and Matt, and they drove around the block to the church. When they arrived, they were met by two men, both firemen, and the captain explained what was happening. The firemen were armed and were guarding the church because of its use as a temporary first aid station.

When they got inside, they were met by a priest dressed in the regular black pants and shirt, with white collar. They stood in the vestibule and Jonas introduced them. "Clive, Matt, Andy, Maddie and Lisa, and you students, this is Fr. Meyers."

The priest put out his hand to Clive first. "John Meyers. It's a pleasure to meet you all," he said as he shook each one's hand. When he got to Maddie, he shook her hand but she said nothing. She just stared into his eyes and held onto his hand. It was as if she was in a trance.

Clive looked at her and said, "Maddie!" and got no response. Fr. Meyers said nothing; he just looked puzzled and continued to hold her hand. Clive repeated, "Maddie!" Still no response.

Matt put his hand on Maddie's shoulder. "Madison"

Maddie suddenly opened her eyes wide as if coming out of a deep sleep, then shook the priest's hand and then smiled, "Yes, I'm glad to meet you."

Clive looked at Maddie and started to say, "What is it with…"

Maddie stopped him in mid-sentence as she turned and glared at him, "Aliston, enough."

Clive just shook his head and said, "Ahh." He then looked at Fr. Meyers and said, "Father, leaving the counselor and students here, it's not going to put you in a bad situation, is it?"

"No," Fr. Meyers said. "We want to help in any way we can—and besides, we could use their help with some things."

"Okay," Clive said. "Then if it's okay with you guys?" Clive looked at the students. They all said yes, and then the group moved onto the main part of the church. Clive removed his hat, as did the others who had been wearing hats, and they all walked to the front. Inside, two of Jonas's men were lying on the two front pews, covered in blankets. There were also several people from the surrounding neighborhoods. Some of them were helping take care of the two men.

Fr. Meyers said, "We will have to stay up here in the church. The basement room was under construction when all this got started. It's not fit down there for man nor beast, if you know what I mean. We moved the food that we could save to a room up there in the choir loft area and the water is down here, but we'll make do. Now all of you pick a place

to sleep tonight. We have enough pews, as you can see."

Andy spoke up first, "Thanks, Father, but we won't be staying. We got to get home."

Clive was about to speak when Maddie said, "Thank you, Father. We'll find a spot."

Clive, Andy and Maddie all started to speak when Matt cut in, "We aren't going to make any decisions about that until I get a call into Janis, and it's time in five minutes." No one said anything. Matt started for the door then turned back to the group "Clive, you want to come with me?"

"Yeah, sure," Clive said as he followed Matt toward the door. Matt turned again and said, "Andy and Lisa, if I get her, I'll call for you. Stay in here for now." Matt and Clive left the church and headed for the jeep.

CHAPTER 23
July

When Matt and Clive got to the jeep, Matt started it. Clive stood beside him. Matt took the mike from the CB radio, turned on the set, then looked at Clive as if to say, "Well, here goes, I hope all is well."

Clive just said, "Matt, make the call."

Matt put the mike to his face and said, "Fallon one, this is Fallon two, do you hear me?" They waited but all they got was a hash sound. Matt said again, "Fallon one, this is Fallon two, do you hear me?" Once again, no response.

Clive said, "Maybe we are early. Your watch could be fast."

Matt shook his head, "Maybe, but I doubt it. Besides, she would be waiting. I know Janis." He keyed the mike again, "Fallon one, this is Fallon two, do you read me?" Nothing but hash. Matt put the mike to his lap for a second, then tried again, "Janis, this is Matt. Please answer." Nothing but hash. Matt tried for several more minutes, as did Clive, but they got no response.

Clive finally reached down and shut off the CB, then Matt shut off the jeep. "We must be too far away. I was afraid this would happen," Clive said as he lowered his head.

"If I could just talk to her," Matt said. "I think I'd feel a lot better."

"Me too, buddy, me too," Clive said.

"Well, what do we do now?" Matt asked.

Clive thought for a few seconds, then leaned on the jeep, looked at the ground, and shook his head. "It's after 6 p.m. and it will be dark in less than three hours." He took a deep breath then continued, "If this was any normal day, we could be home in less than two, but I'd say this is far from normal. If we get stopped as often as we did getting here it will be four a.m. before we get home. I'm not sure I want to be out there in the dark. Not with the kids and Maddie."

Matt looked up at Clive and said, "I'm not sure I can stand an entire night of not knowing, but you might be right. The only thing is, what do I say to the kids? They are going to want to get home and I mean yesterday."

"Yeah, I know," Clive said. "But remember, there is no other light out there now. No street lights, no city lights, no lights at all. A jeep on the road, headlights on, well pretty good target. You know what I mean. Matt we would be sitting ducks out there. But the decision is yours. It's your family. I'll abide by what you want to do, like it or not."

They were both silent for several seconds, then Matt slammed his fist on top of the steering wheel and yelled, "Damn it, damn it to hell." He started the jeep again and turned on the CB. "Janis, this is Matt. Do you hear me? Please hear me." No response, just hash. He put his hand to his forehead and squeezed, then lowered his head to the steering wheel. Clive just stood there.

After several seconds, Matt raised his head again and keyed the mike. He took a deep breath and said, "Janis, this is Matt. I don't know if you can hear me. We are all okay and we have Lisa. It's too late to drive home from Oakland. We will try to call at midnight. Maybe I can hear you then. I want to come home but it's too dangerous at night. I'm sorry. Please be careful. I'll see you early in the morning. Honey, I

love you more than you know. Have a good night. Fallon two out." Matt shut down the CB and shut off the jeep. Clive and Matt slowly walked back to the church. When they got to the door, Matt looked at Clive and said, "Buddy this is going to be a bad scene. You better let me handle this. I need to talk to them alone."

They entered the church and were met by Madison inside the door. "You can't get through?" she asked, as if she already knew.

"No," Matt said. "Nothing. We got nothing."

She put her hand on his chest and whispered, "Go tell them. They are stronger than you know. They will understand. It will be hard, but they will understand." Matt touched her hand and she gave him a quick hug then said, "Go to them."

Matt smiled at her then went inside the church, leaving Maddie and Clive alone.

Maddie walked to the front door, opened it, and looked out at the street in front of her. Clive walked up behind her and stood looking out over her shoulder. "He's a strong man and they are strong kids," Maddie said, without looking away. "They are good people—the best friends you ever had, Clive."

"Yeah, I know," Clive said, as he continued to stare at the street.

"They will always be a part of your life," Maddie said. "Always." She slowly turned to Clive and looked up at him. "The three of them will be fine for now. They all will be fine, all except..." She stopped and looked down at the floor.

Clive took a deep breath and said, "Except, except for what? I mean, why do you think you know everything?" He stopped in mid-sentence as Maddie looked up at him, tears running down her cheeks. She moved in closer to him and put her head against his chest. He did not speak. He just put

an arm around her and stared out at the street in front of him.

They remained there for several minutes, then Maddie looked up at Clive, the tears still on her face. "Clive, please listen to me and please don't be angry with me. We are all going to need you and soon. He will need you."

"Who will need me?" Clive asked in a softer tone. "Do you mean Andy or Matt?"

"I don't want to say," Maddie said. Clive looked a little angry and was about to speak when Maddie placed her index finger to his lips and said, "Shhhhh! I can't or don't want to say." Maddie continued, "I have found that if I say too much it can change the way things are meant to be, and that can be oh so bad at times. Please take my word for this. My word is all I can give you now."

Clive took her hand away from his face and held it. "Maddie, I don't understand. How do you know these things and why won't you tell me? I have pretty much figured out that you know something, but how?"

Maddie placed her hand on his chest and said, "I will tell you but I can't now. It will complicate things, and you and I need to work together—not just for now but on down the road. There will be a need for you then also, and that is the time that I fear the most. For now, please trust me. And one more thing, you must watch your back."

Clive looked and felt frustrated, but something inside him seemed to say, let it go. He looked at her, then wiped one side of her face with his hand. She placed her head against his chest again. He remained silent and held her as he stared out at the street.

Minutes later, Clive and Maddie entered the church and saw Matt near the right front of the church talking to Andy and Lisa. Maddie sat down in one of the pews and watched, while Clive stood beside her. They couldn't hear what Matt

was saying, but Lisa was crying and Andy stood with his head turned to the floor. Matt took both of them in his arms and held them.

Fr. Meyers walked up to Clive and Maddie and spoke, "I know it's hard on the kids but I think you both made the right decision. Going out there tonight is only putting you all in harm's way. Stay here with us tonight. Rest and get a fresh start in the morning. The Lord will protect the rest of the family." He smiled at Clive and Maddie, then turned and walked back to the front of the church, where he was met by Matt, Andy, and Lisa. He put his arm around Lisa and walked her over to the other students; they all gathered around her. Matt stood at the front and talked to Andy.

Maddie looked up at Clive and whispered, "He's right. God will protect them until you are both there again." Clive just looked at her but did not say anything. Matt, Andy and Clive went out to the jeep to get some water and a few items to snack on. Fr. Meyers went to the upper room to get some other food and they all ate a little and tended to the injured firemen. Some of them stretched out on the pews, but Clive went outside and talked to the two firemen who were guarding the building. It was after dark and close to 10 p.m. when he came back inside. They all sat and talked for awhile and the students helped Fr. Meyers go to the basement to get a few more supplies. Matt kept looking at his watch. At about 11:45, he got up and started for the front door.

Clive got up to go with him but Matt said, "It's okay, Clive. I'll call. You stay and rest." Clive didn't answer; he just gave him a thumbs-up sign. Matt was gone for half an hour, but when he got back Clive could tell that he had not been successful just by the look on his face.

He was met by Clive near the front of the church. "Sorry, Matt. I guess I was right, we are just too far. They will be okay. They are better off at camp. Besides, Coop is there."

Matt just smiled and said, "Yeah." He slapped Clive on the back and went up to Lisa and Andy and then lay down on a pew. The church was locked and all were lying down sleeping by 1 a.m.

At about 5 a.m., just before daylight, one of the two guards outside walked around the side of the church to relieve himself. Five minutes later the other guard, getting worried, followed in the same direction. He walked down the sidewalk and then saw, through the shadows, a body lying on the grass. He ran to that position and rolled the body over. It was his partner and he was bleeding from his head. He got up and turned to run back to the church when he was hit across the abdomen with a large pole. It bent him over and knocked him to his knees. He gasped for breath then was hit across the back of the head and fell unconscious to the ground. A dark figure bent down and took his gun and started toward the side of the church.

Clive, Andy and Matt were up before anyone else; they decided to go to the choir loft to get food for breakfast for the group. From the basement came the sound of breaking glass. Fr. Meyers raised his head at the sound, but no one else moved. All were still asleep. Clive, Andy and Matt were too high up in the storage room and did not hear anything. Fr. Meyers got up on one elbow and listened, but he heard nothing. He had just lain back down when he heard a noise again. He sat up, removed his blanket and listened. He got up, slowly walked to the back of the church to a door behind the altar, and slowly entered.

Clive, Andy and Matt had brought out some boxes and set them on one of the choir pews when Clive said to Andy, who was holding his bow in one hand and trying to carry a bag in the other, "You know if you put that bow down you could carry that much easier."

Andy looked at Clive, laughing, and said, "And if you

put down that shotgun you could help me." They both started to laugh when they heard a loud noise from downstairs, like a door slamming open. Everyone in the downstairs pews woke up and sat up as a man came through the door behind the altar. He was in a prison uniform that was dirty and torn and he had Fr. Meyers in a strangle hold in front of him with a handgun pointed at the priest's head.

When Clive saw what was happening, he motioned to Matt and Andy to duck down below the front of the choir rail. He did the same. He put his index finger to his lips and shook his head, "No." When all three of them were down, he moved slowly and quietly to Matt and Andy. He whispered to them to wait and not to move. He turned and looked out over the rail, down at the floor in front of him. The man with gun moved out around the altar, pushing the priest in front of him. Two of the girl students and a couple of the neighbor women started to scream.

The man yelled, "Shut the hell up or I'll shoot the priest." All of them got silent. The man pushed Fr. Meyers out and away from him, directly in front of the altar. He looked at the group of people spread out over both sides of the church and yelled, "Everyone over to this side and all together. I want to see all of you together right here."

Fr. Meyers turned to the man and said, "Please, don't hurt anyone. This is a house of God."

"Shut the hell up, I told you," the man yelled, as he stepped forward and pushed the muzzle of the gun into the priest's face. "Move, move, move," he yelled at the people. "Get over to this side now or I'll shoot your priest here. Now, I said move." Everyone complied and moved into a group to the left side of the church. The priest started to join the group, but the man yelled, "No. You stay with me. I want all their money and any collection money you have here. You

hear me, priest? Now, move."

As the people started to turn over their money, Clive dropped again to below the rail. He called Matt and Andy in close, "I've got to get down to that floor. I can't use this shotgun from here. I'll hit everyone and it's too far for the handgun to be accurate. Matt, you move over to the stairs on the right side then wait for me to get to the stairs on the left. We'll go down and then outside."

Matt said, "The side doors are locked. How do we get in?"

Clive said, "He got in. I'll use his route. You wait at the right side door till I yell for you, then blow the lock with your shotgun."

Andy said, "What about me?"

"You stay here," both Clive and Matt said at the same time.

"But," Andy began.

Clive said, "I said here."

Andy, looking disgusted, said, "Okay, okay."

Matt nodded at Clive then slowly moved low to the floor and over to the right side stairs that led to the front room. Clive moved to the left side door and motioned to Matt to go. He looked at Andy and pointed to the floor and mouthed, "Stay here." They both slowly and quietly moved down the stairs and to the front room. Once there, they unlocked the door and stepped outside. Clive told Matt to search around the right side for where he got in then come back to the front. Clive did the same to the left. Clive found the two guards unconscious, and a broken cellar window, then returned to the front.

"I got nothing," Matt said in a whisper.

"I do," Clive said. "You go to the side door on the right and wait for my signal, then blow that damn lock and get in there. Be careful."

"Yeah," Matt said as he turned and left. Clive ran around

the side again and, with some effort because of his large frame, squeezed into the cellar window and onto the cellar floor. He reached out the window and got his shotgun, then waited a minute for his eyes to adjust. He found his way to a set of stairs that he figured led to the door behind the altar and moved up them slowly. He could see light from the candles in the main church room coming through the partially open door. When he got to the door he pushed it open partway and looked out. He could see the man in the prison uniform and part of the group of people, but not the priest. The prisoner had the gun pointed out in front of him, so Clive figured that Fr. Meyers must be only a few feet away. He looked at his shotgun then his handgun. If he opened the door, he couldn't use the shotgun for fear of spraying the people behind the prisoner. He put the handgun in his right hand and the shotgun in his left. If he had to fire in the direction of the group, one lead bullet was better than many pellets, especially buck shot.

He noticed that Lisa was sitting in the front of the group of people, right in the line of fire. What would he do now? He had to think, and think fast. The prisoner was yelling something about not enough money and he slapped a man who had brought a basket of money to him. Then he yelled that if he got no more money he would call in his partner and have him cut up a few of the girls. He said that he was good with a knife and liked to see people in pain. He yelled, "I said more money and two of you boys strip. We want your clothes."

Clive whispered to himself, "We?" Where the hell was another guy? He didn't see anyone else. He had to think fast. Suddenly, he got an idea. He put both guns on the steps, then removed his hat and slowly took off his shirt. He reached for the corner of the step in the dark and wiped his hand on the surface. He looked at his hand in the dim light. Dirt. He put

some dirt on his t-shirt and his face, then pulled his t-shirt out of his pants and messed up his short hair. He picked up the two guns and pushed them out the door and just behind the altar, out of sight. He took a deep breath, then moved up the steps to the door. He looked out again, then took one more deep breath, pushed the door open and fell out onto the floor. The sudden move took the prisoner by surprise and he turned toward Clive and yelled, "What the hell?"

Clive lay on the floor for a minute, then said, "Hey, man I'm sorry." The prisoner reached out and grabbed Fr. Meyers by the shirt and spun him around. He put his arm around his neck again and placed the gun to his head, then faced Clive and pointed the gun at him.

"Who the hell are you, asshole?" the prisoner yelled as he cocked the handgun.

Clive heard the click and yelled, "Father John, Father John, I'm sorry I got into the wine again. I'm sorry. Please don't be mad."

The prisoner looked at Clive and then pushed Fr. Meyers out in front of him, still holding onto the back of his neck. "Who is he?" the prisoner yelled at Fr. Meyers. The priest didn't answer; he just stood there not knowing what to say. He yelled again, "Who is he?" as Clive got up to his knees, acting like he was weaving back and forth.

Suddenly, a voice came from about the third row back. "He's the janitor and he's drunk again." It was Madison.

"Get out here where I can see you," the prisoner yelled at Clive.

Clive started to get to his feet when Maddie came out of the pew to the main aisle and yelled, "It's okay, Al. I'll help you."

The prisoner, confused by the movement in two directions, turned sideways to Clive, pointed the gun at Maddie and yelled, "Back to your seat, bitch."

Clive made a move for the guns and Maddie yelled, "Get

down everyone," as she hit the floor herself. The prisoner fired at Maddie and the shot splintered the side of the pew just above her head. The people in the pews dove for the floor as the prisoner turned back to Clive.

What he saw was not a drunk but a big man with two guns pointed right at him. He turned the gun toward Clive and Clive yelled, "No," then fired his handgun. The bullet hit the prisoner in the left shoulder and he let go of Fr. Meyers and ran to the side door. When he got to the door he tried to get out, but it was locked. At the same instant, there was a blast from the right and the side door flew open with a shower of wood splinters in all directions. Matt ran into the church through that door, his shotgun up and ready. People were screaming and trying to keep as close to the floor as they could.

Fr. Meyers was on one knee. As he slowly started to get up, the prisoner raised his gun at the priest. Clive yelled, "No," one more time but the prisoner did not stop. Clive pointed both guns at the man and fired before he had a chance to fire back. The shots blew the man up against the door and then to the floor.

There was a second or two of silence, then a shot rang out from behind Clive. He spun around to see Matt duck behind a post as wood splinters burst from the same post. There, standing in the shadows, was a second man in a prison uniform.

The first prisoner hadn't lied. There were two. The second man turned toward Clive as Clive spun around in an attempt to get position. It was too late. The second prisoner had handguns in both hands and he had a bead on Clive with the left hand. As Clive continued to spin around, it was as if everything was in slow motion. Clive saw the muzzle of the gun pointed at him; he heard the hammer click and expected to see a muzzle blast at any moment—probably the

last thing he would ever see. Matt began to rise up again and swing his shotgun toward the man in front of him. Clive could hear himself breathe, but everything seemed to move too slowly. Suddenly, there was a flash of something that passed in front of the second prisoner and his left arm flew to the right and was pinned to the wall. It was an arrow. The second man screamed and for an instant tried to pull his arm from the wall but all he could do was drop the gun in his left hand. He turned the second gun on Matt and raised it to fire.

Clive, Matt and Fr. Meyers all yelled, "No," again and the sound echoed off the church walls. There were three blasts from three different directions and the second man flew into the wall, hung there by the arrow, then dropped his gun. The arrow snapped and he fell to the floor. Four people were left standing, looking at the second man on the floor: Clive to the left, his shotgun still smoking; Father Meyers to the right, making a sign of the cross in the direction of the convict; Matt to the right, his shotgun still raised; and in the center, holding the .30-30, Madison. She looked at the gun, threw it to the floor, sat down, and put her face in her hands. Clive turned and walked first to the first convict and checked his pulse, then over to the second and did the same. Fr. Meyers started to help some of the people up. Some of them were crying and sobbing. Matt slowly sat down in the pew and laid the shotgun on the seat next to him. Lisa ran to Matt, put her arms around him and started to cry. Andy walked down the center aisle near the front and moved to the right to a pew. He sat down, put his bow on the floor, and stared at the altar.

Clive looked over the entire room at all of them. With a gun in each hand, he walked slowly away from the altar and down the center aisle until he was at the last row. He turned toward the front and knelt down on both knees. Sweat ran from his head and face and onto his dirty, wet t-shirt. He

placed the guns, one at a time, on the floor, sat back on his legs, placed his face in his hands, and slowly breathed. As he knelt there, the others could hear him whispering to himself.

CHAPTER 24
September

Janis had finished her painting and was about to start putting her equipment away when the song, "Kiss From a Rose" by Seal came over the radio. It was one of her favorites on that CD. She took a drink from her bottle, then sat and watched Clive as he fished. Matt had fallen asleep again in his chair. She was comfortable for the first time in weeks, but did she have a right to be? After all that had happened and all that was still hanging out there, how could she even think comfortable? She wasn't sure how to feel about how she felt, but she did know that it must be necessary. It must be God's way of saying, "You rest now and put it all on my shoulders. When it is time you will start again, and I will be with you." She sat quietly and watched as the late afternoon sun began to sink in the western sky over Scorpion's Tail. Her mind once again began to drift back to that day at camp. The flames in her memory seemed so real that she could almost feel the heat again.

July

Janis, Sean and Corbin got up quickly and ran low to the ground as the heat from the fireball drove them back. Janis turned back and screamed, "Oh, my God, no." Sean turned back and pulled her by the upper arm back another ten feet

and stopped, putting his hand and arm in front of his face to block the heat.

Bobby Ray had run to the corner of the garage and was laughing like a crazed maniac, yelling, "Look Sean, roast pig, roast pig."

Janis turned to Sean, tears streaming down her now-dirty face and yelled, "Oh yeah, you're in control. Just so much in control. He killed an innocent man. You all did. My God what is wrong with you people?"

She raised her right hand and slapped Sean across the face, then reached back for another swing when he grabbed her by the front of her shirt and pulled her into his chest. "You do that again and more people are going to get hurt. You got that?" Janis did not respond; she just sneered at him. "Did you hear me?" Sean yelled again, as he pulled her so close their faces almost touched.

"I heard you, Mr. 'In-control,'" she whispered, pushing away from him.

Sean let go of her then looked over at Bobby Ray, who was still laughing and yelling about roast pig. Corbin, who had regained his composure, stepped up and pointed his shotgun at Bobby Ray and yelled, "You dumb son of a bitch."

Joey had pushed Coop around the side of the garage, still holding the gun on him. As he got near Bobby Ray, Bobby Ray turned to him and said, still laughing, "Look Joey, look. We got roast pig." Sean stepped in front of Corbin, pushed his shotgun toward the ground, and said nothing. He just glared at him as if to say, "No, he's mine." Bobby Ray was still yelling at Joey as Sean walked up to him. When Bobby Ray turned, Sean grabbed the handgun from him and then grabbed him by the shirt and slammed him back into the garage. He hit Bobby Ray across the right side of the face with the side of the handgun. Bobby Ray's head slammed

off the side of the garage, Sean kicked him in the testicles, and Bobby Ray went to his knees. Sean dropped both of his guns and proceeded to kick Bobby Ray repeatedly as he lay on the ground. He then quickly picked up Bobby Ray, pinned him against the garage, put his hand to Bobby Ray's throat, and began to squeeze. Bobby Ray's eyes started to bulge out as he gasped for air. Corbin yelled to Sean, "Kill the asshole, Sean. Kill him."

Janis started to walk toward Sean and yelled, "No. No more killing—not even him. Enough, enough."

Corbin reached out and grabbed Janis by the back of her hair. He pulled her back, turned her face toward his, and said with a sneer, "No. You stay here, bitch." He forced a hard kiss on her lips as she pushed away, then spit in his face.

Joey pushed Coop closer to Sean, then said, "Sean, she's right. Enough, enough. You're going to kill him." Sean paid no attention but only glared at Bobby Ray, only inches from his face, and squeezed harder.

Joey yelled, "Sean, enough." Suddenly, there was a shot from behind Joey, and Sean let go of Bobby Ray, who fell to the ground. All turned in that direction.

Standing at the corner of the garage was Mose, a shotgun pointed to the sky. For a second or two, all they heard was the burning shed as it fell apart in the flames. Mose said, "What is wrong with all of you? You're acting like you are a bunch of animals. These are good people. We came here to get food and water. They ain't done nothin' to you. I told you when we left not to take that crazy man, Bobby Ray with us, not him or that crazy Herman. Sean, it ain't s'pose to be this way. You ain't crazy like them. You ain't. You're the best man I knowed in that prison. Please Sean, don't be like them kind of people. Don't be crazy."

"Shut up old man," Corbin yelled.

Sean turned to Corbin and yelled, "No, you shut up!"

Janis stepped forward and Corbin pulled her back. She turned and hit his arm, breaking the grip on her. She turned back toward Mose. "Where are my children?"

"They is okay, ma'am," Mose said as he lowered his gun. "They is with Parker. He's awake and seems to be much better."

Janis started toward the house but Joey stepped in her way. She tried to push him aside as Sean spoke up, "No, Joey, let her go. Mose, take her back to the house." When Janis got to Mose, they turned to go. Sean asked, "Is there a hose to put this out and any power for the pump?"

Janis turned and glared at him. "Yes, there's a hose just inside the garage door and I'll turn on the pump."

Sean looked at Mose, "Go with her, and the pump on only, you hear?"

"Yeah, Sean," was all Mose said.

As they turned to walk away, Sean looked at Corbin, then pointed to Bobby Ray, still unconscious on the ground. "Pick up that piece of shit and take him to the house, and no more guns. He gets no more guns until I say so." He then turned to Joey. "Tie up Mr. Coop here and take him to the garage, then tie him to the work bench or something solid till I figure what to do with him."

"Why don't I just take him to the house?" Joey asked.

Sean said, "No, there are more guns in there and he's one feisty old man, ain't you Coop?" Coop just sneered then spit on the ground in front of him. Sean grabbed him by his shirt, "Old man, I know what's on your mind, but you just go with Joey and be nice. I mean real nice. Remember, we have Janis and the kids and Officer Parker in the house. You try anything and it won't be you who gets hurt. You got that, old man?" Coop did not answer; he just continued to stare. "You got that, old man?" Sean yelled as he got closer to Coop's face.

"I heard you," Coop whispered back as he continued to stare.

Sean looked back to Joey. "When you're done with Coop, find that idiot Herman and take him back to the kitchen. No guns for him, not ever. You got that?"

"Yeah, Sean, I got that," Joey said as he turned Coop and headed for the garage.

Sean looked at Corbin. "Let's get the hose and see if we can put this out before the whole damn place goes up." Corbin picked up Bobby Ray by the back of the shirt and dragged him toward the front of the garage. Sean headed for the front of the garage then turned back and looked at the smoke rising high into the air.

"What about that?" Corbin said, as he pointed to the smoke.

"Yeah, I know," Sean said. "Let's just hope no one saw it."

Corbin said, "Sean, the damn fireball went way above the trees. Ya think someone could have seen it?"

Sean stopped at the corner of the garage and looked back, "Okay, we have someone on guard at the end of the driveway till it gets dark, then on the back porch for the night. When you get something to eat I want you out in the garage for the night."

"Well thanks," Corbin said. "You all get a bed and I get Coop in the garage."

"It's only for part of the night," Sean said. "Then I'll come relieve you."

"Why not just take him to the house?" Corbin asked.

"No," Sean said. "I don't trust that old man anymore than I trust Bobby Ray. That old man's trouble. I want him separate from the rest. Now let's get that fire out." Corbin dropped Bobby Ray on the ground in front of the garage. They entered the garage and Janis came out of the room where the generator was. Mose was standing just outside

the room, "What are you doing, Mose?" Sean asked.

"You don't let her go anywhere out of your sight, you hear?"

Mose was about to answer when Janis said, "You got my kids, Sean. You really think I'll try something?"

"Well then, what are you doing?" Sean asked.

Mose spoke up, "Sean, she was just tryin' to see how much gas is left, is all."

"Not much," Janis said as she wiped her hands with a rag.

"You were supposed to kick on the pump and that's it, so what about the gas?"

Janis threw the rag into a trash can. "We got half a tank in the generator. That's maybe four hours, and one more can in the room and that's it. Your buddy Bobby Ray has made quick work of the rest of it. Now the pump's on. Go put out the fire so I can shut it down or we will use more gas. This pump is separate from the one at the house. Two pumps, more gas, or is that too much for you to figure out?"

Sean walked up to her and said, "Yes, I got that. Janis, now go to the house and check on your kids. I'll call you when I need you. Mose, keep an eye on her. She goes nowhere near the gun room, you hear?"

Mose just shook his head then said, "Come on, ma'am. We better get." Joey tied Coop up to the workbench in a chair, then moved any and all tools away from him. He tied Coop's feet together, then tied the chair to the bench. Sean had opened the door and pulled the hose outside. When Joey was done with Coop, he headed back to the house. Corbin grabbed a shovel and he and Sean took the hose and headed to the shed.

As Janis left the garage, she looked at the wooden box that held the CB radio and then looked at the wall clock. It was 6:10 p.m. She had missed the six o'clock call. She wondered what Matt would think or do. She hoped he

wouldn't panic, come back, and race into a trap. She wanted him back very much, but how could she get a message to him about what was going on? In her heart, she wanted to see him, Andy, Lisa and Clive—but not if it meant they would walk into a trap. Not if it meant they could end up like Lenny. The next contact would be at midnight. She had to figure a way to get a message to them. In a way, she hoped they had gotten delayed and would come tomorrow. She had to find a way to talk to them first.

Corbin and Sean hosed down the back of the garage, now scorched black from the heat, and put out the few trees around the shed. Sean hosed down the remains of the shed, then Corbin shoveled on dirt to cool it as much as they could. As Corbin shoveled on the dirt, he could see two burnt shoes lying in the rubble. He shivered all over, then shoveled more dirt in that direction. When they were satisfied that the fire was out, they took the hose and put it in the garage in a pile along the wall. Sean checked the ropes on Coop, then leaned down and looked into his face, "Now old man, I'm going to leave you here alone for awhile. No trouble, or as I said, you won't be the one who gets hurt." Coop just stared back but said nothing. Corbin and Sean checked the generator, then closed the door.

As they started to leave, Coop spoke up, "Sean or whatever the hell your name is. You hurt one hair on Janis or those kids and I'll make it my life's work to hunt you down and kill you. You got that, sonny?"

Sean turned and looked at Coop, then in a low voice said, "Remember, old man, no trouble. You're the one who keeps them safe by what you do. They get hurt, it's because of you."

They turned and left. As they did, Corbin turned back to Coop, "See ya later, asshole."

When the door closed, Coop whispered to himself, "I get

my guns back and you go right after that crazy Bobby Ray, sonny."

Janis went to her room with Mose. Parker was awake but still weak. He had the kids sitting on the floor next to the bed. When Janis entered, they both got up and ran to her. She got down on one knee and held them as they cried. Once they were calmed, she went to Parker and checked his forehead for fever. "I'm fine ma'am," was all Jerry said as he looked up at her.

"No, you're not fine," Janis said as she pulled down the blankets and checked his legs. "You be still and I'll get you some food and water." She was satisfied with the bandages and covered him with blankets again.

"Ma'am, I'm sorry I can't help," Jerry said as he tried to rise up on one elbow.

Janis said, "Jerry, lie down. There's nothing you can do, not even if you were okay. We already lost one of your men. We don't need to lose you."

"We lost who?" Jerry asked. "Not..."

Janis stopped him in mid-sentence. "We lost Lenny," Janis said as she winked at him. "You know Lenny, your old partner. He came looking for you. I'm sorry, but they killed him."

"Lenny," Parker said, now confused. "Partner! But Janis, you know..."

Janis cut in, "Jerry, I'm sorry you lost your partner. I know you are confused, but rest now." She bent over and pulled the blankets up to his neck. As she did, she mouthed the name, "Clive," then shook her head ever so slightly and winked at him.

Jerry looked at her, then smiled and said, "Okay, ma'am, I guess you're right, I am tired. I gotta sleep. I gotta sleep." He squeezed her hand then winked back at her. Mose was standing at the door of the room and the children were in

front of him as he talked to them. He didn't notice the gestures between Jerry and Janis.

When Janis was finished with Jerry, she turned to Mose. "Mose, how did you end up with a bunch like this? You seem like a decent man."

Mose lowered his head to the floor, then took a deep breath. "Ma'am, I been in prison or some kind of jail most of my life. It's the only life I know. I ain't got no home, leastways not no more. My family lived in Virginia, least that's where they say I was born." Janis sat on the side of her bed and the children sat beside her. Mose moved to a chair in the corner and continued. "I got into trouble with a girl when I was young. Sure did love that girl but her daddy hated me, said I was trash. We tried to run away but we had no money so I went and robbed a store. We didn't get far when they caught us. They took her away and I never did see her again. Heard she killed herself. When I got out of jail I just ran away, ended up in Ohio, New York and Pennsylvania and such. Had some jobs but somehow I guess I always got into trouble. Seemed like the only time things was right for me was behind bars. Been in and out, mostly in, most of my life. I guess it's kinda the home I never had."

"But what are you doing now with these people, Mose?" Janis asked. "You are not like them."

Mose shook his head and then looked at Janis. "When the prison got bombed, everyone was running everywhere. I didn't know where to go or what to do. Sean told me to come with him. He ain't such a bad guy, ma'am. He acts tough but he hasta. He wouldn't survive inside if he didn't. You know what I mean?"

Janis shook her head then looked at the floor as she held the children. "Mose, look what's happened. Lenny's dead and the young man with you, if he doesn't get help he may be dead soon too. And us, what are they going to do with us?"

Mose sat forward in the chair, "They won't hurt you, ma'am, not you or the kids. I'll see they don't. 'Sides, Sean won't let them either. He's really not that bad. He's been a good friend to me, ma'am, He ain't like them."

"If he's not like them, Mose, then why are we where we are now? Me and my kids held prisoners, Jerry shot, Coop tied up in the garage, and Lenny dead."

Mose looked at her then said again, "I won't let nuttin' happen and Sean won't either. The rest of them is bad men, all 'cept the kid, just a lot like me when I was young. He got into trouble too but he's a good boy. He ain't had a good life either."

"How did you and Sean end up with the rest of them?" Janis asked.

Mose stood up, walked to the window, and looked out as he continued. "When the terror guys or whatever they are hit the prison, all hell broke loose. Me and the kid didn't know what to do. Sean told us to go with him and we got out. The other ones followed us. Sean didn't want them, 'specially that Bobby Ray and Herman. We all ended up in the woods together. They know Sean is smart. They act like they don't like him but they know he thinks better than them. They say they would get him if they could but they won't 'cause they know he has the smarts up there in his head. They know he can get them away. None of them thinks like Sean." Mose then turned to Janis and walked to her, "Ma'am, you stay away from all of them, you and the kids. Me, Sean and the kid are the only ones you can trust. You make a good effort to stay away from Bobby Ray and Herman, you hear me? Herman got something bad wrong inside his head. He killed his own mom and dad, 'magine that. He's scared to death of little children. Somethin' happened bad to him when he was little. He likes to hurt people, all 'cept kids. As I said, he's scared of little kids. And

that damn Bobby Ray, he's just plain loco crazy. I wonder why God put a man like him on this earth. He ain't got no heart or soul. That man's just pure evil and they say he's got a brother that's worse than him. 'magine that? Whole family must be evil bad. You gotta stay away from them two."

Janis was about to speak again when a voice came from the doorway. It was Sean. "Well Mose, you tell her enough about me and our friends?"

Mose turned quickly toward Sean, "Sean, we was just talking. That's all."

Sean walked to Mose and put his hand on his shoulder. "It's okay, Darnell, just don't let the others hear you. You know how they can get."

Mose turned to Sean. "Sean, you know this ain't right what we is doin' here? These people got no part in this. Let's get what we need and leave these people alone. Too many been hurt or killed. It ain't suppose to be this way, Sean. It ain't right."

Sean just patted Mose on the back and said, "Mose, take the children and play some games or something. I need to talk to Janis."

Janis sent the children to Robert's room with Mose. Sean sat in the chair in the corner.

Janis checked Jerry. He was asleep again. She turned to Sean and put her hands on her hips. "Mose is right. Why don't you take what you need and leave us here alone? We got no way to call for help and no car to go for help. Take food, water, guns, ammo, whatever. Just leave us alone."

Sean paused and stared at her, then got up and walked to her. He raised his hand to her face and she tried to push it away, but he grabbed her hand then gently put it aside. He used his thumb to wipe some of the dirt and soot from her face but she turned away from him. He grabbed her chin and turned her face again toward him. He looked into her eyes

and said, "I don't know who your man is or where he is, but he is a lucky man. Maybe had I met someone like you, my life might have been different." He leaned toward her to kiss her but she turned away. He took hold of her chin again and turned her face toward him, then put one arm around her and kissed her on the lips. She resisted but he held her.

When the kiss ended she looked up at him, then wiped her lips with her shirt and said, "I am a Christian woman, a married woman. Please don't do that again. I thought you said if you couldn't win a woman, you wouldn't have her. Change your mind?"

"No," Sean said, "I didn't. I can't win you, I know that. I just didn't want to spend the rest of my life knowing that I had at least the chance to kiss you and didn't take it. He's a lucky man, your old man. I'd be proud to have you on my arm anytime."

Janis turned away from him wiping her lips again and checked Jerry, then turned back to Sean. "Let us go, please."

"We'll talk about it later," Sean said. "Right now I need you to get Coop and talk him into looking at the kid. He's bad and getting worse."

"You really care about the kid?" Janis asked. "Mose says you are a good man, not like the others. Prove it. Let us go. Take what you want and go."

"I want you," Sean said with a smile. "But I can't have you. You don't need to worry. I'll keep you only for as long as I need you, then you're free. But make no mistake, when I say do what you're told, I mean it. We can't leave tonight. The kid's got to be patched, then rest. We'll go in the morning."

"And us?" Janis asked. "What about us?"

"If I don't need you, you stay. If I do need you, you go till I don't need you anymore."

"And my kids?" Janis asked.

"I'm working on that," Sean said. Then he put out his hand and said, "Come on. I need you to talk to Coop. The kid needs your help, both of you." Janis pushed his hand aside and walked past him out of the room.

CHAPTER 25
September

Janis had finished her painting and awakened Matt. Clive had put away the fishing equipment in the garage. Janis was in the kitchen, making supper with Lisa's help. Matt decided to clean out the fireplace for the evening fire and then get cleaned up. Clive offered to help, but Matt declined. Janis handed him a coffee and told him to please go feed the dog. Robert and Mary came out to talk to Clive for a few minutes, then went on with their playing. Clive fed Ginger, then stood with his elbows up on the top of the dog pen fence and watched the children play.

After a few moments, he walked around the side of the garage and stopped near the back corner. He stood quietly and looked at the forest below as the sun got close to the horizon at the top of the ridge at Scorpion's Tail. The forest was a lush deep green with tinges of color brought on by the approaching fall weather. The sky was turning a pastel shade of pink and orange and a cool breeze moved across the valley floor. Clive was at peace both mentally and physically for the first time in a long while. Most of the day had been good and he knew that he needed this time with these people he loved. They had done all they could up to this point in time; he knew that this time was just a brief pause to rest and think. He knew that they would soon

continue on the search that they all understood could not end until they had answers. The answers had to come, no matter whether they would be good or bad. There had to be some kind of closure for all of them.

What Clive feared most was that if it turned out that the Fallons had no closure, and how would it affect them for the rest of their lives. The never knowing about Andy would be worse than any other outcome. In his heart there was a small glimmer of hope. He didn't know quite why he felt that hope. Was it what Madison Lynn had said or was it a kind of whisper from God? All he knew was that the search for answers had to continue. In the end, they had to know. He also knew that he needed closure. The murders of a year ago had left a deep scar in his mind. What had become of Brian? Was he still alive and out there somewhere? With all of the police help and technology, why had they not been able to find him or Max? The losses that had come with the murders also lay heavy on his spirit. My God, it wasn't only Brian, but also Alice, and how he missed her. In some respects, his life was still turned upside-down. The murders, the lost friends, the attack on America, and the loss of Andy.

In his heart and mind, Clive longed for the calm and peace of days past. As a police officer, some would ask what calm? What peace? But to him, those days of the past were a cake walk compared to what had happened over the last year. He thought about all these things as he stood and looked deep into the forest. The weight of all of it was very great, and yet at this moment in time he was at peace. He was with people he loved, and they loved him deeply. He knew it was that bond that made it all bearable. The whispers came again and again to his mind. How was it, what Maddie had said, "All will be okay, peace will come." He turned and looked at the remains of the burned shed and his mind began to wander back again to that morning in the

church. A part of him didn't want to think about it again, but he knew it must be replayed, dealt with, then filed away in a place far back in the recesses of his mind. They were scars, they were real, they needed tending, then they could be left to fade into the gray.

July

The church was much quieter now, all except for the muffled crying of some of the young students and the women from the neighborhood. Andy was still sitting, his head down, his bow beside him. Matt had calmed Lisa and then walked to Maddie and touched her shoulder. She raised her head and looked at Matt. There were no tears, but the look in her face said it all. She touched his hand, then looked over at Andy and whispered to Matt, "Go to him. He needs both of you."

Matt turned. He and Lisa walked to Andy. The priest met Matt at the place where Andy was sitting and asked, "Are you all okay?"

Matt looked back at Maddie, who was now on her knees, her hands clasped in prayer, whispering to herself. "Yes, I think we all are," Matt said. "What about the others?"

Fr. Meyers looked back at the group and said, "As far as I can see, they are all okay. Not good, but no one was hurt."

"Good," Matt said, then looked back at Clive, who was sitting at the end of the last pew leaning on the shotgun barrel, his head down. "I think we are all okay, but I'm not so sure about him." He nodded in Clive's direction.

Fr. Meyers looked back at Clive, then turned to Matt. "He seems such a good man. Even as a police officer, moments like this must be very hard." He placed his hand on Andy's shoulder, then looked at Matt. "You stay here with your family. I'll go talk with him." Fr. Meyers turned and slowly walked to the back of the church.

When he reached the next-to-the-last pew, he sat down and turned toward Clive. Clive did not move. Fr. Meyers paused for a second, then whispered, "My son, are you alright?" There was no response. Clive just sat, his head hung low, slowly breathing. Fr. Meyers reached out and touched Clive on the shoulder. Clive jumped slightly as if he had just been awakened from a trance or light sleep. He raised his head and looked at Fr. Meyers, but there was no expression on his face. Fr. Meyers spoke again, "Clive, are you okay? Are you hurt?"

Clive took a deep breath, then placed the shotgun and the handgun on the bench beside him. He slowly looked at his hands and arms, then down the rest of his body. He looked back at Fr. Meyers and whispered, "Uh yeah, I guess. I guess I'm alright."

"You don't look alright," Fr. Meyers said.

"I'm fine," Clive said. "Except…" then he paused and lowered his head again.

"Except, for what?" Fr. Meyers asked, somewhat concerned. Clive did not answer. He just sat with his head down. Fr. Meyers touched him again. "Clive, what is it? What is wrong?"

Clive slowly raised his head again and stared into Fr. Meyers' eyes. "That was the second and third man I've had to kill in the last twenty-four hours. That in itself is bad enough, but why did it have to happen here, here in the church? I just don't know what else I, we, could have done. Part of me says I must protect the people but part of me wants to back away."

Fr. Meyers squeezed his shoulders, "Clive, you being here was God's will. Where would we have been if you and your friends had not come here to rest? Yes, even those men's lives were important to God, as all lives are, but some men stray from God. Those men had choices in their lives

and they chose wrong. They had no respect for us and most of all for their God, or they would not have come here to steal in God's house. It was the Lord's will that you be here this day at this appointed time. He sent you to us. To take a life is a bad, very bad thing for anyone to do, but sometimes he uses all of us in ways that must be done. The choice to do what was needed was not yours, it was his. God completes all his good purposes. People will do things that hurt him deeply. Through people like you, he brings good out of evil, light where there was darkness, joy from pain, calm out of chaos and yes, even life out of death. He has touched special people like you. Now, do not grieve. My son, this is a dark night of the soul. But what you do you must do for the good of the weak. You must stay tough, you must dig in, for this may get worse. When he asks you to run against the wind, he will be with you to strengthen you, to sustain you. That's what God does. When we find we have nothing left, that's when we find God is enough.

Clive looked away to the right side of the church and whispered, "Why has he chosen me?"

Fr. Meyers just shook his head and said, "None of us knows why we are called at times in our lives to do what we must, but it is his servants that answer."

Clive turned back to Fr. Meyers, "Called or not, it still cuts me deep when I must do things like today. I have even questioned my choice at times, the choice of being in law enforcement. It has cost me in more ways than you know, Father."

Fr. Meyers shook his head in agreement, then continued. "You were led to be who you are and to do what you do. God has a need for warriors on this earth and he has chosen you. The job you have been given is not easy and you will suffer losses, but it is what he needs you to do to protect some of his children. He has chosen to work through people

like you, not only to protect but to show some of us the way, the right way. My son do not let this time of evil weigh you down. It will pass, as we are told in Psalm 92: 'The wicked may flourish and spring up like grass for a moment, but ultimately they will wither away.' It is God's promise."

Clive took another deep breath, then turned his head up and looked at the ceiling. There on the ceiling was an old worn painting. It was a replica of Michelangelo's painting of God touching the hand of Adam. He stared at it for a moment as one lone tear rolled from the corner of his eye. He turned his head back to Fr. Meyers as he wiped the tear away, "If it is his will for me, then let it be so." Fr. Meyers stood up and put out his hand toward Clive. Clive took it in his and did not shake it, but squeezed instead as he whispered, "Thank you, and when you talk to him next, tell him I said thank you."

Fr. Meyers placed his other hand on Clive's and said, "You can talk to him yourself. He listens to his children. He always hears you, and if you listen closely you will hear him always." Fr. Meyers smiled, then turned and walked to the front of the church.

Clive watched him walk away as he whispered, "Thank you. Thanks, both of you." He turned and once again looked at the ceiling.

Clive disappeared for a while and when he returned he had his uniform shirt on again and appeared to be more composed than he had been. Matt and Andy had gone to get help for the two unconscious firemen who had been guarding the building; they had been brought into the church for first aid. Matt had tried to call Janis again but could not get a response. The bodies of the two convicts were removed from the church; Clive, Matt, Andy, Lisa and Maddie started to prepare for the trip home.

Clive had talked to Fr. Meyers and Maddie. They could

tell that Matt was very uncomfortable with not being able to contact Janis. Andy said nothing, but he just kept staring at Matt with a worried look on his face. Clive finally called all of them to the front of the church. Matt, Andy, Lisa and Maddie sat in the front seat and Clive and Fr. Meyers stood and talked for a moment or two. Clive turned to the four of them and said, "Fr. Meyers is going to take care of the students and the firemen. He has enough help and I talked to Jonas again and he will send more guards here. We will take some food and water, thanks to Fr. Meyers, and we are headed home. I suggest you gather whatever you need. We are leaving in less than half an hour."

Matt stood up and pulled Clive to the side as Fr. Meyers took Andy, Lisa and Maddie to get some supplies. Matt looked at Clive and, with a very concerned look on his face, said, "Clive, I've tried to contact Janis three or four times. I get no response."

Clive looked at Matt and shook his head. "Matt, you know we may be too far for contact. Chances are things are okay there but we are headed home. If we can get moving we could be home in three, maybe four hours, if things are better out there. If not, maybe eight hours or more."

Matt looked back at Clive and said, "We may be too far but something in my gut tells me things are not good back at camp. Don't ask me why I feel this way. I don't know. All I know is I want to get home." He forced a smile, then patted Clive on the shoulder as if to say, "I know you are trying to comfort me, my friend." He turned and walked to where Andy, Lisa and Fr. Meyers were putting items into bags.

Maddie walked up to Clive and stared up into his eyes, "We need to get home as soon as possible."

"Why?" Clive said, sort of sarcastically. "You have a feeling again."

"Yes, I have," Maddie said with a quick response. "When

will you finally get it through your fat head that some things I do know? I told you to watch your back, but did you? Of course not. Why would you ever listen to me?"

Clive broke into a wide smile. Not the response Maddie had figured on. "Calm down," he said. "You were right and I was, well, let's say skeptical."

"Skeptical!" Maddie said, now crossing her arms across her chest again. "You are the most stubborn man I have ever met. The facts are there right in your face. How long will you fight me on this?"

Clive, still smiling, put both hands on her shoulders and looked into her eyes. "Maddie, I don't know what you know or how, but you have my attention, so stop chewing on me. When you get those feelings or whatever they are, please tell me. As I said, you have my attention. Not my total belief, but my attention."

"Well, it's a miracle," Maddie said as she looked at him with a smirk on her face. "Clive Aliston actually believes me."

Clive continued to smile, then put his arms around her, pulled her to him, and hugged her. He whispered in her ear, "You saved my life, dear. Thank you so much for that." He let go of her and looked again into her eyes. "Please, I want you to tell me when you feel something. I'm not sure I understand, but I want to know. As you said, you can explain later."

Maddie unfolded her arms and changed her attitude, then responded, "Thank you for that. And yes, I will tell you. Now, I only have one thing to tell you. I don't know what lies ahead. I guess I'm just not getting it. What I feel is more confusion than anything." She then turned to see where Matt, Lisa and Andy were. When she realized they couldn't hear, she continued. "Something isn't right and I think it has to do with the family."

"Is it part of the confusion?" Clive asked.

"No," Maddie said as she sat down in the front pew. "The confusion is different from what I feel about the family. It's very vague, as if it's just too far from me, but it troubles me more than you know. It's almost as if it's blocking what I'm trying to get about the family. And one more thing," she added. "The feeling of confusion. It seems to have more of a connection to you than to the Fallons."

"To me?" Clive said, looking puzzled.

"Yes, to you," Maddie said. "To you, but I'm not sure. As I said, it's too vague, almost as if it was behind a curtain or in a fog. It's just not clear. I wish I could tell you more and I know this doesn't help with your belief in me but it's all I've got."

Clive looked down at her and realized the concern on her face. "Maddie, all I ask is that you tell me what you know and as soon as you know. I don't understand and I'm not sure I ever will or if I'll accept what you eventually tell me. But I need you to tell me. Can we just go on that for now?"

Maddie stood up and smiled at him, then pulled out her hand to shake his. He took her hand then she put her other arm around him and hugged him. As she held him, she whispered, "Clive Aliston, I may grow to like you yet." She let go of him, then looked him in the eyes and said, "We need to go now."

Clive agreed and the five of them gathered around Fr. Meyers and said their goodbyes. Lisa went to each of her dorm friends and said goodbye. Clive went to Andy and put his arm around him. "You saved my life, Son. You and that bow of yours. I know it bothers you what you did. But sometimes we are put in a place and a time when we are needed. It isn't always our call. You did what you were here to do. Accept it, then let it go. I just got that same advice from a friend. You did good, boy, and did the job. Now let's get home."

They all walked to the back of the church and out the front door. It was daylight, and as they all climbed into the jeep, Clive noticed Maddie looking intently at Andy. He looked at her until she saw him. He gave her a look as if asking, "What? What's wrong?"

She looked at him with a worried look on her face and just shook her head as if to say, "No. I just don't know." Clive climbed into the jeep and Matt started it. They all said their goodbyes again to Fr. Meyers.

As they pulled away from the front of the church, Clive turned and looked back at Maddie. He put his hand on her knee and squeezed, then smiled as if to say, "When you know, I will be waiting." They drove back to the main street, then turned left and started the journey back to camp.

CHAPTER 26
September

Janis made supper with Lisa's help and they all decided to eat on the screened-in porch. Everyone joined in to set the table and the meal was a time of talk and of memories of past events that had included them all at one time or another. There were many references to Andy but none were sad or unhappy. It was as if they were including him, even though he was not present. Even Clive did not find this unusual, for in his mind Andy was still right there with them. When the meal ended, Lisa took Robert and Mary and got them cleaned up for bed. Clive and Matt went to the garage so Matt could show Clive the new CB radio he had just purchased from a farm family who had decided to move away. Janis knew it wasn't the radio that the two of them wanted to talk about. Matt was ready to start the search again and she knew that it would be the topic of their discussion. She cleaned up the dishes, put away the leftovers, and decided to have a cup of tea with honey. After the tea was ready, she moved outside and sat on the top step leading down from the screened-in porch. She sat and looked at the darkening sky and sipped her tea. Her mind went back to that night at camp, the night after Lenny had been killed.

July

Sean and Corbin had put out the fire at the shed and Corbin had gotten something to eat. Complaining, he went out to the shed to watch Coop. After everyone had gotten something to eat, Sean asked Janis if she would talk Coop into taking a look at the kid. He was trying to avoid confrontation. Janis did as she was asked; she and Coop tended to the kid and then again to Jerry Parker.

Janis had missed the 6 p.m. contact time, but it wasn't that contact that she worried about. It was the next one, at midnight. She was afraid that if Matt didn't hear from her a second time, he would hurry home and get caught in the same kind of trap that Lenny had walked into. She had to find a way to talk to Matt. It was either that or somehow get them all away from camp. If Matt did come home, it would be better if he found the place empty than if he walked into a trap. She had to do something. She had guessed that since they were not home by now, it would probably be daylight before they arrived. She knew Matt and Clive well enough to know they probably would not chance the drive home in the dark. She figured that as much as Matt probably wanted to get home, he would not risk Lisa's safety at night on dark roads. Even if Matt wanted to try, she felt sure that Clive would have talked him out of it. She was convinced that she was right, but she still needed to get a message out. How could she get to that radio? It was almost ten o'clock when Sean went out to relieve Corbin at the garage.

Corbin had come back after going to the refrigerator for something to eat, then gone to the living room. Herman was sound asleep on the couch. Janis had just checked on Jerry again; when she came out of the room she saw Corbin grab Herman and pull him off the couch to the floor. Herman, who was in deep sleep, started to protest when Corbin kicked him in the stomach and yelled, "Get the hell out of

my bed, you asshole." Herman curled up into a ball, holding his stomach and yelling with what air he had left. Corbin reached down and grabbed him by the front of the shirt and pulled him up to his face and yelled, "Shut up, you son of a bitch."

Janis said in a low voice, "Corbin, if you wake the children, none of us will get any sleep."

Corbin dropped Herman and started toward Janis, when Joey, who had been out on the porch, came into the kitchen. He had heard the noise and stepped into the living room just as Corbin got face to face with Janis. "The lady's right, Corbin. You wake those kids and it's going to be a long night. Now, use your head man."

Janis stood her ground and looked up at Corbin. Corbin looked at Joey and said, "All right, all right, go back to the porch. I'm going to get some sleep." He glared at Janis and then turned and walked back to the couch. Herman was still on the floor, moaning. He kicked Herman again and said, "I said shut up, asshole." Herman curled again into a ball and covered his head. Corbin grabbed a pillow from the couch and threw it at Herman. "Take that pillow and get over on the floor by that fireplace. I catch you near me and I'll do you right here. You got that, asshole?" Herman took the pillow and slid across the floor to the rug in front of the fireplace.

Joey said again, "Corbin, man, will you hold it down."

Corbin sat down on the couch, then said to Joey, "Go back to the porch and do your job. You want McRoy after you?" Joey looked at Janis and shook his head, then turned and left for the porch. Corbin lay down on the couch and laid the shotgun right beside him.

Bobby Ray was seated in the chair at the end of the room. He had watched what had happened but had not said a word. He slowly pulled up the foot rest on the recliner as he

stared at Janis, still standing at the entrance to the hall. The room was quiet except for Herman's snoring. Bobby Ray watched Janis, as she stared back at him. As she turned to go down the hall, she heard him say with a low laugh, "Good night, darling. Sweet dreams. I'll be thinking about you. Oh, will I be thinking about you."

Janis shivered all over and headed for Robert's room, where Robert, Mary and Mose were sleeping. She slipped into the room and in the dim light she checked the children, then looked at Mose asleep on the floor next to the bed. She knew that he wouldn't let anything happen to them. Mose seemed like such a good old man, worlds apart from the men he was with. She took a blanket from the foot of the bed and covered Mose, then went back to the room Jerry was in and checked on him and the kid, whom they had put on the floor on a large piece of foam rubber. She checked them both for fever, then stood for a moment and looked at the kid, now sound asleep. She whispered, "You're just a baby. How did you end up with these men?" She shook her head, then left the room and went back to the children's room and sat in a rocking chair in the corner of the room. She took a throw that was over the back of the chair and covered herself to the neck, then sat and stared at the children for several minutes. She looked at the clock. It was 10:50 p.m. She had to make a call at midnight, but how?

Janis sat awake, listening to the sounds of the house. The forty-five minutes or so that passed seemed like an eternity, but at about 11:35 p.m., she quietly got up. After checking the children, she again slipped out of the room. She moved quietly down the hall, then from the dark of the hall, scanned the living room. Herman was still on the floor in front of the fireplace; he had his legs pulled up to his chest with his butt up in the air, much like a small child. She just looked at him and shook her head. Corbin was fast asleep on the couch,

with the shotgun clutched in his arms. Bobby Ray was nowhere in sight. The thought of him wandering around sent a chill through her, but she had to make that call. She had to get through. She tip-toed through the living room, then looked around the corner into the kitchen. No one there. She moved quietly through the kitchen, making sure not to run into anything. She knew Joey had been on the porch, so she tried to look out to see where he was. She couldn't see him, but the right side of the porch was too far for her to see without opening the door. She took a deep breath, then slowly opened the door. When it was open wide enough she looked to the right. Joey was lying on top of the picnic table, sound asleep. She thought, "If Sean could see you now, Joey, he would kick your butt." She moved quietly out onto the porch and slowly closed the door. She was between the kitchen door and the screen door of the porch when Joey moved. She froze in her tracks. Joey rolled over, made a few sounds, then continued his deep breathing. She moved to the screen door, then slowly opened it and slipped out onto the back steps. She stopped for a moment and took several deep breaths, then moved down the steps to the sidewalk. She walked the sidewalk to the corner of the porch and looked out at the garage. She could see a dim light from the generator room but she saw no one moving. She looked out at the driveway to the right, but saw no one. The thought went through her mind, "Where is Bobby Ray?"

She waited several minutes, planning what to do, when she got to the garage. How could she make a call with Sean out there? Maybe she could lure him outside and knock him out, but with what? She looked around in all directions for something. She remembered an old walking stick that Matt had always left near the door of the garage. If it was there, it would have to do. She took a couple of deep breaths, then stepped away from the house and out into the driveway. She

was almost to the garage and she could see the stick against the white garage siding, when suddenly she was grabbed from behind and spun around. For just a second, she saw a face. It was Bobby Ray. Before she could do anything, Bobby Ray came around with a punch that hit her solidly on the left side of the jaw. She saw flashes of light and felt herself falling to the ground. She landed flat on her back and her vision faded in and out. First she saw a gray haze, then the stars of the night sky, then a haze again. She felt something pulling on her legs as she was turned and dragged across the driveway and up onto the grass of the back yard. The gray haze came and went and she felt as if she couldn't move anything. Suddenly, the pulling stopped and the next thing she felt was someone on top of her. Her blouse was slowly opened then pushed slowly aside, exposing her chest. She knew she had to move but nothing worked. It seemed like she just couldn't pull herself together. She felt a hand on her throat and another pulling at the snap and zipper on the front of her jeans. The hand left her throat, then like a bolt of lightning all her senses came back. She opened her eyes wide and swung her right hand up in a fist into the side of Bobby Ray's head. The punch took him by surprise and he leaned to her left and moaned. She quickly rolled to the left, pushing Bobby Ray off her to the ground. She rolled to the right and jumped to her feet. At the same time, Bobby Ray was up on his knees and starting to get up. She stepped forward and kicked him in the chest, knocking him back on one hand. He yelled, "You bitch. I'll kill you." She turned and ran toward the garage, but slipped on the limestone in the driveway and fell on her right side. She started to get up when she was grabbed by the back of the hair and thrown to the ground. In a second, Bobby Ray was on top of her again. She put up her hands to block his arms but he pushed them aside and pulled her arm back to punch her again. Suddenly,

from the left, a dark, silhouette appeared. Just as she looked in that direction the butt of a gun slammed into Bobby Ray's head, knocking him to the ground to her right. She rolled away and was about to get up to her knees when a hand grabbed the back of her shirt, pulled her up, and turned her around.

It was Sean McRoy. She pushed at him, trying to get away, but he turned her toward the garage and pushed her back into the siding. She started to scream, but Sean covered her mouth and with his face only inches away said sternly, "Stop. You're okay. You're okay. Stop." She started to calm down, pushed several feet away pulled up her shirt and quickly closed it.. Sean just stood there, put up his hand, palm out, and said, "Calm down. It's over. Calm down." She looked at him, then turned toward the garage and began to cry.

Sean walked over to Bobby Ray, picked him up and pulled him to his feet. "You son of a bitch. What did I tell you." Bobby Ray just looked back, saying nothing, as if he were in a deep fog. Sean shook him with one hand and yelled, "You hear me, asshole?" He pushed Bobby Ray away and Bobby Ray just stood there, weaving back and forth as if he was going to fall down. Sean raised his gun and aimed it at Bobby Ray. "You make one more move toward anyone and I blow your head off, you got that? Now get back to the house."

Bobby Ray slowly turned and started back to the house. Sean started to turn toward Janis when she came running past him and straight at Bobby Ray. She had the walking stick in her hands and when she got close enough, she slammed it down across the top of Bobby Ray's back. The stick snapped in two pieces as it drove Bobby Ray to the ground. The top piece flew past Joey's head as he came down the sidewalk. The other half was in Janis' hand, and

had a long sharp point. Bobby Ray fell face down in the grass. In a second, Janis was on top of him, the stick turned like a dagger. She raised her arms as if she was going to drive the end into Bobby Ray. Then changed her mind. Sean stepped beside her and took the stick out of her hand. Joey yelled, "Sean, let her go. One of us is going to do him anyway. Let her go."

Sean yelled, "No. No more. Enough is enough. Now get that piece of shit out of my sight before I let her go at him." Joey picked up Bobby Ray and started to drag him toward the house. Sean put out his hand toward Janis and she just looked up at him, "Come on," was all he said as he curled his fingers as a gesture for her to take his hand. She did not take his hand but started slowly to get up as she snapped her jeans and zipped her zipper. When she got to her feet, Sean grabbed her and pulled her in close. "Just what the hell are you doing out here? What were you up to?"

"Nothing," Janis whispered into his face. "I just came out for some fresh air. That bunch you have in there could use a bath."

Sean pulled her even closer and whispered back, "That had better be all." He pushed her away and added, "Button up that shirt. I'm getting tired of pulling people off of you. Next time I just might look the other way, or…"

"Or, what?" Janis said, as she proceeded to close her blouse. "Or you might have a go at me?"

Sean looked away for a moment, then clenched his teeth and said, "Get back into that house, and I mean now." Janis sneered back at him then turned and walked back to the house.

When she entered the kitchen, Bobby Ray was sitting in a kitchen chair, his head back, his face covered in dirt and blood, and his eyes closed. Janis looked at the clock. It was 12:07 a.m.; she had missed the call again. Sean came in

behind her. She turned to him and said, "The generator will be out of gas soon. We need to add more or shut it off, one or the other."

Sean thought for a moment then said, "I'll send Joey out. He can do it. You stay here."

Janis said, "Fine. You send him, but he has to shut it off to add gas. That means no light to pour, and besides, it's very hard to restart if you're not used to it."

"Fine," Sean said. "You and I will go, then you get back to that room and I don't want to see you till morning."

As she started back to the door, Bobby Ray moaned and fell sideways off the chair to the floor. They both looked at him but let him lie, and left the kitchen for the garage. Janis had only one thought in mind. She had to find a way to get a call in, but how? She and Sean entered the garage and Janis walked directly to Coop, who was once again tied to a chair and the work bench. She pulled the gag out of his mouth and he took a deep breath, then, in a raspy voice, said, "Thanks, Janis."

She turned to Sean, who was standing about ten feet away. "Do we have to keep him gagged all night?"

"Depends on him," Sean said. "All I've been getting from him is mouth. He promises to shut up, and yeah, no gag."

Janis got down on one knee and looked at Coop. "Promise me you will keep quiet."

Coop started to say, "I'm not…" when Janis put her hand over his mouth and winked.

"Please, Coop. For your own good, just remain quiet." She winked again, then stood up.

Coop looked at Sean, then at Janis. "Okay, dear. But only for you." He then gave Sean a nasty look.

Sean said, "Good old man. Now see that you keep it that way."

Janis turned to Sean, "Can we give him some water? The gag has his mouth all dried out."

Sean walked in closer then said, "Old man, just be glad you got her on your side." He looked at Janis, then added, "You go put gas in the generator. I'll get him the water." Janis turned to go to the generator room and Sean grabbed her arm and stopped her, "You shut it down, put in the gas and turn it back on and nothing else. You got that? You try anything and this old man here is going to pay. We understand each other?"

"Yes," was all Janis said as she pulled away from Sean and headed for the room. When she got inside, she looked around quickly and saw a large crescent wrench on a shelf near the door. She looked out at Sean, who was giving Coop a drink from a bottle of water. She quickly picked up the wrench and placed it on the floor under the generator, then yelled out to Sean, "The lights will be out. Can you come in here and hold a flashlight?" Sean finished giving Coop a drink, then moved into the room. He took a flashlight from the shelf, then backed up away from Janis and stood in the doorway, pointing the shotgun at Coop with the other hand. Janis looked at him and said, "What's the problem? You don't trust me?"

"No," Sean said. "I don't. If I point the gun at you, you would probably try something anyway in the dark. You don't fear much for a woman. Maybe God made a mistake. Maybe you should have been John instead of Janis." He sort of chuckled at his own joke.

"Very funny," Janis said.

Janis leaned toward the generator to shut it off when Sean added, "Remember, the gun's on Coop and it's a shotgun. I don't need to be able to see him to hit him. Don't try and be funny. Fill the tank and that's it." Janis gave him a disgusted look, then shut down the generator. The room

went black. Sean held the flashlight on her as she worked. When the tank was full, she started it again and the lights came on. She looked down at the wrench and knew it would have to wait till later. Her heart sank but she couldn't gamble with Coop's life. When she was finished, she walked out of the room and started toward Coop again. "Where are you going?" Sean asked.

She turned and said, "To tell him good night, if it's okay with you?"

Sean smiled and said, "Fine, but be quick. We all need sleep."

Janis turned back to Sean. "Yeah, we all need sleep. Is Coop supposed to sleep in the chair? The least you could do is tie him up on the floor."

"No," Sean said. "I've had enough trouble from him and you. He stays in the chair. He'll survive." Janis put her hands on her hips and gave Sean a sneer. "I said no," Sean repeated. "Now tell him good night so we can get to bed."

Janis walked to Coop and leaned down and hugged him, whispering in his ear, "In the morning, more gas." She looked into his eyes and winked, kissed his forehead and said, "Good night."

Sean said, "Okay, that's it. Enough of the goodnight. Let's go." Janis turned to walk away and Sean looked at Coop. "No trouble, you hear me? Remember, it's her who could get hurt, old man."

Coop looked at Sean and sternly said, "You touch her or those kids and you deal with me."

Sean laughed then added as he left, "You remember old man, you keep quiet or the gag is back. Now shut up and get some sleep."

Janis and Sean left the garage and headed for the house. As Janis walked out ahead of Sean, she thought to herself, "Matt, don't come till I call you. Please don't come till I call

you." She knew in her heart that she had to make a call in the morning, even if it meant her life.

CHAPTER 27
July

Janis had spent a near sleepless night. The longest period of time that she slept was maybe forty-five minutes. She checked on Robert and Mary and Parker and the kid several times. The clock in the room nearly drove her crazy with its constant tick. It was funny. She had never noticed it before. She had just dozed off in the early hours of the morning, when she was awakened by Sean. "Janis, I need you to look at the kid. Something's wrong." She got up and stretched to get out the stiffness from the night in the chair. Sean repeated, "Janis, I need you to look at him now."

"Okay, Okay," Janis said as she walked past him to the hallway. She went to the bedroom where Parker and the kid were, and put her hand on the boy's head. He was breathing very hard and he had a fever. She tried to awaken him, but got no response. She took a look at the wound on his shoulder, then recovered it. She turned to Sean and in a very serious tone said, "The wound must be infected and the poison is spreading. He has a high fever and if you don't get him help you're going to lose him. You say you are in control. Well, let's see just how much in control you are. Get him some help. He needs a hospital—and soon."

Sean shook his head and said, "No. No hospital. We can't chance bringing anyone else here. Besides, we will be

leaving today."

Janis folded her arms across her chest and glared at him. "You say you care about the young boy. You say you're in charge. Then be in charge and get him some help."

"I will," Sean said. "But no hospital. We have a doctor here anyway. We'll use him."

"He's not the type of doctor you need now," Janis said, adding, "And besides, this boy needs antibiotics and I think we are a little short on those around here."

Sean shook his head and again said, "No. You and I will go get Coop and he will do what he can for the kid."

"Fine," Janis said as she pushed past Sean and entered the hallway. She headed for the living room, then abruptly turned back to Sean, who was right behind her. "You say you care about him. Mose told me you are a good man, yet you refuse to save his life. You say you're in control, but are you really? I can see these men look up to you, but is it false faith they have? Do you really care about any of them or anybody else, or is it just Sean McRoy that counts?"

Sean was about to shout at her when he realized that Corbin, Joey and Herman were awake and listening to what she had said. They all were staring at Sean with questioning looks. Instead of shouting, he repeated, "Let's go get Coop." Janis just shook her head and whispered, "Yeah, you care," then turned and entered the kitchen. As they went through the kitchen she saw Bobby Ray, still lying on the kitchen floor under the table.

As they passed, Sean yelled at him, "Bobby Ray, get up. We need some supplies." He got no response. He stopped and kicked him in the leg to wake him. Sean bent over and repeated, "Wake up, damn it. I said we need supplies. We're leaving soon. Now get up and see what you can put together."

"Yeah, yeah," Bobby Ray said as he looked up at Janis.

"Hi, honey. You have a good night? I did. I had you on my mind." He started that crazed laugh when Sean kicked him again. Bobby Ray looked at Sean and clenched his teeth. "Hey, McRoy, don't do that again."

"Or what?" Sean said as he stared at Bobby Ray. "Or you'll do what?" Bobby Ray said nothing. He just looked at Janis again and smiled, showing his bad teeth. Sean stood back up straight and said, "I didn't think so." Then he added, "Wake up and get up and get help if you need it, but put some food together and start now." Sean and Janis left the house and went to the garage to get Coop. Janis talked to him and he agreed to look at the kid. When they got to the room, Coop started to look at the boy's wounds when Jerry Parker started to get out of bed.

"Whoa, whoa," Janis said as she stopped him. "Just where do you think you're going?"

"The boy's worse off than me," Jerry said. "Put him in the bed. I'll lie on the floor."

"No, you're not," Janis said as she held him on the bed. "You start those wounds bleeding again, then we have two of you to deal with. Now lie back down. The boy will be fine right where he is." Sean had been standing in the doorway, watching. Corbin was right behind him.

Corbin pushed past Sean and sat in the chair at the side of the room. He looked at Parker and with a smirk said, "Imagine a cop that's concerned about a con. Wouldn't have believed that if I hadn't heard it with my own ears."

Janis turned and faced Corbin, "Yeah, you're right. He's concerned. He's concerned because he's a good man. Because he cares about people. Unlike your leader here, who doesn't care even about his friends. All that matters to him is McRoy."

"That true?" Corbin said as he looked at Sean. Sean didn't respond, but his face showed anger. He grabbed Janis

by the arm and started to drag her out of the room.

Coop stood up and started toward them, when Sean, still holding onto Janis, put the muzzle of the shotgun under Coop's chin and whispered, "You try anything old man and she pays for it. You got that?" Coop stopped and said nothing. He just stared at Sean.

Coop looked at Janis, who said, "Coop, I'll be fine. Just help the kid. I'll be fine." Coop bent down and continued to work on the boy. Janis pulled her arm away from Sean, then looked at Parker and said, "Jerry, you stay in that bed. You hear me?"

"Yes, ma'am," was all Jerry said.

Janis entered the hall as Sean spoke to Corbin. "You stay here and watch the doc."

"Yeah, sure," Corbin said, staring at Sean.

Sean followed Janis to the kitchen. Janis turned to say something to him but he turned her back around and said, "Outside." Janis could tell that he was furious.

When they got to the porch, Bobby Ray was picking up some cardboard boxes. He turned and said, "Well, hi honey." It was all he got to say as Sean stopped and glared at him. "Okay, okay," Bobby Ray said. "I'm working on it."

Sean looked at Janis and said, "Outside." He followed her down the steps then pushed her out to a large tree in the back yard. He pushed her to the back side of the tree then spun her around and backed her into the tree. He grabbed her jaw with one hand and squeezed, "I know what you're trying to do and it stops now. You get my meaning? I'm trying to keep things civil here. You realize what happens if they are left to their own devices. I told you I wanted no trouble. We rest, we get what we need, and we move on, no one gets hurt."

Janis tried to pull away, saying, "No one, you mean no one like Lenny." Sean squeezed her jaw tighter and pushed

her harder against the tree.

He moved his face within inches of hers and whispered, "It stops now or I turn Herman or Bobby Ray loose on someone. Don't think you want to see that. Now do I have your cooperation or not?" He gave her a push and let go of her face.

She started to rub her jaw as she whispered, "Okay, I hear you. Just don't hurt anyone else."

"Then we understand each other?" Sean said as he backed away.

"Yeah," was all Janis said.

"Now go help Coop," Sean said as he stepped back away from her. Janis turned and walked back to the house. Sean called Joey out and asked him to see if the truck or Lenny's car would run, then he entered the house again.

As Janis walked through the kitchen, she looked at the clock. It was after 7:00 a.m. She had missed the time again. She had to make a call, but how? Coop did all he could for the boy, but he told Janis he needed medicine and there was no way he should be moved. Janis told Sean, but all he said was "We'll see."

Janis went to the kitchen and started to get some food out of the boxes. Sean followed her in, then sat at the table. "What are you doing?" he asked.

"I'm getting Coop a sandwich, if you don't mind? He hasn't eaten since early yesterday. He's the only doctor you have right now, the only one we all have. I think it might be a good idea to give him something, don't you?"

"Okay," Sean said, "Then he's back out to the garage."

"And what about us?" Janis asked.

"What about you?" Sean asked.

"You said you would let us go when you left. You're planning on leaving, so what about us?"

Just then, Joey came into the kitchen. "Sean, the truck

and Lenny's car have had it. That gunfight between Corbin and Lenny put the end to that. They're all shot up."

Sean looked at Janis. "Are there any other vehicles around here?"

"No," Janis said. "I told you before, my husband has the only vehicle around, and he's not here. He has it."

Joey looked at Sean, "Hey, you know her old man's been gone for at least a day that we know of. Would you leave her and the kids here for any length of time with no car?"

Sean looked at Janis, "When's he due back?"

Janis said, "I don't know."

"Oh, you know," Sean said. "And my guess is it's probably sooner than later."

Sean looked at Joey. "Let's get prepared to leave but I think we'll wait a while, see if Mr. Fallon comes home and wants to lend us his car." Janis said nothing but a chill ran through her. She knew she had to do something quickly. Coop finished his work on the boy and checked Parker again, then he was led to the kitchen and given something to eat.

The children had awakened and Janis fed them and Mose but she told Sean she wouldn't feed the others. They could get food for themselves. Sean didn't argue; he just told all of them to get their own. It was close to nine o'clock when Janis told Sean that the generator was going to need more gas. Corbin entered the kitchen, and he and Sean started to talk about their next move. Janis cut in and reminded him again about the generator.

Sean looked at Joey and said, "Take Coop out and tie him up again. Have Herman clean up around here and have him and Bobby Ray help you push the car and truck out of sight of the driveway. We want it all to look normal when her old man gets here."

Joey asked, "What about the generator?"

Sean said, "Take her with you when you tie up Coop.

Have her gas the generator but don't take your eyes off her or him. I want to talk to Corbin about where we go from here." Sean then looked at Janis. "Remember, no trouble."

Janis didn't respond. She just stared at him.

Sean continued his plans with Corbin and Joey. Coop and Janis headed for the garage. Mose took the kids outside to the swing set and sandbox and started to play with them. Once outside, Janis looked at Mose and said, "Please, if there's any trouble, take them inside."

Mose looked at her and said in soft voice, "No need to fret ma'am. I'll keep these babies safe."

Joey grabbed Janis's arm and said, "Come on. Let's go." As Janis, Coop and Joey entered the garage, Janis remembered the time on the clock in the kitchen. It was 8:50 a.m. It wasn't a check-in time, but she prayed that after three missed contact times, Matt would have left the radio on. She was not sure what she could do, but whatever it was it had to be now.

Joey pushed Coop over to the chair and sat him down. He told Janis to help but Janis said, "I won't do anything. My kids are out there. If I don't get the gas in this thing soon, it will quit and it can be really hard to start when you let it run out of gas. Sean wouldn't be real happy about that."

Joey ignored her statement and said, "Will you get over here and help me!"

Coop spoke up, "Hey sonny, she's right. She won't do anything and I won't either. Now just tie me up and let her put gas in that thing before it stops. Even I have had trouble with it when it runs out."

Joey looked back at Janis with a disgusted look and pointed his handgun at her. "Okay, you put gas in it. I'll tie him up, but you try anything and I'll do him right here, right now, you got that?"

"Yes," Janis said as she turned and entered the

storeroom. Joey tied Coop's hands behind him and to the chair, then bent down to tie his feet. Janis picked up the crescent wrench from under the generator then looked out around the door to see what Joey was doing.

Coop was looking at her and she showed him the wrench. He nodded an okay, then said to Joey, "You have the tie on my one hand too tight. It's going numb."

Joey looked up at Coop and said, "So what?"

Coop looked at Joey and said, "If I can't use my hand later, I'm no good to you to help the kid. Now I'm telling you it's too tight. Please."

Joey finished the rope on his feet, then said, "Okay, okay." He leaned back behind Coop to retie the rope. Janis had been slowly moving toward Joey and was only a few feet away, the wrench in her hand. When Joey finished he stood up and looked at Coop, "That better, old man?"

Coop smiled and said, "No, but this will be." At that second, Janis brought the wrench down on the back of Joey's head. Joey staggered backwards, then slowly turned around and faced Janis. As he did, Janis came down with another swing and the wrench hit Joey in the forehead. He collapsed and hit the floor. Janis paused for a second, then went to the workbench and got a knife to cut the rope holding Coop. Coop picked up Joey's gun and said, "Come on. We got to get out of here. My truck's up on the hill."

"No," Janis said. "There's no time to get help. We have to do something ourselves. I can't leave the children. Besides, I have to contact Matt. If he comes here, he will walk into a trap."

Coop said, "I can't leave you here."

Janis put both her hands on his shoulders and said in a stern voice, "Coop, I can't go. You have to. If they think you went for help, maybe they'll leave and leave us alone."

"Or maybe they'll kill you," Coop said.

"No, I don't think so," Janis said. "Sean may be bad, but not that bad. Now, go. Please go. I have to make a call." She added, "If they think you went for help, they will want to leave here. They will go in the truck or Lenny's car. I think neither will run. If they go on foot, I will lead them away to the ridge. It's where I'll tell Matt and Clive to intercept. If I can contact them. You know the way I'll go. Get away. Hide and watch for what happens next. If they drive off, so be it. If they walk out, I'll use the path to the big oak. If I can get through to Matt, they will need your help. Coop, they have to be close. I can almost feel it. Matt will know where to go."

Coop hugged her, then said, "I hope you're right."

He kissed her on the cheek, and she whispered again, "Go."

Coop ran to the door, and around the side of the garage near the woods. He stopped at the bush where he had left his 10-gauge shotgun and whispered, "They won't be so tough after they get a taste of you." He turned and ran into the forest above the garage.

Janis quickly opened the wooden box that contained the CB radio and turned it on. She watched the door of the garage as she keyed the mike. "Fallon two, this is Fallon one. Do you hear me?"

CHAPTER 28
September

It was close to 11:30 p.m. when Clive rolled over on the couch. Earlier, Clive and Matt had discussed their ideas about what to do next. Janis and Lisa had cleaned up and the kids had played for awhile before bed. All of them were lying down and asleep by about ten or ten-thirty. Clive had lain on the couch for nearly an hour trying to sleep, but so many thoughts kept running through his mind. He finally got up and rubbed his face, then went to the kitchen, poured some water in a cup, and put it in the microwave. He looked around for instant coffee but found none. All he could find was regular tea and chamomile tea. He picked the chamomile, made the cup and then went out on the screened porch and sat down in one of the chairs. He could see the stars through the porch screen, and he put his head back and looked up at them while he sipped his tea. He thought about who else could be out there now looking up at the same stars. Andy? Brian? His mind returned to that morning when they left the city for camp.

July

Clive, Matt, Andy, Lisa and Maddie headed back up through Oakland the way they had come in. The fires were out the city seemed more calm. There was still a large

presence of police and firemen. As they got near the Oakland limits, they saw Jonas standing near a large ladder truck, holding a cup of coffee while talking to the driver. Clive asked Matt to stop. When Jonas saw them, he stopped his conversation and walked to them with a wide smile on his face. When he reached the jeep he said, "Well, Clive, I gather you are headed home?"

"Yes," Clive said. "We need to get there and check on the rest of the family. We haven't heard from them since yesterday."

Jonas said, "I hope they will be fine."

"I know they will be fine," Matt spoke up as he put out his hand in front of Clive and shook Jonas's. "Thanks so much for all you did. I hope your daughter is okay."

Jonas said, "You're welcome, and she is. I just got word this morning that she is in a shelter and she is okay."

"Thank God for that," Clive said as he also shook Jonas's hand.

Maddie looked at Jonas and said, "I knew she would be." They talked for a few more minutes then Jonas told them goodbye and good luck. He said he would try to call ahead to alert the authorities that they were coming and have them pass it on down the line. He figured it might help get them home faster.

As they pulled away, Matt looked at Clive and said, "Now, there's a good man."

"Amen," Clive said as they moved toward Washington Boulevard. As they traveled on they were making much better time on the way back than on the way down to the city. There seemed to be less going on in the way of trouble. As Jonas had promised, some of the road blocks had been notified that they were coming and they were passed through quickly. They traveled down Washington Boulevard up along the Allegheny River. They passed through the town

of Verona and then were stopped in Oakmont. They could not cross the Oakmont bridge as they had done before because of trouble on the other side. After conferring with the local police, they were routed up the hill on the back way and headed in the direction of New Kensington and the Tarentum Bridge. It would take some extra time, but they had no choice. They drove up the hill and passed the huge Oakmont Country Club, then followed the winding road high above the river. As they drove, they saw little to no traffic except for police and fire personnel. They were stopped a couple of times but then moved on.

Clive could see that Matt and Lisa were getting impatient as they continued on. He knew how they felt. The fact that they had not heard from Janis was weighing on his mind also. They came to the bottom of the hill and turned onto Route 366 headed for the Tarentum Bridge and finally back the way they had come. Even with the detour up over the hill from Oakmont, they were making good time. When they reached the Tarentum/New Kensington bridge, they were met by another road block on the New Kensington side of the bridge. They were checked by authorities then told to move on, but they were also told that the way to Bull Creek Road was blocked because of trouble at the Route 28 overpass. Clive thought about the police officers he had met there on the way into the city and hoped they were all okay. They crossed the bridge and were told to turn left and swing down under the bridge to the road along the river. They had just started up the road when Matt pulled the jeep to the side of the road in front of a sign that read, Riverview Memorial Park. Clive looked at him, puzzled, then Matt spoke up, "Clive, I know we said we would leave the CB off, but I'm going to turn it on. It's daylight and things seem to be getting a little better. We haven't heard from Janis since yesterday. I know it's probably because of the distance, but I'd sure feel

better just in case she has tried to get in touch with us and is worried."

Clive reached down and turned on the CB, then looked at Matt. "I think we are all worried, I was going to suggest it myself." Matt smiled at Clive, then put the jeep in gear and started again. They drove along the river through Tarentum, into the town of Brackenridge. They met the Brackenridge police at a T-intersection by the corner of a large steel mill. At that point, they were turned up the hill and given directions to put them back on Bull Creek Road through Fawn Township. It seemed to Clive that even with the delays, just having the CB on made Matt feel better. Each time they heard something on the CB they turned up the volume, but it wasn't Janis.

They moved through Fawn Township and back the way they came. Within half an hour they were back on Route 422 near Butler. They were stopped again near Butler and talked to the police, who told them the way should be clear through West Sunbury all the way to camp. The police said things seemed much better, but there were still pockets of trouble out there and to be on alert. They continued on and drove past the house where they had picked up Maddie. As they drove by, Clive looked up at the house then back at Maddie. She looked back at him but said nothing. They traveled through West Sunbury, and Matt looked at his watch again. It was getting close to nine o'clock, and Matt picked up speed a little. Clive could see the anticipation on his face. They were getting close, maybe an hour or less. They were on the road just past the town of West Sunbury when the CB came alive again, only this time the signal was loud and strong. When Matt heard the words he pulled the jeep to a spot along the road and quickly raised the volume. The voice came on again, "Fallon two this is Fallon one. Do you hear me? Please hear me." Matt looked at Clive with an

astonished expression, then quickly grabbed at the mike.

Andy and Lisa sat forward in their seats and Andy stood up and yelled, "Mom."

Matt keyed the mike and answered, "Fallon one, this is Fallon two. I hear you. Are you okay?"

There was a pause, then Janis came on again. "Matt, don't talk. Just listen. Don't come home. Don't come home. It's a trap. They set a trap."

Matt looked at Clive with sheer terror in his eyes. He was about to answer when Clive stopped him, "She said don't talk."

Janis's voice came on again and you could hear the sheer terror in her words, "Don't come home. Go soon. Tail of the Scorpion. Tail of the Scorpion. Do you hear me?"

Matt heard what sounded like someone throwing the mike around, then dead silence, then only the hash sound. He keyed the mike and almost yelled into it, "Janis, do you hear me?" Nothing but silence. He tried again, "Janis, for God's sake answer me." Still nothing but the hash and silence.

He was about to call again when Clive put his hand out and stopped him. "She's gone, Matt. She's gone. Now what did she mean? What is Tail of the Scorpion?"

Matt took a deep breath. "It's a code we have."

Andy cut in, "Dad, she's in trouble. She wouldn't use those words unless she was in real trouble."

Matt said, "I know."

"Know what?" Clive asked again.

Matt looked at Clive with an intense look on his face. "The Scorpion's Tail is the ridge above camp, way back beyond the pond up in the forest. It's the place we have in our plans if we are in trouble or if we need a meeting place. She's telling us to go there, to meet her there."

"How do you know?" Clive asked.

Matt looked away from Clive and back at Andy, Lisa and Maddie. "It's how she said it. That's how I know."

Before Matt could finish, Lisa cut in. "Uncle Clive, what Daddy is trying to say is she didn't call it Scorpion's Tail. If she had, she would only mean to meet there. She said, Tail of the Scorpion."

Andy cut in, "She wants us to go there, but she's in trouble. She's warning us."

Matt looked at Clive. "We have to get there now, as quick as we can. I know she wants us there first. She's coming. Believe me, she's coming. We need to go now."

Clive tried to ask a question when Maddie cut in, "Clive, just listen to them. Please believe me, we must go now." She just stared at Clive and he shook his head in agreement.

He looked at Matt and said, "Go." Matt pulled out onto the road and floored the gas pedal.

Andy leaned forward and yelled at Matt, "There's a shortcut."

"Where?" Matt said.

"Maybe five miles up the road," Andy said.

"Are you sure?" Matt asked as he looked back for a moment at Andy.

"Yes," Andy said. "I've been there before, but…"

"But what?" Clive asked, looking back at Andy.

Andy shook his head. "It's a dirt road down through the valley and across the creek. It's not the greatest, but it will cut off maybe half an hour."

"Then we'll take it," Matt said as he shifted gears going up a steep hill.

Clive looked back at Andy again and saw fear in his eyes. He reached back and squeezed his leg and said, "What else, Andy? There's something else. What is it?" Andy didn't say anything; he just looked back at Clive.

Matt spoke up, "Andy what is it? What's wrong? If there is a problem you must tell us now."

Andy looked at Clive and said, "The valley, it's a bad place."

"What do you mean?" Clive asked. "Will it cut off the time or not?"

"Yes, it will," Andy said "but…"

"But what?" Matt said, somewhat frustrated.

Andy said, "It's a bad place. No one goes there. It's, it's like a place of evil. The trees are all dead and there's no animals and the smell is bad."

Will it cut off the time?" Matt asked, more sternly.

"Yes, it will," Andy said. "We can make it through, it's just…"

Matt cut in, "Andy we need to get there, now forget the rest of it. You tell me where to turn, you hear."

Andy just looked at the back of Matt's head, then at Clive, and said, "Okay Dad." Maddie reached across Lisa's lap and grabbed Andy's arm and squeezed. She looked at him but said nothing. She looked at Clive, who was looking back at them. He could tell by the look on her face that fear was in her mind. Matt shifted again, up over the top of a hill.

When they came up over the crest of another hill, Andy tapped Matt's shoulder and yelled, "Up there, that dirt road on the left." Matt shifted gears, then made the left turn onto the one-lane dirt road. The road was straight and flat for a time as it cut through the trees on the top of the hill. Matt was moving quickly until he saw the edge of hill out in the distance, and just blue sky and white clouds beyond. He slowed somewhat as Andy spoke again, "There's a sharp right turn at the edge, Dad. Slow down. It's very close to the edge and the hill below is steep. It's almost a cliff." Matt came up to the curve. As Andy said, it was nearly a ninety-degree right turn. He made the turn but continued on a

much slower pace. To the left of the jeep was a steep hill that dropped off in steps or benches of hundreds of feet, to the bottom of a valley covered in thick forest. The road followed the edge of the hill for almost a half mile, then turned right for a distance into the thick forest. Matt had to leave the road in several places because of trees across the road. After several hundred yards, the road turned once again back toward the edge of the hill. It came out of the woods and to a small clearing near the edge. Matt slowed as the road disappeared.

When they reached the edge, Matt stopped. Matt, Clive and Andy got out and looked down the hill at the road as it descended into the valley below. It was very steep and ruts were cut back and forth across it from rain water that had rushed down the hill to the valley floor. Clive looked at Matt, "Can we make it?"

"Yes," Matt said, never taking his eyes off the descending road. "We can, but it will be slow going." He looked at Andy. "Son, are you sure about this? Once we get started, we are committed all the way to the bottom. There's no turning back until we reach the valley floor."

Andy, looking uneasy, said, "Dad, I've been here before. I'm sure but it never looked this steep before—not when I was on foot."

Matt put his hand on Andy's shoulders and looked him in the eyes. "Son, I've been on roads like this before. It won't be easy but we will get to the bottom. What I need to know is, will it cut off the time you told us? If not, we need to go back to the main road now."

Andy stepped forward and pointed out toward the ridges in front of them. "Dad, do you see those three ridges in a row out there to the right?"

"Yes," Matt said as he put his hand above his eyes to shade them from the sun.

"Do you see the last ridge?"

"Yes," Clive said as he looked out in the same direction.

Andy continued, "That high section to the right is where the large oak is. Dad, that's the far edge of Scorpion's Tail. Camp is just beyond. If we go back to the road it will be three times that far by road and we will have to drive past camp and then follow another dirt road to meet Mom at Scorpion's Tail. She said, don't go to camp, it's a trap. Dad, this is the most direct route to the ridge. We can be there in less than half an hour if we don't run into trouble."

Matt turned and looked at Andy, "Okay, Son, if you're sure. But for Mom's sake, please be sure."

Andy paused for a moment, then Clive stepped beside him and put his hand on his back, "Andy, we trust you but you must be sure. If you and your dad are right about what your mom said, then we can't waste any time. We need to be there, well before your mom and whoever they are get there."

Andy looked at Matt. "Dad, I hope we are right. I hope we got the message right, that she is coming there. What if we didn't?"

Matt didn't say anything and neither did Clive. They just looked out at the valleys and ridges in front of them. Matt turned to speak to Andy again when Maddie, who had gotten out of the jeep, spoke up. "We have to go this way, no matter how hard it is. This may be our only chance to help Janis."

Matt looked at her with a questioning look on his face. "Maddie, I've listened to you all during this trip. Like Clive, I don't know how you know what you know or do what you do, but I know you know something. So I'll ask you also, can we make this work?"

Maddie walked up to Andy and put her arm around him then looked at both Matt and Clive. "We have to make it

work, don't we?"

Matt looked at the ground, then, pressing his lips together, he looked back into Maddie's eyes. "Yeah," was all he said.

Andy turned and walked back to the jeep and sat down beside Lisa.

Maddie looked at both Matt and Clive. "Whether you believe me all the time or not, there is one thing you must know before we go. Whatever it is that lies down in that valley frightens me to the bone."

"What is it?" Clive asked.

"I don't know," Maddie said, walking to the edge and looking down into the valley. Matt and Clive walked to her side. She did not look at them, but continued to stare at the bottom as she said, "I feel two very strong things here. One is evil, I'm sure of that. The other, well, I'm just not sure."

"What is it, Maddie?" Clive asked. "We don't have time for this right now."

Maddie turned to Clive, but she was not angry. She closed her eyes and shook her head, then looked up at him again. "It is confusion I feel, that and indecision. It is strong. It goes from good to evil and back again. It is one of the worst feelings I have ever had. I don't know what it is, but it's there. They are both there and it lies between us and the top of that third ridge. We must be very careful. Now, as you said, we need to go now." She quickly turned, walked back to the jeep, and sat in the back next to Lisa. Matt just looked at Clive, then shook his head and turned back to the jeep. Clive looked again into the valley, then opened the slide on his shotgun and checked for the shell in the chamber that he already knew was there. He took a deep breath, then walked to the jeep. Matt put the jeep in gear and they slowly drove over the rise and down the steep grade. They followed the road slowly to the bottom. It was so steep that at times they

had to hold onto whatever they could to keep from falling forward. When they reached the bottom, they all let out a sigh of relief as Matt turned right and followed the road along the creek at the bottom. The road followed the creek for half a mile, crossed the creek and followed the other side for several hundred yards, then began to fade away from the creek to the left. As they got further from the creek, they began to encounter strange patches of fog that hung close to the ground. Another hundred yards and the road made a sharp left and started up a gradual grade.

Matt stopped the jeep as the fog became thicker and the trees all around them, void of leaves, stood as stark gray menacing outlines up ahead. Maddie whispered, "Do you smell that?"

"Yes," Clive said as he looked back at her. "It's a sulphur smell and it's getting stronger."

"Not sulphur," Maddie said, looking at the trees. "More like brimstone."

Lisa leaned forward in her seat and whispered, "Dad, I'm scared."

Matt reached back and took her hand, then looked at Andy. "Are you sure this is the way, Son?"

Andy looked back at him as he handed Maddie the .30-30 and took an arrow from the quiver on his bow. "Yeah, Dad. I'm sure. The last time I was here it wasn't this bad. But yeah, I'm sure."

Matt looked at Clive as Clive put the barrel of the shotgun on the top of the windshield and stood up. He looked down at Matt, "Let's go, but go slow." Matt put the jeep in gear and moved forward slowly.

Andy said in a low voice, "This should only be several hundred yards long then it will come out near the top." As they moved on, the fog got thicker and the smell stronger until it was very hard to see more than ten feet in front of them.

Clive realized that it was very hard to keep on the narrow road so he said, "Stop. I'll get out and walk the road. You follow me."

"No," Andy said as he got out of the jeep. "I'm the one who's been here before. I'll lead."

Matt grabbed Andy's arm and said, "No."

Andy looked him in the eyes and said, "Dad, we need to get out of here and move on now. I'll be fine."

Matt squeezed his arm and said, "You stay in sight. Do you hear me?"

"Yes," Andy said as he looked at Clive, who just nodded at him. Andy moved out in front and started to walk slowly, holding his bow in one hand and motioning for them to follow with the other. Matt heard a click as Clive slipped off the safety of his shotgun. Matt started to move slowly, keeping his eyes on Andy out in front of him. Suddenly, Andy motioned for them to stop. He did not turn around, but just stared into the fog.

Matt whispered, "What is it?"

Andy didn't answer at first; he just listened. He then turned and said, "I thought I heard something, but I guess not. Come on, Dad. Let's move." He continued on ahead. Matt put the jeep back in gear but when he stepped on the gas the back wheels spun in the wet dirt on the slight grade.

Matt put the jeep in four-wheel and then looked up, but Andy was gone. He looked at Clive and said, "Where did he go?"

Clive said, "He's right out ahead. Just move." Matt started to move while straining his eyes to see Andy.

He had only gone a few feet when Andy appeared in the fog, facing them and motioning for them to continue. He said, "Come on, Dad. It can't be much farther. It's…" Something grabbed him from behind. He dropped his bow and was pulled back into the fog and vanished.

Matt stopped the jeep and stood up. He and Clive yelled at the same time, "Andy." Maddie sat in the back, her face buried in her hands. The sound of Clive's and Matt's voices echoed through the fog, then went silent.

CHAPTER 29
September

Janis had awakened around 5:30 and checked on Lisa and the kids. She went to the living room and was surprised that Clive wasn't on the couch. She put a log on the hot coals in the fireplace and stirred them around to get the flame going again. She walked to the kitchen. Still no Clive. She made a pot of coffee and then looked out the back door. Seated in a chair, his head hung down, sound asleep, was Clive. She stepped out onto the porch and shivered a little at the cool, moist morning air. She walked to Clive to awaken him, then decided not to. She went and got the blanket off the couch and gently covered him. She looked down at him and smiled, then kissed him on the top of the head. Janis went back to the kitchen, made a bowl of food for the dog, and poured herself a cup of coffee.

Janis was about to go back out to the porch when she heard a sound outside. It sounded like a cat's meow. She looked at the kitchen window and there, out on the windowsill, was Beau, rubbing himself against the glass. She found a box of cat food under the sink, filled another bowl, then took the bowls and the coffee outside. She set the items on the table, then went back to the kitchen and got her .25 automatic and returned to the porch. As she came down the steps, Beau ran to the bottom to greet her. She placed the

bowls and the coffee on the steps and then picked him up and held him close to her face. He purred, rubbed his face against her, and meowed loudly. She put him down, then walked to the dog pen and placed the bowl of food inside, near the fence. She put the cat's bowl on the outside of the fence and then watched for a moment as the two animals ate on opposite sides of the fence. She smiled, then walked back to the steps and sat down. She picked up her coffee and took a sip. She leaned back on the steps and looked at the now-brightening sky and started to think about starting the search again. She shifted to the memory of that day in the garage when she had made that desperate call to Matt on the CB radio. It all seemed like so long ago, and yet like yesterday.

July

Coop had headed into the woods and Janis had the CB mike in her hand. She called again as she turned and looked back at the garage door. "Fallon two, this is Fallon one. Do you hear me?"

She paused and was about to call a third time when she heard Matt's voice. "Fallon one, this is Fallon two. I hear you. Are you okay?"

For an instant, she felt total elation, then quickly said, "Matt, don't talk. Just listen. Don't come home. It's a trap. They set a trap." Through the door window, she saw Sean walking toward the garage. She turned and spoke again, "Don't come home. Go soon. Tail of the Scorpion. Tail of the Scorpion."

The door of the garage opened and Sean stepped in. She turned to face him, the mike still to her face. Sean, seeing Joey on the floor, ran to her with an angry look on his face. Janis yelled into the mike, "Do you hear me?"

Sean reached for her as she ducked to the left. She made

an attempt to yell again into the mike but Sean knocked it from her hand and pushed her to the floor. He turned and, using the butt of the shotgun, smashed the front of the CB radio, then pulled the plug and pushed the wooden box to the floor in a rage. Janis had gotten to her feet and started to run to the door when Sean reached out and grabbed her by the back of the shirt. He spun her around and reached for her neck but she got away and started to back up toward the side of the garage. Sean blocked the path to the man door. "What the hell did you do?" he screamed. Janis just kept backing up till she backed into the garage wall. Sean walked slowly toward her as he screamed at her again, "What the hell did you do?"

She took a deep breath and yelled back, "I told the police what is happening here, that's what the hell I did."

Sean stopped about five feet from her and started to raise his shotgun. He looked at her with anger written all over his face. As he clenched his teeth he said, "The police don't use CB radios. Now I'll ask again. What did you do and who did you talk to?"

As she looked at the gun raised in her direction, Janis said, "I lied to you. I know where my husband is, and he is with a cop. They are going for help. Now if you intend to use that thing then do it." Sean clenched his teeth again and sneered at her as he quickly raised the shotgun and sighted down the barrel, pointed at her face. She looked at the muzzle end that now appeared to be the size of a large sewer pipe and closed her eyes, expecting her life to end in an instant.

Sean lowered the gun, stepped forward and grabbed the front of her shirt, and violently pushed her into the garage wall so that some of the yard tools fell off the wall. She opened her eyes to see his eyes only inches away. Sean said, "Are you telling me the truth?" She didn't answer. He let go

of her shirt and slapped her across the face with the back of his hand. The blow knocked her to the side as Sean grabbed her shirt again. "I asked you a question, Janis. Don't make me ask again."

Janis reached up and held the side of her face, then used the back of her hand to wipe the blood from the corner of her mouth. She looked into his eyes and in a stern voice said, "Yes. I told you the truth. My husband is good friends with the cops around here, so you can expect a lot of company in a very short time. Now I said if you're going to use that gun, do it now."

Sean pushed her to the garage wall again, then turned for a second and looked at Joey, who was now rolling to his side and moaning. He looked at the chair and the pieces of rope on the floor. "Where's the old man?" he asked in almost a growl.

As he turned back to her, she smiled and said, "He went for help too, just in case I didn't get through. Between him and my husband, I'd say it's going to get real crowded around here soon."

Sean raised the butt of the shotgun to hit Janis, then changed his mind. He took her by the arm and pushed her toward Joey, who was trying to sit up. "Help him up," Sean screamed. She walked slowly to Joey and helped him up. Joey just stared at her as if he was in a trance. "Outside," Sean yelled.

Janis took Joey's arm and led him out of the garage. Sean followed behind. When they got outside, they walked slowly toward the house. At the porch steps, Sean yelled, "Corbin, get out here."

The door opened and Corbin stood at the top of the steps. "What's up?" Corbin said as he looked at Joey, with his head hanging down, still being helped by Janis.

Sean looked at him and said, "Our little friend here

knocked Joey out, released the doctor, and then made a call on the CB radio that we didn't see. The cops may be on their way here now."

Corbin looked at Janis and then started down the steps on a run. "You damn bitch," he yelled as he got to her. She let go of Joey's arm and he fell to the ground. She backed up and then tripped and fell to the ground.

Corbin was stopped by Sean. "Corbin it's too late now for that. Besides, we may need her to get us out of here."

Corbin looked at Sean and said, "Maybe so, but just give me five minutes with her and we'll see if she tries anything again."

Janis stood up, then looked at Corbin and sneered. "Five minutes. That's all the longer it takes for you?"

Corbin yelled. "You bitch," and started at her again.

Sean stepped in his way. "Corbin, it won't matter about that now. We need to get out of here and soon. First, go to the garage and see if you can find that CB antenna and pull it down. I'm not taking another chance. I smashed the set, but the way these people are there might be another."

Corbin said, "Who cares? We are leaving anyway."

Sean said, "Yeah, we are, but do you want someone on the CB telling the cops what direction we went?"

"Okay, okay," Corbin said as he looked at Janis. "You be real glad, honey, that Sean is here. I had my way, your body would be out there in the woods feeding the bugs." He turned and headed for the garage.

Sean helped Joey back up and then pointed the gun at Janis. "Take him and sit him on the porch, then you and I get him some water and some ice for his head. Make no mistakes Janis, you try anything else and this time you die, you hear me?" Janis just nodded and then helped with Joey. They got him water and an ice bag and then Sean called Herman, Bobby Ray, Mose and the children out to the porch.

The children ran to Janis and she sat with them in a chair.

Corbin came back to the house. As he entered the screened porch, he looked down at Janis and said, "No more calls now, lady."

Sean said, "You find the antenna?"

"Yeah," Corbin said, adding, "Her old man's no dummy. The reason we didn't see it is because it wasn't on the roof of the garage. The wire went out the back of the garage and then into the woods. It was on the top of a high tree." He looked at Janis again, then added, "But no more."

Bobby Ray walked over to Janis, then looked at Sean and said, "I told you, you would have been better off if you left her to me. You wouldn't be havin' this trouble and I'd have had a real good time, wouldn't I honey?" he said as he leaned in close to Janis. She just stared at him, then looked away.

Sean said to Joey, "You okay? You feel better?"

Joey removed the ice bag, then looked at Sean, "Yeah, I'm okay now, but I got a real banger of a headache."

Sean looked at Bobby Ray and said, "Sit down. We need to talk and then we need to move quickly." He looked at Herman. "You go out to the end of that driveway and watch the road both ways. You see anything, you tell me. You got that?"

"But," was all Herman got to say as he got up.

"I said go," Sean said. Herman didn't say anymore; he just started for the door. As he did, he side-stepped Janis and the children as he looked down at Mary and Robert. He whimpered as if he was afraid to be too close to them, then he ran out the door, and down the steps, and out to the road.

Corbin looked at Sean and said, shaking his head, "We should have killed that idiot days ago."

Sean said, "Okay, now listen all of you. If she made the call she claims she did and that old man gets to the cops, we

are going to have trouble here in no time. We need to get supplies and a way to carry them. We've got not wheels, so I guess we are on foot again till we can find another ride."

"What about them?" Corbin asked as he nodded in Janis's direction.

Sean looked at Janis as Mose came out and gave Joey some aspirin and water. "Well," Sean said as he got up off the corner of the picnic table. "This lady has just sealed her own fate. She goes with us to show us the best way out of here. Besides, they will think twice before taking a chance shot at us if she's along."

Janis stood up, leaving the kids in the chair. "I won't leave my kids here alone."

"You'll do as you're told," Sean said. "They can't come with us. They'll slow us down too much. Besides, Parker is here."

"Parker," Janis said. "He can't even get out of bed and you want my kids to stay with him?"

Bobby Ray spoke up again as he looked at Janis. "Let me do them all, even the kids—all except her. Then we won't have no trouble. When she gets us out of here, then we won't need her anymore. Then she's mine."

He began to laugh when Sean said, "Bobby Ray, shut up. And no, we don't 'do' anyone. The kids stay. She goes."

Mose turned to Janis and smiled just as she was about to speak. He looked at Sean. "Sean, we can't leave these little ones with Parker. You know that. And the kid, he's in bad shape. You move him and he'll die. You don't want that. I'll stay."

Sean walked to Mose and said, "Mose, you stay and they'll put you back inside. You want that?"

Mose looked into Sean's eyes and then looked at the floor for a second, just shaking his head. He looked up again and said, "Sean, I'm an old man. I'd slow you down too.

'Sides, I don't belong outside. What would I do? The big house is the only life I have ever knowed. These are good people. We don't want nuttin' bad to happen to them. Look at these babies here. We can't just leave them here alone. Let me stay. What can they do to me, put me back inside? No Sean, I ain't goin' with you." He turned and looked at Janis, "Ma'am, you go do what they say. I'll stay and tend to the children, the kid and Parker. They'll be safe with me, ma'am. Safe till the cops come, then I'll give them over. They'll be safe, I promise."

Janis looked at Mose, then took his hand and said, "I know you will take care of them."

The children, who had been silent up to then, started to cry. Mary said, "Momma, don't go. Please, Momma, don't leave us here."

Robert then started, "Mom, I want to go with you."

Janis turned and got down on one knee and held them both, then looked them both in the eyes. "I need to do this to get these men out of here. You stay with Mose. He's a good man. When I'm done, I'll come back home to you just as soon as I can. Now I need you to be brave and do what Mommy asks, please. I'll come back as soon as I can." The children continued to cry, but more quietly.

Sean, who had watched Janis, placed his hand on Janis's shoulder and motioned for her to get up. He then got down in front of the kids and said, "Don't be afraid. Your mom will help us get away from here, then I promise I'll send her home to you." He paused, then he repeated, "I promise." The children just stared at him as he got up. He looked at Mose, then asked again, "Mose, are you sure about this?"

Mose put out his hand and shook Sean's, "You go. I know what I need to do, but you keep your word. You send this here lady back to these little ones. Sean McRoy, you ain't like that. You ain't a bad man. You send her back, ya hear me?"

Bobby Ray said, "Shut the hell up, old man. What happens to her in the end ain't none of your business."

Sean looked at Bobby Ray and sternly said, "No, it's my business. And I'll make the decision."

"Well," Janis said "And what is your decision?"

Sean looked first at Mose, then the children, then he looked into Janis's eyes. "Get us out of here and I'll send you back." Bobby Ray started to protest when Sean put the muzzle of the shotgun against the side of his face, "Bobby Ray, you make one move toward her and we'll leave you where you lay." Sean was about to say something else when he heard the sound of a vehicle coming down the road.

Herman started to yell from the end of the driveway. "Sean, Sean, someone's coming. Hey Sean, someone's coming." Sean, Corbin and Joey stepped out onto the back steps and all of them looked out at the road as a large truck came down the hill at high speed. At first, it appeared that no one was at the wheel, then as it got close to the driveway entrance they saw Coop sit up in the driver's seat. Herman started to back up, still yelling, "Sean, Sean." As the truck sped past the entrance, Coop put the barrel of the 10-gauge on the edge of the window and leveled it at Herman. Herman saw the gun and turned to run. As he did, he slipped on the limestone and fell just as Coop fired. Herman landed face first on the stones, his thick glasses smashing into the ground shattering one lens. The blast from the shotgun passed over his head and kicked up stones and dust just out ahead of Herman and ten feet beyond. The truck continued up the hill on the other side, leaving a large dust trail the length of the road. Herman rolled over and sat up, the lens on the left side of his glasses shattered, and blood, dirt and stones all over one side of his face. He reached up and touched his face with his hand then looked at the blood with his right eye. He screamed and then curled into a ball

on his side and started to cry like a child.

Sean, Corbin and Joey stepped back inside and Sean looked at Janis. "No more vehicles, Aaa? What else didn't you tell us?"

Janis looked at Sean, "I didn't know about his truck or where it was, and I told you the truth. There's no more vehicles around here. Now If I were you, I'd be getting out of here. Even if my call didn't get through, he will."

Sean didn't respond to her. He looked at Mose and said,

"Mose, you want to stay, you stay. Take care of these children and make sure the kid gets help." He looked at Joey. "You okay to go?"

"Yeah, Sean," Joey said, "but I need a gun."

"See what you can find," Sean said, looking at Corbin. "You and Bobby Ray get food, water and ammo and put it all in something to carry it."

Janis spoke up, "There's a backpack in the room where the guns are. You can use that."

"Go," Sean said again to Corbin. Corbin and Bobby Ray went back into the house.

Joey looked out at Herman and said, "Sean what about him?"

Sean walked to the screen and looked at Herman, then said, "He wants to come, fine. If not, fine too. If he comes and causes any trouble we leave him."

Joey said, "Alive or dead?"

Sean just looked at Joey, "Whatever." Joey left and went to the gun room and Janis sat back down with the kids. Sean looked at Mose. "When we get ready to leave, you take them inside. I don't need all the tears and crying."

Mose was about to answer when Corbin came out, followed by Bobby Ray. "Sean, we got food for maybe a day or two and water. We got some ammo but can't carry too much. We need to leave, and now."

Joey came out holding a .22 rifle and a box of ammo, "All I could find," he said, looking at Sean.

Sean said, "Okay, go out and get Herman. Take him to the pond and clean him up, and do it quickly. Give him the water. He needs to do something. He gives you a hard time, call me and tell him when I get there, he dies." Corbin, Bobby Ray and Joey left the porch, walked to Herman, picked him up and headed to the pond. Sean looked at Janis and said, "You and the kids go inside." He and Mose followed them inside.

They went to the room where Parker and the kid were. They were both awake, but the kid was shivering with fever. Sean got down and put his hand on the kid's head, then took a towel that was on the floor and wiped his face. He looked at the kid and said, "Boy, we gotta go. Trouble's coming. You're too weak to travel so I'm going to have to leave you here. I don't want to, but you need help. The cops will give you that. You tell them we made you go with us, you hear me?" The kid started to speak but Sean put his hand across his mouth, "You can't go. You're too badly hurt and I won't let you die out there. You'll be okay, Son. I'm sorry." He removed his hand and smiled at the boy as he placed his hand on the side of his face and said, "See ya, kid." He stood up and walked to Jerry Parker and said, "Mose here is going to stay with you, the boy and the kids till someone gets here. Janis goes with us. She'll be fine. I'm asking you one favor. Tell your friends when they arrive that Mose and the boy were forced to go with us." He looked at Mose, then back at Parker. "We made them go to do all the work. You tell them they helped out here to keep the family and you safe. You tell them it was us who wounded the boy, you got that?"

Parker looked at Sean, then Mose, and finally Janis. Janis nodded her head in agreement. He looked back at Sean. "Okay," was all he said.

Sean asked, "I have your word?"

Parker looked at Janis again, then back at Sean. "My word." Sean stuck out his hand and Parker looked at it then pulled his hand out from under the blanket and shook it. He repeated, "My word."

Sean nodded, then they all left the room except Janis. She looked at Sean and said, "I'll be right there. I won't try anything, believe me."

Sean said, "I'll wait in the living room." Janis walked to the side of Parker's bed and sat on the edge. She took his hand and said, "I'm going with them. I'll be fine. When it comes to the boy and Mose, I agree with Sean. They're good men. Maybe they need a break and maybe we can give it to them."

Parker squeezed her hand and said, "But ma'am, you'll be alone with them."

Janis looked out the window for a second, then back at Jerry. "If I have this figured right, it won't be for long." She winked at him, then bent down and kissed his forehead. She looked him in the eyes and said, "One thing. If this all comes out wrong and I don't make it back, please tell my husband and children that I love them very much. Please."

Jerry looked at her and said, "Ma'am, I'll do as you asked." She nodded at him, then touched the side of his face and left the room. Janis, Mose, Sean and the children went back out to the porch.

Corbin came around the house and said, "Sean, are you ready? We need to go."

Sean said, "Yeah, I'll be right there." He looked at Mose and nodded, then said, "Janis, say goodbye. I'll be in the yard." He turned and walked down the steps.

Janis got down on one knee and hugged the children. They started to cry but she kissed them and said, "I'll be home soon. We will all be home soon. Now you stay with

Mose. He will take care of you." She stood up and looked Mose in the eyes as she wiped one tear away. She held out her hand to him, and he took it in both of his. They said nothing. He smiled, and then to his surprise she hugged him before she turned and left the porch. Mose took the children inside.

They all met in the driveway and Sean looked at Janis. "Now, you lead, and make it the right way. Do we understand each other?"

Janis looked at Sean and said, "I'll take you out and away from the roads that the police will use. I'll guide you to a safe place at a safe distance, then you let me go."

Bobby Ray laughed and said, "Fat chance, lady."

Sean turned and looked at him, then stepped up face-to-face with him and whispered, "You and Herman are liabilities and I should have dumped you both long before this. You try anything, either of you, and I'll leave you both for the vultures. You got that? And this time, I mean what I say."

Bobby Ray just laughed and said, "Okay, Sean. Okay. No need to get mad."

Sean backed away and said, "Okay, then we understand each other."

"What about a gun?" Bobby Ray asked.

"No guns till I say you need a gun. You got that?"

Bobby Ray was about to say something back when Joey said, "Sean, we need to go."

Sean looked at Joey, then at Janis, and said, "Okay Janis, lead."

Janis turned and walked toward the pond, followed by Sean, Corbin, Joey, Bobby Ray and Herman. As she walked away, she looked back at the house. Looking out the windows were Robert, Mary and Mose. She smiled, then turned and continued toward the pond as she wiped tears from her face. Sean looked back and saw the children also, then he looked at Janis's back as she walked out in front of

him. She led them around the pond and onto a path that led into the forest. A few minutes later, she and the group came over the top of a low ridge and she paused. She looked out and up toward the next high ridge in the distance. She could see far off near the top the outline of a huge tree. It was the massive oak at the edge of Scorpion's Tail. In less than one hour they would be at the top of that ridge. As she started to descend into the valley between the ridges she whispered to herself, "Please, God, let them be waiting."

CHAPTER 30
September

Everyone was up and awake by eight-thirty, and the children were out in the back yard playing, as Clive and Matt sat on the back steps and drank coffee and talked. Janis had breakfast ready by nine, and they all sat down and ate. It was another happy mealtime. Janis and Lisa were cleaning up, and the kids wanted to fish. Matt got their poles and walked them to the pond. Clive called the station from his car and reported in, then walked to the pond and watched as Matt got the children ready to fish. He left Matt with the children and told him he needed to walk around the property and try to get the kink out of his neck from a night spent in the chair. Matt said, "I'll be here with the kids." Clive walked to the entrance to the driveway and stepped out onto the road. He looked in both directions, then walked back to the yard, turning his head from side to side to stretch out the muscles. When he reached the property line, he turned and looked back at the house. He thought about what all had happened here just a short time ago. It seemed so unreal. It was again a place of peace and serenity—all except for that gaping hole in their lives. He began to walk along the woods line. As he sipped his coffee, he began to think back to that horrible valley and that day only weeks ago.

July

A split second after Andy vanished into the fog, Clive was out of the jeep with his gun up, headed to where Andy had been standing. Matt had jumped out of the other side, then Maddie got out, the .30-30 in her hand. Lisa got up and yelled again, "Andy."

Matt turned to her and yelled, "You stay in the jeep."

Clive walked to Andy's bow, looked down and said, "Stay here. Protect them."

"But..." was all Matt got to say. Clive repeated, "Stay here." He raised his shotgun, slowly moved into the fog, and vanished. There was complete silence. Matt stood and looked in all directions and Maddie moved to the back of the jeep and held the .30-30 across her chest—although she wasn't sure what she would do with it.

Lisa started to get out of the jeep but Maddie looked back and whispered, "No, you stay." The three of them just waited and listened. All they could hear was the sound of water dropping off the trees to the forest floor. Seconds later, Matt saw something move out of the fog. He raised his gun and waited. Slowly, the person came into view. It was Clive. He was backing up, his hands above his head, the shotgun in one hand.

Matt lowered his gun and said in a low voice, "Clive, what is it?" Clive said nothing. He just continued to back up until he backed into the jeep. Matt just looked at him and repeated, "Clive, what is it?" Movement caught Matt's eye and he turned again to the fog. First he saw Andy, his hands clasped behind his head, a man behind him. The man had Andy by the back of the neck, and had an automatic weapon pointed at the side of Andy's head. The man pushed Andy a few steps further, then stopped. He was about average size and build. He had dark hair and a beard, and he was dressed in what appeared to be camo clothes.

Matt began to move his gun toward him when the man spoke, "Do not move or I will kill the boy." He spoke with a heavy accent and he stared right at Matt.

Clive, never taking his eyes off Andy and the man, said to Matt, "Do as he says."

Andy said, "Dad."

Matt looked at Andy and said, "Andy, do what he says." The man yelled into the fog in a strange language. He got no response, but suddenly two men appeared at the side of the jeep where Matt was standing. They also had automatic weapons and were dressed in camo. A fourth man appeared behind the jeep near Maddie and pointed his weapon at her. She froze in her tracks.

The man holding Andy said, "I want you all to put your weapons down slowly, then back away from them and the jeep. We are going to take your jeep. We will not harm you."

Matt said, "No. We need that jeep now." He stepped toward the man holding Andy.

Clive yelled, "No, Matt. Stop."

The man turned Andy toward Matt and said, "You stop now. You give us the jeep or I kill him."

Matt stopped and said, "Okay, okay," as he started to put his gun on the ground. Clive began to do the same but Maddie just stood in place as if she was frozen solid. The man in front of her said something in the same language but she did not move. The man yelled again as he raised his gun toward her.

Clive yelled, "Maddie, put the gun down. Do as they say." He had no sooner spoken those words when the man in front of Maddie was pulled quickly back into the fog. He screamed as he disappeared and his weapon went off in a loud, long burst of shots. Maddie didn't move. She was unable to. She just stared into the fog. The man who had Andy yelled a name, then suddenly let go of Andy and

dropped his gun. His eyes were opened wide as if in total fear. Andy fell to his knees as the man stumbled past Andy toward Clive.

Only a few feet from Clive, the man fell to his knees, then forward onto the ground in front of Clive. Buried in his back was a short-handled ax. Clive just looked at Matt with a look that said, "What the hell is happening?" The two men to the side of Matt turned toward the fog in a panic and began yelling in their language. One ran into the fog and disappeared. The other turned first toward Clive and Matt, then as he turned to look back to where the other men had been, he was pulled suddenly into the fog and vanished. There were several bursts of gunfire from automatic weapons.

Matt, Clive, Lisa and Maddie all saw the flashes of light from the guns and Clive yelled, "Get down." Matt and Clive dove for the ground and Lisa laid on the jeep floor. Maddie just stood, the gun in her hand as the firing continued, bullets hitting the ground all around her. Suddenly, the shooting stopped and all was silent again. Maddie saw a huge shadow move through the fog in front of her. The gun was knocked from her hand and she fell back to the ground. As if in a trance, she got to her knees and reached out to pick up the rifle that lay on the ground in front of her.

Suddenly, a huge foot stepped on the rifle. She looked up the leg to the person standing there. She suddenly took a deep breath and backed up on her hands, dragging her butt across the ground. She started to let out a sound of sheer terror, "Ahhhh! Ahhhh!" She turned on her side, covered her face and screamed.

Matt picked up his gun and began to turn in all directions, ready for anything. Clive slowly picked up his gun, then walked to Andy, who was still on his knees, with his head down. He squeezed Andy's shoulder and Andy

looked up at him. "Are you okay?" Clive asked.

"Yeah," was all Andy said as he sat on the ground and hung his head again.

Matt went to Lisa and said, "Are you hurt?"

Lisa started to sit up and said, "No, I don't think so." Matt walked to the back of the jeep and bent down to Maddie, who was curled in a ball, but no longer screaming. He squeezed her shoulder and she looked up at him.

He said, "Are you alright?" She slowly sat up then got to her knees and then threw her arms around Matt's legs and squeezed. He could feel her shaking and he helped her up. When she was on her feet she hugged him as if she would never let him go. He finally broke her hold on him. He looked at her and asked again, "Are you alright?" She just stared into his eyes and said nothing. He grasped her face in his hand and asked, "Maddie, are you alright?"

She seemed to come out of it and said, "Oh, yeah. I guess I'm alright."

Clive looked back at the three of them and said, "Stay here. I'll be back." He turned to walk into the fog.

Maddie said, "Clive, no!" Clive turned toward Matt and Maddie and repeated, "I'll be right back." Before she could speak again, he disappeared.

Maddie looked up at Matt and said, "We need to leave here, and I mean now." Matt started to say something when Maddie grabbed his arm and squeezed. She sternly said, "Matt, now. I mean *now*. What I just saw, we need to leave *now*."

Matt took Maddie to the jeep and helped her inside, then walked to Andy. He picked up his bow, helped him up, and handed the bow to him. Andy and Matt walked to the jeep and Andy leaned against the side. Matt turned and scanned the fog but Clive was nowhere in sight. Andy asked, "What just happened?"

"I don't know," Matt said, continuing to look around.

Clive was out in the fog, straining his eyes to see. He had the shotgun out in front of him in one hand and his handgun in the other. He came upon the body of a man and bent down to look at him. He stood up and continued on, found another body, checked it, then moved on again. He had gone a few feet when he realized he wasn't sure of the jeep's location, so he said in a low voice, "Matt, where are you?" He got no response. He repeated, "Matt, where are you?"

This time, he heard Matt's voice. "I'm here, Clive. Right here. Follow my voice." Clive turned to his left, took a few steps, then stumbled over something. It was another body. He bent down and looked at it, only this time he got a shocked look on his face. The man's head was turned around, facing one hundred eighty degrees backwards, and the expression on his face was of sheer terror. He stood up slowly and started to look around, when he caught a movement to his right. He slowly turned. There, for an instant, only four or five feet away, was a face looking back at him through the fog. It was a man about his height. All he had time to see was blonde hair and a full blonde beard. He quickly turned both guns in that direction, but in an instant the face was gone. He strained his eyes all around him in every direction but all he saw was fog. He heard a voice, "Clive, where are you?" It was Matt. He turned in that direction and walked a few yards when he came upon the .30-30 on the ground. He holstered his handgun and picked it up, then continued on. Only a few yards further and he was standing at the back of the jeep.

Matt saw him and walked up to him, "Damn it, Clive. You scared the hell out of me. Where did you go? What did you see?"

Clive handed him the rifle, then shook his head and said, "I'm not sure, but from what I did see, we need to go now."

Maddie looked back at them and said, "Matt, now. Janis needs us." Matt just looked at Clive, then walked back to the jeep.

Clive looked around slowly then walked back and said, "This time I'll lead. Let's go." He walked to the front of the jeep and placed his shotgun on the hood, then bent down and grabbed the man's feet and dragged him out of the way. He looked down at the ax buried in his back, shook his head and picked up his gun. He turned to Matt and motioned for him to move on. Matt put the jeep in gear, then looked back at Andy, Lisa and Maddie. He said nothing; he just followed Clive. Several minutes later, the fog began to fade. Soon, the top of the ridge came into view and the sun began to appear through the tops of the trees. A minute later, they were in full sunlight in a clearing at the top of the ridge. Clive motioned for Matt to stop. He walked back to the jeep and climbed in. Matt looked at Clive and said, "What happened back there?"

Clive looked at him and shrugged his shoulders. "I don't know. I really don't know. My guess is they were terrorists."

"What did you find out there in the fog, Uncle Clive?" Lisa asked.

Clive looked back at her and said, "Four dead men. Just four dead men. The rest I wouldn't even want to guess. Someone else is out there. That I am sure. But who and why, I just don't know." He looked at Matt and then pointed to the ridge beyond. "Is that it?"

"Yeah," Andy said. "That's Scorpion's Tail. Come on, Dad. Let's go."

Clive looked back at Maddie and asked, "You saw something. What was it?"

Maddie just closed her eyes, shook her head and whispered, "I don't know."

Matt looked at Andy, then Clive. Clive just said, "Go."

Matt followed the road into the next valley, along a small stream, then across and up another valley that was just below the top of the ridge at Scorpion's Tail.

Matt stopped the jeep, then looked back at Andy. "What's the best way to get to the top without anyone knowing we are coming?"

Andy stood up and looked ahead. "Go another quarter mile, then the road splits. Take the right fork. It will wind up the hillside and end up in a grove of trees just before the open field. We can check out the area from there."

"Okay," Matt said as he pulled out and continued on.

As Andy had said, the road split and then lapped back and forth up the steep side of the ridge. Several minutes later, the road came up over the crest of the hill to a flat wooded area. Andy said, "Dad, stop here till I go see if Mom's there yet." Andy got out and told Matt he was going to a tree near the edge to climb up and look.

Clive got out and said, "I'll come with you." Andy took his bow and they walked away from the jeep.

Matt was watching them walk away when Lisa touched Matt's shoulder. He looked back and Lisa nodded at Maddie, who was turned to the side, tears streaming down her face. "What's wrong? Matt asked. "The valley's over. We're safe."

Maddie looked at Matt as she wiped her face. "It's not what we have been through. It's what's coming that frightens me."

Just then, Clive and Andy ran back to the jeep. Andy said, "Dad, there's no one there, not anywhere in sight. She's not here yet."

Matt looked at Clive and said, "Good, I guess. I just hope we have this right. If we are wrong, what happens to Janis and the kids?"

Maddie spoke up again. "She's coming. Believe me

when I tell you, she's coming. You need to prepare now."

Matt looked at her and said, "Okay, we'll try it this way. But I'm only going to wait so long, then I head for camp."

Maddie said again, "She's coming."

Matt looked at her and asked, "What you said a few minutes ago… What did you mean?"

Maddie looked at Clive, and Clive said, "Well?" Maddie said nothing. Clive looked at Matt and asked, "What did she say now?"

Before Matt could answer, Maddie did. "I told you before that I felt evil in that valley, that and powerful confusion and indecision that faded from evil to good."

Matt said, "What does that have to do with here and now?"

Maddie looked at Matt, "The evil is gone. I feel it no more. But the confusion is still strong. The fog is gone. It left me when we got out of that valley. It must have been that valley and what is in it that made it so unclear."

"And now?" Clive said.

She looked him in the eyes and said, "She is coming and soon. You will be tested, but…"

"But what?" Matt said.

She looked again at Matt, "Someone is coming to help someone you know."

"And?" Clive said.

Maddie looked at Clive and said, "One of you is in grave danger and may not survive this day."

CHAPTER 31
September

The kids had fished for about an hour and then, growing tired of it, had gone to the backyard to play. Lisa was in her room, reading. Janis had put the roast in the oven and was out in the yard, sitting in a lawn chair and talking with Clive. Matt came up from the pond with the fishing equipment. He walked to the garage and put the children's poles away, started to play with the new CB radio, then changed his mind. He took his handgun from the holster on his side and got an oil cloth out of a ziplock bag in a drawer. He removed the clip and ejected the round in the chamber. He placed them on the workbench and then slowly walked to the window at the side of the garage that faced the pond. He stood there as he wiped the gun with the oil rag and looked out at the pond. He started to think back to what had happened that day on the ridge. Those few minutes that had changed all their lives.

July

Clive looked at Maddie as she sat in the back of the jeep, her head down. "Who is in grave danger, who may not survive?"

She looked at each one of them, then said, "Sometimes these things are not clear to me. Sometimes it comes like a

puzzle with pieces missing. Sometimes I just can't put a name on it. That's when it scares me the most."

Matt looked at her and said, "I have known you for less than two days, but there is one thing I do know. You know something. You have abilities, psychic abilities. I think we have all figured that out by now."

Clive looked away for a moment, then said, "I never believed in any of this mumbo jumbo. I've heard of psychics trying to help the police, but I never put faith in any of it. Now I know you, and I'm not sure I believe even now. Yet part of me has seen and heard you. I may not like to admit it, but you have my attention. Now what else can you tell me? Whatever it is, I need it now."

Maddie looked at Matt again. "She's coming. When she is here, you must stay close to her. Her very life depends on you more than anyone. One of those who comes with her is more evil than the ones in the valley." She paused, then added, "She is not the only one I fear for. There is another, but I can't tell you more. It's as if even the messages I get are confused. It's like, it's like, there is no clear answer. I'm sorry it's all I can tell you. Now you must prepare. The time is growing short." She became quiet and looked away.

Lisa put her arm around Maddie, then looked at Matt. "Dad, do what you must, but all of you beware of everything. I for one believe she feels what is going to happen." Clive just looked at Matt and shook his head. They didn't question her anymore.

Clive motioned for Andy and Matt to follow him. They walked a distance from the jeep, then stopped. Clive said, "Is there a path or road that comes up from camp?"

"Yes," Andy said. "It's out on the other side of the ridge. It comes up to the left of that big oak out there."

Matt then looked at Clive. "If she's coming on foot, that will be the way she comes."

"Is there any other way to camp?" Clive asked.

Andy spoke up. "Yes, there is an old logging road further to the left, but you would need the jeep or some kind of four wheel drive to get up that."

Matt agreed. "He's right, Clive, and we have the jeep. There isn't another vehicle at camp. You know that."

"What if whoever they are came in a four wheel drive?" He just looked at both of them.

"You're right," Matt said. "We need to watch both ways. Now what do we do?"

Clive thought for a moment and said, "Okay, we move the jeep up to the edge of the woods but keep it out of sight. Lisa and Maddie stay with the jeep. You let Maddie have the rifle for protection. I don't think I want her to have a handgun. We all know she's used that rifle at least once." He then looked at Matt, "Is there somewhere near that big tree that you can hide?"

"Yes," Andy said. He looked at Matt, "Dad, you know that big round rock just over the edge of the ridge, the one we sit on sometimes."

"Yeah," Matt said. "It's close to the tree, but just out of sight. I'll go there."

Clive looked at Andy as he handed him his handgun, "Can you use this?" Clive asked.

Andy looked at the gun and said, "Yes, I can. But I'm much better with this." He held up his bow.

"Yes," Clive said. "I've seen that, but we don't know how many we will be facing and how well armed they are. Take it anyway."

Andy took the gun and reluctantly agreed, then added, "This still goes with me," and held up his bow.

Clive nodded an okay then said, "Andy, can you position yourself to watch that road in case they come that way?"

Andy said, "I can watch both. If they come by road, Dad,

I'll wave one hand. If by path, I'll wave with two. If I can see how many I'll try and let you know. You know where I'll be don't you?"

Matt said, "The old tree stand?"

"Yes," Andy said. "They can't see me from there—at least not until they get up to the field."

Matt looked at Clive, "And you, where will you be?"

Clive said, "I'll tell you when we get out there. Now let's go." They went back to the jeep and then moved slowly to the tree line. When they got close, Matt stopped and Andy climbed the tree again to look. He motioned for them to come ahead, that all was clear. Matt moved the jeep just inside the trees and stopped.

Andy climbed down and then Matt got out and turned to Lisa, "No matter what happens, you stay here and out of sight. Do you understand?"

Lisa was not happy but she agreed. He then looked at Maddie as Clive handed her the rifle. "You protect the both of you the best you can."

She took the rifle and just said, "Okay."

Clive turned to Matt and Andy and said, "Let's go." As he turned to leave, Lisa got out of the jeep and hugged Matt, then Andy.

Maddie walked up to Clive and looked up at him, then put her head on his chest and hugged him. Clive put his arm around her and looked over at Matt and smiled. She let go of him, then looked at him and said, "You come back, lawman, you hear me?" Clive looked at her and nodded, but said nothing. The three of them left the cover of the trees and headed across the field. Maddie climbed back into the jeep beside Lisa and put her arm around her, then looked up through the leaves above and whispered, "Keep them safe."

When they got to the center of the field, Matt turned and pointed to the edge of the ridge and said, "I'll be there." He

pointed to the left and said, "See that tree? Andy will be there." He looked at Clive and said, "And you?"

Clive looked around, then saw the picnic table under the tree and said, "There. Right there is where I'll be." Matt just looked at him as they walked to the big tree. When they got there, Clive said, "Help me flip this table over on its side." They turned the table over and then Clive looked at Andy and put out his hand Andy shook it, then Clive pulled him in and hugged him, "Be smart. Be safe," he said. Andy nodded a yes, then hugged his dad and ran to the edge of the ridge where the road came up and started to climb into the tree. Clive turned to Matt, put out his hand again, and said, "Be smart. Be safe."

Matt took his hand and Clive said, "Just try and follow my lead, it's about all I can tell you." Matt gave him a hug, then moved over the edge of the hill to the big rock and sat down where he could see Clive. Clive watched until Andy got into position in the stand, then he waved and Andy waved back. Clive turned and nodded at Matt, then sat down behind the picnic table, concealing himself from the top of the path or road.

Matt sat and watched Clive as Clive first looked at his watch then looked up at the sky, looking for where the sun was. Matt turned and looked at the sun also, then realized that where Clive was put the sun right in the eyes of anyone coming up the path or the road. He looked back at Clive as Clive slowly checked the shells in his gun then took more shells out of his shirt pocket and put them on the ground next to him. He whispered, "Now why didn't I think of that?" He shook his head and smiled as he continued to watch Clive. Clive seemed very calm, almost machine-like as he checked everything. Matt thought to himself, "The man's a real pro. Glad he's on my side." He then whispered, "Be smart. Be safe."

Janis had led the group down through the valley between the ridges and across the creek and was now about halfway up the side of the ridge. The big oak at Scorpion's Tail was less than ten minutes away. In her mind, she kept saying, "Be there. Be there." She wanted so much to see Matt, to be held in his arms again, but she feared what would happen if he and Clive were there. What would the outcome be? She knew Sean had no intention of going back to jail. Neither did the rest of them. If confronted, she knew they would fight, yet she couldn't stop hoping that Matt and Clive would be there.

Janis stopped about three-quarters of the way up the path and looked back at the line behind her. Sean stopped beside her and said, "Keep moving."

Janis did not respond; she just pointed to Herman, who was at the back of the line and lagging far behind as he carried the bag of water bottles. Sean just said, "Damn it," as he waited. They were joined by Corbin and Joey.

When Bobby Ray saw them stopped ahead of him and looking down the hill, he turned and looked back at Herman. He yelled down the hill, "Come on, you piece of shit. Move."

Sean got a disgusted look on his face and told Corbin, "Go shut that big mouth of his. The sound carries all through these woods."

Corbin ran to Bobby Ray just as Bobby Ray turned around. Corbin raised his gun, butt first, as if he was going to hit Bobby Ray. Bobby Ray put his arm up in defense and bent low, anticipating the blow. Corbin didn't strike him, but instead lowered the gun, grabbed him by the back of the shirt, and pulled him up to his face. "Shut up, you asshole. You want the cops to hear where we are? You're worse than that fat piece of crap, Herman. I should have done you both long ago." He let go of Bobby Ray just as Herman reached

their position. He walked to Herman and grabbed him by the shirt. Herman dropped the water bottles and cowered like a child before a beating. "You keep up with us," Corbin sneered at him. "You fat piece of garbage. You slow us down again and I'll do you, man. You hear me?" He pushed Herman, knocking him to the ground. "Now, pick up that water and move your ass," Corbin said as he pointed the shotgun at Herman with one hand. He walked back to Sean. "I don't think they will be anymore trouble," Corbin said.

Sean looked at Janis. "Okay, let's go." Herman picked up the water bottles and the group continued up the hill.

Andy was watching the path and the road when he thought he heard someone yell out down in the forest along the path. He listened intently and was about to believe he was hearing things when a slight breeze moved up from the valley floor. It carried the sound of someone talking. He couldn't make out what was being said but he knew someone was coming up the path. He watched the path intently for several minutes, then he saw movement down among the trees. Slowly, a line of people came into view. He strained his eyes to see who they were but they would vanish in and out of the thick green foliage. He looked over at Matt, who was watching him, and he pointed down to the path to let Matt know someone was coming. Matt nodded that he understood. Clive got up from his sitting position against the table, then waited on his knees, facing the table. Andy watched the line of people as they moved through the thick green cover. The path was beginning to open up and in seconds the first person came into view. It was Janis. Andy had to almost bite his tongue to keep from yelling. He calmed himself, then continued to watch. He counted as the line of people came into view. His mother was being followed by five men. Robert and Mary were nowhere in sight. Andy looked at Matt and waved both arms then he

put up his hand and spread his fingers as far as he could. Matt looked at him and nodded that he understood, then motioned to Andy to hold on or wait by putting up his index finger and shaking it. Matt ducked behind the rock, then looked at Clive. He held up two arms and then five fingers. Clive nodded that he understood.

Clive shifted to one knee, slid the safety off on the shotgun, and looked through one of the slots between the boards of the top of the thick oak picnic table. Andy tried the best he could to hide behind the one side of the V-shaped tree that held the tree stand. He checked that the handgun was secure in his belt, then took an arrow out of the bow quiver and placed it in the bow. Sweat poured from his face and he tried to control his breathing, but he could feel his heart pounding in his chest. Matt waited behind the rock. He kept his eyes on Clive as he wiped the sweat from his forehead. Clive stayed on one knee, not moving, almost as if he had turned to stone. It was funny: Matt, who had just wiped his forehead again, realized that Clive was not sweating at all.

Janis led the group up over the top. When Sean saw the clearing he said, "Okay, stop." He walked in front of Janis and he called Corbin to join him. They stood and looked in all directions for several minutes, then Sean motioned for Janis to come to him. When she reached him he asked, "What is this place."

Janis said, "It's an old picnic ground. It's not used much anymore." As she scanned the area herself, her heart almost sank. She saw no one. Maybe Matt had not gotten the message—or maybe they were just too far away to be here at this time.

Sean looked at her and asked, "Where from here?" Janis, trying not to look disappointed said, "Across the field and down into the next valley. There's an old road there, I think."

"You think?" Sean said. "You better do more than think. You said you knew the way out of here. Now you're not sure?" Janis started to walk away from Sean toward the field. Clive watched as Janis moved away from the group. He was also watching where the rest of them were standing. They were still in the shadows from the trees near the top of the path. Sean yelled to Janis to stop, just as she walked out into the sunlight of the field. Sean called the rest of the group to come up to his position. Janis stood in the sun and looked in all directions.

Clive knew he had to let her see him, but could he do it without letting the others see him? He whispered to himself, "Janis, just a little further out." Sean walked to Janis, leaving the rest of the men in a group at the top of the path. Janis was facing the sun and she covered her eyes for a moment with her hand. Clive, watching her, whispered, "No."

Sean stood in front of her, his back to the sun, and said, "Well, which way from here? And don't tell me you don't know."

Janis looked at him and said, "If I find the road that leads out of here and tell you which direction to go, will you let me go home?"

Sean said, "I'm not promising you anything until I'm sure we are safe. Then I'll let you go. Now, which way?"

Janis said, "I won't know till I get to the other side of the ridge and look down."

"Okay," Sean said. "Now stay here till I get the rest of them up here." He walked away from Janis to talk to the rest of the group so he would not have to yell.

Clive watched the man as he rejoined the group, then he looked at Janis and whispered, "Move, just a little more. Come on, Janis, move." To his surprise, Janis did exactly that. She put her hand above her eyes again and took about ten more steps toward the center of the field. She was looking for

any sign of Matt, but in her heart she felt he was nowhere near her now. Clive could see Janis in the open. He had to make her see him, but how? He looked down at the ground and saw a small flat pebble. He picked it up, then looked at the group of men who were standing, talking intently. He waited for the right moment, then threw the stone as hard as he could in Janis's direction. He had been hoping that it would land near her, but it fell short by about twenty feet. Then, to his surprise, she lowered her hand from her face and looked in his direction. The stone had made a noise that got her attention. Suddenly, she saw him behind the table. Her first instinct was to yell, but she held herself still and in place. She looked back at Sean and the men as they started to walk toward her. She glanced again at Clive, who pointed his eyes at the sun above. She understood. He pointed to his shotgun, then to her to get down.

As Sean and the men got closer to her, Sean realized she was acting funny. He yelled, "Hey, what's going on?" A second later, all the men were in full sunlight. Clive took a deep breath and stood up, the shotgun pointed at the group. He remained behind the picnic table as he yelled, "Stop where you are and drop the weapons." The men were strung out in a line, Sean being the closest to Janis. They all turned and looked in Clive's direction. The sun was in their eyes and they moved their weapons toward the sound of the voice, but they squinted trying to see where it had come from. Clive repeated, "Drop your weapons."

Sean yelled back, "Who are you?"

"The police," Clive said. "Now, do as you're told."

Sean looked away for a moment to his men and said, "Don't move. Hold your place." Sean put one hand above his eyes to shade them, then looked at Clive and then all around. He started to side step toward Janis, who was still standing about ten feet away, looking at Clive. Clive yelled

again, "I said, don't move."

Sean lowered his hand and stopped moving, then yelled back, "I see only one of you. One cop. I think we have the winning hand here."

Matt slowly stood up from behind the rock and said, "You heard the man. Drop your weapons."

Corbin looked in Matt's direction while squinting his eyes. "Two cops. I'm still not impressed."

Clive said, "Janis, move away from them."

Sean said, "No Janis. Don't you move."

Janis began to move away when Sean screamed at her. "I said stay where you are. You led us into this trap. You think I won't kill you for it?"

Corbin spoke up, "Yeah, or maybe we'll let Bobby Ray here have another piece of you." Bobby Ray started his crazy laugh.

Matt could feel the anger boiling inside him. He yelled to Janis, "Did they hurt you?"

Clive yelled at Matt without taking his eyes off the men. "Matt, don't listen to them."

Matt repeated, "Janis, did they hurt you?"

Janis yelled back, "No, Matt. I'm fine. Believe me, I'm fine."

Bobby Ray yelled, "Sean, let's do them both. Then I can have my fun with the lady there." And he laughed even louder.

Then a third voice came from behind them from back in the trees, "Hey Sonny, you won't get a second chance at that lady. I promised you what you would get." Joey and Herman turned around and looked into the woods, but saw no one.

"Three cops?" Corbin said, "You just have me shaking in my shoes. Come on, Sean. Let's do this." Sean started to move again toward Janis and the line of men started to

spread out. Clive knew he had to do something. Sean, Corbin and Bobby Ray were facing Clive and Matt. Joey and Herman were facing the woods behind.

Clive yelled to Sean, "I told you. Stay away from her and drop the weapons. I won't ask again." Suddenly, Herman couldn't take anymore. He started to scream and turned and ran for the path, holding the bag of water bottles in his arms.

Joey yelled at him, "Get the hell back here, you asshole." Herman started down the path when, from the green cover along the side, Coop stepped out, the 10-gauge pointed at Herman. Herman stopped in his tracks, his eyes open wide.

Coop looked him in the eyes and said, "Your days of hurting people are over." Joey saw Coop and turned and fired a shot with the .22 rifle in Coop's direction. The bullet hit a branch near Coop's head. Coop turned and fired the shotgun at Joey but the shot was to the right and low. It hit the dirt at Joey's feet. One of the pellets hit Joey in the foot. He fell to the ground and screamed. Herman, who was only feet from Coop, reached out and grabbed the gun with one hand and tried to pull it away from him, still screaming and crying. Coop pulled the barrel out of his hand, backed up two steps and swung the gun right at Herman. There was a muffled explosion and blood and water from the bag Herman was holding flew in all directions. The blast lifted Herman off his feet and across the path to the ground. He was dead before he hit the dirt on the other side.

Corbin turned his gun toward Clive and Clive saw the move. He ducked quickly behind the table as the blast from the 12-gauge hit the top edge of the picnic table, splintering wood high into the air. Matt turned his gun toward Corbin, who was putting another shell in the single shot. He was about to fire when he saw Sean turn and run toward Janis. He changed his target and swung toward Sean but Clive was just standing up and too close to fire. Matt yelled, "Clive!

Janis!" Clive stood up and looked at Corbin, who was just closing his gun, then looked at Sean who was only feet from Janis. Clive swung toward Sean and fired. Most of the shot went behind him, but one of the pellets hit him in the shoulder. The force knocked him to the ground, but not before he got a hold of one of Janis's feet. She tripped and fell to the ground. Clive started to turn toward Corbin as Corbin leveled the shotgun again at Clive. Matt got off the shot first. It hit Corbin in the upper left leg, knocking him halfway to the ground. He still had the shotgun in one hand and on one knee he aimed again at Clive. Suddenly, Corbin yelled as the shaft of an arrow came through his shoulder. He dropped the shotgun and reached for the handgun in his waistband. He raised the gun just as Clive fired. The shot hit Corbin across the chest and Clive fired again, knocking him back three or four feet. Bobby Ray had been down on the ground, trying to stay as low as he could, when Corbin's handgun landed right in front of him. Joey had gotten up and run from the path as Coop leveled the shotgun at his back. He was about to fire when Bobby Ray, gun in hand, decided to run for it. He turned to head down the path when he saw Coop pointing the gun at Joey. Bobby Ray stopped and fired at Coop, hitting him in the left arm. Coop yelled and fell back but quickly sat up and, with one arm, pointed the shotgun at Bobby Ray. Bobby Ray slid to a stop and yelled, then turned and ran back to the top of the path, just as Coop fired. The shot hit the tree limbs above his head. He dug in and ran faster. Coop, with one good arm, put the shotgun butt first on the ground and pumped it, then started to get up.

Janis got partway up and kicked at Sean, then ran toward the big tree. Sean rolled over, got up, and headed for the woods on the other side of the path. He ducked behind a pile of brush just as Clive got a lead on him. Clive saw Bobby Ray coming from the top of the path. He fired a shot

at Clive, the bullet hitting the picnic table and driving Clive down for a second. Joey turned his rifle toward Matt and was about to fire when an arrow hit the dirt beside him. He turned around, but on his injured foot he fell to the ground in a sitting position. Bobby Ray saw Clive duck. As he ran, he fired a shot at Matt. The bullet hit the top of the rock near Matt. Joey looked up at the tree stand and saw Andy putting another arrow into his bow. He raised his rifle and aimed. Janis saw the move and yelled, "No." Joey fired and the .22 slug hit Andy in the upper right leg. Joey got up and ran toward the woods. Andy fell to the platform of the tree stand, then dropped his bow to the ground. He reached for the gun in his waistband but the pain burned in his leg and he yelled and grabbed his leg instead. Matt had seen Andy fall and yelled, "Andy."

Bobby Ray slid on the loose gravel and landed on his knees. He turned to Matt and pointed the handgun as Matt came out from behind the cover of the rock. Clive stepped out from behind the table and leveled the shotgun at Bobby Ray, yelling, "Hey, asshole." Bobby Ray turned just as Clive fired. The shot hit Bobby Ray in the right shoulder, knocking him backwards. Clive pumped the gun again. Bobby Ray sat up and pointed the gun again at Clive. He got off one shot that whizzed past Clive's head. Clive walked straight at Bobby Ray and, with one hand, fired again. The shot hit Bobby Ray in the chest, knocking him back to the ground. Clive pumped the gun again and to his surprise, Bobby Ray, now flat on his back, raised his head and pointed the gun again. Clive, only feet away, leveled the shotgun again and fired at the same time Matt fired. Both shots hit Bobby Ray in the chest again. Bobby Ray lay motionless and bloody on the ground.

Clive saw Coop come up over the crest of the path and at first turned his gun toward him when Matt yelled, "No."

Coop stopped at the top, his bloody arm hanging at his side.

Suddenly, a shot came from the woods near the tree stand. Janis had run in that direction and Matt had turned to go to Andy also. They both stopped when they saw Sean, his gun pointed up at Andy. Sean looked at all of them and yelled, "You move and I shoot him."

Janis yelled, "No, please." Joey came out of the woods, limping on his bad foot, with the rifle pointed at Janis.

Matt yelled, "Let him go."

"Or what?" Sean yelled back.

"Just let him go," Matt said, lowering his gun. Clive stepped in front of Matt, his gun still raised. Coop walked up to Matt's side and waited.

Janis yelled, "Please, Sean. He's hurt. Please let him go."

Sean looked at Clive, "Let him go so you can shoot us the way you did them. I don't think so."

Clive lowered his gun then said, "You let him go, we let you go."

Sean just laughed and said, "I'm supposed to believe that?"

Clive said, "Yes. You have my word."

Janis started to walk toward Sean. Matt yelled, "Janis, no."

Janis looked at Sean and said, "Let my boy go. You take me like before. I'll go with you."

Matt yelled, "Janis, no."

Clive said, "Wait, both of you. Andy needs you both." He looked at Sean. "You take me and leave the family alone. You can do with me as you will. Just let them go."

"Well," Sean said. "We have a hero here. How nice. No, Mister Police Man, I think I'll just take the boy."

"No," Janis yelled as she started again toward Sean.

Joey yelled, "One more step I shoot the boy," as he pointed the gun up at Andy.

Sean said, "Look, you let us go with the boy. I promise

303

we'll leave him in a safe place."

Janis said, "Please, no. Take me."

Sean looked at all of them and said, "I don't need any more trouble and all of you are trouble. The boy can't do much in his condition. All we want to do is get away. I'll leave him in a safe place." He looked at Janis and said, "I promise."

Janis said, "Please, he's bleeding. Let me tend to him." Sean told Andy to get out of the tree, and with Joey's help he got to the ground. Sean held the gun on Clive, Matt and Coop while Joey put the muzzle of the .22 on Andy's head. Sean told them all to put their guns on the ground except for Clive's handgun. He told Clive to bring the gun to Joey. Janis tore a piece from her shirt and put a bandage around Andy's leg, then got a belt from Matt and cinched it tight. "Now, please take me?" she said desperately.

Sean ignored her, then got Andy to his feet and said to Clive, "You got here somehow and I suspect not on foot. Now where's the ride?"

Matt said, "You're not taking him," and stepped toward Sean.

Sean pulled the hammer back on the gun and pointed it at Andy's head, "Do you want him dead?"

Clive said, "Will you release the boy?"

Sean looked at Clive and said, "As I told her, I promise. She knows I'll keep my word." He looked at Janis.

She looked at Clive and said, "I don't want to but we have to believe him."

Matt said, "Janis!"

Janis looked at Matt, then at Sean, "If I tell you where to go, will you leave him there?"

Sean looked at her. "Janis, I promise. All I want is to get away from here. You have my word."

She looked at Matt, "I believe him." She looked at Andy.

"Son, will you show him the way out of here? He says he'll let you go where I tell him to. Will you go?"

Andy said, "Mom, I'll be fine. Let's just get this over with."

Clive said, "Matt, we have no choice. They will kill him if we resist."

Matt just hung his head, then looked up at Sean. "He's your guide and guide only. You hurt him and I'll hunt you down till my last living day."

Sean said, "Okay, where is the ride?"

Clive yelled, To the woods on the other side of the clearing. "Maddie bring the jeep here and do it now." They heard a motor start, then the jeep came out of the trees. The only one in it was Maddie, and Clive breathed a sigh of relief that Lisa had stayed behind. Maddie drove the jeep to the big tree and got out. She had a terrified look on her face, so Clive walked to her and then tried to explain what was happening. He walked to Sean and handed him the keys but Sean motioned for Joey to take them as he held the gun against Andy's head. Clive looked at Sean and said, "You hurt one hair on his head and you will be looking over your shoulder for the rest of your life. Then one day you'll see me and it will be your time to die."

Sean just smiled at him then said, "I told you, I just want my freedom. I won't hurt the boy unless you make me. Now get back to the group and let us go." Clive turned and walked back to the others. Sean, with Joey and Andy both limping behind, went to the jeep and got in. Joey took the wheel and Sean sat in the back with the gun up against Andy's temple.

Matt said, "I can't let this happen," and started to walk to the jeep.

Sean stood up and pointed the gun at the top of Andy's head and said "No."

Coop, who had been silent, stopped Matt and said, "Matt, he'll kill him." He turned to Sean and said, "So far, you have been a man of your word. Just make sure you keep it this time or all three of us will hunt you down if it's the last thing we do. You had better take our word for that."

Sean sat back down, then looked at all of them. "I believe you and I don't want to be hunted anymore than I want to hurt this boy. I just want to get out of here." He looked down at Andy and said, "Tell them where we will leave you."

Andy looked at Matt, "Dad, three ridges over the flat on the top of the hill there's big rocks. I'll have them leave me there." Andy winced in pain then said, "I'll tell them where to go from that point. Dad, I'll be fine."

Matt nodded his okay and Joey started the motor. He backed the jeep up, then Sean looked at Janis and said, "You'll get your boy back." He looked at Matt. "Mr. Fallon, you are a very lucky man indeed." He tapped Joey on the back and said, "Go." Joey put the jeep in gear and grimaced in pain as he pushed the pedal. The jeep lurched forward, then started out across the field.

Maddie walked up to Clive and said, "He will be protected." Clive just looked at her and she put her arm around him and watched as the jeep disappeared over the other side of the ridge. Matt went for Lisa and brought her to Janis. Janis held her and they both cried. Maddie helped Matt tend to Coop's wound.

Clive looked at his watch and said to Matt, "Ten more minutes and we go get him." Janis filled Matt in on what had happened and where Robert and Mary were. As they waited, Clive walked to the big tree and looked out over the field to where the jeep had disappeared. He whispered, "Be smart. Be safe."

CHAPTER 32
July

Clive walked to the group at the picnic table. Janis was just finishing helping Maddie with Coop's arm. He looked at Matt while putting more shells in his gun. "It's time. Let's get moving."

"What about them?" Janis asked as she nodded to two of the three dead men on the ground.

Coop looked at Janis and said, "Leave the garbage where it lay. We'll take it later."

Matt looked at Janis, and then at the bodies. "Coop's right. We need to get you, Lisa, Maddie and Coop back to camp."

Coop spoke up as he got up from the picnic table. "I'm not going to camp. I'm going with you."

Clive looked at Coop, then said, "No offense, Coop. I'd take you with me if I could—but to tell you the truth, I'd much rather you got these women back to camp. Is your truck anywhere near here?"

"Yeah," Coop said. "It's out on the camp road, parked in the woods at the top. Sure would like to go with you two, though."

Matt looked at him and said, "Coop, I gotta go with Clive. You know that. I'd sure feel better if my ladies here were with you."

307

"Okay," Coop said. "I'll get them there."

Clive looked at Coop and said, "One more thing. When you have them safe at camp, could you see if you can get a call out on Lenny's car radio?"

"How did you know about Lenny?" Coop asked.
Clive looked down at the ground, then back at Coop. "Janis just told me. He was a good man."

"He didn't deserve that," Coop said, adding, "I don't think the radio will work. Those assholes tried to start the car but it was all shot up, same as their truck."

"Check anyway," Clive said. "If it's no good, then pop open the trunk. There should be a spare battery in there. If the radio is still good, it should work. You got it?"

Coop said, "I'll give it my best."

Janis looked at Matt and hugged him, then did the same to Clive. "You two bring my boy back to me. And I want you both back safe too." Coop, Janis, Maddie and Lisa headed back to the path on their way to the road.

Clive and Matt ran across the field to the other rim. Matt stopped and pointed, "There, out there on that third ridge. That's where he should be." Matt and Clive headed down into the first valley, at first at a slower pace. Matt was trying to find a path that he knew led to the road they had been on earlier. When he found it, he and Clive began to pick up speed. When they got to the top of the first ridge, they stopped for several minutes to catch their breath, then continued into the next valley. Halfway up the other side, they came to the road. The path had cut off quite a bit of the road and had saved time. They moved up over the second ridge and into the next valley. They were halfway up the side of the third ridge on the steep road, and had stopped again to take a breather, when they heard shots near the top.

Matt looked at Clive with total fear in his eyes. Neither of them spoke, but Clive felt the same fear. They turned and

ran, at an even faster pace, to the top.

When they reached the top, the trees opened into a flat field. They saw the jeep about three hundred yards away, parked near the big rocks Andy had told them about. Matt started to run toward it when Clive yelled, "No Matt! We move slow now. They have that rifle and we are in the open." He pointed to the tree line to their right. "We go there, he said, and move just inside the tree line." He could tell Matt wanted to get there quickly, but Matt agreed and they ran for the trees. Once in the cover of the forest, they moved toward the big rocks as fast as they could. As they got closer to where the jeep was, they stopped. Clive said he would move in from the far side of the jeep and for Matt to come in from that side. Matt waited for Clive to move further up the tree line, then when Clive waved they both moved out into the open, heading slowly toward the jeep.

As they got closer, they realized there was no movement near the vehicle. When they were within fifty yards, Matt saw two feet sticking out from behind the jeep on the ground. He yelled, "Clive," and started to run. Clive raised his shotgun and began to move more quickly, trying to cover Matt in case it was a trap. Matt reached the jeep first and ran around to where the body was. Clive couldn't see who was on the ground from his position, but he did see Matt's reaction as he looked at the ground. It was a look of sheer disbelief. Matt just stood and stared, not moving. Clive, his gun still raised, reached Matt and then looked down. There, on the ground, was Joey. His body lay, chest down but his face was looking up at the sky, sheer terror in his eyes. His head had been turned a hundred and eighty degrees.

Matt just continued to stare at Joey, as Clive moved to the body and bent down on one knee. Matt slowly moved in closer. Matt said, "My God, Clive, what happened to him? Who could have done that?"

Clive looked up and said, "This is the second time I have seen this today. The first time was in that valley. One of those four men looked just like this. I couldn't believe it then and I still can't believe it now."

Matt regained composure, then said in a kind of panic, "Clive, where's Andy? Andy and the other guy?" Clive stood up and looked in the jeep. On the floor in the back was his handgun. He picked it up and checked it. Three shots had been fired. They must have been the three they heard. He then looked at the seat where Andy had been sitting. It was covered with blood. He just looked at Matt as Matt stared at it too. Matt just looked at Clive. Clive could see the sheer terror in his face. Matt whispered, "Clive, what happened here?"

Clive said, "Don't panic just yet. Let's see what else we can find." They checked all around the jeep, then found footprints in the dust and a blood trail headed toward the large rocks only fifty feet away. Clive reloaded his handgun, put it in the holster, and checked his shotgun again, as did Matt. They both slowly moved toward the rocks. The tracks and blood stopped at the rocks then went around to the left. They followed them slowly, then at a point about halfway around they found the .22 rifle broken in half. The tracks they had followed were joined by two others. There were signs of a struggle. Clive bent down and looked at the tracks. One of the new sets of prints was huge. He looked at Matt and shook his head. At that point, one set seemed to be spaced further apart, as if whoever it was had been running. They followed them to the opposite side of the huge rocks, then three sets of tracks and a blood trail cut away to the left. The fourth set, followed by the set of huge tracks, went into a space between two of the house-sized rocks.

Clive started to move slowly into that channel between the rock walls, followed by Matt. They had gone about

twenty or thirty feet and come to a bend in the path that began to narrow. Clive raised his shotgun into a ready position and quickly made the turn. Suddenly, there in front of him, squeezed in a crevice between the huge boulders about four feet off the ground, was Sean McRoy, his eyes and mouth open wide as if in the middle of a scream. He was covered in blood and a large knife was buried deep into the center of his chest. Matt and Clive just stood and stared in disbelief. Matt looked at Clive and said, "Clive, who did this? My God, where's Andy?" Matt and Clive returned to the spot where the tracks split up. They followed the tracks and the blood trail to the far edge of the clearing and into the forest. The tracks soon went from those of three persons to only two and within several yards they lost the trail. No tracks and no more blood. They searched the area in the woods for half an hour with no luck. They went back to the rocks and started again on the path. Still no luck. They searched the entire field and all around and among the large rocks and the jeep. They found nothing. Andy was gone.

After nearly two hours of searching, Clive told Matt that they needed to head back to camp and try to get help. Matt didn't want to leave the area but reluctantly agreed. The last thing he said to Clive before they left the field was, "How do I tell Janis that he's gone?" They walked back to the Scorpion's Tail and never spoke a word until they reached the big tree.

They sat for a moment at the table and then Clive spoke up, "Matt, Maddie told me that he will be protected. I'm not sure I ever believed in what she says she knows. I think if I hadn't seen it with my own eyes and heard it with my ears, I'd say it was all fantasy. But you know the same as me, she knows something. Call it psychic ability, call it what you want, she knows. I don't understand it or know why but we have to believe it's true. We have to continue to look for

Andy, but we need to believe he will be okay."

Matt, who had been sitting with his head down, looked up and said, "My God, Clive, did you see the blood? If it's Andy's he needs help, and I mean now. And what do I tell my family? What do I say to them? I know what I saw and heard from Maddie, but how can I expect Janis to continue on with that? Clive, she's going to take this hard—and I mean real hard. They all are. How do I tell them he's gone?"

Clive reached out and put his hand on Matt's shoulder as Matt lowered his head again. "Matt, we'll get help. We'll continue to look. You know we won't stop, no matter how long it takes. We didn't find him like we found the others. He's out there. We need to look and look hard but we can't lose faith. Not just for ourselves, but for Janis and the kids. If we doubt our faith, then how can they lean on us?"

They rested a few more minutes, then headed for camp. When they arrived, there were several police cars in the driveway. Coop had hooked up the radio and called for help. To his surprise, he got through. As Matt had predicted, Janis went to pieces upon hearing the news about Andy. He spent nearly an hour in their bedroom with her alone. Lisa and Maddie consoled Robert and Mary the best they could. Mose was handcuffed and sat out on the back porch with one of the officers. Matt had found out what he had done to help Janis and the kids. He told Mose that he would help however he could and that Clive would also. Shortly after they arrived, an ambulance came and took Jerry Parker away. It would soon return for the kid. Coop's arm was tended too, and Coop, with the help of one of the officers, buried the dog. Lenny's remains were left until more help arrived. The bodies of the convicts would wait until they could be retrieved.

The search was started again with help for as long as the light lasted. It began again the next day and continued for

days that turned into weeks. Still, they did not find Andy. The more tired Matt got, the harder he pushed himself. Clive stayed for two weeks off and on, as did Maddie. He was out in the forest every day with Matt, from sunrise to sunset. Maddie helped out at the camp and also in the hunt, but that cloud that obscured her thoughts remained.

She left at the end of the two weeks, and the last person she spoke to was Clive. As she was about to be taken home by Matt, she walked up to Clive, who was standing at the pond. He was covered in dirt and sweat from a long day's searching. He had a bottle of water in his hand and was staring out at the surface of the water. She stood beside him for a few minutes, then looked up at him and said, "Clive, I know how hard this is on you all, but you must keep the faith. I know I don't seem to be able to help right now, but there is one thing I feel strongly about. Andy will be okay. They will all be together again. I feel it. He will be protected."

Clive looked down at her as he put his arm around her shoulder. "I don't know why I believe you, but I do. You know I do. We won't stop looking, but like you, I know he's out there."

She looked out at the pond and said, "When we were in that valley, something happened. You saw something." She turned again and looked at him. "What did you see? Whatever it is, it weighs heavily on you. I can feel it."

Clive looked away at the pond, took a deep breath, and said, "A face. A face is what I saw. A blonde, bearded man looking back at me for an instant. He was there, then he was gone. I don't know what it is but there's something, something about it. It's a feeling I just can't put my finger on." He looked down at her and asked, "And what about you? You saw something too. I've very rarely seen fear like I saw on your face in that valley. What did you see?"

She looked up at him, then slowly walked a few feet to the edge of the water. She turned and said, "What I saw was a man, but not like any man I have seen before. At least, I think it was a man."

Clive walked to her and looked into her eyes, "The fear of it. I can still see it in your eyes, and yet I also see a calm. What is that?"

She put her head against his chest for a moment, then looked up into his eyes. "What you saw, what I saw, the confusion and indecision I spoke of before, the evil, the good… They are all tied together and Andy is in the middle of it."

"How?" Clive asked, surprised.

"I'm not sure how," Maddie said. "The fog that prevents me from understanding it all is still there. It refuses to go. But there is one thing that I feel with certainty: it is out there, out there with Andy. Just remember one thing that I said, even if it's the only thing you believe. He will be protected. He will come home. I just know he will. All will be okay. Peace will come." Clive put his arms around her and they stood at the pond's edge in silence.

CHAPTER 33
September

Matt had come up from the garage with three beers in his hand, one for each of them. Lisa had checked on the roast and called out to see if anybody wanted anything. Janis told her to get a drink for herself and come to join them. She got two more lawn chairs and they all sat in the back yard, talking, while Robert and Mary played in the sandbox.

About fifteen minutes later, they all heard the sound of a vehicle coming down the road. Matt told Janis, Lisa and the kids to go to the porch. Clive and Matt took up positions: Clive behind a tree, Matt at the corner of the porch, each with guns drawn.

The car moved quickly down the road, raising a cloud of dust high into the trees. It made the turn into the driveway and came to a stop behind Clive's patrol car. It was a bright purple Cooper. Janis whispered down to Matt at the corner of the porch, "A purple Cooper?" The door opened and out stepped Madison Lynn Devereaux. When Lisa saw her, she ran down the steps to greet her. They hugged and then walked arm in arm to the back yard, where Maddie was greeted by the children, then Matt and Janis.

Clive stood back and watched, with a broad smile on his face, then Maddie turned to him. She walked slowly to him and into his open arms. She looked up into his eyes and

whispered, "How are you, lawman?"

Clive smiled an even broader smile and kissed her on the forehead, then hugged her tightly for several seconds. When he let her go, he said, "I'm fine, Maddie. How is my favorite psychic?"

She looked at him and whispered, "Fine. Just fine."

Matt got another chair while Janis got Maddie a drink and they all sat and talked. The conversation at first was general, then Maddie looked at Matt and said, "I know you have still been searching. Have you found out anything new?"

Matt shook his head and said, "Not much more than we knew at the beginning. Clive and I have spent more hours than I would like to think about out there. It's all-consuming, and yet we have next to nothing."

Clive added, "We've had police help, fire departments and friends that have put in so many hours. We have alerts and bulletins out everywhere but so far, nothing."

Maddie looked at Janis and asked, "And you, how are you?"

Janis looked at Lisa and took her hand, then looked at Maddie. "We are holding it together, but it is very hard. If I, we, just knew he was okay it would be better. The not knowing anything is the hardest part."

Lisa spoke up as she wiped a tear from her face. "I just don't understand how anyone can just vanish like that. I miss him so much."

Maddie took a sip of her drink and said, "I've tried to clear my mind and I've spent hours in thought about it, but that curtain of fog just won't leave. I've never had this happen before. It was always so frustrating to me to even have this ability. There have been times when it seemed more a curse than a gift. Now, for once, I want it to work and it just won't come to me. I want to help so badly, but no

matter how hard I try there is nothing I can put my finger on. The only thing I feel, and feel strongly about, is that he is out there and he is protected."

Matt looked at her and said, "Maddie, that alone is a great comfort to us. I think that is one of the main reasons our faith is so strong. I, we, know you are a woman of faith, and to have you tell us to have faith, that all will be fine, just makes us that much stronger."

Maddie got tears in her eyes and looked away for a moment. She looked back at Matt, then Janis and Lisa. "I've only known you all for a short period of time, but I've come to love you very much, and I love that boy more than you know. I think the reason why I know he's out there is because his spirit is so strong. It's almost as if he speaks to me and tells me all will be okay." She looked at Clive as she wiped a tear. "And you, lawman, I've even grown to love you, too. Now don't get me wrong, Aliston. You aren't the easiest man in the world to love. Matter of fact, you're just plain stubborn…"

Clive put up his hands, palms out, and interrupted, "Okay, okay, Maddie. I get the point."

They all laughed, then the conversation went on to other things: Coop's recovery, and what they were going to do about helping Mose to get a shortened sentence and a start on a new life. They talked about the memorial service for Lenny and the comeback that the country was making in general. They talked Maddie into staying for supper, then moved the chairs down to the pond, into the shade of the trees.

As they talked, the kids played at the water's edge. Janis had gone to the house for more drinks, and Lisa was helping the kids put a battery in a remote control boat. After a few minutes, Lisa asked Matt if he would get some tools for her from the garage.

Maddie and Clive sat in silence for a time, then Maddie turned in her chair and looked at Clive. She wasn't smiling.

"Clive, I need to say something to you. I need to tell you something."

Clive, realizing the seriousness of her look, said, "What is it, Maddie? Is it Andy?"

"No," Maddie said. "It's you. It's about you."

She was about to continue when they heard Janis say from up near the house, "Someone help me with this tray of drinks before I drop them." Maddie and Clive got up and turned toward her. Matt was on his way from the garage, tools in hand. Janis was carrying a tray of beers and drinks and saying something about the roast when she looked out toward the pond. Suddenly, she froze in her tracks. Her eyes opened wide as if she was straining to see. Her mouth dropped open in a look of amazement then she said, first in a normal tone, "Oh my God." She dropped the tray to the ground then yelled, "Oh my God, Andy." Matt stopped and looked, first at Janis, then in the direction she was looking. Janis started to walk toward the pond, then broke into a run. Matt stood as if frozen for a moment, then dropped the tools and started for the pond. Lisa and the kids heard Janis and watched her as she ran toward the pond. Clive and Maddie turned to see what she was looking at. Up on the hillside above the pond, in a clearing in the trees, one lone person was walking slowly down toward them.

Clive and Maddie strained their eyes in the afternoon sun. Maddie whispered, "Andy."

Clive started to walk toward the hillside, a look of disbelief on his face.

Janis ran past both of them down along the pond, yelling, "Andy. Oh my God, Andy."

Matt ran past Lisa and the kids and yelled, "Lisa, Robert, Mary, stay here till I call you." Maddie walked to Lisa and

hugged her. They were both in tears. Clive watched as Janis jumped across the creek behind the pond and climbed the steep embankment by pulling on tree branches. Matt wasn't far behind her. Clive started to move faster as he stared at the open field. His eyes were on the boy, slowly limping down through the field. He thought he saw someone in the trees behind him. He unsnapped his gun and broke into a run. He followed Janis and Matt across the creek and up the hill on the opposite side. Janis raced through the trees, falling several times, but then getting up and running again. Matt was trying the best he could to catch up to her. Clive kept looking through the trees as he ran, trying to see the tree line above the clearing. Janis ran out of the woods into the field and headed straight to the boy. Matt was still a distance behind, but gaining.

When Janis was only ten feet from the boy, she stopped and whispered, "Andy. My Andy."

The boy stopped his limping gait and stared at her for a moment, then just said, "Mom."

Janis started to walk slowly toward him as Matt stopped beside her and said, "Son."

Clive broke free of the forest and raced toward the three of them, still not taking his eyes off the tree line above the field. When Janis got to Andy, he dropped to his knees and she did the same. She took him in her arms and hugged him. They both began to cry. Matt walked to Andy's side, put his hand on Andy's back, and looked down at him, his eyes filled with tears. He just said, "Hi, Son."

Clive slowed as he got closer to them. He kept looking at the three of them as they hugged each other, but he kept looking up at the tree line also. He stopped beside them and Andy looked up at him and put up his hand. Clive took it and squeezed it and said, "How you doing, boy?" Andy just smiled, the tears streaming down his face, then he continued

to hug his mom and dad. Clive looked up at the tree line and there it was again. Someone was just inside the tree line, watching them. He pulled his gun from the holster and began to move up through the field, first at a walk, then he broke into a run again.

Matt looked up and saw Clive heading for the tree line, gun in hand. He said to Janis, "Keep Andy here. I'll be back."

He pulled out his gun and was about to follow Clive when Andy reached up and took his arm. "Dad, it's okay. They won't hurt us. It's okay."

Matt said, "Okay son, but I'll be back." He started up the field toward Clive. When Clive got close to the tree line, he stopped, his gun pointed out in front of him, scanning the woods. He saw movement in the trees as if someone was moving away from him. He started to move parallel to the trees as he watched the figure appear and disappear in and out of the dark green foliage.

As he slowly entered the trees, Matt reached him. "What is it Clive?" Matt asked.

Clive kept moving and didn't take his eyes off the figure in the trees. "I'm not sure," Clive said. "But someone is out there." He looked at Matt and motioned for him to continue on along the tree line. He said, "I'll go deeper in."

"Clive, be careful," Matt said as he watched Clive head into the thick, dark forest.

Clive moved in and around large trees, through dense foliage, and over huge logs. Every few seconds he caught a movement out in the trees. He was standing next to a large stump when he saw someone moving out to his left. The stump obscured his view, so he went around it. He was in the process of crossing a large fallen log when he heard a noise to his right. He turned quickly and saw a face looking at him from the thick underbrush. It was a man with blonde hair and a beard. It took him by surprise so that he lost his

balance while straddling the log and fell to the forest floor. He held onto his gun as he quickly got up and looked for where the face had been. It was gone. Only the movement of the swaying branches indicated that someone or something had been there. He pointed his gun out in front of him and slowly turned 360 degrees, scanning the forest around him. He saw nothing. He waited for several minutes, listening. There was nothing but complete silence, except for the soft sound of the breeze blowing through the tops of the trees. He watched and listened, then whispered, "Who are you?" He then yelled out into the thick trees, "Who are you?" There was only the silence and the echo of his voice, as it disappeared into the forest.

Clive moved a few steps ahead then stopped again. He wasn't sure where it came from, but he heard himself yell, "Brian. Brian Lasiter." He stood there as flashes of memory cascaded through his mind. The attack on America, the fire fight at the crossroads store, the trip into the city to get Lisa, the house where they met Maddie, the church and the two dead convicts lying on the church floor, the fires in the city, the gunfight at Scorpion's Tail, the empty blood-covered jeep and Sean McRoy pinned in the rocks. He saw the first murder of over a year ago: Jody Miller's body, her throat slashed, and the faces of the other victims. Then he saw Brian in uniform, holding a pool cue and smiling. He shook his head as if he wanted to shake those memories from his mind. He closed his eyes and turned his head to the ground. Suddenly, a hand grabbed his shoulder.

Clive spun around, gun in hand, and there before him was Matt. It must have been the look on his face that scared Matt. Matt backed up two steps, put up his hand and said, "Clive, it's me. Matt." Clive backed up into the stump and just stared at Matt. Matt slowly walked to him and put his hand on Clive's shoulder. "Clive, are you alright?"

Clive said, "Yeah, I'm okay," as he rubbed his eyes and forehead.

"What did you see?" Matt asked.

Clive turned and looked into the forest for a moment then said, "I'm not sure, but…"

"But what?" Matt asked as he stepped up beside him.

Clive turned and looked at him, then said, "I don't know. I'm not sure. Maybe it was nothing. Maybe it's just me. I just don't know." He took a deep breath then he said, "Come on, Matt. Let's go see that boy." They started back out of the forest toward the field, and Clive looked back over his shoulder into the dark trees. He saw nothing but forest. He shook his head and followed Matt out into the sunlight. Matt and Clive joined Janis and Andy and helped Andy down to the camp. He was limping somewhat and had lost weight, but he seemed to be generally okay.

When Lisa and the children saw him, they came running. They were all in tears and didn't want to let him go. They finally got him to one of the chairs and gave him something to drink. Maddie went to him and hugged him. With tears in her eyes she said, "I knew you would be okay. You told me you were okay didn't you?"

Andy just smiled and said, "I thought about you a lot. I was hoping you heard me." They gave him something to eat and checked his wound. Matt decided to go get Coop, since he lived so close, and have him look at Andy. Matt was gone for less than half an hour and while he was gone, Janis took Andy to the house and helped him clean up.

When Matt returned with Coop, they all waited out on the porch while Coop checked Andy's wound and put medicine and new bandages on it.

When Coop was finished, he helped Andy outside to a chair on the porch. The children ran and sat on the floor next to him. They all sat close to him as he sat back in the chair.

Andy kept saying, "It's so good to be home again."

Clive had remained silent for the most part but he finally spoke up. "Andy, I know you're tired but we need to know what happened. Where have you been all this time and with who?"

Lisa said, "Uncle Clive, can't we wait till later?"

Andy looked at Lisa and squeezed her hand, then said, "It's okay, Sis. I need to tell you all what I know." He took a deep breath, then began. "When the men took me in the jeep, they drove the road the way I told them up to the big rocks. I guess the rough road started me bleeding again. I tried to stop the blood but I was getting weak. We stopped at the rocks and the one guy, I guess his name was Joey, tried to help me with the bandage. I guess I passed out. The next thing I knew, the other guy, Sean, pulled me out of the jeep and he and Joey walked me to a spot in the shade. Joey went back for the rifle but he didn't come back. Sean left me sitting by the rocks and he went to see what had happened to Joey. I heard three shots and then Sean came running back. He looked like he was scared to death. He picked me up and tried to run around to the other side of the rocks, but I was getting dizzy again and he couldn't carry me. He put me on the ground and said, 'Sorry kid. I gotta go.' He left me lying there and then I heard a scream and everything started to fade again. I looked up and saw someone looking down at me, but everything was fuzzy. Then everything went black again. I do remember walking with someone's help into the woods, then I think someone carried me. I guess I passed out again. The next thing I remember was being in a kind of bed in a dark, cool place. There was light, but not much. I remember someone giving me water, food and taking care of my leg. I must have been out of it for a long while, but then I remember a man. I never saw him very well but I think he had a beard and maybe blonde hair. He was kind to me and

he always made sure he had food for me and water. I know there was someone else there too, but whoever it was I never saw them.

"After some time I tried to get out of bed and walk around, but the man stopped me. He said he wanted me to stay in bed and I guess I did. I don't know how long I was down but it must have been for a long while. After I started to feel better, the man blindfolded me and took me to some kind of cabin or shack and told me to stay there. It wasn't cool like the other place. He locked me in and told me to rest. He brought food and water. Sometimes we went back to the cool place, but always blindfolded. I guess I don't know where I was. One day at the shack I tried to break out. I couldn't do it, but when the man came back he was mad. He told me that I was to listen to him and that he would take me home if I behaved well.

"Some time after that, he blindfolded me and we walked a long way through the woods, I think. He left me alone and said that I could take the blindfold off a couple of minutes after he left. He said, 'Good luck, kid.' I waited, then I took it off and walked into the field. That's when I saw camp, and you coming for me." Andy started to cry, and reached out for Janis. She held him for a few minutes. Clive didn't say anything. He just turned and looked out the screen at the backyard.

Matt walked up to him and asked, "Well, what do you think?"

Clive looked at him, then back outside. "I don't know what to think," he said, as he shook his head. Matt went back to Andy, and Clive walked down the steps and around to the front of the house. Coop decided he would see if he could get paramedics to come to the camp to check on Andy. He left the porch and went to Clive's car to ask him to call. Clive had already made the call and said they were coming.

Janis thought Andy should go to the hospital, but Coop said they should let the paramedics decide.

The family and Coop stayed with Andy on the porch, but Maddie walked down to the pond where Clive was seated in a chair. She sat in a chair beside him and asked, "Well, what do you think about Andy?"

Clive sat forward in the chair, still looking straight ahead. "Andy will be fine. He's a tough kid and his wound seems to be healing."

"What is it, then?" Maddie asked. "What's on your mind?"

Clive said, "The man that took care of him. I think it's the man I saw in the valley. The same man I just saw up in the woods when we saw Andy."

"You saw him again?" Maddie asked.

"Yeah," Clive said. "Again."

"It bothers you doesn't it?" Maddie asked.

Clive turned to her and said, "I can't figure it out. It's a feeling I just can't figure out."

Maddie looked out at the pond and said, "Clive, I tried to tell you earlier. Something is coming. It feels like a storm is coming, and it's coming toward you." Clive turned and stared at her. She looked him in the eyes and said, "I think we all feel the weight of Andy being missing is gone. It's like a huge rock has been lifted, but that fog remains. The indecision, the confusion, the good, the evil… It's like it's all being funneled now. It's the storm, and it's coming. That which tortures your mind, wraps you up and weighs you down like a cold-heavy wet blanket. Do not let it steal from you who you are. The answer lies beneath. Search and you will end your torment. It's all there: the bearded man, the murders, the unsolved mystery. Somewhere out in those dark clouds are the answers to all that weighs on you. The answers to what really happened a year ago are there. They

are there and so is Brian, out there somewhere in that darkness." She stared intently at him and added. "And death is there. You must be always aware. It can come for you also."

He looked at her, then away at the pond. He just whispered, "I know."

The paramedics came and checked Andy and said he could go be checked out the next day at the hospital. After they left, Janis talked Coop into staying for the roast that she had almost forgotten. Dinner was served in the early evening, out at a table by the pond. The fear and horror of the past weeks faded for a few hours into joy and good feelings shared by all. When the light of day began to fade, Coop got up, said his goodbyes, and told them he would go to the hospital with them in the morning. Maddie had decided to stay the night and help Janis and Lisa with clean-up and anything Andy needed.

Clive said he had to head back to Smith Falls. He slowly walked to his car, followed by the family and Maddie. When he reached the car, he turned and looked at Andy, who was leaning on Matt. He put out his hand and shook Andy's, then pulled him in and hugged him. He said, "I'm glad you're home. I love you, boy."

Andy told him the same, and then Clive hugged and kissed all of them. He sat down in his car and Janis came and knelt beside him. She looked up into his eyes, then hugged him again and kissed him. "Clive Aliston, I love you. Don't you be a stranger, you hear me?"

Clive looked back at her and said, "I love you, dear. And no, I won't." He added, "I'm so glad you're all okay. Now put this in the past and move on, you hear me?" He paused, then looked into her eyes and said, "You know, I think in this life there is more than our fair share of disappointments and pain that we should forget. But the wonderful memories

become the priceless treasures. Treasures of lives shared, relationships lived and the joys we experience." He smiled at her, kissed her fingers and put them in the center of her forehead.

Matt said, "See you later, my friend."

Clive started the car and backed out of the driveway and onto the road. He waved as he pulled away from camp. He looked into his rearview mirror and saw them all waving at him. As he moved up the road he whispered, "And God keep you all safe." He looked into the mirror at himself and said, "And Lord be with me also, for a storm is coming."

EPILOGUE

Nearly two weeks after Andy's return, things were getting back to normal again. Not only for the Fallons and Clive, but for the country itself. The government and the states had started the rebuilding process for all that had been damaged. Most of the escaped prisoners had been either captured or killed—as were the terrorists. Clive was putting in twelve to sixteen hour days, as was the rest of the department. He was tired, but in some ways he felt better.

When he would get a little down he would think of Andy and the Fallons, and it always seemed to make him a little better. He had been notified that he was finally getting a new secretary to replace Alice. He also knew that a new second-in-command would be arriving soon. There were still many things that needed to be changed, not only on a federal and state level, but right here in the county itself. There were even rumors that the sheriff's department itself was going to undergo a complete overhaul.

Most of all, Clive was proud of how America had handled the crisis. A lot of people had died, but America had fought back. Not only with force, but even on an economic level. The financial world did not come close to the problems of post 9/11. It was as if America and Americans said, not this time. Not ever again. The only thing that seemed to be on his mind constantly was what Maddie had said. "It is

now all being funneled. It is a storm and it's coming at you."

Clive had arrived at work on Thursday morning about seven-thirty. He was at his desk, going through the mountains of paperwork that had accumulated through the past weeks. It was close to nine-thirty when he got buzzed by the part-time secretary. "Clive, Jack Duff is on the radio. He says he wants to talk to you about a break-in at the gun store on Route 55."

Clive lowered the paper he was reading and put his pen down. He took a deep breath, then answered, "Ruth, tell him to take care of it. I'll talk to him later. I've got too much on my plate now."

There was a pause, then Ruth came on again. "Clive, he says this won't wait."

Clive took a deep breath, then tapped his fingers on the table and sat back in his chair with a disgusted look on his face. He pushed the button on his radio and said, "Yes, Jack. What's up?"

There was a pause, then Jack answered, "Clive, I'm at the gun shop on Route 55. There's been a break-in."

"And?" Clive said, somewhat sarcastically.

Jack said, "We've got weapons and ammo missing. One of them is real exotic but that's not what I'm calling for."

"What then?" Clive asked.

"I think you need to get down here to see this for yourself," Jack said.

Clive just looked at the radio then answered, "Do you really need me for this Jack? I'm swamped here."

Jack came back on, "Clive, you have to see this. I'm not going to put this over the radio."

Clive could almost feel the urgency in his voice. "Okay, okay," he said. "Give me a few minutes and I'll be there." Clive closed up the paperwork. He stopped at Ruth's desk and told her that he would be at the gun shop on Route 55,

and that if anything important came in she should call him.

Clive left the station and was at the shop in less than ten minutes. He was met at the front of the store by Jack Duff and one of the Smith Falls patrolmen. "Clive, the owner gave me a list of what he thinks is missing. Take a look at this."

Clive took the list and read it. Several handguns, and a competition-grade Weatherby Magnum with a scope and tripod. He looked at Jack and said, "Whoever it is, they like quality rifles."

Jack said, "The list isn't what I called you here for. You have to see this for yourself."

Clive looked at Jack and said, "Okay, lead on." Clive entered the store. Once inside, he looked over the case that was broken into.

Jack said, "It's in the next room, Clive. Come take a look at this." Clive entered the next room. When he turned to the back wall, what he saw almost took his breath away. Painted across the back wall, in large red letters, was the word, "Forever," followed by, "Their tickets must be redeemed." He could almost feel himself turn pale as the blood seemed to drain from his head. He just stared at the back wall and whispered, "A storm is coming."

A Warrior's Knowledge

Adversity, hardship and loss.
All parts of a boot camp, preparing us for the battle of life.
And faith is the ammunition…

—C. William Davis III
Thoughts, Dreams and Fantasies of An Ordinary Man

COMING SOON:

Another Clive Aliston Novel

THE FOREVER MAN II

THE TICKET MASTER

C. William Davis III

Bill Davis plans to continue his Clive Aliston series along with two other full length novels. Since retiring from the industrial electrical and aerospace electronics field, where he did work for the government aerospace and space programs, Davis has focused on his lifelong interest in literature and writing.

A long-time resident of Brackenridge, Pennsylvania, he graduated from Har-Brack High School and earned a degree in Aerospace Electronics from A.T.I. in Pittsburgh.

He has been married to his wife, Linda for forty years and has two children and three grandchildren.

WA